AN UNSEEN PRESENCE

Sarah tensed and looked around, suddenly aware that a hazy shadow had shifted in the corner of her vision.

"Tully?" she whispered, unable to stop the wild shiver that went through her as she looked out the window at the solid gray mass of clouds. The back of her head began to tingle, and the hair on the back of her neck rose.

"Tully!" she said again, louder, forcing herself to be brave even as the feeling got steadily stronger that a dark cloud was hovering behind her, shifting out of sight to one side or the other whenever she turned to try to see it.

Sarah shook her head with disgust at how she was letting her imagination get carried away. "I guess I have to have someone to talk to, huh?"

"That's right," a voice said, clear and close to her ear . . .

HAUTALA'S HORROR—HOLD ON TO YOUR HEAD!

RICK HAUTALA

COLD WHISPER

ZEBRA BOOKS
KENSINGTON PUBLISHING CORP.

To Dominick Abel

ZEBRA BOOKS

are published by

Kensington Publishing Corp.
475 Park Avenue South
New York, NY 10016

First printing: October, 1991

Printed in the United States of America

Acknowledgments

High on the list of *thank-yous* this time is the usual lineup of suspects — those friends who read, dissect, comment upon, and shred my outlines and first drafts. This time out Chris Fahy, Kathy Glad, and Mike Feeney were joined by Matt Costello and Joe Citro. Every last one of them took off the gloves and showed me many of the weaknesses in my original proposal.

Captain Paul McCarthy of the Westbrook, Maine, police department took the time to answer a whole slew of questions about police procedure. By offering details about a policeman's work, he opened up numerous paths the story could take. Of course, any inaccuracies are mine for the sake of fictional development. Thanks to Larry Farrington at the Maine State Prison in Thomaston.

Also, as always, I continue to count on Mike Kimball to bring me up when I'm feeling down . . . as I hope I bring him up when he's feeling down. Ain't the writing life just grand, Mike? At first I thought I'd never forgive him for *insisting* I buy Xy-Write for my computer. Now I can't thank him enough. So Mike — this Bud's for you!

I also want to thank Steve Bissette, who has helped me through a very difficult period by offering his knowledge and his kind words of support. Do yourself a gruesome favor and start reading Steve's magazine *Taboo*.

There are too many other people to start naming them all other than — again, as always — the four people who are *always* at the top of my list for love: Bonnie, Aaron, Jesse, and Matti.

Thanks . . . *all* of you!

Contents

Prologue

Tully

"My hands are clean: the stain is on my heart."
—Euripides

"He's crying! . . . *Again!*" Sarah Lahikainen said. Her voice was tight with anger and frustration as she stared into her dresser mirror and continued to brush her hair the required one hundred strokes.

"What do you think I can do about it?" a thin, high voice asked suddenly from behind her.

Surprised, Sarah shifted her gaze and focused on the reflection of the boy who was sitting in the rocking chair in front of the bedroom window. Slanting rays of the setting sun backlit his head and shoulders with a hard, orange line, making it difficult for her to see his face clearly. He looked no more than a year or two older than Sarah's own eight years. His face was thin and pale in comparison to hers, which was nut brown from the summer sun; but they both had the same thin, wheat blond hair and sparkling blue eyes. Reflected side by side in the mirror, they could almost be taken for twins.

Sarah regarded the boy silently for several seconds. His gradually widening smile exposed flat, white teeth. Then, with a huff of breath, she said, "I have no idea what you could do, what anyone could do about him!" She hiked her thumb in the direction of her baby brother's room, then went back to her brushing, pulling the hairbrush angrily through her hair

11

until she hit a snarl that made her yelp with pain and brought tears to her eyes.

"I suppose you're gonna tell me Brian made you do that, too, huh?" the boy asked. He punctuated his comment with thin laughter.

Sarah stared at him through tears that blurred her vision, but she was unable to say anything because of the tight pressure building up inside her chest.

"Come on, Sarah. Don't you see how silly you're being? You blame your baby brother for just about everything bad that ever happens to you."

A red rush of anger colored Sarah's cheeks. She took a deep, steady breath, then wiped her eyes with the back of her hand before placing the hairbrush carefully on the dresser beside her pink jewelry box. Looking at her own reflection, she noted that, in spite of her efforts, her blond hair still looked limp and thin. Her pale blue eyes were runny and red-rimmed.

"That's because Brian's always causing problems," she said, her voice low and trembling. The dull ache in her chest grew steadily stronger. "Come on, Tully. You saw what he did to me yesterday!" Her gaze flicked over to the reflection of her bed, to the heap of brightly colored stuffed animals and dolls piled up against the headboard. One doll in particular caught her attention with the thin wash of brown stain on the left side of its face. "You were there when he puked all over Missy."

"Yup, I was there all right," Tully said. His smile seemed frozen on his face as he nodded.

"And you can't tell me Brian didn't mean to do it," Sarah said, shaking her head. "You saw him do it!" She wanted to cry just thinking about how much Missy meant to her and now, no matter how many times her mother washed her favorite doll, Missy was ruined. "Now she's gonna have that pukey smell on her forever."

"Come on, Sarah. You can't tell me a one-year-old baby can do something like that on purpose."

"He sure did! He did it because he hates me, just as much as I hate —" She cut herself off sharply, locking eyes with her own reflection. She could see how badly her lower lip was trem-

12

bling, but there was no way she could stop it. "Whose side are you on, anyway? You know Brian hates me! Every time I even sit next to Mommy, he'll start crying and squealing—or he fills his pants 'cause he doesn't want her to pay any attention to me! Especially now that Dad left."

Tully shook his head in amazement. "He's only one year old."

"So? Anyway, Brian's the reason Daddy left in the first place. God I hate him! I swear to God, Tully, sometimes—" She clenched her fists and shook them at her own reflection. "Sometimes I wish Brian was . . ."

"Dead?"

Sarah's head jerked up. She stared intently at Tully's reflection in the mirror, convinced that his lips hadn't even moved when he said the word. She nodded once, ever so slowly, in spite of the chill that shook her shoulders. "Yeah," she whispered. "Dead."

A cold dread that originated in her stomach rushed through her body the instant she said the words. She clenched her jaw to keep her teeth from chattering and squeezed her fists so tight they hurt. Holding her breath, she slowly turned around to face the rocking chair.

It was empty.

Part One

The Darkness Gathers

"I'm afraid of what's always behind me, no matter where I look!"
—Statement made by a seven-year-old,
     when asked why he was afraid of the dark.

Chapter One

Dark Roads

— 1 —

"Sarah! Who are you talking to in there?"

The voice came simultaneously with a rapid burst of knocking on the bathroom door. Sarah Lahikainen turned off her tape recorder. Momentarily flustered, her voice trembled when she answered, "No one, Mom. Just myself."

"Well, would you please hurry it up?" her mother said. The agitation in her voice was obvious, and Sarah had a pretty good idea why. "It's supposed to start raining later, and I'd rather not be driving all night in a storm."

"I'll be right there." Sarah knew the rain wasn't the only reason her mother was in such a hurry. She sat up straight on the toilet and closed her eyes for a few seconds, willing her bladder to release; but her mother had startled her so much she couldn't make herself pee, no matter how hard she tried. Holding her breath, she waited, listening for the soft click-click of her mother's heels as she walked down the hallway back to the kitchen.

Sarah let her withheld breath out in a long, slow whistle. Then, leaning forward, she punched the record/play button on the tape recorder, held the machine close to her mouth, and continued with what she had been saying.

"I just can't believe it. I think that's exactly what she said back then, too, when I was only about eight years old. 'Who are you talking to in there?' Is that a coincidence, or what?" She glanced thoughtfully at the ceiling for a second before continuing. "But ever since I got here to my father's house last week, the first real visit I've had with him in at least five or six years . . . probably ever since they got divorced, I've been thinking about—Oh, God! I can't even say your—I mean, say *the* name out loud!"

Sarah leaned back against the cold toilet seat and shivered as she took a deep breath. Chills danced up her spine like tiny fingertips as she stared vacantly at the silently turning tape inside the recorder. It had been—how long? At least seven years now, since Dr. Wiater had suggested she talk her feelings into a tape recorder as a form of therapy. Pretty much ever since that horrible day when Brian, her baby brother, died.

"Tully. Tully. *Tully!*" Sarah hissed with her mouth so close to the built-in microphone she was positive the name would be distorted on playback.

"There, are you satisfied? I said it. Why the hell am I even thinking about you? It's been so . . . so damned long, I don't know if you were ever really real or what. I mean, who—or what—were you? Just some kind of . . . of figment of my imagination? I don't even know!" Staring at the bathroom ceiling, she sighed deeply. "All I do know is that ever since I got here to my dad's, I've had this . . . this feeling that you're still hanging around. Close by, you know? Sorta like you're still with me, still watching over me, even after all these years." She sniffed loudly. "Is that crazy, or what?"

Voices echoed down the hallway, drawing Sarah's attention. Her mother and Rosalie, her father's new wife, were talking with that buried-just-under-the-surface tension in their voices. Of course, Sarah couldn't blame her mother for being upset; Devin, her ex-husband, hadn't even bothered to inform her that he was getting married again. But then again, Sarah had had a fun week with her dad and Rosalie, and it bothered her that as soon as her mother showed up, that same old tension filled the house like oily smoke.

Flicking the pause button, she cocked an ear toward the closed door and listened. Yup. Now Dad's joined it. Here they go, arguing just like they did back when they were married. That was one of Sarah's clearest childhood memories: listening to her parents fight.

"Wouldn't you think, after all these years, they'd finally get off each others' cases? 'Specially now that Dad's remarried?" she whispered, feeling a cold knot tighten in her stomach. Her hands were slick with sweat as she held the tape recorder close to her face. "Well, I guess old habits just die hard."

The voices from the kitchen rose steadily. Sarah squeezed her bladder one more time, then finally gave up. She stood up, hiked up her panties and jeans, and flushed the toilet. Still, she couldn't quite bring herself to leave the bathroom. Not just yet. Not until she calmed down and tried to put into words a few more of her thoughts about Tully.

Unpausing the tape, she spoke again. "So what is it, huh? What's making me start thinking about you now, after all this time? Is it just listening to them argue that gets me so . . . so mad?" She sniffed loudly, aware of the tightening panic inside her. "Why? Why am I even thinking about someone I can hardly even remember—someone I haven't thought about in years? I don't even know how much—if any of it—actually happened. Were you even real? Maybe I used to have an older brother who died or something." Her throat nearly closed off. "Whew! That's a thought! But I sure as heck can't ask my mom about it . . . not after what happened to Brian. But what do I remember?"

She moved over beside the sink and hiked one leg up onto the counter. Resting the tape recorder on her thigh, she closed her eyes and rocked gently back and forth as she continued speaking softly into the microphone.

"Well . . . I sure do remember what you did to Myrtle. Aww, poor Myrtle." Her eyes stung with tears as she shook her head sadly from side to side. "I couldn't have been more than four years old, but I remember the day she scratched my arm like it was yesterday . . . and how mad I was at her. I still have the scars."

As if to prove it to someone standing there beside her, she rolled up the sleeve of her right arm. Through the blur of her tears, she stared at the three faint white lines that ran up the

19

inside of her arm from her wrist almost all the way to her elbow joint.

"I must've been older—maybe five. It was definitely before
Brian was born. It's surprising how clear I remember some
parts of it. And boy oh boy, do I remember how much that cat
scratch stung! Especially when my mom put that peroxide on
it. It must have been peroxide 'cause I remember watching it
foam up like Alka-Seltzer. And I remember being scared that
the foaming meant I had rabies. But most of all, I remember
how mad I was at Myrtle—that she could have done something like that to me."

Tears flowed freely from Sarah's eyes. Sniffing, she wiped
her nose and cheeks with the back of her hand before forcing
herself to continue.

"But I think the worst thing was what you did to poor, old
Myrtle . . . my cat." She heaved another, deeper sigh. "You
should have known how much I really loved her, and that I
was just mad at her for scratching me. I never really wanted
her dead. I just said that 'cause I was mad at her. You know
how people can say *I wish you were dead* when they're angry and
not really mean it. I'll bet every kid in the world has said that
about their parents at least once in their life. But I never,
never wanted you to kill Myrtle or do what you did to her."

The memory of how she and her mother had found Myrtle
rose in Sarah's mind. She covered her mouth with her hand,
fearful that she was going to vomit. She squeezed her eyes shut
as she relived the horror of the day her mother, having noticed
a streak of pink running down the side of the toilet, had lifted
the cover and found Myrtle, her head twisted horribly to one
side, her eyes hanging from their sockets like glistening pearls
as she floated belly-up in water that reeked of Sani-Flush.
Myrtle's blood had turned the blue water a sickening prune
purple.

"And of course I got blamed for it! Even now, I don't think
my mother honestly believes I didn't do it. Who else could
have done it? You were nowhere around when it happened,
and Brian—poor, dear Brian—wasn't even born yet. So I
think that even after all these years, Mom's convinced I killed
my cat . . . that I was mad at her for scratching my arm, so I

twisted her neck and stuffed her into the toilet. And you, Tully. I remember, just as clear as day, shouting at you, accusing you of killing Myrtle when you showed up in my bedroom the next day. That was when my mother called out to me, *Who are you talking to in there?* The exact same words she just used."

Sarah sniffed with dark, twisted laughter.

She straightened when she heard footsteps coming down the corridor again. Glancing nervously at the door, she finished her message, hissing into the microphone. "But I know *you* did it, Tully, wherever the hell you are now, I know you killed Myrtle 'cause I was mad at her, and I —"

She cut herself off when her mother knocked loudly on the bathroom door.

"Come *on*, Sarah! I want to get going now!" The tension in her voice was wire-tight.

"I'm all set," Sarah said, forcing herself to sound chipper. For emphasis, she flushed the toilet a second time, using the sound to cover the noise she made when she turned off the tape recorder and stuffed it into her backpack. Slinging the pack over her shoulder, she opened the door, smiled widely at her mother, and said, "Let's hit the road."

— 2 —

Route 26 was one of many back roads leading out of Hilton, Maine. It was narrow and curving as it cut through the dense forest which, farther west, near the New Hampshire border, became part of the White Mountain National Forest. The air was heavy and moist; thick tendrils of fog drifting low to the ground made the driving much more difficult for Marie Lahikainen, who sat hunched over the steering wheel, peering into the night ahead. High above, fast rushing storm clouds streaked across the sky from the south, masking the thin crescent of moon. Towering pines lined both sides of the road, and the lack of streetlights cast everything into inky darkness. The car's headlights, even on low beam, reflected off the silvery walls of fog, hardly helping as Sarah and Marie headed back to their home in Westbrook.

"So, you seemed to like Rosalie well enough," Marie said.

21

Her mother's voice was still wound tight, and Sarah knew just how loaded her comment was.

"She's okay, I guess," she said. She wanted to say that she thought her father could have done better but decided not to give her mother any extra ammunition. "I think she's kind of protective, you know? Real possessive about Dad, like she didn't want to have to share him with me, but we got along okay."

Marie bit down on her lower lip and said nothing. Sarah took a deep breath and continued.

"I just don't see why, as soon as you showed up, you had to start ragging at Dad, I mean, he—"

"I didn't start anything," Marie said sharply, frowning as she glanced over at her daughter. "I simply commented that he should have at least shown me a little bit of respect and had the common courtesy to let me know he had gotten married again before I showed up. I don't exactly care for those kinds of surprises. And you—you could at least have phoned me sometime last week and told me about it. Can't you understand how awkward I felt, walking in there and meeting her for the first time?"

"Yeah, sure," Sarah said, "but she was really nice to you. She didn't—"

"Well, what's she supposed to do? She won! She's got him."

Sarah started to say something but remained silent.

"And I don't really appreciate you defending her either," Marie added.

Sarah fought to keep back the accusation she had been about to let fly. Her hands tightened in her lap as she stared blankly at the road ahead. Neither one of them seemed willing to discuss the matter any further, so the only sounds were the car's whining engine, the tearing hiss of tires on wet asphalt, and the sporadic *slap-slap* of the windshield wipers.

"Uhh, Mom . . ." Sarah began, clearing her throat and twisting in her seat to glance at her mother.

"Yes?" Marie said, keeping her gaze fixed on the road ahead. In the dim wash of light from the dashboard, Sarah could see her mother's jaw muscles clench and unclench. The circled reflection of the speedometer

22

danced like twin full moons across the lenses of her glasses.

"I — uhh, I kinda have to go to the bathroom," Sarah said.

"What?" Marie shouted. She let her breath out with a hissing sputter as she glanced again at her daughter. "I thought that's what was taking you so damned long back at your father's house."

"Well, I did go — I mean, I tried to, but I couldn't. I gotta go bad now."

Marie's grip tightened on the steering wheel. Sarah knew her mother was more upset about her ex-husband than she was about having to stop now. She could understand her mother's desire to get as many miles as possible between herself and Devin and his new wife, but she really did have to go.

"You don't think you could wait until we get to Bethel, do you?" Marie asked. "There's got to be a restaurant or gas station where we can stop."

"I really gotta go bad," Sarah replied, leaning forward and crossing her arms over her lower abdomen. "It'll only take me a minute. I was just so uptight once you got to the house I couldn't do anything."

"Lord knows you flushed the toilet enough times," Marie said.

"Please, Mom?"

"I swear to God, Sarah," Marie said with a low, angry sniff. "You sure do have a way sometimes."

"Thanks a lot, Mom," Sarah muttered as her mother slowed the car and pulled over onto the gravel shoulder of the road. Even before the car was fully stopped, she had her seat belt undone and was swinging open the car door. The dome light inside the car came on, stinging her eyes as she stepped out into the moist night. The fog swirled in the red glow of the taillights, and for just an instant, Sarah thought she saw a human shape forming in the hazy glow. In spite of the warm spring air, she shivered as she looked out at the impenetrable blackness of the woods.

"Don't go so far you get lost," her mother yelled when Sarah started up the slope and into the woods.

"Don't worry," she replied as a wave of nervousness

crested inside her. "I just want to be out of sight in case someone else comes along."

"You expect to see someone else foolish enough to be driving this road this late at night?" Marie said. She leaned across the front seat and slammed shut the door Sarah had left open.

Sarah had been about to remind her mother that *she* was the one who had showed up three hours late to pick her up, and *she* was the one who had put a sour finale to the weekend by arguing with her ex-husband; but with the car door closed, she wouldn't have heard her anyway. Still seething with slow-burning anger, Sarah picked her way carefully through the dense brush, walking up the sloping hill until she found a good spot where she could still see her mother's parked car down on the road. She had just unzipped her pants and was scooching down when the curve of the road behind them began to brighten. Another car was approaching.

"Damn it!" she muttered. She pulled up her jeans and zipped them shut before darting around behind a large tree. Clinging to the thick trunk, she stared down at the dark road and waited for the car to go by.

The light coming up behind her mother's car got steadily brighter, turning the wall of fog a bright silver. Within seconds, twin circles of approaching headlights appeared like hooded eyes out of the mist. The light swept down the road, illuminating the dark walls of trees that lined the road. Sarah had the impression the car was exiting a long, dark tunnel. The tires whined loudly on the wet road.

What had at first been mere irritation at almost getting caught peeing in the woods suddenly shifted to sharp apprehension when the car, instead of passing by, glided to a stop directly behind her mother's car. For several seconds — seconds that seemed like long, sludgy minutes — it just sat there, idling. The glaring wash of its headlights illuminated every detail of her mother's car and sent spikes of light reflecting off the chrome, but Sarah could make out none of the details of the other car.

Clinging close to a thick tree, Sarah stared down at the two parked cars. After a moment, the driver's door of the dark car swung open. Someone got out. In the diffused glow of the headlights, it looked like a thin, young man. He slammed the car door shut and started walking toward Marie's car with a long, confident stride. When he was close to the car, he said something, but it was muffled and lost in the distance.

Fear, cold and clammy, gripped Sarah's stomach. She was nearly frantic, not knowing what to do. Should she run down to the car in case her mother needed her help? Or should she go off and hide somewhere, protect herself and hope her mother could do the same? She wanted to believe this guy would prove friendly, that he had stopped to see if her mother had a flat tire or something; but an alarm was sounding in her mind, warning her that this guy meant only one thing—trouble.

He came up close to Marie's car, leaned down, and said something to Marie through the opened window. Again, Sarah couldn't hear what it was. The dull glow of the dome light almost—but not quite—lit up his face when he suddenly snapped the car door open. Sarah couldn't tell for sure, but her mother either stepped out or was pulled out of the car onto the road. A scream threatened to burst out of her but, sucking in a lungful of moist air, she crouched beside the tree, careful to make as little noise as possible.

"Oh, no. No car trouble at all," she heard her mother say as she straightened her shoulders defensively. Marie might have taken a step back from the man but she was blocked by her car. Even at this distance, the tension in her mother's voice was obvious—much worse than what Sarah had heard back at her father's house. Sarah craned her head forward to hear everything that was said.

"Kinda unusual, though, to see anyone stopped out along here. Not unless they run out of gas or somethin'," the man said. His voice had a deep, threatening resonance that grated on Sarah's nerves.

"No, my—I mean, I just stopped here to go to the bathroom," Marie said, raising her voice.

Sarah knew her mother was afraid, and was cuing her to stay quiet and out of sight.

"Well, hey," the man said, stepping closer to Marie. "Don't let me stop you. Here." Without warning, he lunged at Marie,

25

his hands grabbing at her skirt. "Lemme help you get that off."

Marie tried to spin away from him, but he caught her up short, spun her around, and grabbed her. She cocked her arm back and swung her elbow at him, but the man easily deflected the blow. Holding her from behind, he pinned her arms to her sides.

"What the hell's the matter with you?" he said as he leaned close to her ear. "I'm just tryin' to be friendly, tryin' to help you out a bit." He reached around in front of her and ran the back of his hand across Marie's face. "I wouldn't think of hurting such a pretty lady like you."

"You don't want to be doing this," Marie said, her voice rising several octaves higher as she jerked her head away from his touch. Even with the harsh glare of the headlights, the intervening fog made everything look like a two-dimensional shadow play, with two dark figures pressing close together. Sarah could imagine her mother's fear-widened eyes glistening as the driver leaned close to her. She was irritated that she couldn't make out any details of the man's face.

"Just what in the hell do you think I want to be doin'?" the man asked menacingly. His hand came around to the front of Marie's blouse and lingered over the top button, making his intentions all too clear. Gripping the collar, he pulled down hard. The sound of tearing cloth filled the night. Sarah watched, horrified, as her mother struggled against the crushing hold the man had on her. Her shoes scuffed in the roadside dirt as he dragged her to the back of the car and slammed her facedown onto the trunk. The impact knocked Marie's glasses off and sent them skittering across the trunk before they fell to the ground.

"Well," he said with a deep, malicious laugh. "I guess I just gotta do something about making you more appreciative of the help people offer you."

Pressing Marie down hard against the trunk, his back was to Sarah as he undid his belt and zipper and let his pants drop to his ankles. When he was ready, he raised Marie's skirt, tore off her panties, and positioned himself behind her.

"Consider this the penalty for trying to piss on the side of the road," the man said as he kicked Marie's legs wide and

26

thrust forward with a vicious grunt.

A hot flood of vomit rushed up into Sarah's mouth as she cringed behind the tree and watched the dark silhouettes. Every sound was dulled by the fog, but the stark light of the headlights made it all too real. Her mother's face was pressed flat against the trunk, distorting her screams. Sarah's vision blurred with tears, but she strained to look, trying to make out any details of the man. She clamped her hands over her ears in a vain attempt to block out the savage grunting noises he made as he thrust harder.

Sarah rocked back and forth on her knees as she watched the horrifying scene on the road. The night clamped down around her like a shroud, pressing so tightly inward she was afraid she was going to suffocate. Sharp jabs of pain centered between her eyes speared through her head.

This isn't really happening! her mind screamed. *This can't be happening!*

She was swept away by the disorienting feeling that it was a dream, a terrifying nightmare, and she would wake up soon. How could something like this be happening to her? To her mother? They had just been driving home to Westbrook, and all she wanted to do was go to the bathroom.

In spite of the shrouding fog, she could see her mother splayed across the trunk as the dark figure of the man thrust repeatedly into her. She could hear her mother's strangled cries for help and the man's throaty grunts of animal pleasure as he built toward release.

"Tully."

The first time Sarah said the name, it sounded foreign to her ears, as if someone else had spoken it nearby in the misty woods. Frantic with fear, she looked around, but her eyes met with only the impenetrable darkness of the woods and the lowering sky above the trees.

"Tully?" she whispered again through lips as dry as sand. "Tully? You aren't here, are you? How could you be?"

Unable to convince herself that she was alone, Sarah looked behind her, scanning the woods, trying frantically to pierce the dense darkness and swirling tendrils of fog. She both wanted and dreaded what she might see, but she saw nothing.

27

Her attention was pulled back to what was happening down on the roadside. With a loud groan, the man satisfied himself, then stepped back, pulled up his pants, and buckled his belt. With one hand, he kept Marie pinned down against the car trunk.

"Jesus Christ, Tully! Why can't you be here now?" Sarah hissed. She reached down to the ground; her fingers clutched the soil, digging into the forest floor, but all the while she was imagining having that man under her power so she could hurt him. Rip him apart with her bare hands.

"Where the hell are you when I really need you, Tully?" Sarah said with a deep-belly moan. "I didn't need you back then, not when I was mad at Myrtle . . . or at Brian. But I need you *now!* Where the hell are you?"

The sound of her mother's wracking sobs filled the night. Sarah wished she could force herself to close her eyes, to stop watching, so she could picture Tully as clearly as she could in her mind: his thin blond hair, his pale blue eyes, his wide-toothed grin . . .

"Why can't you be here now that I really need you?" she whispered as hot tears streamed down her cheeks. "Why? Why?"

With sudden, shrill laughter, the man rolled Marie over onto her back and leaned over her. "You liked that, huh?" he shouted.

Sarah watched him as he folded his arms across his chest, stepped back, and looked down at her. Marie stayed where she was, lying flat on the trunk, immobile. Sarah wished to God she could make out the features of his face, but through her tears, he was nothing but a dark smear against the night. Her mother wasn't moving at all; she looked like a disposed doll, too helpless to even move.

"But you know? I ain't quite done yet," the man said with a deepening tone of voice. Pinning Marie down with one hand, he lifted his foot up onto the bumper, reached down to the side of his boot, and pulled up his pant leg. With excruciating slowness, he extracted a long-bladed hunting knife from his leg sheath. Holding it up high, he let the headlights glint off the polished blade.

"Jesus Christ! *No!*" Sarah whimpered when the man flipped the knife around and pointed the blade downward, poised mere inches above her mother's throat.

"Well, we've had our little fun," he said with a twisted edge in his voice. He glanced up and down the road, then turned back to Marie, allowing the blade to drop perilously close to her exposed neck. "It's just a little personality quirk of mine, but I just don't like the idea of leaving any loose ends behind, if you catch my drift."

"Come on, Tully! *Please* come to me!" Sarah murmured weakly. Her throat felt like it had been flayed.

Sarah watched, stunned, as the driver rolled her mother onto her stomach, grabbed a fistful of hair with one hand, and wound it around in his fingers a few times for a good grip. When he jerked her head back, something in Marie's neck cracked, sounding as loud as a gunshot in the night.

"This'll just take a second here," the man said, looking over his shoulder at the road behind him. "I wanna make sure you don't tell nobody about me." He laughed savagely as he pulled back hard on Marie's hair, forcing her to look upward at the cloudy night sky. Sarah stared in numbed disbelief at the agony, the lifeless horror that glowed in her mother's eyes.

With a quick motion of his wrist, the man brought the blade around toward Marie's face and with a single flick drew the blade across her throat. A hot gush of blood as black as India ink shot over the trunk. When Sarah heard the sickening, gurgling sound that issued from her mother's opened throat, she screamed.

"Son of a bitch!" the man said, glaring up the hillside into the misty woods as the echoes of Sarah's scream faded away. He released his grip on Marie's hair and let her drop. Her head hit the trunk with a hollow drum sound before she slipped slowly onto the ground. "Sounds to me like I ain't the only one out here."

Chapter Two

The Chase

— 1 —

Branches lashed Sarah's face, and darkness closed around her like a net as she ran up the slope, deeper into the woods. Her fear-heightened senses strained to catch the sounds of the man chasing after her. He seemed to be closing the distance between them rapidly. Rain-slick leaves matted the forest floor, making her footing uncertain. In the enclosing dark, she bumped into unseen trees and tripped over invisible roots and rotting deadfalls. Whenever she fell, the stinging aroma of decaying vegetation filled her nose and throat, spurring her panic even higher. Her heart hammered fiercely in her ears as she fled from the pursuing man.

"You're making this too damned easy for me!" he shouted. "You sound like a goddamned cow barrel-assing through the woods."

Panting heavily, Sarah stopped a moment to get her bearings, reminding herself that she had to keep going uphill.

"You know you ain't gonna get very far," the man hollered. His voice boomed like a cannon shot through the foggy night. "So why don't you just give up now before you hurt yourself in the dark? You don't wanna fall down and break your leg or anything, now, do you?"

Sarah choked back what she had been about to yell at him, knowing he was only goading her to reveal where she was. But she did start moving more slowly so she wouldn't make as much noise. She reached out in front of her face to bat away the unseen branches, mentally thanking her pursuer for the advice; the last thing she needed to do right now was trip and twist her ankle so he *would* find her.

As Sarah moved through the dense growth, her mind continually replayed what she had just witnessed: her mother had been raped and then slashed with a knife. She knew she was probably dead back there on the road, but Sarah couldn't let go of that faint spark of hope that — somehow — her mother might still be alive. She tried not to remember the jet of blood and the horrible gagging sound her mother had made as her throat was slashed. Just before she started to run, she had seen the man drag her mother's body over to the side of the road and roll her down into the ditch. Through her panic, she just wished to hell she had gotten at least a glimpse of his face — *anything* to help her identify him later . . . if she made it through the night alive.

She forced herself to take deep, even breaths. The night air was like fire in her lungs. Her leg muscles screamed with the agony of running up the steep wooded slope, but fear spurred her on. The damp brush soon soaked her jeans from the knees down, and the extra weight dragged her back with every stride. Her sneakers made sickening, squishy sounds on the spongy ground. She could feel her arms and face were slick with something — either mist and mud . . . or blood. She stung where unseen branches had cut her, but she didn't let up; she knew exactly what this man would do to her if he caught her.

"Come on," he shouted from somewhere far behind her. He sounded as if the chase was beginning to tire him. "You know, the longer you run, the madder I'm gonna be once I finally do catch you."

"Fuck you!" Sarah shouted. Her voice was ragged with exhaustion. It echoed, sounding dense and close in the foggy woods.

"Ah-hah!" the man yelled triumphantly. "A little girl. So it

31

was *you* off in the woods going pee-pee while your mother waited at the car, huh?"

Fearful that he was still just trying to lure her into giving herself away, Sarah didn't reply. Instead, she lowered her head and pumped her arms, redoubling her efforts in spite of the screaming pain in her body. It sure as hell wouldn't take him long to run her down if he knew which direction to go.

When she saw a thick, dark clump of brush up ahead, she didn't hesitate; she dove headlong into it, heedless of the pain as the branches whipped her face. Snuggling down flat on the wet forest floor, nearly numb with panic, she waited, panting and shivering. Again, the cloying smell of rotting leaves filled her nose and throat, gagging her. She nearly screamed when she imagined herself lying dead on the forest floor. She sucked her breath in hard and pursed her lips to stifle a coughing fit. At least he couldn't hear the rapid-fire hammering of her pulse.

"Come on, little girlie," the man called out. His voice echoed from several directions at once in the fog-shrouded woods. Sarah cowered on the ground, fearful that he knew exactly where she was, and any second now he would grab her from behind, pull her out of her hiding place, and do to her what he had done to her mother.

"You don't have to worry, little girlie," the man yelled, sounding even closer. "I promise I won't hurt you."

Sarah shook violently as she hugged even closer to the ground. Feverish prayers filled her mind, urging him to pass on by and not notice her. Her mind and every muscle in her body had been pushed far past their limits. She knew she couldn't take much more. If he didn't go past her soon she was going to scream . . .

The heavy tramp of the man's footsteps sounded louder, closer, pummeling the ground like a horse's hooves as he charged up the hill. Sarah shut her eyes tightly, forcing back her tears and the trembling hitching of her breath. She knew she had to stay as calm as possible and not make a sound. If she was going to survive the night, the next *minute*, she had to think clearly. She had to get rid of all fear and fill herself with thoughts of —

Tully!

The name came to her as clearly and as sharp as it had come earlier tonight, in the bathroom of her father's house just before she and her mother left. The skin on the back of her neck crawled as she fought the illusion that *she* hadn't thought the name . . . someone hiding behind her had whispered it in the darkness. A prickling rush of fear danced like needles up her spine. At that same instant, a heavy, wet splattering sound filled the woods as rain began to fall. She could still hear the man's steadily approaching footsteps. The spongy forest floor seemed to vibrate with each heavy step as he came closer to where she cowered in the darkness.

Tully . . . Tully . . .

She squirmed on the ground in terror when she sensed something moving behind her. Turning slowly so as not to make any noise, she tried to pierce the pressing darkness. What if the man had a friend with him, and he had managed somehow to sneak around behind her?

For just an instant, the black night intensified, pulsating with energy as it solidified into a lurking, menacing, vaguely human shape. But as soon as Sarah thought she saw it, it quickly whisked away like wind-blown mist.

"Jesus Christ!" Sarah whispered, unable to stop herself.

"Was that *you*, little girlie?" the man called out above the steadily rising splatter of raindrops. His voice was high-pitched and taunting, and he sounded really close now.

Looking down the slope, Sarah could barely discern his form as it shifted against the solid black wall of trees. He wavered in and out of view, elusive, like a puff of black smoke. One second he was there; the next, he wasn't. Whimpering deep in the back of her throat, she nestled her face into the damp ground and closed her eyes tightly. If he caught her now, she didn't want to see. She was determined to keep her eyes closed.

"I know you're around here somewhere," the man called out teasingly. The sound of the rain grew deafening as heavy drops ripped like thousands of bullets through the leaves. Wet branches snapped underfoot, sounding like distant gunfire as he came even closer to where Sarah was hiding.

"You know I'm gonna find you, so why don't you just come out now? You don't want to get all wet and cold, do you?"

Against her will, Sarah opened her eyes and again stared down the slope at the man. Her heartbeat froze in her chest when she saw him standing right there in front of her, no more than six feet away. If she even took a breath now, he'd hear her. She didn't even dare blink her eyes for fear that it would give her away.

"I'm losing my patience with you, little girlie," the man called. His voice wafted toward her with an eerie warble, sending icy spikes of fear through her.

"This isn't any fun for either one of us now, is it?" the man shouted. "Well? Is it? Think about how nice and warm and dry you could be."

Think about how nice and silent, cold, and dead I could be, Sarah added.

This close, she could clearly hear the sound of his labored breathing, but she still couldn't make out any details of his face. It was hard to keep focused on him, but she did see the dim outline of the knife in his right hand. The same knife he had used to kill her mother. She tried not to imagine the thick stain of blood that must be on the blade. But she was willing to chance seeing her mother's blood if only there would be enough light so she could see this man's face. All she wanted was to get out of this alive and find out who the hell this bastard was so she could make him pay . . . pay with his life for what he had done to her mother!

But no! Sarah thought. *How can my mother be . . . dead?*

Her eyes burned as she glared at the dim outline of the man, all the while earnestly willing him to drop dead right there in front of her. No, not dead; she wanted to see him fall to the ground and be torn to pieces — sliced and shredded, the way he had sliced her mother. She wanted to see and hear him suffer, thrashing and screaming in pain before he died a slow and agonizing death.

When Sarah saw another hint of motion behind the man, she thought at first that her vision was blurred from the rain and her own tears. But the longer she stared at it, the clearer it became; there was . . . something hovering silently behind

34

the man. Gazing into the deep well of blackness, Sarah tried to make out what it was, but she couldn't quite pin it down. It wasn't so much something she could see as it was something she could *feel* . . . a cold, menacing presence, drifting in the fog, shifting and condensing as it wafted up the hill behind the man's back.

"You know, I'm startin' to get really pissed off!" the man shouted. "Honest to Christ I am!" He slapped the knife blade in the flat of his hand a few times, making a wet *whop-whop* sound.

Sarah was unable to tear her terrified gaze away from the dark shape as it grew larger and darker behind the man. A numbing sense of imminent danger, of cold dread, filled her, making her shiver wildly. She almost cried out, but her throat was closed off, forcing her to remain silent while she watched with mounting terror as the hazy darkness behind the man contracted and deepened until it took on an indistinct human shape.

"I can wait around here all night if I have to," the man shouted. "Rain don't bother me none!" When he cupped his hands to his mouth and directed his voice uphill, Sarah realized he had no idea where she was hiding. If she could just stay completely quiet and wait . . .

"But you know, the longer I have to wait, the sorrier you're gonna be once I do find you," the man yelled. "And you know I'm gonna find you—eventually." He repeatedly slapped the knife blade against his hand as he craned his head forward, listening and watching. Suddenly, he twitched violently and, whirling around, struck a defensive posture with his knife at ready.

"What the—" he grunted. Crouching and quickly dodging to one side, he sliced the air viciously several times. The blade made a sharp whickering sound with each pass.

Sarah could see that his arm and knife passed right through the hazy cloud behind him, but he seemed not to notice. Above the hissing rush of the rain, she heard him laugh softly under his breath as he muttered, "Gettin' a little jumpy there, ain't yah?"

After scanning the woods around him, he started moving

slowly uphill again, away from where Sarah was hiding. He seemed not to notice the black shape that trailed behind him. As the thick night swallowed him, Sarah had the distinct impression that the black cloud shimmered and dissolved like smoke.

But once the man had disappeared up the hill into the darkness, Sarah still didn't dare let out her breath in relief. She was determined to stay where she was, for hours if she had to, just to make sure he wasn't hiding behind a nearby tree, waiting for her to reveal herself.

While she waited in shivering silence, even with the violent scene of what had happened to her mother fresh in her mind and her teeth chattering from the cold rain, she couldn't stop wondering what she had just seen. Had there really been some kind of dark cloud there behind the man? Was it possible? Or had it been nothing more than an illusion, a trick the darkness and her panic had played on her? But no, there was no denying that it had been there. The man had reacted to it, too. He'd turned and defended himself, but he had acted as if he hadn't even seen it.

Shivers raced up Sarah's back, and tears sprang from her eyes when she wondered if it might have been her mother's ghost, out to get revenge on her killer.

In her heart, she knew — even if she couldn't quite accept it yet — that her mother had to be dead back there on the road, in the ditch where the man had thrown her. Sarah had seen her throat slit open and blood gush from the wound. That hadn't been her imagination. Even if the knife wound hadn't killed her right away, she would have bled to death long before another passing motorist might have found her. On a dark road, on a night like this, so late and so far out of town, who in their right mind would stop to help anyone? She sniffed loudly in spite of the raw burning in the back of her throat.

"You know I'm gonna get you!" the man shouted, but now his voice was faint with distance. Still, Sarah stayed where she was, letting the grief pour over her, colder and harder than the rain.

"And you know you're gonna be one sorry little girlie when I catch you!"

His voice faded off into the night. Finally, long after she could no longer hear the man shouting in the distance, she began to believe that he was truly gone. She shifted quietly into a sitting position, feeling every muscle and joint creak with cold and damp. Hugging her legs, she vigorously rubbed her arms to restore some sense of warmth as she fought to stop her teeth from chattering. Cold and hollow anguish reached to the very core of her soul and wrung her out until, even with the cold rain washing her face, she no longer had tears to cry.

Unable to stand the tension any longer, she leaped to her feet. Pins and needles made her legs go numb, making her stagger for balance. Her eyes, throat, and lungs felt as if they were filled with water, as if she were drowning. Every muscle in her body screamed in anguish as she forced herself to start down the slope toward the road. She was dimly grateful when she didn't come out of the woods near her mother's parked car. Her mind had created its own horrifying image of her mother's ravished corpse back there, lying in the ditch as plump raindrops beat against her. She started down the road back toward Hilton, running faster and faster until she wasn't even aware of who she was or what she was doing — all she knew was the horror of what she had seen. And as she ran, she was convinced that the man who had killed her mother was close behind her, his knife raised high and ready to strike.

Chapter Three

The Hunt Begins

— 1 —

Elliott Clark returned to the Hilton police station from his patrol shortly after midnight. Twelve-seventeen on the log sheet. Half an hour later, he was sitting in the lounge area with a steaming cup of coffee in hand when he heard his name called over the intercom. Not much ever happened in Hilton, so he felt no particular hurry or concern as he poured his coffee down the drain and headed up the stairs to the main lobby. It was probably another call from Carol, asking him where this month's alimony check was. As soon as he saw the girl waiting by the dispatch window — he guessed she was fifteen, maybe sixteen years old — he suspected otherwise.

Her torn, rain-soaked clothes, dirt-smeared face and hands warned him this meant real trouble. She was sitting on the edge of the chair closest to the dispatch window, her hands wedged tightly between her knees. Her face was pale and strained, and her shoulders shook violently as she sobbed. Tears carved thin streaks through the grime on her cheeks. She jumped and raised her arms protectively when the heavy metal door clanged open, and Elliott entered the room.

"Hello, I'm Patrolman —" Elliott said, starting toward her. As soon as she looked up and saw him, she wailed loudly, leaped to her feet, and rushed to him and collapsed in his arms. Stunned, Elliott could do nothing but smile an embarrassed grin at the dispatcher as he returned her embrace. Her blond hair was matted to her skull from the rain and smelled woodsy as he patted the back of her head and muttered reassuring words.

"Hey now. Take it easy there," he whispered as he pushed her away from him and stared into her terror-glazed eyes. "Just take a second here to calm down and tell me what—"

"It's my mother!" the girl wailed. Her voice rose, high and fragile, hitching between breaths. "This man—we stopped by the side of the road—I had to—go to the bathroom, and this—this man stopped and he—he killed her! He killed my mother after— after doing terrible things to her!"

"Come on into my office here," Elliott said kindly, "and tell me exactly what happened." Before leading the girl away, he nodded to the dispatcher and said, "Better get McCulloch on the horn. And notify the staties. I think we're gonna need some help."

With one arm still supporting the girl, he fished his keys from his pocket, unlocked the door, and started down the corridor toward his office. The girl stumbled several times as she walked along beside him. When he shoved open his office door, she practically collapsed into the chair by the desk. Her face was pinched with fear and misery, but still Elliott couldn't help but notice how pretty she was. He went back out into the hallway and filled a paper cup with fresh water from the cooler.

"Now just try to calm down," he said. He gave her the cup, and she drank greedily. "You have to tell me exactly what happened, when and where. First off, what's your name?"

"Sarah—Sarah Lahikainen. My father is Devin Lahikainen. He lives out on—"

"Sure, sure, I know who your father is," Elliott said mildly as he sat on the edge of his desk. "He lives out on Ridge Road, and in just a bit, I'm going to send someone over there to pick him up so he can come down here. But first, you have to tell me again—slower, this time—exactly what happened."

Sarah looked at him, her pale eyes red-rimmed and glistening. After taking a deep, trembling breath, she shook her

39

head savagely and said, "I don't know where—not for sure. We were somewhere out of town a bit—leaving my father's house. We had to stop 'cause I had to go the bathroom."

"You told me that part already," Elliott said mildly. "First of all, are you positive your mother was killed?"

Gnawing at her lower lip, Sarah nodded several times. "She has to be—" Her words caught in her throat, and she buried her face in her hands as violent sobs wracked her body.

"But you have no idea where you were, huh?"

Sarah looked at him over the tips of her fingers and shook her head violently. "No—I probably could show you, though. I think I could."

Elliott considered for a moment, but before he said anything, his phone rang. He picked it up and snapped, "Yeah." After a moment, he nodded and said, "Okay" and hung up.

"Look, Sarah." He leaned toward her and placed his hand reassuringly on her shoulder, surprised by how compelled he felt to comfort her. "I'm going to have to leave you with Mrs. Harrison while I drive out to pick up your father. The front desk just phoned him and he's home, so I'm going to bring him down here, if that's all right with you." He studied Sarah closely, trying to gauge her reaction, knowing that if there truly had been some kind of trouble, family members—especially estranged family members—were always prime suspects.

Sarah looked at him with pain-filled eyes. "I want to see my father," she wailed, again burying her face in her hands and sobbing uncontrollably as she leaned against his shoulder.

She seemed so frail, so helpless, Elliott thought his heart was going to break as he gently patted her shoulder again and whispered softly, "Don't you worry, honey. I'll be right back with your dad. And then, as much as I don't like it, I think you're going to have to show me where this all happened."

—2—

"Who was that, honey?" Rosalie Lahikainen asked lazily. She pulled the rumpled sheet up over her sweaty naked body as she sat up in bed and ran her fingers through her curly brown hair. As soon as Sarah and Marie had left, she and Devin had gone upstairs to bed, but they hadn't spent the time sleeping.

"That was the . . . police," Devin said, his voice tight and threatening to break. The blood drained from his face as he stared out the bedroom window and carefully replaced the phone. He was silent as he sat on the edge of the bed, staring blankly out at the darkness for a moment; then, shivering wildly, he turned to look squarely at her. His hand trembled as he reached out for her. She took his hand and gave it a firm, gentle squeeze as their eyes met.

"There's — uh, there's been some kind of trouble," Devin said. "Elliott Clark's on his way over."

"Trouble?" Rosalie said, clutching the sheets tightly around herself. "What kind of trouble?"

"With Marie and Sarah." Devin suddenly lurched off the bed, stumbled, almost fell, and then started pulling on his jeans, which he had casually tossed to the floor beside the bed two hours ago. "The dispatcher didn't say exactly what, just that Elliott was on his way over. Sounds to me like there might have been an accident."

"I hope everyone's all right," Rosalie said softly. They stared at each other silently for a long time, both of them at a loss for words.

Devin began pacing back and forth beside the bed, all the while running his fingers through his hair. He picked up his shirt from where he had dropped it, but before he could put it on, he heard a car pull into the driveway. Looking out the window, he saw the town police cruiser parked at the foot of the driveway. Rain danced on the slick driveway as the cruiser's windshield wipers slapped back and forth. Still bare-chested, he ran downstairs, taking the steps two at a time. He got to the front door just as the doorbell rang. The instant he flung the door open, he knew by the expression on Elliott's face that this was more than an accident.

"I'm sorry to have to tell you this, Devin," Elliott said, "but there's been some trouble. We think your ex-wife may have been killed."

Devin absorbed the news in stunned silence for several

heartbeats. Then, swallowing noisily, he said with a shaky voice, "And Sarah?"

"She's fine," Elliott replied. "Pretty shaken, needless to say, but she's fine. She's down at the station now." Briefly, he told him about Sarah's appearance at the police station and what she claimed had happened.

It was never easy to break this kind of news to anyone, and even though Elliott didn't know Devin Lahikainen very well, the fear and pain he saw in the man's eyes — especially when he mentioned his daughter — cut him to the quick. After reassuring him that Sarah was safely under protective custody at the station, Elliott waited on the doorstep while Devin went upstairs to finish dressing.

Back in the bedroom, Devin quickly told Rosalie what little he knew. His fingers were shaking so badly he couldn't button his shirt, so finally, in frustration, he tossed it aside and simply pulled on a T-shirt.

"When will you be back?" Rosalie asked, shrugging her shoulders helplessly.

Unspoken worry darkened her usually bright eyes, but as concerned as she was for Devin, and as worried as she was that something bad might have happened to Sarah, whom she had genuinely tried to get to know over the past week, she found she couldn't forgive Marie for the scene she had pulled earlier that evening. She had just met Marie for the first time tonight, and she had approached that meeting with every intention of trying to be at least cordial, if not outright friendly. But Marie — just like Devin had predicted all along — displayed nothing but resentment and barely masked hostility. After baiting both of them, Marie had finally ended up in a shouting match with Devin. Although Rosalie felt a stirring of guilt for having such thoughts and feelings, they were undeniably there.

"Should I come with you?" she asked. "Maybe I can help." Before Devin could answer, she swung out of bed and stood there naked. Her hands fluttered nervously in front of her as she glanced around the room for her discarded clothes.

"No, I don't think that would . . . help any," Devin said. He paused a moment and stared at her, remembering with a twist

42

of melancholy the pleasure they had just shared. "Either way, it's going to be a long night . . . and next couple of days. You might just as well wait here."

"Do you expect me to be able to sleep?" she asked.

Devin could tell she was struggling to keep the angry edge out of her voice. He stared at her as strong, cold fingers gripped his heart and squeezed. "I'll be back as soon as I can," he said softly. "Please . . . I just want to be alone with Sarah right now."

He was close to tears as he walked over to her, embraced her stiffly, and gave her a quick kiss on the cheek; then he ran down the stairs, grabbed his raincoat from the front hall closet, and slipped it on as he walked out to the cruiser with Elliott. Through the rain-smeared car window, Devin looked up at the dull yellow light spilling from his bedroom window and the dark silhouette blocking it. Neither said a word as Elliott backed out of the driveway and drove downtown to the station.

After an agonizing reunion at the station, which made both Sarah and Devin break down in tears, they all got back into the cruiser. Sarah had washed up and changed into clean, dry clothes. She sat with her father in the backseat as Elliott headed out of town on Route 26, following the directions Sarah gave him. The rain-slick road glistened like silver in the headlights. Once out of town, they passed a few isolated houses and farms, all with their lights off, and then entered the dark, lonely stretch of woods.

About two miles past the last house, Elliott eased up on the gas when he saw the dark shape of an abandoned car up ahead. He pulled to a stop on the side of the road, being careful to angle his headlights so they didn't illuminate the crime scene. He looked over his shoulder at Sarah but found himself at a loss for words and shifted his gaze over to Devin. Then he picked up his emergency flashlight from the dashboard, opened the car door, and stepped out.

Rain beat down on him, making loud popping sounds on his rubber rain slicker as he approached the abandoned car. His flashlight beam weaved back and forth, scanning the roadside. He could see some indication of a struggle in the dirt, but the torrents of rain had pretty much washed it away. Elliott's heart skipped a beat when he caught a flash of white off to one side. Looking down into the narrow ditch, he saw Marie Lahikainen. She lay on her back in inches-deep gutter water, her face and clothes splashed with mud and blood. Her hair was slicked back in shiny, dark ringlets. The black, gaping slash across her throat was stretched open wide, looking almost like a second mouth. Her sightless eyes reflected back the light with a dull, silvery glint.

"Oh, shit!" Elliott muttered as a deep chill reached inside his slicker.

He knew he didn't have to go down there to make sure she was dead, so he turned and walked slowly back to the cruiser. As he eased himself onto the car seat, he found he couldn't even look at Sarah or Devin as he picked up the radio microphone and clicked it on.

"Yeah, uh, Tony we got a ten-forty-eight out here. About five miles out on 26 toward Andover. Notify Augusta and get Hank and one of his boys to help me secure the area. You might want to contact Andover, too, and ahh—we're gonna need an ambulance and a tow truck. Over."

The dispatcher acknowledged Elliott's message and then signed off with a curt "Over and out."

Although generally in a case like this the husband or ex-husband was considered a prime suspect, Elliott was confident that Devin Lahikainen had had nothing to do with his ex-wife's murder. He knew Devin had been home with his wife, and unless Devin was a superior actor, he had genuinely broken down when he had been told what had happened.

"We'll have to wait until the ambulance and some help shows up," Elliott said. His voice had a slight tremor as he turned around to face Sarah and Devin. "Once the Criminal Investigation Division gets here and everything's covered, we can head back to the station." Feeling a strong surge of compassion, he looked at Sarah and asked in a softer voice, "Do you think you're up to handling some questions from one of the detectives?"

Biting her lower lip, her expression tight, Sarah nodded. "I think so."

"Good," Elliott said.

Devin had his arm over Sarah's shoulder and was squeezing her tightly. He locked eyes with Elliott in a silent exchange of concern. As they waited, a dull silence broken only by the patter of rain on the car roof and bursts of static-filled chatter over the radio filled the cruiser.

"You know, this isn't going to get any easier, Sarah," Elliott said after a while. "This questioning back at the station—it can get pretty grueling."

"I want to be there, too," Devin said. His voice sounded unnaturally tight and dry.

Elliott nodded agreement. "You have to be. We can't interview a juvenile without a parent or guardian present."

"I think I can . . . can handle it," Sarah stammered.

Finding it difficult to look at her, Elliott shifted his attention back to the police scanner and stared at it blankly as he listened to the radio traffic. "The CID should be here soon," he said, more to himself than to either one of them.

As much as she tried not to, Sarah couldn't stop looking up ahead at the black hulk of her mother's deserted car. She was dimly grateful her mother's body wasn't in sight, but that only made it seem possible—somehow—that she still might be alive. Her eyes burned as hot tears coursed down her cheeks and a restless, winding fear filled her when she remembered the pure terror of watching from the woods as her mother was brutally raped and then murdered. And then the memory of running . . . running for her life and hiding so that man wouldn't do the same thing to her. She could barely think about it without wanting to scream—scream until she either passed out or died.

"Tully . . ." she whispered softly, barely aware she was speaking aloud.

"What did you say?" Elliott asked. He turned around quickly and looked squarely at her.

Sarah shook her head, trying to fight back the steadily mounting waves of numbing fear that were crashing inside her. In spite of all the horrors she had seen and felt this night, nothing reached deeper into her mind with cold, sharp claws than the memory of seeing that black, vaguely human shape

45

drifting through the woods and hovering threateningly behind the man who had been chasing her.

"No — I, uhh —"

"You said a name. What was it — Terry or something?" Elliott said, pressing. "Did your mother say that? Maybe she knew who the guy was." He knew he shouldn't push her too hard, but what if she had unconsciously repeated a name she had overheard?

"Oh, no — no," Devin said as he pulled Sarah closer to him. "She said *Tully*. That was the name of her make-believe friend back when she was a little girl."

The mere mention of her childhood brought fresh tears to Sarah's eyes when the realization hit her — again, and just as cold and hard — that her mother was lying dead somewhere there up the road. Her shoulders shook as agony cut through her like a scalpel. She looked back and forth between her father and the policeman, desperately wishing either one of them could remove even a fraction of the panic and pain inside her. She couldn't stop her startled yelp when she glanced straight ahead and caught a trace of motion up by her mother's car.

"Is that —" She cut herself off sharply, unable to finish her question as she stared into the darkness ahead. For a panic-filled instant, she thought she had seen something move.

What if it was her mother, still alive, struggling to stand up? Or if that wasn't her mother, what if it was . . . Tully?

The memory of seeing that shadowy figure gliding through the rainy woods made her shiver wildly.

"What is it?" Elliott asked, instantly tensing. His hand dropped to his service revolver as he looked out at the road. Night and the heavy rain were all he could see.

Sarah kept staring up the road, even though her vision was blurred by her tears. She was positive she had seen something — a dark movement against the night forest either behind or beside the car.

"No. For a second there, I thought I saw someone . . . up by the car," she rasped.

"C'mon," her father said reassuringly even as he flashed a worried glance at Elliott. "You've been through a lot tonight, honey. You—you're probably just imagining things."

"The two of you stay here," Elliott said as he grabbed his flashlight with one hand and unsnapped his revolver with the other. He went back out into the night. The brief blast of the dome light before he shut the door stung Sarah's eyes, sending spinning red circles across her vision. Feeling faint, she watched tensely with her father as Elliott started up the road again toward the car, sweeping his flashlight beam back and forth in wide arcs as he went.

"Do you think he might still be out there?" Sarah asked her father. Devin assumed she meant the man who had killed Marie, but then she shakily added, "Do you think Tully could be out there?"

—3—

The rain fell in a steady, heavy downpour. Tensed and ready to respond, Elliott stayed well away from Marie's car as he checked both sides of the road for fresh footprints or any other indication that someone was still in the area. He glanced at the glowing dial of his watch several times, irritated at how long it was taking the backup and investigators to show up. He knew that every minute they delayed, more valuable evidence was washing away—if it wasn't already completely destroyed. The road and woods were silent except for the steady hiss of rain, but even so, he couldn't shake the feeling that Sarah had been right. He could almost feel that someone was nearby, hidden by the darkness, watching his every move. He shivered, commanding himself to stay calm, but he couldn't forget the old police maxim: "They always return to the scene of the crime."

Whenever Elliott glanced at the dead woman sprawled in the ditch beside the road, he cringed, thinking about the agony and horror Sarah must have experienced—and would have to live with the rest of her life. His heart felt hollow and cold. This was the part of police work he truly detested—having to maintain such professional detachment while dealing with people who were experiencing misery and suffering—especially people like Sarah, who were so

47

innocent, so vulnerable.

Fifteen minutes later, the ambulance arrived. Shortly thereafter, the sheriff's department from Bethel, two patrolmen from Andover, and the state detectives and evidence technicians all showed up. Elliott went back to the cruiser along with Detective Gary Simpson while the sheriff's men and the ETs set about establishing the crime scene.

"Sorry about what happened," Detective Simpson said tonelessly as he eased himself into the front passenger's seat. He was a heavyset man who looked as if he would sweat even on a January morning. Hooking an elbow over the car seat, he turned to face Sarah and Devin. "I don't suppose we need either one of you for a positive ID of the victim."

Devin made a thick grunting sound in the back of his throat as he shook his head.

Turning to Elliott, Simpson said, "Looks to me like they've got things pretty much covered. We might as well head on back to town so we can get started."

The area was alive with strobing red and blue emergency lights as Elliott turned the cruiser around and headed back to the Hilton police station. As they drove away, Sarah couldn't help but turn around and look back. Staring out the rain-streaked rear window, she watched the silently receding figures of two men as they set up a barricade blocking the road.

What in the name of Heaven was that hazy black shape hovering in the darkness of the woods while she cowered on the forest floor?

What if it had been Tully?

What if he had come because she had called him?

And what if she was the one who had made him do those horrible things to her mother because *she* had been so angry at her?

Chapter Four

The Lineup

– 1 –

Sarah spent the next two hours at the station telling Detective Simpson and Elliott everything she remembered. She repeated, time and again, in as exact detail as she could recall, the precise sequence of events. She wasn't sure why, but the first time through she decided not to mention the shadowy figure that had drifted out of the darkness from behind her and had hovered beside the man who had been chasing her. It seemed too strange, too crazy to have been real; she dismissed it—as well as any possibility that Tully had been there—as something her overstressed mind had created. As exhausted as she was by the night's events, she certainly didn't want to say anything that might call her mental stability into question. The interrogation lasted until well past three o'clock in the morning.

"But you never got a clear look at this man, is that correct?" Simpson asked for the umpteenth time.

Biting her lower lip and shaking her head, Sarah muttered, "No . . . not at all. It was really foggy, and I had gone quite a ways into the woods." The bright lights in the room stung her eyes, making her wince. She needed to sleep, but she was positive that if she were to lie down now, she wouldn't be able to drift off—not with the tormented memories she had. She began to wonder if she would ever be able to sleep again.

"And once this 'strange man,' as you keep calling him, got out of his car to talk with your mother, you went even farther into the woods. Right?"

Sarah nodded.

"Why did you do that? Once you knew he might mean trouble, didn't it cross your mind that you should try to help your mother — or at least see who he was so you could identify him later?"

"She was scared, for Christ's sake!" Devin snapped. He, too, was exhausted, and Detective Simpson's incessant repetition was grinding his nerves down to the core.

"I — I tried to. Honest!" Sarah answered bravely. "But my mother said something that sounded like she wanted me to stay out of sight —"

"That was when she told the man that she had stopped because she had to go to the bathroom, saying it as if she was alone, right?"

Sarah nodded tightly.

"As if she knew he meant trouble?"

"That was obvious right away," Sarah said. "I could tell that just from the way he was approaching the car. He had this real cocky swagger when he walked, like he thought he was really cool. And the way he talked to her." She wiped furiously at her eyes with the sodden tissue in her hand and then grabbed a fresh one from the dispenser on Elliott's desk.

"Don't you think we've been over this enough?" Devin asked, glancing up at the clock on the wall. "I think the only thing Sarah needs right now is a good night's sleep."

"Just a bit more," Simpson said with a cold, hard tone of voice. He wiped the flat of his hand over his sweaty face as he considered for a moment. Turning to Sarah, he asked, "Do you think you'd be able to identify this man in a lineup?"

Sarah had seen enough police shows to know what a lineup was. She thought for a moment, mentally replaying the events of the night. Everything had been so hazy and had happened so fast, she was beginning to question the accuracy of her own memory.

"I — I'm not sure," she said with a raw scratch in her

50

voice. "I guess I could try."

"Well, then," Simpson said, turning to Elliott, "I think we're going to have to do a bit of legwork and see if we can rustle up as many suspects as we can find and just hope for the best."

Throughout the interrogation session, Elliott had remained seated quietly in a corner of his office. He found himself staring intently at Sarah most of the time, unable to stop watching her. Detective Simpson's comment caught him off guard.

"Yeah, I guess so," he said.

"So — ? Are you releasing her into the custody of her father now?" Simpson asked.

Even though he still had a few lingering doubts, Elliott nodded. It may simply have been the stress of the situation and the late hour, but he thought he detected a submerged tension in Devin Lahikainen that bothered him a bit.

"Then I reckon you're free to go home now, Sarah," Simpson said.

Sarah stood up and shakily walked over to her father, immediately breaking down when he put his arm around her. Covering her face with her hands, she sobbed and cried out, "I don't have a home anymore!"

Devin crushed her against his chest and vigorously rubbed her shoulders. "There — there; you know darned right well you can stay with me and Rosalie. You have a home as long as I'm alive."

Sarah looked up at him, her face slick with tears, her eyes glazed with misery.

"I know we haven't spent all that much time together the past few years," Devin went on, "but now — "

Before he could say any more, Sarah collapsed against him, folding into his arms as she cried.

— 2 —

After giving Sarah a full week to recover, time enough to bury her mother and at least begin to absorb her grief, Detective Simpson asked her to come down to the police station early one morning. She spent the better part of two hours poring over mug shots with Simpson. Her eyes were still red and burning from crying as she sat down in a small, unlit room and watched through the two-way mirror as seven men walked into the squad room and stood silently under the bright lights. It took a great deal of effort for her to concentrate and study each man individually. She had seen so many faces, read so many descriptions, and had so many twisted, tormented nightmares that she no longer trusted the few fragmentary memories she had of that horrible night. The image of that man, laughing like a maniac as he chased her through the sodden woods, calling to her to give herself up before he got too mad, had grown in the dark recesses of her mind until he had become something almost supernatural. He had transformed into a towering, menacing shadow that hovered constantly at the edge of her awareness, following her . . . stalking her . . . waiting to pounce on her the instant she let her guard down.

"Is he out there?" Detective Simpson asked flatly.

He knew they were grasping at straws now. So far, he and the rest of the investigating team had come up one hundred percent dry for suspects. Area questioning had been a dead end as had all attempts to lift clear tire casts, footprints, or fingerprints from the scene of the crime. The results from the semen residue indicated that Marie's assailant was A-positive blood type. And that was all the police had.

Biting her lower lip, Sarah glanced over at her father, who was sitting beside her in the darkened room, then scanned the line of men a second time. One thing she was positive of was how good it felt to have him here, just as good as it felt to have Elliott Clark with her. She tried squinting, to remove some of the details so she would see the man more as she had seen him that night — a dim, watery silhouette, but even that failed. She wanted to believe that she would be able to sense his presence if he were close by; but for all she knew, the man who had done those horrible things to her mother could be standing right there in front of her and she'd never even realize it!

"No, I — I can't — "

She cut herself short when a rush of chills rippled up her arms and gripped her lightly on the back of the neck. Her breath caught in her chest and started to strangle her as the steady flutter of her pulse turned into a heavy hammering in her ears. Icy cold formed in the pit of her stomach, radiating outward like spider's legs.

I think he's here! she thought but was unable to say it aloud. *Tully.*

Waves of dizziness washed through her as she squirmed in her chair. Her hands went numb as she squeezed them between her knees. The tingling spread down her arms and legs like cold fire as her breathing became shorter, shallower. Without moving her head, her eyes darted from side to side, looking first at her father, then at Detective Simpson, and finally at Elliott Clark. Their faces were blank, expressionless, as if nothing was happening.

He's right here . . . He's right behind me.

Sarah wanted to turn and look behind her, but she didn't dare. The four walls of the room seemed to press in on her, stifling her.

"I know how tough this must be for you, Sarah," Detective Simpson was saying. His voice seemed to come from far away — as if he were in another room. "But I want you to try as hard as you can."

Staring helplessly straight ahead, Sarah could faintly see herself, her father, Elliott, and Detective Simpson reflected in the polished surface of the observation window. Their reflections looked like pale apparitions superimposed over the lineup of men, like a photographic negative — thin and washed out. And hovering behind her left shoulder was something else — a fifth reflection, but not of another person . . . just of a cloudy silhouette, a hazy, gray splotch that blotted out her view of one of the men in the lineup.

With an anguished moan, she stood up suddenly, knocking her chair over, and slapped both hands across her mouth. A scream was born and died inside her mind. From far away, she heard the clatter of metal on concrete as her chair scraped against the floor. It sounded like the prolonged, tortured wreck of a car in slow motion.

"Sarah? . . . Are you all right . . . ?"

The voice — it might have been her father's — seemed sludgy and distorted.

It was the last thing she heard before the darkness pulled her down. She wasn't conscious when Elliott lunged forward and caught her just before she hit the floor.

— 3 —

"Are you sure you're up to this?" Devin asked. He and Sarah were downstairs in the kitchen, waiting for Rosalie, who was upstairs putting on her makeup.

Sarah smiled as she straightened out her father's necktie and brushed a tangle of lint off his shoulder.

"Of course I am," she said. "I felt like a complete idiot yesterday — fainting in front of you and Elliott, but I'm fine now — just fine." The hollow tone in her voice wasn't convincing even to herself.

"Sleep well last night?"

She nodded. "Terrific," she lied; it had been another night of twisted nightmares. "Now will you please stop worrying?" She gave her father a good-natured swat on the shoulder. "I think it's important that we —" She cut herself off when her voice caught in her throat.

"That we get on with our own lives, right?" her father said, trying to complete the thought for her.

Sarah nodded, thought what she had intended to say was how important it was for her and Rosalie to try to get to know and like each other. Over the past week, tension had been running high in the house, and things between her and her stepmother were quite strained. Sarah had suggested that the three of them go out to eat at the White Crane, a fancy restaurant in town, just so they could get out of the house and, if possible, put the investigation behind them . . . at least for an hour or two.

"You're something else, you know that?" her father said, smiling broadly.

Sarah smiled back at him, but the instant their eyes locked, their smiles faded. With a sigh, Devin pulled her close to him.

"Oh, baby," he whispered. His eyes misted over as he ran his hand down the back of her head. "You just don't know how much I wish things had been different between me and your —"

"I know that," Sarah said, quickly cutting him off before he

54

could say the word *mother.* Just thinking the word made her eyes sting. She looked up at him, trying her best to stop her lower lip from trembling as tears filled her eyes. She wanted to say something brave and reassuring, but she had no idea what.

When they heard Rosalie's footsteps on the stairs, they went into the hallway to meet her.

"What a great dress," Sarah said politely. "It looks so summery."

"I figured—what the heck? Why not rush the season a little?" Rosalie smiled as she flounced the floral print dress. Tossing her head from side to side to fluff her thick, curly hair, she walked over to Devin. "Do you like it?"

"You look beautiful," he said softly as he put his arms around her and kissed her.

As the kiss lengthened, Sarah felt a stirring of discomfort. Glancing at her wristwatch, she cleared her throat noisily and said, "Hey, guys—I hate to break anything up here, but our reservations arc for eight o'clock."

The three of them linked arms, walked out to the car, and drove downtown to the White Crane. Even after they were seated and had ordered drinks and appetizers, though, Sarah's discomfort continued. She felt a twist of guilt when she realized she was thinking how much she wished her father had never married Rosalie. It wasn't that she didn't like her new stepmother; she seemed nice enough, at least as much as Sarah had gotten to know her. Over the past few days, Rosalie had earnestly tried her best to be compassionate and helpful. But other than the week she had spent with them last spring, this was the first time Sarah had an opportunity to see her in a situation other than the excruciating circumstances of her own mother's rape and murder and the subsequent investigation, and she was filled with grave doubts about what would happen next. She had spent almost all of the last week or so with her father and Rosalie. But, school would be ending in a week and a half, and Sarah was nervous about moving in with her dad and Rosalie. She wanted to stay in Westbrook with Kathy Meserve, her best friend; she dreaded the thought of leaving all her friends behind. They were the last link to her former life, when her mother was alive. No matter how hard Rosalie tried, she

55

would never come close to replacing her mother in Sarah's affections.

As dinner went on, Sarah became increasingly withdrawn until, by the time the main course was served, she was quiet and morose, hardly speaking even when asked a direct question. She picked a little at the stuffed lobster on her plate. As soon as her father and Rosalie were finished eating, and her father had slouched back in his chair to enjoy a cigarette, she asked if it was all right if she went outside for a bit of fresh air.

"Just hurry on back," he told her, his eyes shimmering with affection, his brow creased with concern. Sarah got the unsettling impression that he was putting all of this on, that after spending just about every waking minute with her for the past weeks, he would much rather be spending this time alone with Rosalie. As she wended her way between the crowded tables and out the front door, Sarah was stung with fresh pain; she began to see herself as the albatross in the Coleridge poem.

A full moon was riding high in the sky above a dusty cushion of clouds. A light breeze made Sarah shiver as she closed the restaurant's double doors gently behind her and wandered down the curved walkway toward the road. The sound of conversation and clinking silverware from the restaurant soon faded away, leaving her wrapped in muffled silence that magnified the clicking of her shoes on the asphalt. She knew she could cry if she wanted to; no one was here to see her; and even if there was . . . so what? More than anyone else she knew, she had a right to cry, and she didn't have to tell anyone — even her father — the real reason grief and loneliness were wringing her heart.

But it was more than grief and loneliness; she knew that much. She was filled with anger. Right now, she was angry at her father for remarrying. Just as angry as her mother had been that night. It didn't matter whom he had married or how nice she was; Sarah felt her mother's memory was being betrayed simply because her father was sleeping with someone else.

And she was angry at Rosalie, maybe even more than she was at her father. At least her father was doing whatever he could to help her. He had been nothing but supportive and caring since that horrible night. Throughout the interviews with Elliott Clark and Detective Simpson, the mug shot reviews, and that horrible lineup yesterday, he had been right there with her. Every night, when she couldn't get to sleep, he would stay with her, talk to her, hug her long into the night just to let her know that she wasn't alone.

Rosalie, on the other hand, was different. Sarah could see that, of course, she didn't have a deep, emotional stake in what had happened. If anything, her father had probably filled Rosalie with lies about her mother. But no matter how much Rosalie tried to cover it up, Sarah was convinced she resented—yes!—resented how much of her father's time and attention she was taking up. She was convinced that Rosalie dreaded that she would be living with them permanently. Her stepmother certainly never said or did anything to reinforce this impression, but Sarah felt it was there just below the surface every time Rosalie even looked at her.

But most of all, Sarah was angry at the man who had done this horrible thing to her life—the man who had tormented and killed her mother and left her feeling as though, no matter how long she lived, she would never again feel the joy, the happiness of being alive. As deeply as she could hate anyone, she detested this unknown man who had cast a black cloud over her life that would never lift. And she twisted with guilt whenever she thought of Tully—Tully who might have been there that night, who might have somehow caused it all to happen.

Sarah turned the corner and walked slowly up the hill, carefully feeling her way along the unlit sidewalk. Through the opened kitchen windows at the back of the restaurant, she could hear the clank and clatter of dishes and silverware, and the shouted commands of waiters, waitresses, cooks, and dishwashers. She paused by the back stairway and stared down into the small garden area where, once the summer arrived, White Crane customers could eat outside on the patio. The garden was dark now, lit only by the light spilling from the kitchen windows. Before she continued her walk, a figure moved behind the lighted screen door at the back of the restaurant, drawing her attention.

"Yeah? Well *fuck* you!"

The angry voice startled Sarah. It filled the night, echoing dully from inside the back entryway, demanding her attention. The person standing there was obviously a young man, tall and broad-shouldered. She watched as he stood defiantly with his fisted hands held low and tensed at his waist.

Another, deeper voice from inside the kitchen said something, but Sarah couldn't quite make it out.

"I swear to Christ I didn't take your *fucking* money!" the young man shouted. His voice broke with vicious hostility and anger. "Why the fuck would I need to steal money from you?"

Again, the other person said something in so low a voice Sarah didn't quite catch it, but she clearly heard the young man's response.

"Yeah, well who the hell needs this fucking job anyway?"

The rusty spring on the screen door shrieked as the young man flung it open and stormed out into the night. Before the screen door could snap shut, the person he had been arguing with stopped it with his hand as he leaned out.

"You're *fired!*" the man yelled. "You hear me, Griffin? *Fired!*"

"Fuck you!" the young man shouted over his shoulder. "You can't fire me. I quit." Snorting with laughter, he turned and started up the stairs, slamming his feet heavily on each step as he pounded his fists on the railing.

"I'm warning you. I'm going to talk to the police about this," the man leaning out the back door yelled. "You can't get away with this!"

"Yeah, well you can't prove shit!" the young man replied. He was halfway up the stairway to the street when he turned, reached behind his back, undid the apron he was wearing, and balling it up, flung it down at the man in the door. Coming unseen out of the darkness, it hit the man squarely in the chest. He shouted and staggered back in surprise, letting go of the screen door, which slammed back and bumped him in the face.

"I swear to God, Griffin!" the man shouted. "I'm gonna tell the police everything!"

"Ahh—fuck you!"

As the young man turned and started back up the stairs toward the street, Sarah was filled with a cold, nameless dread. She wasn't sure why; all she knew was, she had to

58

make sure this man didn't see her . . . and he was heading straight up the stairway toward her.

Looking frantically around, she spotted the hedge that lined the sidewalk beside the restaurant. For a frozen moment, she considered ducking in there and hiding until the man was gone. Steely fingers of fear gripped the back of her neck, and sweat stood out on her brow. It was too late to hide! He would see her or hear her before she could move a muscle. Spinning around quickly, she started briskly back toward the front of the restaurant, knowing that the best she could do, without being too obvious, was pretend she had been out for a walk and hadn't heard a thing. If the man went the same way she was going, she might even slow down to a casual pace, smile at him as he passed her by, and say what a pleasant evening it was. But she didn't dare turn to see which way he went once he reached the top of the stairs. Clenching her teeth so hard her jaw muscles ached, she listened for his approaching footsteps above the steady hammering of her pulse in her ears.

When she rounded the corner, she was finally able to force herself to glance over her shoulder. She couldn't see a thing other than the dark tunnel of the unlit street, but—thankfully—she could hear his heavy footsteps as they faded away into the night, moving away from her. She let out her breath in a long, loud whistle but, even now, couldn't resist the chilling thought that he hadn't really walked away. He was still out there, lurking in the dark, watching her.

Why the hell am I so damned jumpy? she wondered even though she already knew the answer. The horrors of that night on the deserted road a mile out of town would stay with her for the rest of her life; there was no escaping them.

Still feeling as though unseen eyes were staring at her out of the darkness, she hurried back into the brightly lit restaurant and forced herself to smile and pretend she was happy for the rest of the evening.

Chapter Five

Valley View

— 1 —

On a chilly, rainy Saturday afternoon in late July, Sarah was home alone for the first time since her mother's death. Her father and Rosalie had driven to Rumford for lunch before continuing on to Waterville to visit Devin's mother, who was in a nursing home there.

Sheets of rain beat against her bedroom window as Sarah sat cross-legged on her bed with her tape recorder in her lap. She was trying to focus her thoughts, but as soon as she tried to put her feelings into words, nervousness would make her voice tremble. Nervousness? Or was it anger at being left alone in an empty house? Her eyes glazed with tears, blurring her view as she stared out over the field at the distant gray line of trees across the river. The trees were swaying to the fitful gusts of rain-laden wind. Especially when it rained, Sarah couldn't help remembering what had happened that night almost two months ago.

She punched the button on the recorder, and the tape started to turn. Clearing her throat, she began to speak. "I have to be honest—at least with myself when I'm doing my tapes," she said in a broken whisper. "I mean, I know what I'm doing is probably wrong. It's not like it's Rosalie's fault that she married my dad or that any of this happened. I mean, I can't very well blame her for my problems, right?"

A chill shook her shoulders. She glanced nervously at the closed bedroom door behind her. Ever since she had moved to Hilton, she felt anxious, vulnerable, skittish. A lot of the time, she felt as if she were being watched. Several nights, especially during the first few weeks in her new bedroom, she had awakened in the middle of the night convinced someone was hiding either under her bed or in her closet or just outside her window. Too scared to get up and check or even to call out to her father, she would lie there in the dark, worrying and wondering why she felt so . . . so . . .

"Haunted," she whispered as the tape silently turned. "I feel like this house, maybe this whole town is haunted with . . . with memories of my mom."

Her throat closed off with a loud, hitching sound. Rubbing her eyes viciously with the heels of her hands, she sniffed loudly but forced herself to continue.

"And of course I know none of this is Rosalie's fault. It isn't hers or anyone's fault that my mom . . ."

Again, her throat closed off as though she were being strangled.

". . . that my mom . . . *died.*"

The last word was no more than a puff of air, but saying it finally made her break down. Collapsing forward onto her bed, she buried her face in the crook of her arm and wailed, letting the torment of weeks of anguish and loss consume her all over again, as fresh as if everything had happened just yesterday. The tape continued to run, recording the agonized sounds of her crying. After a while, once the initial sting of pain began to fade, she sat up, wiped her eyes with the sleeve of her blouse, and continued talking.

"I can't kid myself about Rosalie. I know exactly what I'm doing," Sarah rasped. "It's like something straight out of a fairy tale, you know? I'm putting all the bad things I feel onto my stepmother, as if she's some kind of . . . of wicked witch-queen or something. Like today, for instance. I mean, for weeks I had plans to go down to Westbrook and spend the weekend at Kathy's. Ruth and Louise were gonna be there, too. And then when Kathy called and said her father had to work a double shift at the mill, and we'd have to cancel unless I could get a ride down, who did I take it out on? Why, Rosalie, of course. Why am I being such a creep? As if Rosalie doesn't realize what I've been through, how much I miss my old friends."

She sighed deeply, twisting with guilt but still feeling a needling barb of anger at Rosalie.

"But it isn't just her. She isn't the one who wouldn't change their plans so they could give me a ride to Westbrook. But I can't say as I blame Dad, either. He couldn't just change their plans. They had already told my grandmother they'd be coming to visit her this afternoon. They couldn't not show up. But still . . . it just doesn't seem fair!"

She swatted the mattress with the flat of her hand.

"I mean, if only Dad would help me buy me a car so I could get around on my own. He says he doesn't want me driving off to Westbrook by myself. Probably he's afraid what happened to Mom might happen to me. But he uses the excuse that he has to save money to get me through college after next year."

Sarah snorted and wiped at her eyes. She had calmed down enough to remember to push the pause button while tried to sort out her thoughts. For several seconds, she stared blankly at the yellow wallpaper. Once she was ready, she took a deep breath and started the tape moving again.

"I mean, as if telling me they're going to visit Grandma in the nursing home makes it any different. Sure, sure—she's my father's mother, and he's lucky that she's still alive, unlike my moth—But there are things I just can't stand about Rosalie! Like that she tricked my father into marrying her, and that she doesn't even want him to spend any time with me. I know I'm making a lot of this up, but sometimes when I look at her, I can just imagine how much she hates me—because of what happened. I think she's just

62

waiting for the next school year to be over so I'll be off to college, and she'll have Dad all to herself. I guess it's okay to say that. Sure, there are a lot of little things she does that niggle me, but sometimes I get the feeling she has it in for me big time, you know? Because I had to come here and live with them. Like it's nothing more than some kind of interruption or inconvenience in her life that my mother was . . . was killed!"

Sarah's anger and grief grew razor-sharp for a moment. She sucked in air between her teeth and clenched her hands into fists. With a gut-deep sob, she punched the bed again, hard enough to make the recorder jump.

"And when I think about how . . . how damned lonely I feel—"

Tears and frustration choked her. She sniffed loudly, frowning at the bad taste in the back of her mouth.

"And when I think about how much I miss my—my mom . . . how I can't stop remembering what I went through, the terror she must have felt before she died, trying to protect me! And then I think back to how much it hurt when I was a little kid, and they were going through their divorce. That can't be Rosalie's fault, but whose fault is it?"

She wiped under her nose with the back of her hand.

"Maybe I should be mad at the police. They're never going to catch that man. Never! Oh, yeah—sure. They say they're doing their best to find him, but their excuse is that by the time they got there, the rain had washed away all the evidence. They say he must've been a drifter, just passing through town. Maybe—but if he was a drifter, how come he didn't take the money in mom's purse? I think the cops don't want to find out who it was. Maybe they would just as soon pretend it never happened! As long as nothing else like that ever happens in their sleepy little town again, they can just brush it all under the rug. . . . But I *can't* . . . goddamn it, I can't because it's my mom who died!"

Sarah tensed and looked around, suddenly aware that a hazy shadow had shifted in the corner of her vision. Her

63

finger was poised above the pause button but she didn't stop her recording.

"Tully?" she whispered, unable to stop the wild shiver that went through her as she looked out the window at the solid gray mass of clouds. The back of her head began to tingle, and the hair on the back of her neck rose.

"Tully!" she said again, louder; this time followed by a tight laugh. "Damn it, Tully! That's when I first started talking to you, wasn't it? Back when Mom and Dad were having all their trouble?" She laughed again, forcing herself to be brave even as the feeling got steadily stronger that a dark cloud was hovering behind her, shifting out of sight to one side or the other whenever she turned to try to see it.

Sarah snorted and shook her head with disgust at how she was letting her imagination get so carried away. "I guess I had to have someone to talk to, huh?"

"That's right," a voice said, clear and close to her ear.

With a shriek, Sarah leaped off the bed and spun around, almost losing her balance and falling to the floor. Her eyes widened in shock when she saw the young man sitting in the rocking chair by her closet door. Although he looked older now, she instantly recognized him.

"Jesus Christ, Tully! What are—? How did—? How did you get in here?"

The young man shrugged his shoulders before flipping a thin strand of blond hair away from his eyes. His face was winter-pale, the skin almost translucent. He stared at her with unblinking blue eyes that crackled with intensity. His pale, long-fingered hands rested on the arms of the chair. His feet were wrapped through the chair rungs as he shifted his weight forward and back, rocking slowly. The rocker creaked on the wooden floor with a steady cadence.

"I've been here all along," he said, smiling that same old wide-toothed grin of his. He looked older now, still a year or two older than she was. Maybe . . . well, if she was seventeen, he must be eighteen or nineteen.

"But you—" Sarah stammered. "I mean, I haven't seen you—I haven't even thought about you for years . . . at least, not until recently. Only since I came to my dad's. Where'd you come from?"

Tully shrugged again, holding his hands in the air and wiggling his fingers like a magician proving he had nothing up his sleeves. "All I can say is, I've been around. I knew you were angry and needed someone to talk to." His blue eyes momentarily clouded over; then he shook his head and finished, "So here I am. I'm ready to talk."

"I just—You aren't . . . I can't believe this," Sarah said, shaking her head and shivering with nervous laughter as she glanced down at the tape recorder. It was still churning away. "I mean—you're not even real! You can't be real! You're just somebody I—I made up when I was a kid."

Tully's grin widened. "You mean you didn't see me in the woods that night?"

His question jolted her. She frowned deeply, then opened her mouth and was about to say something, but Tully cut her off.

"You know which night I mean, don't you?" he asked. His voice was low, almost threatening. "The night you were hiding in the bushes while that man was chasing you." He sat back as though surprised. "You mean, you didn't see me there?"

Sarah's throat made a tight choking sound. "You were— How could you—? That couldn't have been you!"

"Ah-ha, so you did see me."

"Well—yeah, I saw something," Sarah replied. "But I thought it had to be all in my imagination."

"Do you think what happened to your mother was all in your imagination, too?" Tully asked. He leaned his head back and laughed loudly without the faintest trace of actual humor. Sarah's blood ran cold.

"Yeah, I was there all right," Tully said. "I saw exactly what happened."

"Sometimes I even thought maybe you made it all happen."

Tully's smile tightened for an instant, then faded. "I saw everyone who was there, but I—"

65

"You mean you saw him? You saw who killed my mother?" Sarah asked with sudden intensity. She leaned forward, her hands clenched into fists. "You have to tell me who he was! *Tell me!*"

Tully smiled again and nodded, but even as he opened his mouth to speak, he began to fade. "I don't know if you don't know," he said, his lips moving in slow motion. A sparkling halo of yellow light blossomed behind him, brightening as it surrounded and engulfed him. Then, with a hollow *pop* sound and a shimmering of light, he vanished.

For a long time, Sarah sat poised on the edge of her bed, staring in disbelief at the empty rocking chair. The space where Tully had been still vibrated, wavering like a heat haze that gradually faded away. Her mind was a roaring blank, and she lost all sense of where she was as she wondered how — and why — Tully had come to her after all this time. What had called him back? Had she willed him back into existence, simply by thinking about him and talking to him as if he were real? Or could the emotions she was feeling — grief, anguish, and anger — somehow have brought him back? Was that what gave him new strength? Or perhaps, as he had said, maybe he had simply "been here all along."

Been where? Sarah wondered. *Has he been with me all these years, watching over me without my even knowing it? Or is he just something I've made up because I'm lonely and scared?*

What finally pulled Sarah back to awareness was the sudden loud *click* of the tape recorder shutting off when it reached the end of the tape. She could barely control her trembling hands as she pressed *reverse*, let the tape rewind all the way back, and then pressed *play*. Cold disbelief cut her like an ice-edged sword when, throughout the tape, the only voice she heard was her own. But disbelief was replaced with soul-deep shivers when, for the entire last half of the tape, the whole time she was talking to Tully, she could hear the steady *squeak-squeak* of the rocking chair runners, moving slowly back and forth . . . back and forth . . .

Devin wrinkled his nose as he walked with Rosalie down the corridor of the Valley View Nursing Home in Waterville. As much as the Valley View administrators insisted this wasn't a hospital, the antiseptic smell and the cold, sterile walls made him think otherwise. Devin had never liked hospitals, so he wasn't exactly wild about the prospect of visiting his mother. Ester Lahikainen had been in Valley View since early last winter, following hip surgery. Because Devin had been the one to put her here, he felt quite a bit of guilt about her present situation.

"Oh, by the way," Devin said as they rode the elevator to the second floor, "I haven't told her anything about what happened to Marie. It'd probably be just as well, if we didn't mention it."

"I wasn't planning on bringing it up," Rosalie muttered. The tight expression on her face revealed how much she was looking forward to this afternoon's visit.

They got out of the elevator and started down the corridor. Passing through the dual wooden doors, they proceeded to the next to the last door on the left. Devin sucked in a deep breath before knocking, then pulled the door open and held it for Rosalie as he called out, "Hello, Ma. It's me, Davy."

The room was dimly lit. Thick plastic-backed curtains blocked out the daylight except for around the edges, which glowed with dull gray light. Rosalie stayed a step or two behind Devin as he cautiously approached the bed where the frail old woman lay. Her eyes were open, but they appeared to be focused somewhere well beyond the vanilla-colored acoustic ceiling tiles. A dull ache of loneliness struck Devin when he glanced at the array of family pictures on the bed stand. There was one of him, Marie, and Sarah from the week they had spent in North Carolina so many years ago. The gentle sucking sound of his mother's breathing was unusually loud in the otherwise quiet room.

"So tell me, Mom, how have you been feeling?" Devin

asked. He sat down on the edge of the bed and took her hand in his. Patting her wrist lightly, he let his fingertips trace the soft, blue lines of her veins.

"I've been better," Ester Lahikainen said with a voice cracked with age. "I've been better." Her eyes snapped into focus for an instant as she looked from Devin to Rosalie; then they glazed over and shifted back up to the ceiling.

"Well, I've been thinking about you a lot," Devin said. He signaled with a flick of his hand for Rosalie to step closer to the bed.

Ester's expression clouded as she strained to raise her head from the well of the pillow, but she soon gave it up and dropped back down after struggling for only a second or two. The tip of her tongue darted out and licked her pale upper lip before she said, "Is that Marie with you? You've done something different with your hair."

Rosalie shook her head as though startled and glanced quickly at Devin, trying to gauge by his reaction what she should say or do.

"No, no, Mom. This is Rosalie, my new wife. You remember me telling you about Rosalie, don't you?"

"Hello, Mrs. Lahikainen," Rosalie said softly in a flat, toneless voice.

Ester's lips moved silently as she twisted her head from side to side, but neither Devin nor Rosalie understood what she was trying to communicate.

"Oh, yes . . . Sarah . . . and you, too," Ester said. One side of her mouth twitched, almost smiling even as her gaze drifted toward the closed curtain where nobody stood. Her eyes went unfocused. "Yes—yes, my little darling, Sarah . . . and our little *haamu*."

Rosalie glanced again at Devin, her eyes silently asking him what the hell his mother was talking about, but he simply shrugged. Rosalie had never known Ester when she was well. Seeing someone who had deteriorated like this made her feel queasy and nervous. With a twinge of guilt, she couldn't help thinking that at least Sarah's own mother had been spared a long, painful decline at the end of her life.

For a moment, clarity returned to Ester's eyes as she tried again to sit up in bed. Devin went to the foot of the bed, pulled out the cranking mechanism, and turned it so the top half of the bed rose up. Ester's eyes brightened as if she just now realized she had visitors. Smoothing the sheet that covered her stomach and legs, she glanced over at the clock beside the bed and said with a bright, chipper voice, "Well, well, morning already?"

Rosalie and Devin both nodded and looked at each other, neither one bothering to tell her that it was already late afternoon.

"You've grown up since I saw you last, Sarah," Ester said.

"No, Ma. This isn't Sarah," Devin replied. There was a trace of exasperation in his voice. "This is my new wife— Rosalie."

"Your wife's name is Marie," Ester said. "Didn't she and I go to Sunday School together? I remember a Marie. Did you know that?" She sighed deeply. "That was a long time ago . . . a long time ago . . . back before the war."

Devin caught Rosalie's baffled glance and looked helplessly back at her.

"So, Sarah—you must be married by now, aren't you?" Ester asked. "And is this your young man?" She was still looking straight at Rosalie, but her eyes kept twitching from side to side, as if she were looking at several people in the room at once.

"No, Mom—Sarah will be a senior in high school this year," Devin said. "But this isn't Sarah—this is Rosalie."

"I know that!" Ester snapped, looking harshly at her son. "And I'd know my little Marie anywhere!" Shifting her gaze back at Rosalie, she went on, "Remember that time you and I got caught cheating on our spelling tests? That was you, wasn't it? Was Mrs. Hildonen ever mad at us!"

With a not so subtle prompt from Devin, Rosalie nodded agreement even as she rolled her eyes ceilingward. Devin could clearly read the revulsion in Rosalie's glance, but before he could say something to draw his mother's attention away from her, there was a soft knock on the door behind them. Devin and Rosalie both turned around to see a young woman sticking her head into the room.

"Mr. Lahikainen? You have a phone call in the lobby. It's your daughter."

"Could you stay here and talk to her?" Devin asked Rosalie. "I'll be back in a jiffy."

"Oh, yeah — sure," Rosalie said, looking nervous enough to bolt out of the room. She watched longingly as Devin left, and the door whooshed shut behind him. Trembling inside, she turned to face Ester again. As soon as they made eye contact, Rosalie felt an almost overwhelming wave of dizziness. She put her hands to her forehead and shook her head, waiting for the light-headed sensation to pass.

"So, are you two going to stay with me for the afternoon, or is this going to be a quick say 'hi' and run? I can't remember the last time you came to visit me here."

"Actually . . ." Rosalie said, a deep tremor in her voice, "I — I've never been here before." Afraid she was going to fall down, Rosalie grabbed the bed railing for support. "You see, I just met Devin — less than two years ago. Until recently, I was living in Montana."

"Oh? And are your mother and father back together?"

Rosalie looked at Ester, not at all sure who she was talking about. A shiver raced up her back to the base of her skull. She shook her head and tried to push back the almost total sense of disorientation that had gripped her. Panic was churning in the pit of her stomach, threatening to burst out at any moment. It was as if, as soon as Devin had left, the air in the room started to thicken and a wild, completely crazed gleam lit up her mother-in-law's eyes.

"You know, I've been wanting to tell you about all of that, Sarah," Ester went on, not at all aware of Rosalie's rising panic. "You have to be nice to him, you know. He's only there to help you, but he can hurt anyone — including you — if he gets angry."

"Devin — ?" Rosalie said, her voice no more than a gasp. "Devin wouldn't hurt *anyone*." Her voice reverberated as though she were speaking down the long, echoing tube of a tunnel. The light in the room was dimming with each passing second, and the floor seemed to be rippling under her feet as if she were standing on a drifting ice floe. She had the unnerving sense that the darkness of the room was coalescing, condensing behind her. She was convinced someone else was in the room with her, standing behind her, but she was too scared to turn around and look. She wanted desperately to see who it was, but every muscle in her body was frozen into immobility. Her attention was riveted by the wild glimmer in Ester's eyes.

"You know, it's been with our family ever since . . . ever since forever," Ester went on. "At least, that's what my father and grandfather told me."

"I —"

That was all Rosalie could say as cold, powerful pressure tightened around her throat. The tension building up behind her eyes made her vision pulsate with every hammering beat of her heart. She imagined strong, dark arms encircling her chest from behind and squeezing ever tighter as they forced the breath out of her.

Suddenly, from behind her, there came a loud *thump* and a brilliant burst of light. In a roaring rush that was magnified until it sounded like a freight train, the door slammed open, and Devin entered the room.

"Everything's all right at home," he said, shutting the door behind him. To Rosalie's fear-heightened senses, his voice exploded and rippled like thunder. "Sarah just wanted to know if we planned on being back for supper. She sounded a bit nervous. She was probably calling just so she could hear my voice." He chuckled as he walked over to his mother's bedside. He didn't notice anything was unusual until he glanced at Rosalie and saw how pale and shaky she was.

"Hey, hon —? Are you feeling all right?" he asked. Concern darkened his brow.

Rosalie moved her lips, trying to say something, but the only sound to come out was a wet-sounding gasp. The choking sensation had started to fade, but she still had the feeling that — even with Devin here — there was someone unseen in the room with them, and she couldn't shake the suspicion that Ester had seen who it was and been talking to him. With fear-widened eyes, she started walking toward Devin. Each trembling step felt like her last until she pitched forward and collapsed into his arms.

"Hey, hey," Devin said, hugging her tightly as he glanced worriedly at his mother. "Take it easy, honey. God! Your skin's as cold as ice."

"I don't feel so well," Rosalie stammered. "I think I have to sit down."

With Devin supporting her, they went over to the chair beside the window. When Rosalie slumped down onto it, the cushion made a loud *whooshing* sound, but she barely noticed it as she closed her eyes, tilted her head back, and forced herself to take steady, deep breaths.

"What happened? You were fine when I left you," Devin said. He knelt down beside her and gently rubbed the back of her hand.

Rosalie nodded, then reached up and started to massage her throat. "I don't know what came over me," she said. "One minute I was fine. The next thing I knew, I felt like I was choking or something." She thought it foolish to mention that she had been absolutely convinced there was someone in the room with her, someone who had grasped her from behind and started squeezing her chest so she couldn't breathe.

From her bed, Ester muttered something indistinguishable. She mixed English with Finnish, so Devin didn't catch it all, but she was saying something about how she had to tell Sarah about our *"pikku haamu,"* our little *haamu.*

"I just want to get the hell out of here," Rosalie whispered. The wide-eyed, fear-filled look she gave Ester said it all. "I—I never did very well in hospitals."

Devin eased his arm around Rosalie to help her stand. She trembled in his grasp as they started toward the door.

"Hey, Mom, I think we'll be going now. Rosalie's not feeling so well," he said.

"All right, dear," Ester said. From where they stood near

the door, it looked as though her eyes were closed. "Nice to see all of you again. Come back and visit me soon, okay?"

— 3 —

Devin and Rosalie got back home a little before nine o'clock only to find Sarah sprawled on the couch, half-asleep with the TV blasting away. She sat up when her father came from the kitchen into the living room.

"Hey, you didn't have to wait up for us, you know," her father said. "You should have gone to bed." He leaned over the back of the couch and gave Sarah a hug and kiss.

"Where's Rosalie?" Sarah asked.

"Oh, she's sitting in the kitchen for a minute before heading up to bed. She's not feeling so hot. I think she's got a flu bug or something. It hit her really hard this afternoon while we were visiting your grandmother."

"So how's mumu doing?"

"Not all that much better, I'm afraid."

"Umm," Sarah said, frowning. "Well, I hope it didn't ruin your time away — Rosalie being sick, I mean."

"It didn't help any," her father said with a thin laugh and a shake of his head. "If she isn't back in gear in a day or two, I'm going to take her to see the doctor."

Just then the kitchen door swung open, and Rosalie, looking pale and drawn, shuffled toward the stairway. Her eyes had a clouded look to them when she nodded a silent greeting to Sarah.

"Can you make it by yourself, or do you want some help?" Devin asked.

"I'll make it," Rosalie said weakly.

"I'll be right along," Devin replied as he watched her trudge slowly up the stairs.

"God," Sarah said, once she heard Rosalie close the bedroom door upstairs. "She looks terrible." Considering how badly the day must have gone for them, she decided it was best not to mention what had been bothering her all day. After much consideration, she had decided that she must

73

have fallen asleep and dreamt that she had seen a grown-up Tully, although that still didn't explain the sound of the rocking chair on the tape playback. There could be no other explanation . . . not unless she wanted to consider the possibility that her father's house was haunted.

"So, you handled everything okay today?" her father asked as if he sensed that she was holding something back.

"Sure." Sarah said with a false brightness. "It got kind of lonely around here, though." Nervously, she looked away from him.

"Well, Rosalie and I are back now," he said, ruffling her hair. "Besides, school starts in a month or so. I'll bet you make plenty of new friends then."

"Yeah," Sarah said listlessly. "That's just what I need—some new friends."

Chapter Six

Dark Clouds

Taking in a deep breath, Rosalie eased the screen door shut behind her as she looked out across the back lawn leading down to the river. From the back porch, she couldn't quite see the small stretch of sandy beach, but she knew Sarah was down there, swimming and sunning herself. Clutching her folded towel tightly against her side, she started out across the grass. In spite of the sun beating down on her, she shivered and pulled her shirt collar up tightly around her throat.

She had only one thought in mind: she wanted to have a talk with Sarah. The pent-up frustration and rage she felt coming from her stepdaughter was making her sick at heart. The three months following Marie's death had been tough—on all of them. Up until now, Rosalie had had no idea how to deal with the anger she felt directed at her; she hadn't even dared talk to Devin about it. But day by day, it was getting worse instead of better. This morning, after Devin had left for work, Rosalie had decided to tackle the problem head-on.

As she followed the well-worn path across the lawn and through the thin stand of trees down to the beach, she couldn't help thinking how many times she and Devin had said they would come down here some night to go skinny-dipping. They hadn't had a chance to yet, at least so far this summer, because of the horrible thing that had happened to Marie. It was like a lot of things they had said they would do and then never found the time. And now, summer would be over in a few weeks. Rosalie sighed as she considered lost opportunities and further steeled herself not to lose this chance to connect with Sarah, to deal with her right up front and honestly. Also, she wanted to explain why she had been so sickly and run-down lately; she had found out two weeks ago that she was pregnant and, on doctor's orders, had quit her job at the mill.

She found Sarah, wearing a modest one-piece bathing suit, lying flat on her back on a towel spread out on the sand. Her tanned skin glistened with tanning lotion, beautifully setting off her hair, which was bleached nearly white from the summer sun. A paperback book with a lurid cover lay open, facedown on the sand beside her.

From the edge of the woods, Rosalie regarded Sarah in silence for a few moments. She alternated between genuine affection and pity for the girl and twinges of guilt over seeing her stepdaughter as nothing more than an immature, self-centered, and self-pitying little girl. Even keeping in mind the horrible things Sarah had witnessed last spring, Rosalie thought at least some of her actions were inexcusable.

"Hi, Sarah," she said. She was trying to sound cheerful, but her voice was husky with tension as she walked toward her across the burning hot sand.

Squinting from the bright sunlight, Sarah sat up and leaned on her elbows as she regarded Rosalie expressionlessly. "Oh," she said. "Feeling better?"

"A little bit. I thought maybe some sun would help knock the last little bit of this flu out of me. Mind if I join you?"

When an answer wasn't immediately forthcoming, Rosalie flapped out her towel and spread it over the hot sand, not too close to where Sarah lay. She took off the blouse she was wearing, exposing the skimpy black bikini that

76

barely covered her full figure. She looked down at her stomach, imagining how it would swell as the baby developed.

"It's as much your beach as it is mine," Sarah said softly, as she closed her eyes and eased back onto her towel. "Probably *more*."

Rosalie bristled but held back her sharp retort. Heaving a deep sigh, she sat down on her towel, hugging her legs as she looked out over the swift-moving river. A thick-boled tree, stripped of its leaves and most of its branches, had washed up on the sand. The dark silhouette of its gnarled roots looked like twisted bones against the shimmering water. Several swallows were weaving and dipping over the river, scooping up insects. From the surrounding woods came the incessant singing of birds. Rosalie took a deep breath, trying to let the serenity of the river soothe her nerves.

"It's so pleasant down here," Rosalie said after a moment. "Now that I'm not working, I should come down here more often while the weather's still good."

Rosalie's clasped hands tightened around her legs, turning her knuckles white as she shifted her gaze over to Sarah. The twisted, sour expression on Sarah's face bespoke volumes: *No, don't start coming down here more often. It will ruin it for me!*

"So—umm, how are you feeling about school starting soon?" Rosalie asked, then inwardly cursed herself for not getting directly to the point. Why couldn't she just say, *So tell me, Sarah, why don't you like me? Why do you act like you hate me so much?* Or else start out on a more positive note and tell her about the baby.

"I can't really say I'm looking forward to it," Sarah replied tightly. "I still miss my—" She cut herself off sharply and shifted uneasily on her towel.

"I remember how scared I was when my family first moved out to Montana," Rosalie said. "I was only ten at the time, but I remember feeling as though we were moving to the edge of the earth." She giggled softly to herself. "Well, you know what they say—Montana isn't the end of the world . . . but you can see it from there."

Sarah's expression remained impassive, and the silence stretched out uncomfortably long between them.

"You know, if you haven't got all the school clothes you need," she went on, "maybe you and I could drive down to the Maine Mall sometime. I'll be needing a new wardrobe soon, too. As a matter of fact, I don't have anything planned for the rest of the day. How about after lunch we drive to South Portland?"

Sarah bit her lower lip and shook her head. "I dunno," she replied sleepily. "I'm feeling pretty comfortable right where I am."

"Well then, maybe sometime next week." In spite of the cool breeze blowing in off the water, the air was close, stifling. Waves of heat crashed over her, hammering down on her shoulders like liquid lead. The glare off the sand made her eyes feel as if she had been crying. Without warning, a subtle current of panic began to stir inside her. She looked around frantically when she suddenly realized that the swallows were gone, and the woods had grown strangely silent. The only sound, was a faint rushing *hiss* that could have been the water at the river's edge . . . or the blood pulsing in her head.

"Do you—" she started to say but fell silent, left with the disorienting impression that she hadn't spoken aloud.

The warmth of the sun beating on Rosalie's back suddenly cut off. She looked up, expecting to see that a cloud had drifted in front of the sun, but the sky was a clear, vibrating blue. Shivers raced up her back as she shifted forward and struggled to stand.

"I think . . . maybe . . . I . . ."

Her legs felt like frayed rubber as she grabbed her blouse and towel, and stood up. She looked frantically toward the house. It look impossibly distant.

"The sun's kind of getting to me," she said in a tight,

raspy voice. "I think I'll . . . head on up to the house."
Again, she had the distinct impression she hadn't even
spoken aloud, but Sarah, still not opening her eyes, simply nodded and grunted her agreement.

"I—I'll see you for lunch," Rosalie said, and with that
she left the beach, practically running. She dashed
through the woods and across the lawn, feeling curiously
detached from her body, almost as if she were in a dream.
Trembling wildly, she burst through the screen door and
rushed into the living room to collapse onto the couch. As
wave after black wave of fear mounted inside her, she
squeezed her eyes tightly shut and lay there, trembling
with her face buried in the couch cushions.

—2—

"There, see? She's not so bad."

With a startled cry, Sarah kicked her legs up as she
jerked into a sitting position. Her eyes quickly scanned
the beach, trying to locate whoever had spoken. Her vision was blurred by the pulsating red afterimage of the
sun on her retina.

The voice—a man's voice—faint and teasingly familiar,
had sounded far away, barely audible over the distant rush
of wind in the pines and the droning of insects. At first
she didn't see anyone and was trying to convince herself
she had imagined hearing the voice; then she looked down
toward the water. Against the backdrop of sunlight glittering off the water, she saw the rippling silhouette of a
washed-up tree trunk. It took her a moment to realize the
dark tangle wasn't just torn-out roots; someone was sitting
on the base of the tree.

A knot of tension formed in Sarah's stomach as she
glanced up at the house over her shoulder. It was more
than a hundred yards away across the field. If this person
meant trouble and she had to run for it . . .

"Well . . . ? Don't you agree?" the person said mildly.

Sarah still couldn't tell who it was; he looked thin, nearly transparent with the glittering water behind him, dazzling her eyes. Then, in a flash, recognition dawned.

"Oh, Tully. It's you," she said. "God, you surprised me. I thought I was alone down here." Feeling suddenly vulnerable, sitting there in just her bathing suit, she folded her arms across her chest.

"Well, you should know by now that you're never truly alone around here," Tully said. His laughter sounded surprisingly deep and hollow. A wave of chills raced through Sarah as she strained to see his face, but he still was nothing more than a wavering dark smear against the moving water behind him. The distorting light made him appear even thinner than usual.

"No, I just wasn't expecting anyone. Rosalie was here a while ago but she left."

"Oh, yes . . . *Rosalie*," Tully said, nodding as he stood up and walked slowly toward her. Just the way he said her name sent a hot bolt of anger through Sarah.

"So, do you want to be alone or not?" Tully asked. When he was about ten feet away from her, he dropped down into a cross-legged sitting position so fast it startled her.

Not knowing what to say, Sarah remained silent. She clenched her hands into fists and cast her eyes down at her toes as she wiggled them into the sand.

Placing his hands on his knees, Tully leaned back so the sunlight illuminated the flat planes of his face as he took a deep breath. His blond hair fell back, brushing against his thin, naked shoulders.

"Ahh," he said, sighing with deep satisfaction. "To be alive on a day like this."

Sarah almost said, *But you're not alive! How can you be? I made you up!* but then thought better of it.

"If you want to be alone, you can tell me," Tully continued as he rolled his head back and forth, scanning the heat-hazed summer sky. "Of course, there are some things you *don't* have to tell me."

"Oh, yeah? Like what?"

"Like what you've been thinking about Rosalie. I already know how you feel . . . about her." His voice was light, but there was a dark undercurrent of threat in it.

Sarah stiffened but said nothing. Her clenched fists were slippery with sweat and tanning lotion.

"You know, you *have* to be honest with me, Sarah," Tully said. He turned and looked directly at her with a hard, piercing gaze. His blue eyes seemed almost like holes in his skull through which she could see the blue sky beyond. "You can admit how much she pisses you off."

Snorting with laughter, Sarah shook her head in denial. "She doesn't piss me off," she replied, tasting the lie like acid on her tongue. "We're still just getting to know each other. That's all."

"Yeah—right," Tully said. He laughed again, but he continued to look at Sarah with a cold, unblinking stare. "You know you don't believe that, so don't even say it, all right?" He paused a moment to let that sink in. "I'll bet even now you're thinking she just came down here to bother you, right?"

Sarah considered a moment, then nodded. Her gaze drifted past him to the tree-lined horizon. At the very edge of the sky, she could see fat, purple thunderheads piling up.

"Yeah—maybe," she said. "Even when she asked me to go shopping with her, I don't think she really meant it. I think she was just baiting me."

"Is that so?" Tully asked, his eyebrows curving upward. "You didn't even pick up on what she was hinting at?"

"Wha—? What do you mean?"

Tully sniffed with laughter. "That she's pregnant."

Sarah stiffened.

"Oh, yes," Tully went on. "That's why she came down—to tell you that. Only she didn't quite dare to." He leaned forward, peering straight into her eyes. "So, how does that make you feel?"

Sarah tried to deny the flood of anger and jealousy that swelled up inside her. Her first thought was, if that was true, if her father and Rosalie were going to have a baby, that would only further push her away.

"You want the truth?" she asked, fighting hard to control the trembling in her voice.

"Nothing but."

"I think if she *is* pregnant, she did it — like everything else — to drive a wedge between me and my father. You have to admit that, ever since I moved in with them, she's been pulling some subtle — and some not so subtle things — to let me know how much I'm in the way . . . at least as far as she's concerned."

"Come on now, Sarah," Tully said, smiling grimly as he pressed the point. He shifted his weight forward just as a slow rumble of thunder sounded in the distance.

"You know it's true, Tully," Sarah snapped. "She doesn't even want me in her home — *her* home! Not mine! Not my father's!"

"It's as much your home as it is hers," Tully said mildly. "Probably *more.*"

Sarah shivered, hearing him echo her comment to Rosalie about the beach. Her clenched hands tingled, but she couldn't stop them from trembling. She wanted to stand up and leave right now, go back to the house, just leave him here, but her legs felt weak and unstrung, as if they wouldn't even support her.

"*More* hers than mine," Sarah said bitterly. "I think she's playing mind games with me. You can't honestly tell me you don't see it."

"But don't you think relationships like this are awkward, that they take time?" Tully asked archly. "It has to be just as difficult for her as it is for you."

"Yeah, well, I'm working on it!" Sarah snapped.

Another roll of thunder filled the air. Tully's smile widened but still didn't display a shred of humor. "So am I."

"No," Sarah said, no more than a whimper. "I didn't mean—"

Sighing deeply, Tully looked up at the rounded bank of dark clouds moving ever closer. "Remember that Saturday a couple of weeks ago, when the two of them went off for the day and spoiled your plans to go visit your friends down in Westbrook?"

Against her will, Sarah nodded as another, stronger wave of chills tingled through her body. She crossed her arms tightly over her chest, collapsing herself inward as she stared at Tully's profile.

"I knew how mad you were that day, and I tried to help you then because I figured you blamed Rosalie for your not being able to go down to Kathy's house."

"What do you mean *help* me?" Sarah asked sharply. She nailed him with a harsh stare. "I don't *need* any help."

Tully laughed again, louder. Holding his hands up as though he were completely helpless, he said, "That's why I'm here—to help you. No matter what you say, I know what you think about her. It's written all over your face."

"I—I don't hate her," Sarah said, a bit unconvincingly.

Tully smirked. "I was there with your dad and Rosalie when they visited your grandmother at the nursing home. Your grandmother—your *mumu*—she saw me, too. I know she did because she kept talking to me. I don't think Rosalie knew what was going on, though. Both she and your dad figured your mumu is . . . you know." With his forefinger, he made tiny circles in the air around his ear.

Sarah shivered wildly when a third peal of thunder sounded, louder and closer. The air seemed to change in an instant, becoming heavy and oppressive. Her arms broke out with goosebumps when she recalled how sick Rosalie had been when they returned that evening. Even after several days in bed, she was still looking weak and shaken. Could it be true? Was she pregnant?

"Maybe I'm the one who's crazy," she whispered, more to herself than to Tully. She picked up her shirt from

83

where she had left it beside the blanket and hurriedly put it on.

"But I can help you if you want me to," Tully said, looking at her with a cold, earnest stare.

"I told you—I don't want any help!" Sarah said. "Especially your kind of help!" She took a deep, shuddering breath. "And I—I'll never forgive you for what you did!"

"Are you talking about Myrtle again?" Tully asked.

"No! You know damned well I'm not!" Sarah shouted. "I'm talking about what you did to *Brian!*" Even as she said her dead brother's name, a hot, choking sensation grabbed her by the throat. The air around her felt charged with static electricity.

Tully glanced away from her, his face clouded with thought. Sunlight glanced off his pale forehead and cheeks, making them look like slick ice.

"Brian . . ." he said dreamily. "Ohh, that's right . . . your baby brother Brian . . ."

"I know you did it!" Sarah shrieked, lunging forward and shaking an angry finger at him. "I know you killed him. No matter what you say and no matter what the doctors said, I know you did it!"

"Oh? And just how do you know that?" Tully asked. Icy sarcasm returned to his voice.

"Because it was just like what you did to my cat," Sarah replied. "Only that time you were a bit more careful to make it look like an accident."

Tully shrugged. "I don't see how you can say it was my fault when you were the one who said you wished he was dead."

"*Wished!* I wished he was dead because I was mad at him for throwing up all over my doll!" Tears blurred her vision as she looked at Tully, trying to read any trace of human feeling behind his vacant blue eyes. "I spent three years in therapy after Brian died, two days a week, all because I was convinced I had gotten my wish . . . that somehow *I* had killed him!"

84

Tully shook his head from side to side as though baffled. "Well, you did, didn't you?" he remarked coolly. "You know what they say—be careful what you wish for; you just might get it."

"So you admit it!" Sarah snapped. "Brian didn't choke on his rattle, like the doctor said. You suffocated him because you thought I really meant it when I said I wished he was dead. Right?" She shook her fists in frustration. "God damn you, Tully! Damn you to hell!"

"You know what I think, Sarah?" Tully said mildly. His voice was as distant as the wind in the trees, as if he wasn't even listening to her. "What you have to do is start thinking of me in a different way. If you ever thought I was just some imaginary friend or something, well— maybe you were wrong about that."

"Then who the hell are you? *What* the hell are you?"

Again, Tully shrugged. He looked at her, his steady stare reaching right inside her and gripping her heart until it felt cold and motionless.

"Maybe I'm a part of you that can do things you can't or don't dare to do," he said in a low, steely tone. "In some ways, maybe I do need you, but . . ." He exhaled slowly and shook his head thoughtfully, letting his words drift away on the hot summer breeze. "But I'm not so sure . . ."

Fuming with anger, Sarah stood up and began folding her beach towel. She picked up her book and then, wheeling around, pointed her finger at him. "Well, I'll tell you this much right now, just so you don't misunderstand me!" she shrieked. "I don't want you to help me! Not with my problems with Rosalie or with anything else."

"Somehow, I don't quite believe you," Tully said softly.

"Yeah, well, maybe I needed you when I was a kid, but not anymore. I don't need or want you anymore!"

Tully smiled but said nothing as his gaze shifted over to the tumbling, gray storm clouds on the horizon. Thunder boomed like a cannonade along the river valley.

"I don't know about that," he said. "I'm not even sure you have a choice about it. I think maybe, whether you want me to or not, I'm going to have to help you."

Sarah's mind went blank. She could think of nothing else to say, so she turned on her heel and started walking toward the house. Her feet kicked up fantails of sand behind her. At the edge of the woods, she stopped and turned around toward Tully, prepared to yell and scream everything she had just said all over again — a dozen times if she had to. Her words got caught in her throat and died there when she saw that he wasn't there. She was alone on the beach.

— 3 —

The weather turned unseasonably cold heading into the Labor Day weekend. On Friday afternoon, thick clouds blew in from the west, and by evening, heavy rain was falling. Devin had made plans to drive with Rosalie and Sarah up to Quebec for one last summer vacation fling over the weekend, but considering the weather and that Rosalie still wasn't feeling up to par, he canceled everything. Complaining of a headache, Sarah went to bed early on Friday night, so that left Devin and Rosalie, sitting in the living room, watching the fire Devin had started in the fireplace to cut the chill.

"You know, I think she's really nervous about school starting on Wednesday," Devin said. He had his arm around Rosalie's shoulder and was holding her tightly as they sipped on the whiskey sours he had made for them. "I can't say I blame her, though. She doesn't know any of the kids around here. I suppose it's partly her fault for not trying to make friends this summer, but that's gotta be pretty difficult."

Rosalie said nothing as she stared blankly at the flames. All day long, a tight, cold pressure had been building in her chest, making it difficult for her to take a deep

86

breath. The palms of her hands were cold and clammy. She wanted to go straight to bed but was convinced—just like the past few nights—that she would end up lying there, staring at the ceiling.

"And, not to mention what happened to her mother last spring," Devin added. Shaking his head, he heaved a deep sigh before draining his glass. "God damn! I don't see how she's ever going to get over that. But that's why I don't think we should tell her yet about you being pregnant. I think she's got enough to deal with as it is."

Rosalie grunted, only vaguely following what he was saying.

Devin placed his empty glass on the floor beside the couch, then slid his hand from Rosalie's shoulder down to her waist and gripped her tightly. Leaning close, he kissed her behind the ear. "Come on, honey. You seem awfully quiet tonight. Are you still feeling lousy?"

Rosalie shrugged and shuddered as she took a shallow breath. She wanted to pull away from Devin's touch but didn't even have the energy to do that.

"Sarah's probably asleep by now. I was hoping maybe we could fool around a bit," he said, laughing softly. "We'll probably want to have all the fun we can now, before you get too big."

Rosalie sniffed but said nothing.

"You still don't think Sarah blames you for us canceling the weekend, do you?"

Again, Rosalie shrugged and said nothing. The flickering flames in the fireplace drew her attention and held it like a magnet.

"Well, she certainly can't very well blame you for the weather," Devin said, a bit more harshly. "I think you both are going to have to try a lot harder to connect. Maybe we should tell her about the baby. Maybe that would give her something positive to focus on. I know I'm happy as can be about it." He rubbed her lower belly vigorously and laughed.

For just an instant, Rosalie glanced at him, then turned back to the fire. She was listening to her pulse, racing thin and fast in her ears.

"Oh, I don't know," she muttered, shifting again, sinking deeper into the couch cushions. "I just feel so . . . so *blah*."

"Well, I'm dry. How about you?"

In answer, Rosalie held up her glass. It had barely a sip missing. Devin stood up and snatched his glass from the floor. Before heading to the kitchen, he opened the fireplace screen, stirred up the coals, and dropped two more logs onto the blaze. Flames leaped up, sending out a shimmering wave of warmth.

"Ahh—that's better. Cozy," he said. "Be back in a jiffy."

Rosalie shifted her gaze without moving her head, tracking him as he left. She didn't know whether she wanted to stay here with him or go upstairs to bed just to be alone. Right now, either option seemed dismal. She had no idea what to do with herself. One thing for sure— she wished she wasn't feeling so damned nervous about being pregnant. She was only thirty-five years old; there was still plenty of time to have a baby or two with Devin. But why, then, had she been so damned miserable during the first months? She shuddered whenever she thought she might have conceived on the night Marie had been raped and killed.

But it was more than that.

For the past few days—no, the past few weeks . . . maybe even ever since Sarah moved into the house, Rosalie had been feeling . . . uncomfortable. Almost all the time, now, she felt restless and impatient. Naturally, a lot of it centered around Sarah living with them. Rosalie still regretted not trying harder to connect with her. Even this morning, down by the river, her overtures had turned out horribly. And all of these unresolved and unspoken feelings left her feeling hollow. More often than not, just being in the same room with Sarah seemed to cast a pall over everything.

"You sure you don't want a freshen-up?" Devin called from the kitchen.

"No thanks," Rosalie replied, surprised by the force of her voice. She continued to stare into the fire, watching as the tongues of flame licked over the dark logs.

She wondered if maybe the drink was getting to her. She had never been much of a drinker and had agreed to have one with Devin tonight only because their weekend plans had been ruined. She probably shouldn't be drinking at all because of being pregnant. Hell, whatever it was, she couldn't deny or ignore the nervous tremors racing through her body. Her thoughts and emotions were tangled and twisted, and she was genuinely afraid that sometime soon—maybe when Devin asked her a simple, innocent question, instead of answering him she would start screaming and not be able to stop. Close to tears, she squinted her eyes tightly shut, staring at the blurred orange flames and concentrated hard on pushing back her bad feelings.

But it didn't do any good.

The pressure building up inside her was almost intolerable. Rosalie knew with a gut-churning certainty that sooner or later it was going to explode. Either that, or else the pressure outside of her, surrounding her, would squeeze inward unrelentingly until she finally succumbed. Try as she might, she couldn't shake the feeling that someone else was in the room with her. Not just now, but all the time. Even when she knew she was home alone, when Sarah was off somewhere and Devin was at work at the mill.

"God damn it!" she hissed, feeling the words like sand between her dry lips. "What the hell is the matter with me?"

Tears started to build up in her eyes. She put one hand over her mouth and bit down hard on her forefinger. No matter what she thought about, she couldn't stop the tremors that were building up inside her. Her breathing came in raw, ragged gulps, and her stomach felt as if cold hands were hugging her from behind, squeezing . . . squeezing ever tighter.

Rosalie jumped when she heard the sudden whine of the blender in the kitchen. Although every muscle in her body complained, she forced herself to sit up and look around toward the kitchen door. Her breath caught in her chest, and her eyes widened in shock when she saw Sarah, standing behind the couch.

"My God," Rosalie said, no more than a gasp. "You scared the crap out of me, sneaking up behind me like that."

Sarah didn't say anything. She just stood there, looking at her with a dull, blank stare. Rosalie's pulse rate shot up, hammering loudly in her ears when she realized that there was something definitely wrong with Sarah. Her skin was as white and shiny as polished stone; her eyes were glazed, as if she were blind or else focused on some object far, far away; and her wide smile, with absolutely no trace of humor, exposed flat teeth that made her look like a ravenous animal.

"Sarah! Jesus Christ, Sarah!" Rosalie whispered. "Wha—what's *wrong* with you?"

The expression on Sarah's face remained as motionless as if it were carved in stone . . . or a porcelain mask. The air between them crackled with electricity. At last, with stunning impact, Rosalie realized that this wasn't Sarah. The thin blond hair framing her face was too short, and the face, although it certainly resembled hers, had a strong masculine cast to it. The bony shoulders and thin arms looked as if they belonged to a scarecrow, not a living, breathing human being. As she stared at it in horror, Rosalie found she couldn't even think of it as a person.

A faint whimper escaped from her throat, but that was the only sound she made as she pushed herself up off the couch and stood, trembling, facing this . . . this *thing*.

90

Her back was to the fire as she watched with mounting terror as the figure moved slowly toward her.

The motionless face leered out at her from a dark, churning mass that looked like thick, oily smoke condensing between her and the kitchen door. It blocked out most of the light coming from the kitchen. Rosalie wanted to scream for help, but she was transfixed by the thing's ice-blue, unblinking eyes and its frozen, evil smile.

Rosalie's legs almost collapsed when she took a quick step backward. She was desperately trying to convince herself that she was imagining this, but with every throbbing pulse of her heart, the marble-white face loomed closer toward her out of the darkness. Terror cut through her like a stinging blade when she saw two pale, bony hands rise up and reach toward her as the glowing blue eyes widened with anticipation.

"No . . . please," Rosalie rasped.

She took another few steps backward but stopped when she banged into the fireplace mantel. A bolt of pain raced down her arm, making her hand go numb. The heat from the fire singed the backs of her legs, but it didn't come close to removing the chilled tendrils of fear that coiled like a nest of snakes in her stomach.

The face seemed to suck the darkness out of the room and into itself, getting stronger . . . and larger. The baleful blue glow of the eyes burned white hot as skeletal hands reached out for Rosalie . . . coming closer . . . closer . . .

"Please . . ." she whimpered.

She was unable to tear her gaze away from the figure as it shifted toward her, seemingly passing right through the couch. Her retreat was blocked by the wall. Unable to make the slightest sound, Rosalie could only watch in horror as the thin, white hands reached out for her. Spikes of numbing cold tore into her when the bony fingers touched her chest and started pushing her back against the wall. Looking down, she saw that the hands were plunged

91

wrist-deep inside her chest. Intense pressure caved her ribs inward as both arms pressed in halfway up to the elbows. There was no blood—no gaping wound in her chest; just long arms, reaching out of the darkness and reaching through muscle and bone with an irresistible force.

Rosalie grimaced with pain as tears flooded from her eyes. She wanted to scream but was strangled into silence when she felt one of the hands curl around her heart and grip it with a relentless embrace.

Wave after numbing wave of nausea swept through Rosalie as the pressure steadily increased inside her and the pale blue eyes came right up to her face. The heavy thump of her pulse echoed like distant drums in her ears, but each beat was growing fainter and weaker as her heart strained against the ever-tightening grip. With a sudden tug, the figure pushed upward, lifting Rosalie into the air. Her feet dangled helplessly above the floor. Every nerve, every muscle in her body was screaming in agony beneath the brutal pressure. Her heart twisted in the icy grip, trying to pulse, trying to force blood through her arteries, but the cold and the fear had stopped everything as if she had been frozen.

Her eyes wide with terror, Rosalie stared into the cold fire of the blue eyes that loomed in front of her. A frigid blast of wind swept over her face just as her lungs collapsed, and the air inside them went stale. The beating of her heart was nothing more than a fleeting memory as the pressure lifting her off the floor suddenly released. With a feeble moan, she dropped to the floor just as Devin, a fresh drink in hand, walked back into the living room. The instant he saw her hit the floor, he dropped his drink and ran over to her; but even before he propped her head in his lap, he knew . . . she was dead.

Chapter Seven

The White Crane

— 1 —

Even though the sun was shining brightly, Devin could hardly see the road ahead as he and Sarah drove away from the cemetery. Tears blurred everything. The funeral service for Rosalie and her unborn child had been simple and short, attended mostly by friends from the paper mill. Paul Kennedy, the minister from the Lutheran church Rosalie attended, had conducted the brief service. He had invited Devin and Sarah over to his house afterward, but they had declined. Sarah was grateful for that; she was having a difficult enough time coping as it was.

"I probably should have told you about the baby before now," Devin said. His voice was weak, completely broken.

Sarah looked at him, feeling her insides go ice cold. "Well, I—uh, I already knew she was going to . . . to have a baby," she said softly.

"You did? How'd you know that?"

"She—umm, Rosalie told me," Sarah replied as hot tears filled her eyes. "One day . . . she and I went swimming down at the river."

"Oh," Devin said. His expression froze, and his grip on the steering wheel tightened so hard his knuckles turned white. "It's just that I—I don't! *Damn* it!" He pounded the steering wheel with the heel of his hand. "I wish I knew why the hell I didn't insist she go to the doctor, especially after she complained about feeling so run-down and weak all the time."

Sarah wanted to say something reassuring, but her mind was a raging turmoil of grief and guilt, wondering how or if what had happened to Rosalie has any connection with what she had told Tully that same day.

"I know—I know it wouldn't have made any difference," Devin went on as he wiped his eyes with the flat of his hand. "She had a complete physical as soon as she found out she was pregnant, and I just thought—like she did—that she was just run-down from her body adjusting to the pregnancy. But I should have known something was wrong after that day."

"Wha—what day?" Sarah asked. Her voice shook because she feared in her heart that she knew exactly what day he meant; that day Tully had told her he had been with them at the nursing home and had "tried to help."

Devin sighed heavily. "This all started . . . back during the summer, when Rosalie and I went to visit my mom in Waterville," he said, sniffing back a fresh flood of tears. "We didn't want to tell you about it because we didn't want you to worry, so we used her having the flu as an excuse. Hell, at the time, I didn't think much of it. I thought she was just woozy from being in the nursing home and seeing my mother the way she is. But Rosalie was pretty sick, you know? Her system had never been all that strong. That's why the doctor made her quit work as soon as he found out she was pregnant."

Flustered, Sarah looked out the side window as the scenery slid silently past. Her mind filled with the memory of the day down by the river, how Rosalie had tried so hard to talk to her, how she had offered to go school shopping with her, how she had been trying so hard to tell Sarah she was pregnant. The guilt Sarah felt at how

94

she had brushed Rosalie off, ignored her, stung Sarah like salt on an open wound; but below that was something else . . . a darker stirring of worry and guilt.

Jesus Christ, Tully, she thought, staring at her eyes, reflected in the window. Her heated breath fogged up the side window, blurring the scenery. *What the hell have you done, Tully?*

"I—I knew she wasn't well," Sarah said, "and I guess being pregnant and all."

Devin shook his head, then with a tight grunt, brought his fist down again on the steering wheel, hard enough to make it vibrate. "Goddamn it all!" he wailed. "Goddamn it!" He was silent for a moment, then said softly, "And do you want to know the . . . the worst thing about it all?"

"What's that?" Sarah asked as the churning guilt inside her grew blacker, almost thick enough to taste.

"Well, you know, because of Rosalie's age and all, we had to do amniocentesis. You know what that test is, don't you?"

Sarah shook her head.

"Well, it's to test to see if the baby has certain congenital diseases, but from that test, we found out that it was a boy." He glanced at her with glistening eyes. "You were going to have a baby brother, Sarah. And we were—we were going to . . ."

His voice shattered as fresh tears sprang from his eyes. The tears filling Sarah's eyes spilled over as well. A cold twist of guilt filled her chest. She knew she was crying not only for her father . . . but for herself and her own mother as well. But the tension coiling up inside her was unbearable as she waited for her father to gain control of himself so he could continue.

"We were going to name him . . . Brian," Devin said. The last word was nothing more than a raw whisper. "Damn! If only I had done something about it sooner!"

95

"You did everything you could," Sarah responded. "You couldn't have known." She sniffed back her tears as she touched her father lightly on the crook of the arm.

Devin shook his head dejectedly and said, "Yeah, I suppose so. At least I have to believe that. After the autopsy, the doctor said it was almost inevitable because of the condition of her heart." He blinked his eyes rapidly, trying hard to fight back the tears. "He said . . . even if she had known how bad her heart was, without an operation it was just a . . . a matter of time before it gave out. I guess we're lucky to have had the . . . the time together that we did have, right?"

"Yeah—absolutely," Sarah whispered. "You sure are."

She couldn't stop thinking about her own twisting guilt as she watched the silently passing roadside out the window as they drove toward downtown Hilton. In the dark recesses of her mind, a tiny voice was whispering—*You did it! You know you did it!*

"And we have to remember what Pastor Kennedy said," Devin went on. "We have to have faith that all of this is—somehow—all part of God's plan. And no matter what else happens—" He reached out and rested his hand gently on Sarah's shoulder, letting his fingertips massage the back of her neck. "We still have each other. Right, kiddo?"

Sarah's voice choked off when she tried to answer. She turned to look at her father, but as she turned her head, a flickering of motion in the backseat caught her attention. The pit of her stomach went cold when, for just an instant, she imagined Tully was sitting in the backseat, behind her father. She imagined his smile widening as he looked at her with a steady, unblinking stare and held up his hands in a shrug as he winked at her.

96

The night was cold and still. A thin crescent of a moon hung low on the horizon. The streetlights lining Hilton's Main Street cast feeble shadows as falling leaves blew along the gutters. Alan Griffin and Lester LaJoie, both dressed in dark clothes, crouched in the bushes at the bottom of the stairs beside the back door of the White Crane.

"What—are you going pussy on me?" Alan asked sharply.

"No," Lester said. "I ain't going pussy on you. I just don't think you should—"

"Well, I don't think you should be giving me any shit about any of this, all right? Either you shut up and do as I say, or else you leave . . . and you can find yourself some other connection. It's that simple."

"I just don't see why you had to wait this long. Christ, the asshole fired you last summer."

Alan snorted with laughter and shook his head with insufferable sadness. "Lester my boy—don't you think if someone broke into his place a few days after I got my ass fired, he and the cops would put two and two together? This is more my style, to lay back awhile and let things cool off before I take care of business. That way there's no connection, you see? Besides, I have to take care of this before I attend to something else that's starting to bug me . . . something that might take a bit more time."

"What's that?" Lester asked.

"None of your damned business," Alan replied coolly. He jabbed his forefinger at Lester's chest. "It's just someone else I have to have a little talk with before she says the wrong thing to the wrong person." He laughed softly and added, "But you can read about it in the papers like you did about her mother last spring, okay?"

Lester shook his head as though thoroughly confused. "I don't get it."

"It's just as well, Lester my boy, just as well." Alan said, snickering. He stood up and started toward the door. The gasoline can he was carrying sloshed heavily at his side. "If you're coming, come on."

Lester stood up but hesitated before following. "You know, Al, I just don't think this is such a good idea. What if Hartman is still around?"

"LaJoie, you are *sincerely* beginning to piss me off! How long do we have to plant our asses out here and watch before you realize he ain't here? I, for one, am freezing my tail off." High laughter rang out in the night. "I need a little bit of heat to warm myself up."

"But his car's still parked out back."

"So he walked home," Alan snapped. "He only lives up the street."

Shaking his head, Lester took a step back into the shadows. "I dunno, man. I mean, I can understand that you're bent out of shape that Hartman fired you—"

"He accused me of stealing money from the register!" Alan hissed.

"Well . . . did you?" Lester asked shakily.

Alan sighed deeply as he put down the can of gasoline and walked over to his friend. Placing his hand firmly on Lester's shoulder, he brought his face up close, letting his alcohol-tinged breath wash over him.

"Of course I did, but that's not the point!" he said. "That's not the fuckin' point at all!"

"I just don't think we have to . . . torch the place," Lester said, his voice whining a register higher than normal. "Christ, man, if we got caught, we could end up doing hard time!"

Alan laughed, low and deep in his chest. "Lester, Lester, Lester," he whispered as he shook his head. "We've done plenty of things that would put us away. Why, just the cocaine you're holding for me now would put both of us in Thomaston if we got caught. Christ, with your record, you don't even want to get caught spitting on the sidewalk."

Lester chuckled and tried to pull back, but Alan slipped his hand behind his neck and held him fast.

"So just lighten up, will you?"

Lester stiffened and wondered if the term "turning state's evidence" applied to what he was thinking he would do if they did get caught tonight.

"Hey, what are you worrying about, anyway?" Alan continued. "You help me out with this, and I'll help you out with your problems."

"I don't have any problems," Lester said in a grave voice.

"Yeah—right. None except for that monkey you got riding on your back. But don't worry. I'll keep you supplied . . . as long as you back me up on this tonight. It's no sweat. We'll be out of here in a few minutes. I don't see your problem."

"I said I'd come with you tonight to trash the place," Lester replied tightly. "I never said nothin' about helping you burn it down."

"Let's say it was a last-minute inspiration," Alan said, laughing darkly. He made a fist that bunched up Lester's coat collar as he spun him around and dragged him roughly forward. "Now, you're gonna go through this with me, or else I'll make sure things aren't so comfortable for you."

Lester tried to speak, but his collar was choking him. As Alan pulled him toward the restaurant door, his feet scraped loudly on the asphalt walkway.

"Now," Alan said once they were in front of the screen door. "I want you to jimmy that door open while I plan exactly what we're gonna do. Think you can handle that?"

Lester was about to protest, but he stopped himself, knowing damned well how uncomfortable Alan could make him if he copped out now. Taking the large screwdriver he had brought with him, he knelt down and started working on the lock.

—3—

Henry Hartman had been waiting in the White Crane front office for over three hours, and Estelle still hadn't shown up; she hadn't even called him. He understood that she might have trouble getting away from her husband, but the last five or six times now, she had been a no-show and hadn't bothered to call until the next day. He was beginning to think she wasn't going to divorce Tony after all; maybe all along she'd been playing him for a fool. Sometime after eleven o'clock, with three whiskeys in his gut, he turned out all the lights, sprawled out on the office couch, and fell asleep. The sound of dishes shattering on the kitchen floor pulled him back to consciousness.

Hilton wasn't exactly the kind of town that had a high crime rate; and the White Crane, in spite of Henry's pretensions, wasn't exactly the kind of restaurant that did a bonanza business, especially after Labor Day, once the tourists were back home. Henry had never felt the need to keep a revolver in his desk drawer. The thought that he might need one someday had just never crossed his mind . . . at least not until now. He quietly swung his feet to the floor and tiptoed across the carpeted office to the door. He couldn't believe the mayhem that was going on in the kitchen. A small part of him wanted to believe this was all a bad dream.

"Jesus H. Baldy-eyed Christ," he muttered as he eased the office door open and looked out into the darkened kitchen area. At first, he only saw one person, standing by the dish rack and scooping stack after stack of plates off the shelves. Each crash was deafening as porcelain exploded across the tile floor.

"You lousy son of a bitch!" Henry muttered.

Although it didn't really look like him in the dark, Henry had a pretty good idea who this was. It had to be Alan Griffin, the dishwasher he had fired months ago for having sticky fingers near the register. Henry weighed the wisdom of going right out there and confronting him but decided against it when he noticed someone else over in the corner, piling up the dirty dish towels by the salad bench.

After watching for a moment, he realized that this other person was preparing to start a fire. Sweat broke out on his forehead as he eased the door shut, tiptoed back to his desk, picked up the phone, and pressed the quick-call button for the police station.

— 4 —

Ever since the night of Marie Lahikainen's murder, Elliott had driven out to the scene of the crime on Route 26 at least a couple of times a week while on patrol. He wasn't sure why, but something about that night still galled him. He knew it wasn't just the horror and brutality of the rape and murder. In the line of duty, he had seen a few cases that were worse. And as much as he tried to deny the effect it had on him, it wasn't just the pain and suffering he had seen in Sarah Lahikainen's eyes that motivated him. Although, try as he might, he couldn't stop thinking about how defenseless she had seemed . . . and how compelled he felt to try to help and protect her.

He probably felt that way because he still had an unsettled feeling about what had happened that night, as though something had been overlooked by him, by the

101

state detectives, by the sheriff's men — by everyone involved. With each passing week, it looked less and less likely that the investigation would ever turn up any suspects; but Elliott had a crazy notion that, if he came out here, it would hit him — the piece of the puzzle that everyone else had missed.

Or it might be something else . . . something he could barely dare let himself feel. He couldn't deny he felt strong stirrings of affection for Sarah Lahikainen even though she was almost young enough to be his daughter.

As Elliott drove slowly past the ditch where, just a few months ago, he had found Marie Lahikainen's body, the night dispatcher's voice crackling over the police radio suddenly grabbed his attention.

"We have a break-in in progress at the White Crane on South Main Street. Car Three, do you copy? Over."

"This is Car Three. I copy. Got any particulars on that, Dan? Over."

" 'Fraid not much," Dan responded. "Henry phoned, says he was working late in the office. Two men are busting up the kitchen. He says it looks like one of them might be fixing to start a fire."

"On my way. Over and out," Elliott said. He flipped on the blue lights and stepped down hard on the accelerator. As he sped back toward town, he radioed the sheriff's department in Bethel and asked for support. Within three minutes, he was rounding the corner onto South Main. A hundred yards up ahead on the left, he saw the darkened building. Turning off the siren and flashers, he slowed to a stop by the front door. Before getting out, he radioed the station again, asking Dan to advise the sheriff in Bethel that he was at the White Crane alone, and he was going in.

Drawing his service pistol, Elliott stepped out of the car and cautiously approached the front door of the restaurant. At least from the outside, nothing appeared out of the ordinary, but he wasn't about to let his guard drop just yet. Peering through the line of windows, he could see the rows of deserted tables, their white tablecloths glowing dully in the dark interior. Crouching low, he made his way slowly around toward the back.

Before he came to the back door and saw that it had been broken open and was hanging from one hinge, he heard a loud crash echo from inside the restaurant. This was followed by a high-pitched burst of laughter. Holding his revolver at ready, Elliott stepped cautiously into the darkened entryway. The sounds of destruction were deafening, so he made no attempt to mask the noise of his approach.

"Pin him down," someone inside shouted. "I'm just about ready here."

That was all Elliott needed. He rounded the corner, instantly sized up the situation, and shouted, "All right! Police! Hold it right where you are!"

He recognized the two intruders immediately — Alan Griffin and Lester LaJoie. Lester was sitting on Henry's chest, pinning him to the floor as he held a long screwdriver up under Henry's chin. Alan was standing beside a long wooden table next to a large pile of cloth napkins and tablecloths thrown on the floor. The smell of gasoline was so strong it made Elliott's eyes water.

"Aww, shit!" Lester shouted when he saw Elliott's gun aimed directly at him.

"You don't want to make this any worse than it already is, Lester," Elliott said calmly. "So why don't you just ease yourself up off of him?"

From Alan's direction, Elliott heard a faint *click*. Glancing to one side, he saw the blue teardrop flame of a butane lighter. Swinging his arm around, he shouted, "Don't be a fool, Griffin. I'm not alone."

Taking this as his signal, Henry made a loud grunting sound and kicked up at Lester. The sudden movement

103

knocked the screwdriver out of Lester's hand. It clattered across the floor as the men began to scuffle. Elliott took one step forward, braced his aim, and shouted, "I said hold it, Lester!"

In that instant, a rushing roar sounded from behind him, sucking the air past him in a hollow concussion. Bright orange flames billowed up like a mushroom, filling the kitchen with flickering light and hammering heat. Lester rolled away from Henry, grabbed the screwdriver from the floor, and then dove at him. Without hesitation, Elliott crouched and squeezed the trigger once, firmly. The revolver kicked hard in his hand with a deafening report as the bullet caught Lester in midjump and jerked him violently backward. He twisted in the air and hit the floor hard, facedown. His feet skittered on the tile but didn't find any purchase as he rolled over and sat up. He clasped his hands over the dark stain that spread slowly down his shirt.

"Jesus Christ! You *shot* me!" Lester howled.

Elliott gave him scarcely a glance as he turned toward Alan, his revolver cocked, aimed, and ready. "I'm warning you, Griffin. Freeze right there!"

The pile of napkins and towels was blazing high, filling the kitchen with sooty smoke. In the silence that lengthened between them, the smoke alarm suddenly went off with an earsplitting blare, making everyone jump.

"Get the fuck over there, and put your hands against the wall! *Now!*" Elliott said. He had to shout to be heard above the whining alarm. Bracing his aim, he waited until Alan was spread-eagle against the wall before turning around.

Henry scrambled to his feet and was staring in horror at Lester, who was still flopping around on the floor, splashing in his own blood. The wounded man's face looked like a white balloon as he stared helplessly at Elliott with fear-rounded eyes.

104

Keeping his revolver aimed squarely at Alan, Elliott edged his way over toward the wounded man.

"Jesus Christ, man! I'm dying! You *shot* me!" Lester screamed.

"You ain't gonna die," Elliott said. Then, glancing at Henry, who was cowering in the corner by the sink, he asked, "You all right?"

Henry nodded vigorously. "Yeah—yeah—least I think so."

"I assume that alarm sounds down at the fire station."

Henry nodded and said, "Yeah—yeah. I'll go turn it off."

"Good idea," Elliott said as he knelt down beside Lester. Rolling him onto his left side, he jerked the man's hands roughly behind his back, then quickly handcuffed him. "You can lay right here and wait for your ride to the hospital," he said callously. "I gotta take care of your buddy over there."

He walked over to Alan, who was standing with his face to the wall, his arms raised high over his head. After running a quick frisk, Elliott yanked Alan's arms behind his back and slapped on a pair of cuffs. Spinning Alan around, he pushed him back hard enough to slam his head against the wall.

"So, you think you're gonna come along and not give me any trouble? Or should I leave you here to roast in this nice little fire you got going?"

Alan's upper lip curled as if he were about to spit into Elliott's face. "Fuck you, asshole," he snarled.

Elliott chuckled even though the smoke in the kitchen was about to choke him. "Oh, no, my friend. I'd say *you* were the asshole. And after this, I think you'll be looking at a bit of vacation time up in Thomaston."

"Fuck you!"

Elliott laughed as he jerked Alan toward the back door. From outside, the sound of wailing sirens grew louder as the fire trucks rolled up to the restaurant. As a team of firefighters burst in through the front door of the White Crane, two men Elliott recognized from the sheriff's department in Bethel came running into the kitchen through the back door. Their revolvers were drawn and held at ready.

"I believe I'll need someone to escort this gentleman to the hospital," Elliott said, indicating Lester with a nod of his head. He didn't want his voice to give away how near to collapsing he was. "Any volunteers?"

The braying fire alarm suddenly went silent, and Henry rejoined them in the kitchen.

"Henry—I think you'd better go along, too," Elliott said, "just to get checked out before you come by the station. I assume you'll be pressing charges."

Henry nodded vigorously and tried to reply but couldn't make a sound.

Elliott waved the dense smoke away from his face. "You might want to douse that out, boys," he said, indicating the flickering glow inside the restaurant. "Nothing much—just a pile of gas-soaked rags."

He grabbed Alan's cuffed wrists and pulled up hard enough to get a satisfying wince of pain on the young man's face. "I'm going to be a bit busy myself, booking this asshole down at the station."

106

Chapter Eight

Visiting Hours

— 1 —

"Let's see — how does breaking and entering, aggravated criminal mischief, attempted arson, and accomplice to attempted murder all sound?" Elliott said, looking through the bars of the holding cell at Alan. "And that's just for starters. With your past record, I'm sure we can dig up some other little tidbits to make sure you're out of circulation — at least for a little while."

"Fuck you," Alan muttered. He gripped the jail cell bars with both hands and gave them an ineffectual shake.

"Is that all you can ever say?" Elliott said. He shook his head as though deeply saddened. "I swear to God; people these days sure do lack imagination."

"You don't want to *know* what I'm imagining about you." Alan hissed between the bars.

"Can't say as I care much, either. I'm satisfied just knowing you'll be getting a court date real soon, and then you'll be on your way to a glorious future stamping out license plates."

"They don't make license plates at Thomaston anymore," Alan snapped.

"Considering the company you keep, I'm sure you'd know," Elliott said over his shoulder as he headed out of the holding cell. The door slammed shut behind him, and he went up the stairway to the lobby.

"I think I'll go on over to Mercy to see how the other guy is doing," Elliott said to Dan, the night dispatcher, as he walked by the waiting room window toward the front door.

Dan glanced up and nodded. "I just got a call from there. They say the wound wasn't bad at all. Just a puncture in his gut. They don't even think he'll be there a week. Just got to keep an eye on it in case of infection."

"Well, whoop-dee-doo," Elliott said. "How about Henry; any word on him yet?"

"They gave him a quick checkup and sent him home," Dan replied. "He was pretty shaken up, but that's all."

"Good," Elliott said. He paused at the front door, then pushed it open and stepped out into the night.

Once he was outside, he leaned his head back, looked up at the stars, and took a deep breath of the cool night air to clear his head. As much as he tried not to let it affect him, he was deeply shaken by what had happened at the White Crane. He had fired his revolver during arrests before, but always overhead, as a warning. Never, in the line of duty, had he ever wounded anyone. Although he had maintained a rough cop exterior during the scuffle with Lester and Alan and the subsequent booking down at the station, it had been second-nature: a result of his training. Inside, he'd been shaking, was still shaking. Seeing a young man—How old was Lester? About twenty-five?—down on the floor with a hole in his stomach was something he had never bargained for when he became a town cop eight years ago.

He felt more in control by the time he pulled into the Mercy Hospital parking lot. From the front lobby, he took the elevator up to the third floor and walked down the hall to where Kyle McKinnon was sitting guard outside Lester's room. He had his chair leaned back against the wall and was sipping coffee as he thumbed through a back issue of *People*.

"How's he doing?" Elliott asked, hesitating outside the door before looking inside.

"He's in quite a bit of pain, but the doctors say he's not in any real danger," Kyle said. "He's drugged to the gills now. Pretty much the way he likes it, I guess."

Elliott shook his head. "Ain't it a shame the way we have to work so hard to protect low-life like him, when it's the honest, decent citizens who suffer."

"I guess that's why they call it *criminal* justice," Kyle replied, " 'cause they're the only ones who get any justice."

"Well, we'll see about that when we get him into a courtroom." Hitching up his belt, Elliott swung the door open and entered the darkened room. The first thing he noticed was the gleaming metal of the handcuffs that held Lester's wrist to one of the railings of the hospital bed. An IV feed was stuck into the taped back of his other hand. A thick pad of gauze showing a faint, pink flower of blood was taped to his side. An oxygen tube was taped to Lester's upper lip.

As Elliott came over to the side of the bed, Lester's glazed eyes swung over and looked at him. For an instant, the man's stare hardened, but then his eyes went unfocused, glazed over, and rolled upward.

Why didn't you freeze when I told you to? Elliott wanted to say. He knew both Alan and Lester from around town as troublemakers. They had reputations as small-time drug dealers, and both had a string of priors, mostly for dealing, hot-wiring cars, and petty theft. Alan was clearly the leader of the two. Lester was just one of those guys who seemed born to be some wiseguy's flunky. And now, here he was with a bullet hole in his gut while Alan was all in one piece down at the station.

After staring up at the ceiling for a moment, Lester

lowered his eyes to Elliott again. He brightened for a moment and tried to say something, but his lips were dry and cracked, and the steady hiss from the oxygen tank obscured whatever it was he whispered.

"I told you to freeze," Elliott said, feeling uncomfortable under Lester's steady gaze. "I didn't want to shoot."

Lester's head twisted from side to side, making a faint crinkling sound on the pillow. His long, greasy hair was matted down with sweat. The stubble of beard made him look like a derelict on death's door.

"You wouldn't be here right now, you know, if you didn't hang out with that asshole Griffin."

Again, Lester's mouth moved, but nothing was intelligible. Elliott knew the boy was flying high on pain killers and probably wouldn't make sense even if he didn't have the oxygen tube stuck down his throat.

"Well, look at it this way," Elliott said, reaching out and patting Lester gently on the shoulder. "You'll get a chance to rest, get that wound all nice and healed up before you have your day in court. And I'm going to try like hell not to feel too guilty when I testify against you."

Lester made a strangled, slurred sound in the back of his throat. The boy's eyelids fluttered and then closed as Elliott turned and walked toward the door.

– 2 –

Lester was flying high in a dreamy, drugged haze. Whenever he opened his eyes, the dim light in the room wobbled and blended into thick orange rivers. His entire awareness was filled with a loud hissing sound that wavered in and out like a storm wind. He felt curiously disoriented, as if he were perpetually falling over onto his right side. Several times he had the panicky sensation of drifting out of his body, of leaving himself behind as he hovered up near the ceiling and looked down at his body.

He was too out of it even to wonder whether he was alive or dead . . . or somewhere in between.

One second that cop was standing there, looking down at him, laughing hysterically at his condition. The next second he was gone. Then he was back again, only now he looked different. His face was thinner, paler, and his eyes seemed impossibly bright. As he leaned over the bed, the pale skin of his face began to slough off like a snakeskin, exposing the dull gleam of worm-pitted bone. His lips peeled away, and his face dissolved as if it were evaporating under an invisible blast of heat.

I thought I told you to leave, man.

The words rang clearly in Lester's mind as if he had spoken them aloud.

Don't you think you've done enough to me already?

The skull-faced cop leaned over his bed but said nothing as he slowly shook his head from side to side.

Don't I have to have a lawyer here? You can't make me say anything unless I have a lawyer here.

Skull-face smiled widely, exposing large, flat teeth that glowed. The pale eyes, deep in the bony eye sockets, were twin whirlpools, spinning in ever-widening circles, like some crazy cartoon character. The cop leaned his head back and let loose with a loud, roaring laugh.

You son of a bitch! You shot me! Jesus Christ! What are you going to —

Lester's eyes widened with terror as he watched Skull-face raise one bony hand high in the air and flex his fingers like a piano player about to play. A few last shreds of rotting flesh dissolved and disappeared as if blown away by the wind. The room wobbled and blurred as the skeletal hand reached out and touched the padded bandage on Lester's stomach.

No, don't! That hurts when you touch it!

Unblinking eyes stood out like sickly yellow balls as they shifted from Lester's stomach and locked onto his

111

terror-filled gaze. Lurching forward with a deep grunt, the skeleton suddenly drove his hand down hard. It passed through the bandages and into the wound. Lester couldn't make a sound as numbing, cold fingers tore through his flesh. Pain spiked through him as the finger-nails gouged and tore through layers of muscle and fat, digging and twisting deeper . . . deeper up under his ribs. Fresh blood bubbled out of the wound in a warm gush.

Please! . . . Don't! . . .

"I told you to freeze," the skeleton face whispered, its jaws clicking maddeningly as the lipless grin came up close to Lester's face. The pale eyes swelled like overinfla-ted tires until they split open, spilling thick, yellow fluid down the bony cheeks. "I didn't want to shoot."

. . . please . . .

Stinging pain sang along every nerve in spite of the painkillers. The room killed with the sound of shredding flesh and crunching bone. Above the hissing of the wind that filled his ears, Lester could hear something else — a heavy hammering sound.

. . . thump . . . thump . . . thump . . .

The room and everything in it dimmed — everything except for the grinning skull face that hovered above him.

"You wouldn't be here right now, you know, if you didn't hang out with that asshole, Griffin," Skull-face said thickly. "Well, look at it this way. You'll get a chance to rest, get that wound all nice and healed up before you have your day in court. And I'm going to try like hell not to feel too guilty when I testify against you."

With a quick jerk, the skeleton yanked his hand out of the wound and held up something dripping and red in front of Lester's face. White lines of gristle and muscle were veined with twisting black and blue lines. Beneath the oozing blood was a tangle of pink meat that still twitched with a faint pulse. Fiery, spinning pain engulfed Lester.

"Recognize it?" Skull-face asked, holding it close to Lester's face. Then he shook his head. "Naw . . . probably not."

Skull-face laughed softly as he left the bloody thing slip slowly out of his hand to land on the floor with a dull *plop*.

Lester could no longer focus his eyes, but he could still hear the softly fading *thump* . . . *thump* . . . *thump* of his heart. The darkness of the room suddenly collapsed inward with a soundless implosion that pulled him down.

— 3 —

Just as the door was swinging shut behind Elliott, a shrill beeper and the sound of breaking glass sounded from Lester's room. Kyle was instantly on his feet, and Elliott turned and shouldered open the door as a nurse came running toward them.

"Something's wrong," she shouted, a look of deep concern creasing her face. "His monitor just went flatline."

Elliott was first in the room, followed by Kyle and the nurse. When he saw Lester, sprawled halfway off his bed, he staggered and had to grip the door edge to keep himself from falling down. Lester's head was still on his pillow, but his legs were splayed awkwardly on the floor, half-twisted around. The handcuffs had prevented him from falling out of bed altogether. The pads of bandage covering his stomach had been torn away, and thick gouts of blood pumped from the open wound. Blood stained the twisted sheets and splashed onto the floor in a widening pool.

"Christ on a cross!" Elliott muttered as his stomach did a sour flip-flop. The nurse and Kyle looked as if they were close to fainting, too.

Lester's free hand was making feeble grabs at his stomach, pressing back against the gaping wound as if he could somehow close up the hole and stop the heavy flow of blood. His eyes were as dull as lead as he looked first at the nurse and Kyle; then he locked eyes with Elliott.

"Why did you do this to me?" he whispered, his voice no more than a sputtering hiss.

— 4 —

"You realize that this is entirely unnecessary, don't you?" Police Chief Charles Beckworth said. He held the single sheet of paper with both hands as he glanced over the top of his glasses at Elliott, who stood at attention in front of Beckworth's desk. Soft afternoon light filtered through the slats of the Levelor blinds of his office window, spreading bars of faint lemon light on the window sill and floor.

"I—umm, I'm not entirely convinced it isn't, sir," Elliott replied stiffly. He was holding himself back, afraid that, if given the opportunity, he would let his anger fly. As far as he was concerned, the department had ruined him—his life, his marriage, even his sense of his own personal integrity. And if it wasn't the department's fault, then it was Lester LaJoie's for dying in the hospital.

"I suppose I don't have to tell you how confident I am that the internal investigation will exonerate you—completely."

"I know that, sir."

"And that being suspended with pay is the best I can do for you until the completion of the investigation."

"I want to thank you for that, sir."

"For Christ's sake, Elliott! Will you drop this *sir* shit?" Beckworth said with a snap. "And stop standing there like this is some kind of military review or something. Have a seat."

"Thank you," Elliott said, almost adding sir again, but then he simply pulled back one of the two chairs in front of Beckworth's desk and sat down.

"I've got to tell you, as a friend, that if anything, resigning from the department will only make the situation look worse, not better."

"I'm aware of that possibility," Elliott replied with a cool detached tone of voice. "I just think that . . ."

"Yes?" Beckworth said, prompting Elliott when he let his voice drift away.

"I was going to say that I think, no matter what the department finally concludes, there will be people around town who will say how suspicious it looks, that a suspect in an attempted arson case coincidentally dies right after the arresting officer, the man who wounded him, has visited him in the hospital."

"But we know that you didn't do anything in that hospital room, correct?"

Elliott remained silent for a moment. "Come on, Chuck," he said tightly. "You've known me a lot of years."

"I just have to ask."

"Well, you must know that I couldn't do anything like that," Elliott said. "Christ! Half—more than half the reason I'm resigning is because I can't handle the thought that I"—his voice choked a moment before he could continue—"that I shot him. I *killed* him!"

"And what the fuck were you supposed to do?" Beckworth asked sharply. "Stand there and let him skewer Henry with that frigging screwdriver?"

Elliott shrugged and whispered, "I don't know. I mean, if Lester had been planning on hurting anyone, don't you think he would have had a weapon on him? A gun or a knife or something?"

"A screwdriver that size can do some pretty serious damage." Beckworth heaved a heavy sigh. "Look here, El. I know this is rough as shit on you, but it's the kind of thing you can't be queasy about if you decide to be a cop. Understand? Your job, which as far as I can see you did one hundred percent right, was to protect Henry. If that means you have to shoot someone, then so be it. That's what you're trained to do, for Christ's sake!"

"I know that," Elliott said. "But in the long run, who the fuck's gonna care if one trigger-happy cop loses his job because he shot some punk, huh? Just so long as things get back to normal in town. That's all anyone really cares about."

"So what's the big fuckin' deal?" Beckworth said. "Let the investigation run its course, and you'll be back on the force in a couple of weeks, tops."

Elliott shook his head slowly and, narrowing his eyes, stared at his boss. "Did you ever do it?" he asked. "Did you ever have to shoot someone in the line of duty?"

Beckworth heaved another heavy sigh. "No I never have. But in my time as chief, I've seen more than my fair share of officers who have."

"But you've never had another human being lined up in your gun sites," Elliott said edgily. "You've never had to pull the trigger and then see that glazed-over dead look in another human being's eyes."

"I've also seen more than my fair share of dead people," Beckworth replied coolly.

"But never when *you've* been the one to do it!" Realizing he had both fists clenched at his side, Elliott forced himself to release them. "I—I'm not so sure I want that kind of responsibility, or jeopardy, or whatever," he finished in a tight whisper.

Beckworth looked at him and nodded sagely as he placed the letter of resignation squarely on the blotter in front of him and smoothed it with the flat of his hand.

"So then," he asked thoughtfully, "if you quit the force, just what *are* you going to do? What are your plans?"

Elliott shrugged and shook his head. "I doubt it

116

will be any more police work."

Beckworth was silent for several heartbeats then his face suddenly lit up. "Wait a second! I have an idea. I just thought of something. A good friend of mine—Jim Avery—is head of the campus police at the University of Maine in Orono. I'll bet you a six-pack I could pull a string or two and get you a job up there."

Elliott's face remained expressionless.

"It'd be a perfect situation for someone like you," Beckworth continued, growing increasingly excited by the idea. "You wouldn't even have to carry a gun. You can spend your days ticketing cars parked in the faculty parking lot and cruising by fraternity parties that are getting a bit too rowdy. What do you say? Want me to give Jim a call?"

Elliott considered a moment, then shook his head. "I don't know," he said. "I mean, right now, all I want to do is go home, have myself a couple of beers, and try to forget all of this shit. If you'll excuse me." He rose from the chair and stuck his hand out across the desk to his boss. They clasped hands and shook firmly.

"Thanks," Elliott said, "for your support in all of this."

"No sweat," Beckworth replied as Elliott turned and started for the door. "But promise me you'll think about it, okay? Avery's just one phone call away."

"Yeah, sure," Elliott said. "I'll think about it."

—5—

Throughout the first few weeks of school, Sarah was quiet, withdrawn, and nervous. She spoke only when spoken to, and made no effort to get to know any of the students. She was downright miserable about spending her senior year at Hilton Lake Regional High School. She would have to spend the entire year as an outsider— the "new kid," as she heard in passing more than once

117

while walking from class to class. Being an outcast really hurt, especially after being so tight with her circle of friends back at Westbrook High School. She couldn't adjust to the idea that she didn't know anybody here, and just about no one seemed interested in getting to know her.

Most of the students scrutinized her from a safe distance, but few would come anywhere near her. Some of them were at least pleasant enough to chirp a quick "Hi" when she looked directly at them, but few bothered to introduce themselves. On the other hand, at least no one was being overtly mean to her either. Sarah was positive it was because they had all heard about what had happened to her and her mother, why she was living in Hilton in the first place, and how her stepmother had died just three days before school started. In many ways, this silent treatment was worse that being teased because it made her feel like such a nonentity.

Everyone ignored her except for Jennifer Killborne. If anything, Jennifer seemed too anxious to become Sarah's friend. As much as Sarah wanted to be nice to her in return, she could easily see why Jennifer didn't have any friends. She was thin, pale, and not terribly attractive, and she seemed to have a sour, pinched expression on her pimply face all the time. Jennifer took great pride in proclaiming herself as being too good to be stuck her whole life in a "podunk, boon-dock, hick" town like Hilton; and she let everyone know that she was too smart to socialize with dummies who would probably end up working their lives away at the corner gas station or, more likely, the National Paper Products mill, just like their divorced parents.

On Friday afternoon of the second week of school, Jennifer and Sarah were sitting by themselves on the hillside beneath a tall pine tree at the back of the school yard. Sarah was nibbling at her tuna fish sandwich and watching the groups of friends as they hung around, smoked cigarettes, and talked and joked together. As lonely as she felt, she found herself wishing Jennifer would just go someplace else to eat her lunch and leave her alone.

"So, don't you think Mr. Merrill is giving us too much homework for so soon in the year?" Jennifer said. "God! He's such a queef!"

"Umm," Sarah replied with a shrug. "He's not so bad."

"Well, I think he's a queef," Jennifer said, pressing the point. "He doesn't even know the material he's supposed to be teaching us. I bet I know more about ecology than he does."

Sarah grunted before taking a long sip of diet soda just so she wouldn't have to say anything. She glanced at her watch, noting that there was still more than fifteen minutes left for lunch. Well, at least Jennifer wasn't in her next class, American Literature.

"And the way he goes on and on about stuff—like that lecture he gave us on acid rain this morning. Geeze, I mean, as if I care!" She shook her head disgustedly. "What a queef!"

For the sake of conversation, Sarah was about to ask Jennifer exactly what a queef was, but she let her question drop and focused, instead, on the groups of students hanging around the parked cars. She couldn't help remembering how she and Louise and Kathy would have been right there in the center of it if this had been Westbrook.

But it wasn't Westbrook, and Jennifer's constant chattering was getting on her nerves. Sarah took a deep breath to push back the flood of anger that was rising inside her and looked over at one group where several boys, all wearing Hilton High football letter jackets, were standing around one good-looking blond girl.

Jennifer followed her gaze. "Oh, that's Lisa Ruckner," she said with an exaggerated wince when Lisa's flirting laughter rang through the crisp air. "She is such an idiot! Look at the way those guys hang around her. God, they're like animals in heat or something!"

Sarah frowned but said nothing.

"She thinks she's so cute. Look at her! Just look at the way she teases them, acting like a coy little slut. She makes me want to ralf!"

"Come on, Jen," Sarah said, shortening her name because Jennifer had told her how much it irritated her whenever anyone did that. She was all set to confront Jennifer, to tell her that she was jealous because Lisa could attract guys, something Jennifer probably would never do; but her voice choked off, and she was suddenly afraid to speak. The anger building up inside her crested like a black tidal wave. Sarah was suddenly filled with mean, hateful thoughts, all of them directed at Jennifer.

"Geeze—what was that?" Jennifer asked. She shivered wildly and rubbed her upper arms as she glanced from Sarah to the group of students lolling around the car.

"What was what?" Sarah said, her voice tight and dry in the back of her throat.

Jennifer's eyes widened with shock as she looked frantically around them, as if she expected to see someone. "I—I don't know," she said, her voice wavering. "For a second, there, I had this really weird feeling, like there was . . ." She narrowed her eyes and gave Sarah a suspicious once-over and shook her head again. "I don't know. I just got the shivers." She forced a laugh and tried to inject bold confidence into her voice. "It's what my mother always calls 'having a goose walk over your grave.'"

"Pleasant thought," Sarah said, unable to stop her frown from deepening. She, too, couldn't push aside the feeling that something was different . . . something was definitely wrong.

"Oh, no," she muttered when she shifted her gaze

120

down to the students and saw Tully standing behind one large group that was gathered around several parked cars.

Tully glanced up at Sarah and gave her a wide smile. His face was as white as marble, and his pale blue eyes sparkled in the sunlight. Sarah's eyes widened with shock when Tully raised one hand and pointed a bony forefinger straight at Jennifer and nodded.

With a quick twist of her body, Sarah leaped to her feet. Her sandwich flew out of her hand, and her foot kicked over her soda can, spilling its contents onto the ground. She stood there, her arms tensed, as if she were coiling up, getting ready to run down toward the students.

Jennifer looked up at her with a bemused smile. "What is it, Sarah? she said, snickering nervously as she looked back and forth between Sarah and the other kids.

"No. No! I—I," Sarah muttered. Her eyes were fixed on Tully as she shook her head back and forth. She started to move forward, then drew to an abrupt stop. Her breath came in short, tortured gulps. Her hands— her whole body were suddenly cold and trembling.

"What the heck's the matter?" Jennifer asked apprehensively. "God! Now you're acting like a queef."

"I've got to—stop him. He has to get away from me!" Sarah muttered. Her words vibrated low and deep in her throat, struggling to get out.

Again, Jennifer looked fearfully from her to the group of kids around the cars.

"Will you please sit down?" she said. "God, if anyone hears you, they'll think you're crazy or something. Come on, Sarah! Sit down!"

"No, I—I can't! I have to stop him! Control him! I didn't mean it!" Sarah whispered. Her voice resonated with tension and worry as she stood there, wringing her hands helplessly. Her eyes were riveted on Tully, and she

121

could feel her own raging anger being reflected right back at her. His smile widened as he raised his eyebrows questioningly. His teeth glinted in the sun like an animal's bared fangs.

"Come on, Sarah! Stop it, now! Will you? You're scaring me." Her voice rose to a high, insectlike whine. Any minute now, she expected to see Sarah drop to the ground and start twitching and foaming at the mouth. When she looked to where Sarah was staring, she didn't see anything unusual at first. Then, in an instant, she saw . . . something. For a second, there was just a wavering gray haze, like thin smoke. It was swirling up from underneath one of the cars parked behind the group. As she watched, the cloud steadily thickened and darkened, uncoiling into the clear blue sky.

"Oh, my God! That car's on fire!" Jennifer shrieked. She leaped to her feet and tried to run down to the parking lot, but Sarah snagged her by the arm and held her back.

"No!" she yelled. "Don't go down there!" Her fingertips dug painfully into Jennifer's wrist and wouldn't let go as she stared fixedly at the group of students.

"Get away from there! That car's on fire!" Jennifer yelled as she pointed wildly at the car, all the while struggling to break the grip Sarah had on her arm.

A couple of the kids looked over at her, then looked in the direction she was pointing, but Jennifer could tell by their confused expressions that they didn't see the danger.

"The blue car there! Look! It's on fire!" Jennifer yelled, still pulling to get away from Sarah.

"You can't go down there!" Sarah said firmly. "He'll kill you if you do! It's my fault. I have to control him!"

"What? What the heck are you talking about?" Jennifer asked, looking at her with absolute shock. "Those kids have got to . . ." Her voice faded to nothing when she looked back at the car. There wasn't even a lingering trace of smoke. A couple of the kids frowned at her, shook their heads, and laughed while everyone else just went on doing what they had been doing. Stunned into silence, Jennifer shook her arm out of Sarah's grip. Exhaling loudly, she sat back down onto the ground.

"What the hell . . . was that?" she asked, shaking her head tightly. "I thought for sure I saw smoke."

"I—I'm not sure," Sarah said. Her voice was still wobbly, but she was getting herself back under control.

"Those kids—" Jennifer said, cutting herself short. "I'll bet all of those kids are laughing at me."

"It doesn't matter," Sarah said softly. "Let them think whatever they want." She looked from Jennifer to the group of students, not at all surprised to see that none of them were paying any attention to either of them. She unclenched her fists and eased herself back down onto the grass as the numbing waves of panic gradually receded. She picked up her sandwich, brushed the grass off it, and took a small bite. As she chewed, she could only think of one thing: Tully was gone. He had come, responding to her anger at Jennifer, and she had controlled him. She had made him go away.

Chapter Nine

Cell Mate

— 1 —

"Hey, you don't get away from me that easy!" Alan shouted.

Rolling over quickly, he threw aside the coarse woolen blanket and swung out with a clenched fist. He missed entirely but followed up with a wide, sweeping kick. Again, he missed, and the momentum carried him, his blanket, and his top sheet off the bed and onto the cold prison floor. He landed flat on his back, hard enough to knock the wind out of him.

"Hey, man — calm down," Larry Mosley said sleepily from the top bunk. Larry was the other prisoner sharing the segregation cell with Alan; both of them were waiting for individual cells to become available in the East Wing, the "low-rent district," as the prisoners called it, where all the "cherries" first went after being admitted to the Maine State Prison.

Alan fought frantically to untangle himself from the sheets. He was tensed and ready for an attack, but hearing Larry's voice, definitely sleepy and coming from the top bunk, soon convinced him that he was in no immediate danger.

"Kinda jumpy down there, ain't yah?" Larry said.

Alan grunted, still coiled and ready to fight if necessary. Sweat dewed his skin, and his breathing came in fast, dry gulps.

"Yeah, I guess so," he said after a moment.

"Ahh, fuck it. Everyone around here gets a little crazy, sooner or later," Larry said. "You just got to learn to find ways to relax yourself."

Bunching his sheet and blanket under his arm, Alan got slowly to his feet, all the while shifting his eyes suspiciously around the narrow confines of the cell. In a seven-by-nine-foot room, there weren't many places to hide; he didn't see anyone else, but he couldn't dispel the feeling that someone had been standing beside the bed, leaning over him as he slept. He didn't dare voice his suspicion that Larry might have come down from his bunk and tried to attack him.

"Hey, man! You're disturbing my dreams, if you don't mind," Larry said with an angry edge in his voice.

"Sorry about that, but I just had the feeling someone else was in here," Alan said.

"There's no one here 'cept you, me, and my bitch," Larry said.

Alan stood beside the bed for a moment, his fists still clenched, but there was no motion from Larry's direction. Finally, he lowered his guard a bit, then bent to spread his sheet and blanket over the mattress.

"And anyway, you've been snoring since I turned the light out," Larry said. "I just been up here, talking to my bitch!"

Alan knew exactly what he meant. Every night, Larry drew a pair of eyes and full, lush lips on his right hand with a blue and a red pen. "Talking to his bitch" meant he was making the crude woman's face on his hand do what Lizzie, his girlfriend, couldn't do for him right now.

"Yeah, sure," Alan said as he climbed slowly back under the covers, fluffed his thin pillow, and laid his head

125

down. As his muscles unwound and he started to relax, his confusion cleared, and he realized what had happened.

"I was just having a dream . . . about—"

He cut himself off abruptly when a razor-edge image from the dream came back to him.

He was chasing after that young girl through rain-soaked woods. He finally caught her, threw her down, and sat on her, pinning her shoulders to the wet, spongy earth. Just as he was reaching for his belt buckle, getting ready to do to her what he had done to her mother, she had . . . changed, somehow. Her expression subtly shifted. Not into someone else's face, really. The change seemed to happen only deep inside her eyes. The look of stark terror, which he had been so thoroughly enjoying, was replaced by pale, angry, staring eyes that swelled with violent intensity. Like a sudden blast of heat from a furnace, the change surprised him, making him pull away from her for a moment. In that instant, she twisted and slithered out from under him and started running again. But before he could get up and start after her, he sensed something else . . . someone coming up on him from behind.

Alan lay there, staring up at the sagging, bouncing bottom of the mattress above him. Larry's movements made the metal frame of the bunk bed squeak terribly. Alan tried his best to push out of his mind the stark dream image of the girl's face, but it lingered, filling him with a dull, gnawing sense of loss . . . of lost opportunity. He clenched his hands into fists and pounded them together as he lay there in the darkness, thinking how royally pissed off he was about how things had turned out. Just too damned bad he hadn't caught up with her that same night. Then maybe his dream would have come true; he could have screwed her first and then used his knife on her like he had on her mother. Even after that night, he'd had his chances—plenty of them—but he hadn't taken them. The timing hadn't been right until it was too damned late.

From newspaper accounts of the incident, Alan had learned her name—Sarah Lahikainen. And from the telephone book, he had easily found out where she lived—in Hilton, out on Ridge Road with her father, Devin Lahikainen. And from tracking her down, following her around, he knew exactly what she looked like—medium height, blond hair, blue eyes, and one hell of a nice body—nice tits, and a firm, full ass. Ever since that night, Alan had spent a lot of his waking hours thinking about her. At least two or three times a week, he would go out to the Lahikainen house, hide in the woods, and watch the windows. It was fairly easy to figure out which one was her bedroom window, so he'd position himself on the edge of the woods where he could keep watch, all the while imagining how much fun it would be if only he could gain entry. But in all that time, even once school started, she never seemed to be home alone—at least whenever he was around. He had been starting to get impatient, following her around, waiting to catch her in a situation where it would be just the two of them; but then he blew it by getting arrested that night at the White Crane. Now, he feared his chances were gone for good.

"Goddamn it," Alan whispered in the darkness. The palms of his hands hurt from squeezing them so hard.

The bed stopped squeaking, and Larry said angrily, "Will you *please* shut the fuck up?"

"Fuck you!"

"No, fuck you!"

"Yeah, you just try fucking with me," Alan said with a snarl.

"You ain't exactly my type, asshole," Larry snapped. "Too goddamned skinny, for one thing. But I'll tell you this much: you'd better watch yourself before you go mouthing off to the wrong person around here. It might not be so good for your health, if you catch my drift. Now, would you please just shut your fucking mouth so my bitch can finish what she started?"

Alan wanted to say more but instead let his breath out in a long, slow whistle. He stared up at the darkness, hardly aware of the bunk bed swaying from side to side.

"Umm-umm, that's good, baby," Larry murmured from up above. "Who taught you how to do that, anyway — your little sister or your mama?"

Alan sighed heavily and scrinched his eyes tightly shut. Once most of the prisoners turned out their lights, even the slightest sound echoed throughout the cell block. Sleep just wouldn't come to him, so he opened his eyes and just lay there, looking at the dim light glowing in the corridors outside the bars. This was only his eighth night in prison following his conviction on all counts, and already the monotony of the days and nights was getting to him. He knew he was going to have to adapt quickly; otherwise — like Larry said — he would lose his mind or else say the wrong thing to the wrong person. By his lawyer's best estimate, he still had something like five hundred more nights to go before he could even think about getting out. It was going to be a long stretch.

But even with his eyes wide open, staring into the darkness, his mind filled with fantasies of his own. He couldn't stop imagining Sarah's face, floating in front of him like a white balloon in the darkness. Her pale, blue eyes stared at him with a mocking, gloating look, as if to say: *I did it, you lousy son of a bitch! I got away from you!*

— 2 —

"Hi, Dad." Sarah was standing in the doorway of the

128

living room, looking in at her father as if she didn't quite dare enter the room. He was sitting on the couch with his feet up on a hassock while he read the *Portland Evening Express*. An empty coffee cup was on the end table beside him, and the sports section from the paper was spread out on the floor where he had dropped it.

"Hey, how you doing, sweetheart?"

Sarah took a deep breath and said, "I—uh, I think we have to talk."

Devin lowered the newspaper and patted the couch cushion beside him, signaling for her to come over and sit down. "So tell me, what's on your mind?"

"A lot," Sarah said, sighing heavily. She moved into the room but avoided the couch and instead lowered herself onto the easy chair opposite her father. She sat stiffly on the edge of the chair with her hands folded between her knees. Her fingers were braided together so tightly her knuckles turned white.

"What is it—something about school?" he asked.

Biting her lower lip, Sarah shook her head dejectedly. "No—school's going all right I guess."

"Something outside of school then?" He looked at her earnestly. "Is it about a boy?"

Again, Sarah shook her head.

"Well then—what is it? You know you can talk to me about anything."

Tensing her shoulders, Sarah squeezed her eyes shut before beginning.

"Well, I've been thinking a lot about Rosalie and . . . and Mom lately, and I—"

"Hey, hey," Devin said. He threw the newspaper aside and came over to her. Standing beside the chair, he reached down and gently rubbed her neck and shoulders. "I know . . . I know how hard it must be for you." His own eyes stung as he looked down at her bowed head. He took a deep breath and for just a moment his eyes went unfocused as he looked out the window. Autumn had stripped the trees bare, and the view was gloomy, desolate. "I understand how you feel, honey. I still miss them, too. I just think this is something that you never really get over."

"Yeah, but it's . . . it's more than that," Sarah said in a shattered whisper.

Inside, she was burning to tell him everything—tell him about her suspicion that Tully—or *she*—might have done all of these horrible things, might have caused people to die . . . even as far back as when Myrtle and Brian died. She wanted to tell him that she thought maybe her getting mad at her mother and at Rosalie was what caused them to die. Objectively, she knew the idea was crazy, but her heart told her differently; it seemed as if whenever she directed her anger at anyone, they died shortly thereafter.

And there was more. She wanted to tell her father how, ever since she had moved to Hilton, she had had the feeling that somebody was lurking nearby, almost all the time, watching her. At times she thought it might be Tully, but at other times it felt like it might be . . . someone else. And she wanted to tell him how just last week, ever since that day she had controlled Tully, commanding him to leave her and Jennifer alone, she had felt liberated . . . as if that menacing, lurking, unseen presence was suddenly no longer around, no longer watching her.

But as much as she wanted to say all of this, she couldn't. The words formed in her mind, but as she sat there, feeling the quiet strength of her father's hands massaging her back, she found that she couldn't even begin.

"You gotta understand," her father continued, "I mean, your mother and I—well, it's no surprise that we hadn't gotten along for a lot of years, even after the divorce.

130

God, even the few times a year when we saw each other, things were always pretty—" He cleared his throat. "Pretty tense. I still feel terrible that she and I argued that . . . that last night. I suppose in a lot of ways it was my fault for not telling her that Rosalie and I had gotten married. But you know, at the time, I figured it'd just give her one more thing to be upset about."

"Oh, I don't blame you for that," Sarah said. Her voice was nothing more than a strangled whisper as she thought about all the things she couldn't say.

"But, hey—you gotta remember the good times, too," her father said brightly. "The happy times. They can help you make it through when you're feeling so lonely."

Lonely? Sarah thought, sighing wistfully. *Dad, you don't know the half of it.*

"I mean, in spite of the problems your mom and I had, I think I always did—and always will—love her in a way. . ." Devin blinked his eyes and looked up at the ceiling before continuing. "Because we had . . . you." He gave her shoulders a tight squeeze.

Me . . . and Brian, Sarah thought as her heart did a cold flip-flop in her chest.

"Oh, I know you loved her," Sarah said, forcing a smile as she twisted around and looked up at him. "Even though you two couldn't stand living together. But there's . . . there's something else."

"What?" he asked.

Sarah bit down harder on her lower lip to stop it from trembling. She had no idea how to tell him she was positive she had caused her mother's and Rosalie's deaths because she had been angry at them. No matter how convinced she was of that, it just didn't make sense whenever she tried to say it out loud. The only time she could was when she was talking into her tape recorder.

"Hey, these things take time," her father said. "Day by day, the pain—at least the immediate pain—will lessen."

131

He gave her another bracing pat on the shoulder, deeply pained as he looked at her and saw how close she was to breaking down. "I'll bet in another month or two, you'll be doing just fine."

Sarah opened her mouth but was unable to speak. She realized with a cold twisting in her stomach that, as much as he loved her, he had no idea who she was; he had no idea what she thought and felt and dreamt. There was a breach—of years, if not love—between them, and it sickened her to think that it might already be too late to heal that breach.

He turned her around to face him and held his arms out to her. In a flash, Sarah was out of the chair and hugging him. Her shoulders shook violently as he folded her into his embrace and stroked her hair and murmured comforting words.

But all Sarah could think was, *Is he really gone? It's almost too good to be true, but is Tully really out of my life forever?*

—3—

The whining sound of power tools filled the work area. Pale winter sunlight streamed through the windows, spiking the dust-filled air with golden beams and casting harsh shadows across the floor and underneath the work benches. After several months of working in the wood shop, Alan was finally getting used to the pervasive smell of wood stain and varnish, but he knew he would never get used to the noise. Even when he wore protective headphones, his ears would ring for hours after his stint in the shop.

Day after day, week after week, for four hours a day, he operated a lathe, turning out chair and table legs for the prison furniture shop. The work had a mind-numbing effect so, once he got the hang of the machinery, he could pretty much do his job without thinking about it.

132

The only good thing about the noise was that it was so loud it blocked out every other sound. Alan liked that because it left him alone with his own thoughts as he worked.

And he had plenty to think about.

He received his hometown newspaper, the *Hilton Register*, every day, always just after lunch. For half an hour before his work shift, he would carefully scan the newspaper, especially the local news. He wasn't exactly sure what he was looking for, but it always made him feel tense, wound up with expectation.

Any day now he expected to see some hint, some mention of the ongoing investigation to find out who had raped and killed Marie Lahikainen last June. He was nervous about that; now that he had been convicted of one crime, the police just might put two and two together and make the connection. Although that concerned him, it didn't bother him as much as Sarah Lahikainen did . . . and the fact that she was still alive. Maybe all he was looking for was a mention that she had been run over by a steamroller or something. That certainly would have given his day a boost.

Whenever he thought back to that night last spring, nearly a year ago now, he had to chastise himself for not catching up with her when she bolted off into the woods. It galled him that he hadn't run her down and cut her throat . . . after having a bit of fun with her, of course. Although he clearly remembered that it had been raining and as dark as pitch that night, events had gradually become distorted in his memory until, after a while, he was absolutely convinced Sarah had not only seen him but had also identified him. She had gone straight to the police with a description of him, and the cops knew he had done it.

The only thing they didn't have was proof. That was the only reason he had never been arrested and charged with the crime.

Shortly after entering prison, Alan had learned that Lester LaJoie had died of his wounds from the night at the White Crane. At first, Alan's only thought was that he hated to lose such a good customer for the drugs he dealt—not to mention the stash someone must have found when they cleaned Lester's personal belongings out of his apartment. But after a while, what had happened that night at the restaurant seemed to fit into the bigger picture. Alan became increasingly convinced that the whole thing had been a setup to nail his ass and send him off to prison. That's why he was in jail now. Sarah had tipped off the cops, and Lester, probably by driving a bargain with the cops to leave his ass alone, had set him up to get arrested. So catching that bullet and dying in the hospital served the little bastard right, Alan thought bitterly, and the conclusion seemed inevitable: the police couldn't convict him on one thing, so they'd put him away for something else. It was as simple as that! And that bitch Sarah Lahikainen had started it all . . . simply by getting away from him that night.

"But you won't get away from me forever," Alan muttered, unable even to hear his voice over the whine of machinery as he stared blankly at the wood turning in the lathe.

Someone snagged his shirt sleeve from behind and gave it a tug. Surprised, Alan turned quickly, ready to fight if he had to. He eased up when he saw his former segregation cell mate, Larry, signaling by tapping his watch that work period was over; it was time to shower up before recreation period.

Alan nodded and, without removing his ear protectors, indicated that he wanted to finish turning out this last chair leg before knocking off. Larry shrugged and left as other men deserted their work stations and, under the watchful eyes of the guards, started filing out the exit.

No matter how frustrated he felt, in some ways, Alan thought this stint in prison was doing him some good in at least one regard; he had loads of time to think about things and plan exactly what he would do to Sarah Lahikainen once he got out of prison. She would, after all, have to pay for putting him here.

"Yes-sir-ee," Alan whispered as he watched the wood turn and imagined that it was Sarah's throat beneath the wide chisel blade . . . that it was Sarah's skin, not soft, white pine, curling up like a potato skin as he peeled her throat ever so slowly.

"You *are* going to pay, you bitch, come hell or high water. And I don't care if you move to California and change your name or even change your goddamned face, once I get out of this fucking place, I'm going to find you. And when I do, I'm going to do *this* . . ."

He pressed the lathe blade down hard, gouging deeply into the wood, ruining the chair leg.

"And *this*."

Another, harder thrust of the blade took a V-shaped chunk of wood out of the leg.

"And *this!*"

He pushed down so hard against the blade it knocked the leg onto the floor. It bounced and rolled ten feet before coming to rest beneath one of the drill presses. Alan turned off his machine, took off his ear protectors, and went to retrieve it. Just as he was bending over to pick up the chair leg, a hand clamped down hard on his shoulder. Tensing, he turned but quickly dropped his fist when he saw Ben Alexander, one of the prison guards, glaring at him.

"You got a problem here, Griffin?" Ben asked, eyeing him narrowly.

Alan's face was flushed with anger. His hands were tingling, just itching to wrap around someone's throat and squeeze, but he knew this wasn't the time or the place or

135

the right person.

"Uh—no. No problem at all," he stammered.

Ben gave him a silent once-over, then cleared his throat as he backed away and indicated the door with a nod of the head. "Well, just watch it," he said. "You look a little tense to me. You gotta learn to relax."

Chapter Ten

Party Hardy

— 1 —

The music was loud and distorted. Sarah could hear it nearly a block away as she walked up Depot Street toward Lisa Ruckner's house. It was a bit after ten o'clock, and the graduation party was in full swing when Sarah arrived. For the past few weeks, she had been waiting for Pete Bishop to ask her out. She knew he wanted to, but his terminal shyness had prevented it. She hadn't wanted to go to Lisa's party but had changed her mind about it at the last minute . . . mostly because Lisa Ruckner had grown to be—well, certainly not a close friend, but friendly enough over the past few months. Sarah and Jennifer were barely speaking to each other, but Sarah couldn't honestly say she missed her; actually, she hoped Jennifer wouldn't be here tonight. The only person she was looking for was Pete Bishop.

"Hey, babe, what's happenin'?" Randy Potter asked as she made her way through the crowd standing on the porch outside the kitchen door. The boy was wearing a Baltimore Orioles hat with the bill pointing backward, a shredded gray sweatshirt, and jeans with ragged holes in both knees. Sarah recognized him from around school and town, but about the only thing she knew about him was his name. Throughout the school year, he had never even bothered to speak to her.

Blushing, Sarah smiled and nodded, but said nothing as she pushed past him. As she entered the house, she heard someone behind her whistle and say, "Hey, lookin' foxy tonight!"

It was either Randy or the boy he was standing with, but she didn't turn to see.

The noise inside the house was deafening. Blaring music squelched all but the loudest shouted conversations. The kitchen counter and table were spread with food — little sandwiches, bowls of chips and nuts, and assorted treats. Beside the refrigerator, a large washtub was filled with ice cubes and cans of soda. Thin blue rafts of cigarette smoke drifted just above head level, swirling as people moved around. Occasionally Sarah caught the sweet tang of marijuana smoke, but most of the kids seemed intent on guzzling from the beer bottles and wine flasks they were surreptitiously passing around. A few people uttered quick greetings to Sarah, to which she smiled and replied quickly, but she couldn't stop feeling incredibly self-conscious; it seemed as though every pair of eyes was on her as she picked up a can of Pepsi, snapped the flip top, and moved through the crowd.

A few couples were dancing in the living room while other couples huddled close together on the couch and easy chairs. Sarah quickly scanned the crowd but saw no one she could talk to — as if there was anyone here she could truly call a friend. Her heart ached when she thought that, right now, a few hours' drive south, all of her true friends were probably having their own graduation party in Westbrook.

"So — you come here alone?" The voice was loud, almost a shout to be heard above the music.

Sarah turned around, hoping against hope to see Pete's face; but as she did, the strong smell of alcohol hit her full

138

in the face. Disappointment swept through her when she realized Randy Potter and his friend had followed her into the living room. She shrugged and flickered her eyes around the room, fighting a surge of dizziness.

"You know, I was just saying to George . . ." Randy hooked his thumb and indicated his friend standing one step behind him. "This is my buddy, George Dunbar. But I was just sayin' to him how it seems kinda odd how you're always hanging out by yourself. Why's that?"

One blasting song stopped, but after a brief silence, before Sarah could reply, another started up again, so she simply shrugged.

"Hey! This is the new album by Rabies!" Randy said, smiling broadly as he indicated the stereo with his thumb. "Wanna dance?"

Dancing was just about the last thing Sarah felt like doing, but it beat standing alone in the corner somewhere, watching everyone else have fun. She nodded and followed Randy out to the center of the floor, where they began jostling and bouncing with the other kids. The music had no discernible flow other than a heavy down beat, but Sarah did her best to move to it. Lost in his own world, Randy looked like someone with a serious nervous disorder as his body jerked spastically to the off-beat.

One song ended and another began. Before Randy realized it, Sarah wandered away. She tried to avoid George, but he followed her, keeping a short distance between them. When Randy realized he was out there strutting his stuff on his own, he looked around until he spotted Sarah and George. He walked over toward them, scowling.

"Had enough already?" he said. Arching his eyebrows, he added, "Maybe you got a better idea of something we could do." Looking past Sarah, he signaled for George to back off. Then, patting his hip pocket, he said, "My brother just scored some bitchin' weed. Wanna slip out for a doobie?"

Frowning, Sarah shook her head. "No thanks. I—uh,

I'm unstable enough without drugs," she said. Randy missed the joke entirely.

"Well then," he said, pressing closer to her. "What say you and me see if we can think of something else to do." He wiggled his eyebrows and leered at her.

Sarah started to back away, but within three steps she bumped into the wall. Looking frantically left and right, she could see no way to get away from Randy without causing a scene. What a fine way to finish up the year at school, she thought.

"Look, uh—Randy, I really appreciate the offer," she stammered, "but I just came to see everyone. I'm just not in a party mood."

The dark room and hammering music closed in on her like a steel trap. With her back to the wall, and the nearest doorway straight across the floor through the knot of dancers, Sarah had to fight back hard on her rising surge of panic. Randy's face loomed in front of her like an idiotic, grinning moon. His breath reeked of alcohol, and his glazed eyes glowed with a dull, lambent light.

"What the hell do you mean you're not in a party mood?" he said. Twisting his body, he swept his hand to indicate the thronging living room. "This is a party, man! Graduation!" Clenching his fists and shaking them, he wailed, "It's time to party hardy!" Before Sarah could reply, he stepped right up next to her, pinning her against the wall. Lowering his voice, he slurred, "Unless you wanna slip out and create our own little party. Maybe that's what you're looking for."

Biting her lower lip, Sarah shook her head vigorously as hot anger surged inside her.

"Well then what do you wanna do?" Randy said, his face darkening. "I don't wanna start any rumors—or spread the ones that have already started—but you ain't a lezzie, are yah?"

Sarah's face went blazing hot. She tried to say something, but her voice wouldn't work. Was that it? Everyone at school thought she was a lesbian? Maybe that was something Jennifer had started . . . or maybe Jennifer was gay, and hanging around with her had started the rumors.

"Well?" Randy said. His hands went around her waist and pulled her tightly against him. "You sure as shit ain't bad-lookin'. I don't see what's your problem."

Sarah stared at him with fear-widened eyes, shaking her head from side to side. Her heart did a cold flutter in her chest when she remembered that night just about a year ago when someone came on to her mother like this. Randy's slurred voice echoed in her ears like someone else's voice . . . a deeper voice from another lifetime ago . . .

"What the hell's the matter with you? I'm just bein' friendly, trying to help you out a bit. I wouldn't think of hurting such a pretty lady like you."

The words rang in her memory like a deep-throated bell.

" 'N just what in the hell do you think I want to be doin'?"

He's going to do something! Sarah thought, twisting inside with black, bottomless anger at both Randy and the man who had hurt and killed her mother. *Just like what happened to my mother, this guy is going to see how far he can go . . . or else push it all the way!*

And Sarah knew all too well how far that was.

"Please," she said. Her voice was no more than a faint whisper against the music as she struggled to control her fear and anger. Her entire body was tingling as she twisted away from Randy's grasp and looked frantically around the room for help. Everyone was occupied and didn't even notice what was happening to her—everyone, that is, except for one boy, standing at the far end of the room, leaning against the wall, and watching them. A cold shock hit Sarah the instant she recognized him.

"Tully! Oh, Jesus!" she muttered as she fixed her gaze on the unsmiling face and unblinking eyes watching her. "No, Tully . . . please."

"Huh?" Randy said, casting a careless glance over his shoulder. "What is it, you already got a boyfriend? Or

141

maybe you have a *girl*friend. Hey! What's the fuckin' difference? I won't tell if you won't. Tonight, let's party! Let's have ourselves some fun!"

He reached out with both hands and grabbed her. One arm encircled her back, crushing her against him while the other hand mauled her breasts. His cold, wet lips mashed against hers in a smothering kiss. Sarah almost vomited when he slipped his tongue into her mouth. It felt like a bloated, twitching slug. Forcing her against the wall, Randy started grinding his hips against hers, applying a steady, throbbing pressure. The hardness of his crotch rubbed painfully against her thigh.

Drowned out by the music and her rapidly cresting fear, everything in the room dropped away except for Tully's steady stare, which Sarah could see over Randy's shoulder. She couldn't close her eyes or even look away. Distantly, she felt Randy tug her blouse up before he slipped his hand in underneath and cupped her breasts. He moaned like an animal in her ear as he gave her a rough squeeze.

"Hey, now," he said, breaking off the kiss and pulling back an inch or two. "That's a little more like it." The alcohol fumes of his breath made her dizzy, but not as dizzy as the spiraling fear of just knowing Tully was there in the room.

"No—please," she said, her voice rasping deep in her throat. *"Please* go away. You don't know what you're doing!"

"Who says I don't?" Randy growled. He didn't notice that Sarah was looking past him, her gaze transfixed by Tully's pale, unblinking eyes. Drifting in slow motion, Tully started to move toward them as a cruel, thin smile split his face. His wide, flat teeth caught what little light there was in the room and reflected it back like cold moonlight.

Randy leaned forward to kiss Sarah again, but she squirmed away from him. His hand was still under her blouse, and it caught her up, practically dragging her back into his arms.

"Come on," he said, moaning low. "Give it up. You never

142

know until you try it."

"You don't . . . you don't know . . . he'll hurt you!" Sarah said. Her voice was no more than a strangled gasp as she fought back her anger. "Please, Randy . . ."

Randy was about to say something, but just then the blaring music ended with a series of crackling pops, like a string of firecrackers. Everyone in the room looked over at the stereo, where yellow light flickered and heavy, black smoke was billowing out of the component cabinet. The smoke rose to the ceiling, hanging like dense fog. The turntable and CD player crackled, then erupted into flames. A sharp, static hiss was followed by a rumbling boom.

"Oh no! Fire! Fire!" several voices shouted.

"Mom! Dad! The stereo's on fire!" Lisa's voice shrilled above the mayhem.

In an instant, all the party-goers were racing toward the nearest door. Through his drunken haze, Randy slowly sized up the situation, then clamped his arm around Sarah and directed her to the front door, practically pushing her over as they ran. In the confusion, people knocked into each other; a few threw punches to get someone out of their way. Just as Sarah and Randy stumbled out the front door, Sarah heard the hollow hiss of a fire extinguisher. She wanted to look back, but Randy dragged her across the front lawn. Panting from the exertion, they finally stopped under one of the large maple trees down by the street.

"It's all right!" a voice shouted from the house. Sarah looked up and saw a man standing in the front doorway, waving them back in. "It's already out. There's no danger."

Sarah looked nervously at Randy, who still had one arm around her shoulder, clutching her tightly against him. He turned her around and pressed her hard against the tree.

Randy snickered as he glanced over his shoulder at the house. Groups of kids were starting to filter back to the party. "We was leavin' anyway, weren't we?"

"No—*we* weren't!" A cold, hard voice sounded frighteningly close to Sarah's ear. Stifling a scream, she turned to

143

one side and saw Tully, standing behind the tree. A look of pure malice underlit his face as he stared at Randy.

"Did you say something?" Randy asked. He frowned with confusion as his eyes shifted from Sarah to a spot behind her on the tree.

Unable to speak, Sarah shook her head.

"Come on, then," Randy said. He stepped back and slid his hand down to grip her arm just above the elbow. He was just turning to leave when he was stopped in his tracks, jerked back as though he had been fetched up on the end of a rope.

"What the—?"

Tully was no longer there. In his place, a swirling black cloud spilled out from behind the tree like a tornado of dense smoke. Thick enough to obscure the lights of the house, it condensed into two distinct arms that reached out of the shadows and embraced Randy. A soft, strangling sound came from his throat.

"No, Tully!" Sarah shrieked. "Please . . . don't do this!"

She started backing away, her hands fluttering near her face. She stumbled on the uneven ground in the dark and almost fell.

A voice, as clear as if it were in her head, said mildly, "But I have to do this, Sarah. He was going to hurt you, and you were mad at him, right?"

"No! I wasn't!" Sarah yelled. "I can handle him!"

Randy struggled silently against the enfolding black cloud. His face and hands were white smears against the night as he struggled to release himself. Sarah watched in horror as the dark figure lifted Randy clear off the ground, kicking violently. One shoe flew off his foot. Randy's mouth was open, but the only sound that came out was a deep-bellied grunt, as if the figure were crushing the life out of him. Before long, Randy's pale face was lost in spinning swirls of black mist.

"Please, Tully!" Sarah said, snorting loudly as tears dimmed her vision. "Please . . . I don't need your help! I

144

don't want your help! I want you to go back to—to wherever the hell you came from! Leave me alone!"

For a flickering instant, the mist thinned. Sarah could see Randy's body, jerking and twisting violently, as if he were falling; then, the instant she felt her anger at him rekindled, the mist deepened and he was caught up again.

"Go away, Tully! Leave me alone!" Sarah shouted. She darted forward and swung her fists wildly at the mist, but her hands passed through it unhindered. Randy's throat was making a deep, bubbling sound, as if he were choking on saliva . . . or blood.

A burst of light suddenly illuminated the end of the road. Frantic with fear, Sarah looked as a car came speeding out of the darkness toward them. The black figure holding Randy moved swiftly across the lawn toward the curb. In the darkness under the tree, it paused, hovering as the headlights steadily brightened. Then everything happened at once.

When the car was no more than ten feet away, the figure spun around once. Randy's arms and legs flailed helplessly in the air as he sailed straight out into the path of the oncoming car. Sarah's scream was lost in the harsh squeal of tires trying to stop on slick asphalt. Then a loud, wet *thump* filled the night as Randy's body punched out one of the headlights. Sarah watched in horror as he rolled and tumbled on the road, flopping and twisting into impossible poses before finally coming to a rest. The car skidded to a stop, its one headlight brilliantly illuminating the long, red streak on the pavement that ended at the mangled shape that had once been Randy Potter.

—2—

Like every other family of that year's graduating class, Sarah and her father attended Randy Potter's funeral on the day before graduation. It rained throughout the orations delivered at the high school gym and all during the

145

slow procession out to Pine Grove Cemetery, where Sarah's stepmother was buried. Alluding, no doubt, to the rumor that Randy's alcohol blood test had measured well over .3, the minister offered a few words about the tragic waste of youth and its potential. The next day, at commencement, Randy was eulogized again as being an inspiration for next year's and all succeeding years' seniors to promote "chemical-free" graduation parties.

Right after the funeral, Devin had to go to work at the mill. Sarah knew she should spend some time making sure her clothes were ready for graduation the next day, but her mind was preoccupied. She spent the rest of the afternoon sitting on the back porch, listening to the rain beat on the roof as she talked into her tape recorder.

"I have no idea what I'm going to do," she said shakily. "I don't know if I should see a psychiatrist or what."

The cold hollowness she felt from being out at the cemetery only reminded her how much she still missed her mother. It was just over a year ago that she had been killed, but the pain was as fresh as if it had been yesterday. All Sarah could think was—*My mother should be here tomorrow to see me graduate.*

Looking toward the river, she shivered when she recalled seeing Tully down there that day last fall . . . just before Rosalie died. Tears as hot as acid filled her eyes, blurring her view.

"I mean, I'm not even sure I know how much of this is in my imagination or real. How could it be real? It's not possible that I can see someone who isn't there. Not unless I'm crazy. And it plain old doesn't make sense. It's impossible that if I lose my temper, this . . . this *person* will come and kill whoever I'm mad at. That's—"

Her voice cut off, and she had to fight hard against the rush of anxiety that gripped her.

"It's crazy, pure and simple," she said, sniffing loudly. "And it's even crazier for me to think I can control this imaginary thing, whatever the hell it is. I mean, am

I responsible for it? For five deaths now?"

A dull ache throbbed in her chest whenever she thought how impossible it was for her even to broach the subject with her father. She had tried so many times, but the words just wouldn't come. Why? she wondered. Did she mistrust her father? Was she afraid of how he would react? Would he put her in a mental institution or something? Or would he blame her and hold it against her, too?

"How can I expect him to believe what I'm not even sure I believe?" she asked, whispering into the tape recorder microphone. "Jesus Christ, Tully. . . . What in God's name *are* you?"

Shivering, she looked out over the rain-beaten grass to the dark fringe of woods, half expecting to see Tully standing there under the trees, his pale face and steady, glassy stare watching her from the shadows.

Until the graduation party, Sarah had thought she'd gotten rid of him, had gained control of him. For most of the winter she'd never had even the slightest feeling that he was around, hovering just out of sight. At the party, when Randy had come on so strong to her, she must have let the reins slip—by letting herself get so angry at Randy, she gave Tully the crack he needed to come back.

"I don't need you anymore, Tully," Sarah said, her voice as low and trembling as a roll of thunder on the horizon. "I'm going to college in the fall, and this is my chance to start all over again, where no one knows anything about me or what's happened to me. And I'm not going to let you ruin it for me. I'm not going to let you back, Tully! If I have to, I'll spend every damned second I'm awake concentrating on keeping you away! And who knows . . ."

She paused and, smiling weakly, looked up at the twisted gray rain clouds.

"Maybe if I get mad enough at you, you'll turn all of your energy against yourself. Wouldn't *that* be something." She stood up, fighting the trembling in her body as she scanned the backyard and shouted.

"Do you hear me?" Her voice echoed dully from down by the river. "Do you hear me, Tully? I'm never going to let you hurt anyone for me again . . . *Ever.*"

Part Two

The Darkness Beckons

"If that thou be'st a devil, I cannot kill thee."
— Shakespeare

Chapter Eleven

Meeting Michael

— 1 —

In late August, Sarah and her father drove up to the University of Maine in Orono. Alice McCoy, Devin's new girlfriend, also came along with them. Autumn was already tingeing the air with a crispness. The maple trees along College Avenue displayed bright splashes of yellow and red against the brilliant blue sky. A thin, blue haze of smoke from burning leaves drifted in the air. Almost every house along Fraternity Row had a football game in progress on the front lawn. The campus was choked with cars and vans as parents and students busily unloaded their baggage and carted it up to their rooms. Sarah had been to the campus once before for orientation during the summer, so she directed her father to Hancock Hall, her dormitory on Munson Road.

"I'll bet you're pretty excited about all this, honey," Devin said as they waited in line for a chance to pull into the turnoff in front of the dorm.

Sarah was busily gnawing at her lower lip as she scanned the frenzied activity. Laughing students greeted each other, hugging and slapping each other on the back. It looked as though everybody knew everybody else, and Sarah couldn't stop thinking that — again, just like in Hilton — she was going to be the "new kid."

"I'm kind of nervous," she said softly.

"Boy, oh boy," her father went on, not even responding to Sarah's comment. "I wish I'd had this kind of opportunity back when I was fresh out of high school. But no-sir! It was straight to work at the National Paper Products mill for me — first in Westbrook, then in Hilton."

The mere mention of Westbrook made Sarah brighten. "That's right," she said with a rising note of excitement, "Kathy Meserve, my best friend from Westbrook, is a freshman here this year, too. I'll have to look her up."

"Let's get you unpacked first," her father said with a laugh.

"Oh, I'm sure you'll make plenty of new friends here," Alice piped in. Sarah glanced at the back of her head — as she had throughout the drive — and frowned. What seemed most important, to Alice, if not her father, was to dump her off and leave as soon as possible for their own trip up to Quebec. Sarah hadn't known Alice long enough to have a solid opinion of her. She was attractive enough — perhaps too attractive. She was tall, blond, and very well proportioned, very pretty. In some ways, she seemed much nicer than Rosalie ever was, but there was a vacantness about her that Sarah didn't like. She wondered if her father was involved with Alice just for the sex; the woman didn't have much else going for her.

The snarled traffic in front of the dorm didn't seem to be getting any better, so Devin finally slammed the gear shift into *park* and turned off the engine.

"Okay," he said, rubbing his hands together. "Everybody out. It's not that far. We can carry everything from here."

Sarah already knew her room assignment — Room 218. It was on the west side of the building overlooking the parking lot and the Stillwater River. If the elevator was half as busy as the driveway, it would probably be faster for them to carry everything up the two flights of stairs. But no matter how excited her father tried to pretend he was about all of this, Sarah was suspicious that he, too, was anxious to drop her off and be on his way. If she hadn't been so nervous and excited about starting college, she might actually feel hurt, maybe a little bit angry about it all.

Alice took it easy while Sarah and Devin did the lion's share of the work. Even so, it only took them five trips up and down to get all the suitcases, boxes of bedding and books, and her trunk up to the room. All Sarah knew about her roommate was that her name was Martha Lewis, and she was a sophomore from Windsor, Connecticut, majoring in elementary education. When they got to the room, they found that Martha had left a Post-it note stuck to the mirror, informing Sarah that she was off visiting a friend and would meet her tonight, after supper.

Almost as soon as they were finished unloading the car, Devin gave Sarah a long hug and kiss good-bye, then he and Alice took off, leaving Sarah alone in her dorm room. An upperclassman, Martha had arrived a day or two before. She had already hung curtains in the window, and her side of the room looked at least habitable. Sarah's half looked as stark and sterile as a hospital room with a bare blue and white stripped mattress cover, an empty desk, and no stuffed animals, posters, or anything else to give it a homey touch. She stared blankly at the pile of her possessions, which seemed pitifully small now, in spite of the labor it had taken to bring them up to the room. Outside her door, the corridor echoed with the bustle of activity, banging of doors, and labored grunts as people struggled down the hallway with luggage. She knew she should roll up her sleeves and get busy unpacking, but instead she swung her door firmly shut and sat down on the edge of her bed. Supporting her chin with her hands, she stared at the bare tile floor, fighting back her tears of loneliness.

—2—

"I swear to Christ, I'm sick of all of this!" Alan said as he plopped down hard in the recreation room chair, leaned back, and crossing his legs at the ankles, fished a cigarette out of the pack in his shirt pocket. After lighting a wooden match with his thumbnail, he took a deep drag and let the smoke drift lazily out his mouth as he studied the other five inmates. They were playing a seemingly endless round of Five-Card Anaconda, one-matchstick ante, five-stick limit. A skinny guy nicknamed Squeaker, because of his notorious farts, was cleaning up tonight.

"You in the next game?" Larry asked, looking at him over the fanned top of his cards.

Alan smirked as he took another drag off his cigarette and blew smoke up at the ceiling. "Yeah—just give me a second. I wanna check through the newspaper." His daily *Hilton Register* had arrived late, and he hadn't had a chance to check through it after lunch.

"What are you looking for, a wedding announcement to find out your old lady's hooking up with someone else?" Larry said.

Alan snorted blue smoke and said, "I don't have an old lady . . . never wanted to get tied down."

"To any one *woman*, that is," Larry said. "Now, if the right *guy* came along . . ."

Everyone at the table chuckled except Alan.

"Up yours!" Alan said, his mouth curling into a sneer. "No, I'm just sick and tired of waiting! I've got a couple of weeks left here, and I just can't wait to get out of this hellhole."

"That's right, you're out of here soon. Is it true what I heard, that you actually requested one last body cavity search?" Squeaker asked.

"Up yours, too!" Alan said, frowning as he peeked over the top of the newspaper and jabbed his middle finger at him. "No, it's just sometimes I get to feeling like—I don't know, fidgety or something, like there's someone always watching me."

"There is, asshole; they're called prison guards."

"No, I mean like even at night, and when I'm alone in my cell, sometimes I get this . . . feeling, like maybe this place is haunted, you know?"

Squeaker rolled his hips to one side and let out a long, rising fart. Everyone including Alan groaned and waved their hands in front of their faces.

Larry laughed out loud as he slapped a guy named Joe Bailey on the back. "Oh, I don't know 'bout it being haunted," he said with a forced Southern accent. "How 'bout you, Joe—you seen any spooks 'round here?"

"Keep laughin', white boy," Joe said, his dark face scowling as he held his cards close to his chest. This was his third straight losing night, and he was feeling edgier than usual. Looking at Alan, he said, "You probably been getting spring fever, yah know?"

"It's fall, in case you hadn't noticed," Alan said.

"No, I mean you be gettin' all *fevered* 'cause they gonna *spring* yah soon."

"I'll tell you what it is," Larry snarled. He shifted the toothpick he'd been chewing from one side of his mouth to the other. "It's your goddamned paranoia getting to you. You feel like you're being watched because *you are* being watched. Every fuckin' second of your life." He nodded toward the surveillance camera in each corner of the rec. room. "You mean to tell me this is normal, to have people searching you all the fuckin' time, and going through your cell every time you leave it?" He sneered and shook his head, casually flipping his middle finger at one of the cameras. "You'd be loony if you didn't think you were being watched."

"And look on the bright side, sunshine," Squeaker said, sneering to himself. "You're getting out of here after only— what? How long you been here?"

"Eleven months, give or take." Alan took another drag and practically spit the smoke out of his mouth. "Fuckin' lawyer couldn't get me any less."

"Did pretty good far's I can see," Squeaker said. He had quite a reputation as a jailhouse lawyer. "I figured you were good for eighteen months, minimum."

"You know, that's why, when lawyers die, they bury 'em ten feet under . . . 'cause deep down, they good people." Joe snickered at his own joke but then looked at Alan with an intense earnestness. " 'Sides, I don't see what you're bitchin' 'bout." He shook his head with disgust. "Eleven months ain't nothin' compared to how long I'm gonna be doing here."

"Yeah, well—I didn't shoot any clerk at a liquor store either," Alan said. He cringed as soon as the words were out of his mouth, thinking that he'd be growing old here with Joe, Larry, and the rest of them if the cops ever nailed him for that night out on Route 26. His hand was shaking as he took another deep drag off his cigarette and flicked the ash onto the floor.

"If you're gonna fuckin' smoke, I don't see why you can't use an ashtray like everyone else," Larry said.

Alan shifted forward and made a show of dropping his cigarette to the floor and crushing it out. For emphasis, he rubbed his foot back and forth a few extra times. "This whole place is an ashtray. Worse than an ashtray. It's a fuckin' *sewer!*" He settled back into his chair and started flipping through the newspaper.

"Sewer's the word, all right," Stan Montagne said. His cards hadn't exactly been hot tonight either. He kept glancing over at Squeaker as if he expected to see him palming some extra cards.

"One stick to you, Squeaker," Larry said, scowling as he cupped his cards facedown on the table.

"So, what you gonna be doing once you get out of here anyway?" Joe asked.

Alan kept the newspaper in front of his face, still turning pages as he replied. "I don't know. I don't have any family to speak of back home. No wife or nothing. I suspect the little business I had going is pretty much fucked up by now. I don't know, maybe I—Holy shit!"

"What, did you find that wedding announcement?" Larry asked.

Alan slowly lowered his newspaper, unable to believe what he had just read. His pulse was running high and fast in his ears, and his hands got clammy as he scanned the short news item a second time. It was an article about seven graduates from Hilton Regional High School who were just starting their freshmen year at the University of Maine in Orono.

The second student mentioned was Sarah Lahikainen, who intended to major in English.

"No I, uhh — Hey, Squeaker, you'd know about the prerelease center up in Bangor, wouldn't you?" Alan asked. It took effort to keep the excited tremor out of his voice. "What's it like anyway? What do they do for you up there?"

Squeaker shrugged. "Like any other release center. They put you up. I think they use the old nurses' dormitory at Eastern Maine Medical now. And they help you line up a job. You can stay there awhile — least until you adjust back to civilian life."

"Yeah? What kind of jobs can you get?" Alan asked, even more interested as an idea got clearer in his mind. His hands crinkled the newspaper as he looked expectantly at Squeaker.

"Oh, like anywhere — mostly shit jobs, working for the highway department or maybe at the university. I hear it's easier to get a university job if you register for courses — what they call the Division of Basic Studies."

"But the jobs, you mean like grounds work or something?" Alan asked.

Squeaker nodded. "Yeah, that or something in one of the cafeterias or janitor in a dorm or something. Stuff like that."

"Well, well, well," Alan said. He surprised everyone at the table when he tilted his head back and burst out laughing. Then, rubbing his hands vigorously together, he leaned forward and said, "Deal me in on the next hand. I'm feeling lucky tonight."

Looking around at the circle of bemused faces, he smiled contentedly to himself and said, "I guess that's what I'll do after I get out, then. I think I'm gonna go to the university and get myself an education. Yes-sir-ee . . . a college education."

— 3 —

"That's the word for it, all right."

It was the third week of school, and Sarah was sitting on her bed, leaning against the wall with her tape recorder in

157

her lap. Several textbooks were spread open around her, but she hadn't been able to concentrate on anything after reading the brief letter from her father. Three weeks, and this was only the second note she had received from him; a letter should be at least more than three sentences long. True, both envelopes had a check for fifty dollars enclosed, but the money didn't come close to soothing the hurt of the hastily scribbled note promising to "write more when I have the time."

A wave of anger at her father made her twist with guilt and a tingle of fear as she spoke into the microphone.

"I know I shouldn't expect him to make me the center of his life — not anymore anyway. He has his own life, just like I'm trying to make a new life for myself. Just because he's my father, it doesn't obligate him to accommodate me in his life. That's expecting way too much from him. Maybe I've expected too much all along. What I have to do now is brace myself and move ahead, and not spend any more time looking back — especially with regrets. Regrets are useless, wasted energy."

But as much as she had wanted it to be a new and exciting experience for her, Sarah was finding college to be a lonely experience. True, Martha was turning out to be a great roommate. She had been in the same room last year, so she had everything they needed to make the place more than comfortable. There were curtains on the windows, a braided rug on the floor between the beds, posters on the walls, and dozens of little touches, such as a vase of flowers on each bureau. And although she was finding the work much harder than in high school, she was doing well enough in her classes. But no matter how hard she tried, Sarah couldn't get rid of the gnawing feeling that she had lost forever the life she had, and she had no idea what kind of life she was going to find. Right now, it sure as hell looked like a long and lonely road.

Clearing her throat, she began to speak again. "All my life, I've felt like I — like I've been — "

The sound of footsteps approaching the door and a key sliding into the door lock made Sarah cut herself off short.

Her throat constricted as the tumblers turned, the lock clicked, and then the doorknob twisted.

"Hey! What're you doing in here?" Martha said as she burst into the room, followed by two of her friends, Rachel Patterson and Elaine Carrio. Flustered, Sarah shook her head as she turned off her tape recorder and sat up straight on the bed.

"Just—umm, just doing a bit of homework," she said tightly.

"On a Saturday afternoon? You're not sick or anything, are you?"

Sarah shrugged as she forced a laugh.

"Did I hear you talking to yourself?" Martha asked, eyeing her narrowly as she dropped her sweater onto her bed and then opened her closet. "Or do you have a guy hiding in here? Maybe he's stashed under your bed." She leaned down, lifted the edge of the bedspread, and glanced under the bed. "Hmmm—no one there. You weren't talking to yourself, were you?"

Sarah shook her head.

"You must know what talking to yourself is a sign of— don't you?" Martha said. She pulled a different sweater from the top shelf of her closet and put it on.

Sarah took a shallow breath and shrugged again.

"Talking to yourself, my dear, is a sign of insecurity. Am I right, girls?"

Both Rachel and Elaine laughed and nodded.

"It's a sign that you've been working too hard," Martha continued, pinching her chin sagely.

She walked over to the bed where Sarah was sitting and, hands on her hips, loomed over her as she surveyed the pile of books and papers surrounding her roommate.

"Yup," Martha said, glancing over her shoulder at her two friends and nodding. "This girl is working too damned hard. What she needs is to get out and, if she can manage it, have a little bit of fun. Who knows—maybe we can find her a fella' . . . after we find ours, of course."

Sarah was about to protest, but Martha grabbed her arm

159

and tried to pull her gently off the bed.

"We have come to the conclusion that there aren't enough men — at least the right kind of men — at the library this afternoon to warrant us busting our tails pretending we're studying on the weekend, so we're heading to Bangor to see what's shaking."

"Nothing ever shakes in Bangor," Rachel said.

"True, true; but we're gonna give it our best shot, aren't we?" Martha finished for her. "You want to come along, Sarah?"

Biting her lower lip as she looked from one face to another, Sarah tried to gauge if they really wanted her to join them, or if they were asking just to be nice. She shifted uneasily on the bed and gestured helplessly at the stack of books surrounding her.

"I don't think so," she said weakly. "Not today."

"Not today?" Martha burst out. "If not today, then when? I don't mean to be rude, but how many times have we asked you to come along with us, and every time you say, 'not today — not tonight.' Sarah, my girl, I'm beginning to worry about you."

"I'm just not . . . feeling all that up," Sarah said.

"That is exactly my point," Martha said. She jiggled Sarah's shoulder hard, as though she were trying to wake her up. "You're not gonna get any better, sitting around the dorm feeling crappy about yourself. You've got to get out, girl. Have a little fun once in a while! You can start by trying to smile!"

Sarah smiled but shook her head more assuredly. "Not right now, Martha — really. I appreciate your offer, but I have to finish up a few things here."

Martha finally gave up. Heaving a deep sigh, she looked at her friends and shook her head. Then, softening, she looked directly at Sarah and said, "Seriously — are you sure? We're just gonna fool around at the mall for a couple of hours."

"I'm sure," Sarah replied.

"Well, don't like up for me," Martha said. "You never know. I just might get lucky and bump into Mr. Right."

160

She went over to her bureau, ran her brush through her hair a few times, and then, after giving Sarah one last, inviting glance, swung the door shut. Sarah jumped involuntarily when the door slammed. Tears welled up in her eyes as she listened to their laughing voices fade down the hallway. Once the dorm was quiet again, she took a deep, shuddering breath and looked blankly at her tape recorder.

"Damned right!" she whispered after pressing the button to start recording again. "Abandoned."

She let her gaze drift over to where slanting sunlight stabbed through the brightly colored leaves of the maple trees that grew right outside her window. Through her tears, they were nothing more than bright smears of color. She sniffed and wiped her eyes with the back of her hand as the pain welled up inside her with a cold ache.

Sarah snickered as she shook her head and said, "Yeah, even good old Tully. Whoever — or whatever — you were." Her vision clouded, and for an instant, the view outside her window dimmed as though a dark cloud had passed in front of the sun.

"I know this much; you couldn't have been real," she whispered into her tape recorder. "I just made you up because I was so . . . so damned lonely! *Abandoned* . . . by everyone I ever loved . . ." An icy chill took hold of her stomach as a wracking sob sounded deep in her chest. "And now even you, Tully — even you have deserted me."

She smiled, recalling the Lily Tomlin record Martha had played for her a few nights ago, where Lily makes the astute observation that, "We're all in this alone."

"You got that right, Lily girl," Sarah said as she clicked off her recorder. She took out the tape and locked it away in the box where she stored her other tapes. Looking dejectedly at the stack of books on her bed, she heaved a deep sigh and said again, "Boy oh boy, did you ever get that right. I've felt abandoned my whole damned life."

"You look like you could use a study break."

The voice, speaking so close behind her, made Sarah jump as she turned around quickly. For a panicked instant, she expected to see Tully smiling blankly at her; the voice had sounded almost like his. She let out an exaggerated sigh of relief when she saw, instead, the boy who sat beside her in Fundamentals of Speech class.

"I'm sorry," he said, smiling widely. "I didn't mean to scare you." After looking up and down the rows of practically empty tables in the Fogler Library study room, he asked, "Is this seat taken?"

Blushing, Sarah indicated that it wasn't. She had noticed this boy the first day of class, but all she knew about him was that his name was Michael. From the first speech he gave, she figured he was a sophomore, majoring in philosophy. The chair made a loud squeaking sound on the wood floor as he pulled it out, slung his book bag onto the table, and sat down.

"We haven't met—formally, that is," he said, still smiling as he held out his hand for her to shake. "My name's Michael Shulkin. We're in—"

"Speech class together," Sarah finished for him. She took his hand, pumped it lightly once or twice, then let it go. She scooped aside her textbooks and notebooks to make room for him.

Michael opened the flap on his book bag and took out two cans of Pepsi. "I had a feeling you might be thirsty," he said. He held the can beneath the table top and pulled back on the tab. The can opened with a loud hiss. He passed it to Sarah, who smiled her thanks.

"Why would I be thirsty?" Sarah asked, eyeing him narrowly as she raised the can to her lips and took a sip.

Michael smiled and said, "Because I've been watching you, and you've been licking your lips. I figured, either you have an incredible reading problem, or else you're getting nervous working on your first speech."

"What, are you psychic or something?" Sarah asked, blushing again.

"No," Michael said. "But you've been sitting here, mouthing the words of whatever it is you're writing. Doesn't take a Sherlock Holmes to figure that much out."

Sarah placed the can of Pepsi on the table, but Michael quickly signaled for her to hide it.

"You'll want to keep that down. They don't like people eating or drinking in here."

Sarah nodded, then broke eye contact with Michael and looked back down at her notebook. "It's my speech, all right. I can't believe how nervous I am about doing it."

Michael sniffed with laughter. "That's why I volunteered to do my first one right away. I wanted to be over and done with it."

"Come on! You can't tell me you were nervous," Sarah said, laughing tightly. "You delivered your speech like a professional politician."

"You mean I sounded like I was lying through my teeth?"

They both laughed out loud at that one, but Sarah blushed, realizing that they had both been checking each other out. She couldn't deny the warm feeling she got just sitting here, talking to Michael. In class and the few times she had seen him around campus, usually in the Bear's Den, taking a study break with his fraternity brothers, he seemed so confident, so secure. She couldn't help wondering why he was taking time to talk to her.

"Well, you had me convinced we should stop boycotting Cuban products," Sarah said. "Although I can't say I'm anxious to try smoking a cigar myself."

"I don't know about that. I think a woman smoking a cigar looks kind of sexy." They both laughed again, this time drawing an irritated *shush* from someone sitting a few tables away. "Anyway, that's the only thing philosophy majors are good at," Michael said, lowering his voice. "We can talk like we know what we're talking about even though we don't have the foggiest idea. Besides—haven't you noticed that Professor Fisher smokes cigars? I figure he's the kind of person who can

163

really appreciate a Havana cigar, and he'd give me an A just for saying so."

Sarah burst out with laughter again, once again drawing a quieting hiss from a student. Michael grabbed the strap of his book bag and, leaning close to Sarah, said, "Come on — I meant it when I said you looked like you needed a study break. Why don't we go over to the Den to finish these sodas?"

"Yeah," Sarah said as a gush of warmth filled her. "Why don't we?"

Chapter Twelve

Making Moves

—1—

It was bound to happen . . . eventually, Sarah thought.

Night after night for at least a month now, the janitor had been checking her out. He went around with a stainless steel pushcart filled with dusting and cleaning supplies, but something about him — it might have been his military-looking crew cut . . . or the distant, hard look in his eyes — but there was something about him that Sarah didn't like. Even when she moved from one study lounge in the Student Union to another, it seemed to take him no time at all to find her. He'd spend way more time than seemed necessary, emptying ashtrays and wastebaskets or polishing and straightening the tables and chairs.

On most week nights, Sarah and Michael studied together in one of the lounges in the Student Union. Maybe she was being paranoid, but on those nights it seemed as though this janitor made himself scarce, kept his distance. Only on the nights when she was alone, usually when Michael had something to do at the fraternity house or some other obligation, would this man hang around wherever she was . . . too many times for comfort. Sarah could feel him staring at her; whenever she would look up, he would quickly turn away and pretend to be busy. But he never looked away quite fast enough. She always caught a glimpse of his cold, blank eyes. His presence was starting to bug her. And she was getting scared of him.

One snowy November night, Sarah was huddled in an overstuffed chair by the window. Michael was supposed to be back within half an hour, but right now, she was the only person in the room. The streetlight outside the window glowed with a blue nimbus of falling snow. A bare branch of the tree outside was tapping like a skeletal hand against the glass. The sound set Sarah's teeth on edge. She was all set to get up and move when—for the third time tonight—the janitor showed up. The wheels of his cleaning cart squeaked wickedly, sounding like someone raking their fingernails down a chalkboard. Sarah froze. She stared at the opened book until the words all blurred, all the while wishing to hell this guy would just get his work done and leave her alone.

"Mind if I take that for you?" the janitor asked, indicating the full ashtray on the table beside her.

Without looking up, Sarah shook her head. A dry knot filled her throat. She almost told him she didn't care because she didn't smoke, but she remained silent.

The janitor dumped the crushed cigarette butts into the waste can, wiped the ashtray clean with a damp cloth, and then slid it back onto the table.

"What are you studying there that looks so interesting, anyway?" he asked, craning his neck so he could see the textbook open in her lap.

Sarah shifted nervously, feeling his eyes were fastening on her, not her book. Flustered, she shrugged and, still not daring to make eye contact, muttered, "Just my American Lit."

"Oh, yeah. American Literature. I'll probably be taking that next semester," the janitor said. There was a bright lilt to his voice that sounded entirely fake and forced to Sarah. Just beneath the surface, she sensed a razor-sharp edge of nervousness.

166

"That's nice," she said, still not daring to look up.

An awkward silence descended between them, but the man didn't move away to continue his job. The back of Sarah's neck flushed with heat as she imagined him staring intently at her. She wished desperately that Michael would show up so this creep would leave.

"Yeah," the janitor said at last. There was still that subtle, steely tone in his voice that grated on her nerves. "I'm in the Basic Studies program. What are you studying?"

Heaving a sigh, Sarah closed the book on her finger and, sucking in a deep breath, forced herself to look up at him. "Nothing, right now," she said, exasperated. "I *was* reading American Lit." She struggled to disguise the trembling in her voice.

The janitor snickered and said, "No, no—I mean, what are you majoring in?"

Steeling herself, Sarah sucked in another breath and, still looking at him, said, "English Lit." She looked back down at her book and added, "Now please—if you don't mind . . ."

Either he was dense and didn't get the hint, or else he plain wasn't going to take it. Either way, he just wasn't going to give up. He just stood there, towering above where she sat. The light behind him cast a hazy shadow over the book in her lap, but she resisted the shiver that danced up her back.

"You know," he said as he snapped his fingers and then pointed at her, "there's something about you that seems kinda familiar. Do I know you from someplace?"

Again, Sarah looked up at him. Unable to stop the flood of images from the horror movies she had seen, she wondered if this guy was simply a bit soft in the head or if he was truly dangerous. She had read in the newspapers just last year about Bliss Marshall, the young actress going to Bowdoin, who had been kidnapped while out jogging. Sarah couldn't help but wonder if this guy might be the same kind of nut case who might try something crazy like that.

"I don't think so," Sarah replied coolly. With the light behind him, it was difficult to see his face clearly, but now
that he mentioned it, there was something about him that
struck her as familiar. It filled her with a dull sense of
dread.

"So tell me, where're you from?" the janitor asked. He
was still standing slightly behind her.

"I'm from—uh, Portsmouth, New Hampshire," she said.
She hoped the tremor in her voice wouldn't reveal that she
was lying.

"Portsmouth, hmmm? Nope. Can't say as I've ever spent
any time in Portsmouth . . . other than passing through on
the turnpike, that is."

"Well, then . . ." Sarah said, watching the shadow of his
head on her book as he nodded thoughtfully. She thought
she detected a teasing, taunting tone in voice

"No, I'm from a little doo-hickey town in Western Maine
called Hilton. You probably never even heard of that
place."

As soon as he said the name, the blood drained from
Sarah's face. The air in her lungs went stale, and her pulse
started beating like a cheap tin drum in her ears. She
clenched both hands into fists to stop them from shaking as
she slowly looked up at him again.

Sarah took a deep breath and held it. "I can't say as I've
heard of the place."

"Not surprised at that," the janitor said, laughing softly.
But he still didn't move away from her. "But if you've never
heard of Hilton, and I've never spent any time in Portsmouth, I'm wondering why the fuck—excuse me, I meant
to say—why the heck you look so familiar."

Sarah shrugged tightly, wishing to God this man would
just leave her alone.

"I mean—no kidding, I feel like I know you from someplace," he said, his eyes narrowing as he snapped his fingers
a couple of times. Someone passing by in the corridor drew

his attention. He looked over his shoulder at the door, then backed away quickly. With a casually tossed off, "Catch yah later," he took his cleaning cart and walked out the door.

As soon as his shadow slipped away from her, the heavy oppression lifted off Sarah. Every nerve in her body was tingling as she listened to the wheels of his cleaning cart go *squeak-squeak* out the door and down the corridor. Heaving a deep sigh, she leaned her head against the chair back and stared sightlessly up at the ceiling. The branch scratching against the dark square of window drew her attention. It took a long time for the steady hammering of her heartbeat to slow down.

−2−

Elliott Clark was sitting alone at the small table in the kitchenette of his second-floor, one-bedroom apartment on Burnham Street in Old Town, Maine. His right hand, slick with condensation, was curled around a beer can—his fourth of the day. Through the streaked window, he could see the dark, hulking mass of the Old Town paper mill. Thick columns of steam and smoke belched from the chimneys, blending into the lowering gray of the sky. Even with all the doors and windows tightly shut, the choking, rotten egg smell made it into the apartment. Elliott wondered if it was merely chance or a serious quirk in his personality that always brought him to live in towns that had major paper mills.

While he slipped on his beer, he stared at the radio telephone in his other hand. The phone was switched on, and for the last five or ten minutes, his thumb had been poised over the last digit of Carol's phone number. Like most nights, he felt a deep need to talk to someone—maybe even his ex-wife. But even with a skinful of beer, he couldn't bring himself to push the last number. He hadn't spoken with her for a couple of months now—not since the day he called to tell her he had resigned from the Hilton police

169

and had taken a job as a campus cop at the University of Maine.

Maybe the beer was making him feel melancholy, a bit homesick; maybe the dreary November weather was depressing him; maybe the job as a campus cop at the university was simply too tame, and he genuinely missed active police work . . . or maybe he was just plain old lonesome. Other than the people he met at work, he didn't know anyone in the area. He was uprooted, adrift, and had no one to socialize with. Whatever the hell was bothering him, he was thinking how nice it would be, now that he was off work for the day, to hear a warm, friendly voice.

Maybe even Carol's.

"Naw," he muttered. He pushed the chair back and stood up, took a swig of beer, wincing at the warm taste, and began pacing back and forth across the kitchen floor. With each step, he slapped the telephone into the flat of his hand. His grim and lonely thoughts were interrupted by a sudden burst of static from the police scanner, which he kept turned on day and night on the kitchen counter.

Elliott paused and listened as the Old Town Police dispatcher reported a "minor scuffle" in progress at the Rat Hole, one of the local bars. One officer was on the scene, and another was on his way. As he listened to the calls going back and forth, a faint smile played across Elliott's face. During his time on the Hilton force, he had responded to plenty of calls like this. He could easily imagine what the situation was and how the officers were handling it. He couldn't stop thinking about—and already beginning to resent—the relatively tame situation he found on the Orono campus. Tagging student cars parked in the faculty lots and watching the crowds at concerts and football games weren't exactly overwhelming challenges.

"Is that all it is?" he said in a low, hissing voice. "I miss the job? I miss being a player?" He snickered softly. The fact that he always listened to his police scanner whenever he was home was answer enough. In the back of his mind, he left open the possibility that, come spring, he might put in an application at the Old Town and Orono police stations, just in case an opening came up.

In the darkening gloom of his apartment, he replaced the radio phone on its base and clicked off the police scanner. He considered having another beer and watching some TV, but then decided that he needed to be around people. He got into his car and drove to Orono, to Pat's Pizza, where he usually spent an hour or two after his shift, sitting downstairs in the bar. He'd nurse a couple of beers and watch the college kids—especially the college girls. They didn't look like that when he was young and cruising. He knew that sitting in a college bar half-stewed wouldn't do him any goddamn good, but it was better that sitting home alone getting drunk.

Elliott was just settling down in a booth in a darkened corner when a young woman walking into the bar caught his attention. He didn't see her face at first, but as soon as he saw the shoulder-length blond hair, he felt a jolt of surprise . . . and hope.

Is that her? he wondered. *Can that be Sarah?* He knew she was on campus but hadn't seen her yet; he figured it was just a matter of time before they bumped into each other.

This girl was with a guy who wore a Sig Ep fraternity jacket. They walked over to a booth at the opposite side of the room. As she shucked off her winter coat, she almost turned so Elliott could see her face, but not quite. His hand clutched the beer glass tightly as he raised it to his mouth and took a slow sip, all the while studying the girl's back.

He watched as the guy stepped to one side so his date could slide into the booth. Then he sat down in the booth beside her. A waitress came over to the table and took their orders for drinks after checking the boy's ID. The girl was obviously too young.

After the waitress moved away, the young woman looked up and scanned the barroom. Recognition hit Elliott.

"Jesus Christ, it is!" Elliott said, loud enough for the two men at the table next to him to give him a suspicious glance. He considered going over to say "hi" to Sarah, but after some deliberation decided not to. She probably would have forgotten him by now, and anyway, even if she hadn't, considering the circumstances under which they had met, seeing him would probably just upset her. Why go and dredge up the horrors of that night—for her or for himself? Thinking about it now, maybe what happened to Marie Lahikainen had just as much to do with his decision to quit the police force as his shooting of Lester LaJoie.

No, Elliott decided; it would be best just to pretend he hadn't seen her. He'd just finish his beer and get the hell out of here. Maybe if he got back to his apartment early tonight, he wouldn't have as bad a hangover in the morning.

But before he could get up and leave, someone else entered the bar. This person was wearing tight, faded blue jeans, and a ratty-looking T-shirt underneath a battered black leather jacket. A cigarette dangled from one corner of his mouth, leaving a thin trail of smoke that wreathed his shoulder as he walked up to the bar, leaned one hand on the edge, and slapping down a bill, loudly ordered a beer.

It was going to take more than a short haircut to disguise Alan Griffin's face. That sneer and that cruel, hard look in his eyes were the same as they had ever been—maybe worse after a year in Thomaston. Elliott had followed the situation enough to know that, after serving only a portion of his three-year sentence, Alan Griffin had been released and was now working as a janitor on campus while taking Basic Studies courses. He had seen him around a few times but hadn't bothered to speak with him.

Elliott clenched his fists as he watched Alan. It could have been coincidence that Griffin and Sarah—both from his hometown of Hilton and both now in Orono—might show up in the same bar at the same time, but Elliott

172

wasn't the kind of person who trusted anything that even smelled of coincidence. No policeman worth his salt ever did.

Alan took the glass of beer from the bartender, snubbed out his cigarette, and tilting his head back, downed half of it in several large gulps. Then, after wiping his mouth with the back of his hand, he turned around and casually scanned the barroom. His eyes narrowed as he glanced from table to table, apparently looking for an empty seat. But there was no denying Sarah's reaction when she and Alan made fleeting eye contact. Elliott's throat went suddenly dry.

The eye contact between Alan and Sarah lasted only a few seconds, but Elliott could feel it, practically see it crackling in the space between them. Alan's mouth twitched into a smile as he nodded to her. Sarah looked quickly away, obviously displeased that he was even in the same room as she was.

Alan pushed off the bar and made a point of pressing close to the table where Sarah sat as he sauntered to the back of the room. Sarah's boyfriend didn't seem to notice anything unusual going on when Alan sat down at the table closest to the back door, hooked one foot in the rungs of the chair opposite him, and sat back to nurse his beer. But Elliott noticed that Alan kept flicking his gaze back at Sarah, watching her with a hard glint in his eyes.

Elliott's first impulse was to go over to Alan and ask him what the hell he thought he was doing. Sarah's discomfort was obvious. She shifted in her seat as if she could feel Alan's eyes drilling into her back. She sat with her shoulders hunched, looking tensed and ready to run out of there at any moment.

But Elliott realized that, like it or not, he had absolutely no right or authority to question Alan's presence in the bar. His police authority ended as soon as he left the campus. Just because Alan had served time, it didn't mean he couldn't come into a bar and have a few drinks. If Elliott even spoke to him, he might end up on the receiving end of a harassment suit.

"Let it ride," he whispered to himself. "Just let it ride. None of your damned business anyway."

He drained his glass and placed it carefully on the table among the wet rings and soggy napkins. He considered having one more beer, but seeing Alan Griffin had spoiled whatever mellow mood he might have been close to attaining. Heaving a heavy sigh, he eased himself up from the table and started for the door. He was brought up short when, above the noise of conversation in the bar, he heard someone call his name. Turning, he locked eyes with Alan, who was staring at him with a wide smirk spread across his face.

Elliott's expression remained impassive as he nodded a silent greeting in return. Ever so slowly, Alan raised his hand, extending his middle finger in Elliott's direction. Elliott smiled grimly, shook his head, and very precisely mouthed the words "Fuck you" before turning and walking out of the bar.

– 3 –

Two hours later, Sarah and Michael were sitting side by side on the small couch in Michael's room at the fraternity house. Michael had his arm around her shoulder and was holding her tightly against him as they talked. Sarah hadn't been able to get served at Pat's, so they had left shortly after they'd arrived. Back at the fraternity, Sarah had drunk two glasses of red wine in the course of an hour. She wasn't used to drinking, and before long, she was dizzy. Everything she said was slurred as she snuggled into Michael's embrace, hugging him tightly and praying that the room would stop whirling around.

A single blue light bulb cast an eerie glow, like a thin coat of paint, over everything in the room. Michael's face and his hand holding hers looked ghastly white in the weird lighting. The fingers of his other hand twirled through her hair. Sarah found it difficult to focus on his face or anything else in the room, so she closed her eyes and let her mind drift in a spinning haze.

Soft music was playing on Michael's roommate's stereo. Their conversation skipped lightly over various subjects; but even through the alcohol buzz, Sarah suspected what Michael was really after. The way he held her hand and pulled her closer to him, his heated breath on the side of her face . . . all of it was incredibly disconcerting even as it sent a tingling thrill through her. This was the first time she had come up to his room, and she was angry at herself for foolishly letting him get her half-crocked.

No, she thought sternly, trying her best to focus her thoughts. *Michael didn't force me to take a single drink. Maybe I wanted to get tipsy . . . or felt I had to just to have the courage to come up here.*

She realized that while she had been drifting with her thoughts, Michael had been going on and on about something; she wasn't even sure what. He looked at her, his expression softening. Before she could ask him what he was talking about, he leaned toward her. Both arms went behind her back and gently pulled her to him as his mouth sought hers. Their kiss was warm and lingering. His hands, long-fingered and strong, massaged her back, kneading her shoulders as his hug tightened.

"No, I . . ." She pulled away; but before she could protest further, he kissed her again. One hand moved slowly around to her side, down to her waist, and then started easing up to her breasts. Sarah's head filled with giddy thoughts and dulled anxiety as Michael gently caressed her, his fingers becoming more insistent. Memories of the graduation party with Randy Potter sent a stirring of guilt and anger through her. Michael broke off the kiss and nuzzled his face into the crook of her neck, his breath hot on her skin. A wave of shivers raced up her back.

"I never thought I'd feel this way about anyone," Michael

175

whispered heatedly. His lips danced a hot line up the side of her neck.

Torn between temptation and fear, Sarah wiggled and tried feebly to push him away. She couldn't deny how aroused she was, but she was also filled with apprehension. She moaned but could say nothing as hot rushes warred against the icy knot of anxiety in her stomach. She told herself she wanted to be doing this; she truly did. This might even be love, but there was also something about all of this that seemed wrong, somehow . . . and dangerous!

Michael's hand slipped down to the edge of her blouse, tugged it out from under her belt, then slid up underneath. His fingertips were hot as he traced the rounded curve of her breast and then moved up underneath her bra.

The coiled tension in her stomach began to spread, roaring into a burst of anger. Where she had felt warmth and loving caresses, she now felt a blossoming frost.

"Come on, Sarah," he whispered heatedly. "You know how much I love you."

"Please, Michael . . ." she said, her voice tightening as she tried again to push away both him and her rising anger. "It's not that I don't want to, but I—"

She cut herself off sharply when she saw something move over Michael's shoulder. A splotch of light glowing eerily pale resolved out of the dark corner of the room and zoomed at her as it snapped into focus. Before Sarah could catch her breath to scream, she saw Tully's face, staring at her out of the darkness. Like a pale, full moon, it hovered in the dark, weirdly underlit by pale, blue light. His shoulders, his arms, his chest took form until Tully was standing there beside the closet door. His arms were folded across his chest as he smiled thinly and watched her with glowing, unblinking eyes.

"Oh, Jesus!" Sarah said. She pushed back harder against Michael, knocking him off balance. The hand he had under her blouse pulled back, ripping the fabric.

"Oh, shit! I'm sorry!" Michael said.

Sarah stared at him, her whole body trembling.

"Come on. I was just—" He shook his head as though to clear it. "I don't know what came over me. Maybe I . . . maybe I've had a bit too much to drink."

"Please!" Sarah screeched. "Leave me alone!"

Her eyes were wide with fear as she stared past Michael's shoulder. The blue light shining on Tully's face pulsated with every slamming beat of her heart.

"Okay! Hey, I'm sorry, all right?" Michael said, holding up his hands as if he were resigning. "Really, I just kinda lost control there for a second. I didn't mean any—"

"Goddamn you!" Sarah wailed, shaking her clenched fists in front of her face as hot, red anger filled her mind. "Leave me alone!"

She grabbed her head with both hands and stared, terrified, past Michael at Tully. The dim blue light in the room made his grinning face look like a mask, floating in the darkness.

"Jesus Christ," Michael said, sounding angry as he spun off the couch and then started pacing the floor. "I said I was sorry, all right?"

Tears blurred Sarah's vision. Everything in the room rushed into a swirling blue and black whirlpool—a whirlpool with Tully's death-pale, smiling face at its center. A sickly sour taste bubbled up from her stomach into her mouth. Whimpering, she kicked her legs out and scrambled wildly, pressing her back against the couch, trying to get as much distance as she could between herself and Tully.

"Come on, take it easy, will you?" Michael said. "I'm sorry I tore your blouse. And I—I didn't mean to try to force you or anything. Honest."

Sarah said nothing as she glared at him in the darkness.

"If you want, I could take you back to the dorm now." His voice was low, edged with genuine concern that he had pushed too hard. "I—I have a shirt you can use. I wasn't, you know, trying to force you into . . . into anything you didn't want."

"Just . . . just leave me alone!" Sarah said in a broken voice before covering her face with her hands and pressing herself flat against the couch back. Sobs racked her body, and she was completely unable to stop the violent tremors that rushed through her.

"Please," she whimpered. *"Please! Just leave me alone!"*

Chapter Thirteen

Stalking

— 1 —

"I'll be right back," Michael said as he heaved himself up off the couch where he had been slouched next to Sarah. He dropped the book he had been reading onto the couch and twisted his head back and forth to work out the kinks.

"Where are you going?" Sarah asked with a trace of tension and irritation in her voice. Ever since that horrible night more than three weeks ago at Michael's fraternity house, she had felt increasingly unnerved and edgy, and more than a bit distrustful of him and his motives. Of course, Michael had apologized profusely for coming on so strong to her. He had sent her flowers, cards, and other small gifts nearly every day for the past three weeks. Although Sarah had accepted his apologies and tried to convince herself he truly loved her, she couldn't deny the strong element of doubt that had entered their relationship. She tried to convince herself this was a natural part of a relationship as it got more "serious," but she wasn't so sure how much she could trust Michael anymore.

Other things were bothering her as well. For a long time now, she had been convinced Tully was out of her life forever. Seeing him in Michael's room that night had instantly destroyed any newfound confidence or security she might

179

have been feeling. She often wondered if she would have given in to Michael's sexual advances that night if she hadn't seen Tully, watching them with such obvious disapproval. She didn't trust Tully or Michael or even herself anymore. Whenever she felt even the vaguest stirrings of anger or hostility, she fully expected to turn around and see Tully's unblinking stare, boring into her from some darkened corner.

But Sarah also had another good reason to feel threatened whenever Michael wasn't around. Although he was making a point of avoiding her, she knew that creepy janitor was still watching her. That night at Pat's had been one of many times she had looked up and seen him, staring at her as if she were some kind of trophy he lusted after. It seemed as though she caught glimpses of him wherever she was, both on or off campus.

Michael leaned forward, kissed her lightly on the mouth, and said, "I just gotta go make my bladder gladder."

Sarah blushed as a rush of panic about being left alone in the study lounge swept through her. It was late, almost time for the Student Union to close. They were the only ones left in the room. She wasn't sure she could handle it if she saw that janitor or Tully.

"Can I—"

"I'll be back in a just sec," Michael said, turning away before Sarah could get up and go downstairs with him to the restrooms. She smiled thinly, not wanting to appear too nervous.

She snuggled down deep on the couch and tried to force her attention back onto the book she was reading—*Moby Dick*, for her introductory literature class. Even with Michael there, she hadn't exactly gotten swept up by the story; with him gone, she felt suddenly very vulnerable. She hadn't read even a full paragraph before she heard the shuffle of footsteps and the *squeak-squeak* of the cleaning cart's wheels outside the study lounge door.

"Is that all you ever do, is study?"

Sarah had only heard him speak once before, but his voice was all too familiar. The forced tone of joviality instantly grated on her nerves.

Pretending to be absorbed in her reading, she didn't bother to look around as the janitor sauntered around the perimeter of the room emptying the ashtrays and wastebaskets. Sarah tried to imagine herself a turtle, pulling her head down between her shoulders.

"What's that you're reading anyway?" Alan asked. When Sarah didn't immediately answer him, he added, "Looks like an awfully big book."

"No pictures either," Sarah said, surprising herself.

"Huh—yeah, well, I suppose not," Alan replied. Leaving his cart behind, he moved around so Sarah could see him. Sliding his hands into his pants pockets, he rocked back and forth on his feet as he looked down at her. For a second or two, she focused intensely on her book, but finally shifted her eyes up at him.

"Is there something you want?" she asked, her voice tight with control. She regretted the words as soon as they were out of her mouth. She knew damned well what he wanted!

Without missing a beat, Alan smiled thinly and said, "Yeah, well—actually, there is something I want." He looked ceilingward for a moment, then back at Sarah with a piercing gaze. "I was thinking I'd like to talk to you a bit. Mind if I sit?" Without waiting for her answer, he slid one of the chairs away from the table and sat down, straddling it backward. He draped his arms over the chair back, letting his hands dangle loosely in front of him.

"Actually, I do mind," Sarah said. She shifted her eyes back to her book as soon as it was obvious he wasn't listening. "I have an awful lot of reading to do for a test tomorrow morning, and I—"

"Ain't that the bitch of it, huh?" Alan said, shaking his head as he leaned forward. "You work, work, work, and what the fuck—I mean, what the hell for, huh?"

Sarah was silent, not even daring to look at him.

181

"We ain't met properly yet," he said. He leaned forward, extending his hand for her to shake. "My name's Alan — Alan Griffin." His eyes narrowed as though he was watching for her reaction.

Ignoring his hand, Sarah nodded and said, "My name's Sarah." Chills prickled the back of her neck as she glanced over at him and added, "Now, if you don't mind?"

"How's this college stuff going for you anyway?" Alan said, completely ignoring her brush-off. He bounced one leg rapidly up and down, making his chair squeak. "I don't know if I told you, but I'm just doing this job nights and going to class during the day. It was something my parole — well, something I figured I'd do to get out of the rut my life had kinda fallen into."

Marking her place with her finger, Sarah closed her book and, sighing deeply, looked him straight in the eyes. On the surface, he seemed nice enough, polite and friendly; but something about him bothered her . . . bothered her deeply. Every time she saw him, she got an undeniably powerful and negative feeling she could never quite nail down. It was almost as if, no matter what expression was on his face, he was constantly scowling. Even in the bright light of the study lounge, there was a dark cast to his face as though he were standing inside a thick shadow.

"You're a freshman, right?" Alan asked, looking at her eagerly.

Sarah nodded, then sat up and glanced quickly over her shoulder at the door. If only Michael would hurry up and get back! She was convinced Alan had been lurking around outside the study lounge all evening . . . probably every damned night she and Michael studied here. And she knew damned well he'd been just waiting for this opportunity.

"Look — umm, Alan," she said, lowering her voice, "I'd love to sit here and chat, but I really have a lot of reading to do before that quiz tomorrow."

"Hey!" Alan replied, leaning back and slapping his thighs with his palms. "I just wanted to shoot the bull for a bit. I don't mean no harm by it or nothing'."

Where the hell is Michael? Sarah wondered. Gnawing cold filled her stomach as she glanced at the doorway again. It shouldn't be taking him this long. What if he bumped into some of his fraternity brothers and was down in the Bear's Den, having a quick beer?

"You see, I'm not taking the kind of classes you're taking," Alan said. "I'm in the Basic Studies program 'cause — well, hell, you probably figured out I ain't exactly scholarship material."

Sarah shrugged, frantically wondering, *What the hell do you say to someone like this?*

"But you know, in the last year or so, I kinda got straightened around. I decided that I was gonna go straight and really try to get myself an education."

"That's . . . nice," Sarah said. She shifted her feet off the couch to the floor, grabbed her purse, and stood up quickly. Blood drained from her head and whooshed in her ears. She was afraid the sudden motion would throw her off balance and she would pass out, but she forced herself to turn and walk slowly toward the door.

"I have to go check on something," she said over her shoulder. Without waiting for Alan's response, she strode quickly out of the study lounge. She was practically running by the time she reached the stairway. She didn't care that she had left her books behind on the couch; all she could think right now was that she had to get away from Alan Griffin.

— 2 —

Alan was ripe, royally pissed off.

"Who the fuck do you think you're kidding?" he muttered after watching Sarah spin around the corner and out of sight. He listened to her receding footsteps click on the linoleum floor as she ran toward the stairs as if he were chasing after her.

"Yeah, well, all in good time, sweetheart—all in good time!" he whispered as he sat there, clenching and unclenching his fists until the hallway was quiet. Then, looking glumly at his cleaning cart, he sniffed with twisted laughter as he pulled a cigarette from his shirt pocket and lit it. Leaning back against the table, he considered just how pissed off she was making him. It wasn't that she was doing her damndest to ignore him, acting like he didn't exist. It was the head game she was playing, as if she didn't even recognize him . . . as if she hadn't recognized him right from the start.

Alan was pissed off about a few other things, too, like that asshole fraternity guy who was always hanging around her. He looked like such a little dickweed with his wire-rim glasses, his faggoty-styled hair, and his pinched-looking, smug, rich asshole face! Who did he think he was, anyway? He certainly wasn't man enough to satisfy any of Sarah's stronger urges. Maybe that's why she looked so tense, so wired all the time. If she was hanging around with a needle-dick like that, she probably hadn't had a good, solid fucking from a real man in a long time.

"And you'll get it, sweetheart," Alan muttered. He took a long drag on his cigarette and angrily blew the smoke up at the ceiling. "I'm going to take my time and make sure I do it right, but you're going to get it again and again and again before I kill you just like I killed your mother!"

He leaned forward, considered crushing his cigarette out on the floor, but then smashed it into the ashtray on the table behind him. Groaning, he eased himself up out of the chair and started back toward his cleaning cart. As he passed the couch, his attention was caught by the stack of books and notebooks Sarah had left behind.

"Sarah . . . Sarah . . . my dear Sarah," he muttered, cautiously eyeing the doorway before picking up one of her books. He idly flipped through the pages, all the while listening for her return. He dropped the book he was looking at and picked up one of her notebooks. Chuckling softly as he flipped through the pages, he took the pen from his shirt pocket and, on the very last page, scrawled in big block letters:

YOU KNOW YOU WANT ME.

"Ain't life just grand?" he said, snickering under his breath as he closed the notebook and dropped it back onto the couch. "And ain't it just wonderful the way it comes around in these tight, little circles?" His laughter grew stronger as he pushed his cleaning cart over to the table, picked up the rag and a spray bottle of cleaner, and started wiping the table top. Whistling through his teeth, he did a shrill, off-key rendition of "It's a Small World."

— 3 —

Sarah was scared, but that soon changed. After waiting outside the men's room door for a few minutes, she checked for Michael in the Bear's Den. A couple of his fraternity brothers told her he had been there but had gone off with some friends to dig out a car out of a snowbank. The Student Union was closing soon, and she knew she had to go back upstairs to get her books. As she walked out of the Den, hot anger replaced the cold fear twisting in her gut.

"Thanks a shitload, Michael!" she whispered as she cautiously approached the stairs. That jerk janitor was undoubtedly still up there, waiting for her to come back. Her hands were slick with sweat as she started up to the third floor.

It was late, well past eleven o'clock. The building was practically deserted. As she mounted the stairs, faint voices echoed in the stairwell from down below. As far as Sarah knew, she and Alan Griffin were the only ones up here.

She knew, just by the way he looked at her, sliding his eyes up and down the length of her body, that he wanted her. She also knew that a man like his wasn't *attracted* to a woman. He had the hardened face and manner of a con-

185

vict; he looked like the kind of man who was used to taking whatever he wanted, and society be damned.

At the top of the stairs, Sarah froze in midstep when she heard soft laughter ringing through the hallway. At first, she couldn't tell if it was coming from upstairs or down; then a voice echoed low and rumbling in the hallway from the opened door of the study lounge. She couldn't quite make out the words, but she knew who it was.

"God damn you, Michael," she whispered as she narrowed her eyes and clenched her hands into fists. "Why did you have to take off like that?"

Her legs trembled beneath her. She knew there was no way she could oppose a man like Alan. He wasn't all that big, but she had noticed the sharply defined muscles of his forearms as he sat straddling the chair. She knew, if he took it in his mind to do anything to her, she'd be powerless.

She approached the opened door cautiously just as another sudden burst of laughter echoed from the room. She heard a voice say, "And ain't it just wonderful the way it comes around in these tight, little circles?" followed by the loud *slap* of something dropping. Then his laughter rose even louder. Sarah didn't doubt for a second that it was Alan. The squeaking sound of his pushcart wheels set her teeth on edge, but she sucked in a sip of breath and forced herself closer to the doorway.

This is crazy, she thought, trying to command herself to have courage. *I'm being totally paranoid.* But that didn't stop the shivers from racing through her when she heard him start to whistle "It's a Small World."

Sarah held her breath until it burned in her lungs, but she couldn't force herself to round that corner and enter the room. The old joke—*Just because you're paranoid, doesn't mean they're not out to get you!*—rang in her memory. Closing her eyes, she leaned against the wall, willing her rapidly pounding pulse to slow down, but it did no good. Just knowing Alan Griffin was in there, and she would have to see him again, made her stomach twist into a cold, hard knot. And the anger she felt directed at Michael almost made her choke.

The squeaking wheels of his pushcart caught her attention. Her eyes snapped open, and she looked frantically at the door, fully expecting to see Alan's pale, thin face leering out at her. The sound of the cart's wheels got louder. He was coming toward the door!

With a suppressed grunt, Sarah pushed herself off the wall and started running toward the stairs as fast as she could. She bit back the scream that threatened to burst out of her. Afraid she might trip and fall, she didn't glance back over her shoulder to see if he had seen her or if he was coming after her. She grabbed the banister and used it to swing her momentum around and down the stairs, expecting to hear the cadenced *slap-slap* of his feet behind her and to feel his hand catch her from behind.

Sarah's shoes clicked loudly on the stairs as she raced down to the second floor. She paused only a moment on the landing to look in both directions, then started down to the first floor. At the bottom of the stairs, she rounded the corner in a sharp turn and ran smack into someone. The impact knocked the person back several steps, and Sarah, surprised and thrown off balance, pinwheeled her arms crazily to keep from falling.

"I'm sorry," she said, her voice nothing more than a raw rasp. When her vision cleared and saw blue uniform of a campus cop, her heart dropped. She didn't know whether to be relieved or more frightened.

"Hey, hold on there! What's the problem?" the policeman said as Sarah started inching away from him. All she could think was she had to get away from Alan, she had to find Michael, but she stopped in her tracks when she realized who she was looking at.

"Oh, my God—it's you!" she said. She was trembling and panting heavily as a hot flush of blood rushed to her face. She took a deep breath and wiped the back of her hand across her sweat-slick forehead.

187

"Son of a gun," Elliott said, smiling widely. "Well, if it isn't Sarah Lahikainen." He looked at her admiringly for a second, then continued, "You know, I'd heard you were on campus and figured it was just a matter of time before we bumped into each other, but I didn't expect it to be quite so literally. I didn't hurt you, did I?"

"Oh, no. I was in a—a hurry to find a friend of mine," Sarah said, still panting.

"Well, the Union's closing in five minutes," Elliott said after checking his wrist watch. "You'd better make it quick."

Sarah was ready to leave, but still she stood there, staring at him with a bewildered expression. In an instant, her mind flooded with painful memories of the night her mother had been killed. But even as fresh tears started to fill her eyes, she remembered how concerned and caring Elliott had been throughout the drive to and back from the crime scene, and all during the interrogation with Detective Simpson and the fruitless months of investigation that followed. In some ways, he had been more sympathetic than her own father had been.

"What's the matter?" Elliott asked, taking one step closer to her. "You look upset."

Sarah looked downward, still choking on her fear, but it didn't take long to decide that she could trust Elliott completely. In a few sentences, she told him about the janitor who seemed always to be hanging around, watching her as if he were stalking her.

"I know exactly who you mean," Elliott said, even before she was half finished. "Alan Griffin, right?"

Biting her lower lip, Sarah nodded. "Yeah—he introduced himself," she said. "I just don't like the way he looks at me."

Elliott's expression hardened as he glanced up the stairway toward the third floor. "Well, to tell you the truth, I don't blame you. I had more than my fair share of run-ins with Alan back in Hilton, and . . ." He paused a moment, considering his words. "Let's just leave it at this. He's a bad dude, and you'd be pretty smart to avoid him if at all possible."

"Believe me, I'm trying," Sarah said, cringing. "But he's up there in the Taylor Lounge right now, and I left my books up there. I don't know if I dare to—"

"Why don't I go on up there with you so you can pick up your books?" Elliott said. His smile reassured her—at least a little bit.

"Thanks," Sarah said. "You know, my boyfriend went out a while ago to help someone, so his stuff's up there, too."

Elliott nodded. "No problem," he said as he and Sarah started up the stairs side by side. "But if you want a little piece of advice, I'd start studying at the library or someplace else. You know, someplace where there's a lot more people."

"Don't worry, I will."

"And another thing," Elliott said. They both stopped halfway up the stairs and looked at each other. "I'll be keeping a careful eye on our friend Griffin from now on, but if he ever calls you or start bothering you—in any way—you let me know, all right?" He placed his hand firmly on her shoulder. For an instant, she had the impression that he had wanted to put his arms around her and hug her. She glanced at him longingly, wanting to cry out all of the tension inside her, but she braced herself and continued up the stairs. They reached the third floor landing and walked boldly to the Taylor Lounge. When they entered the room, they found Sarah's and Michael's books still there, undisturbed on the couch. The wastebaskets and ashtrays were clean, and it looked as though the tables had been hastily wiped. Alan Griffin was gone.

"I want to thank you, Mr. Clark," Sarah said, smiling grimly after she had gathered up their things and was ready to leave. She clutched her notebook protectively to her chest.

"That's Elliott, if you don't mind."

"Sure—thanks, Elliott."

"If you'd like, I could walk you back to your dorm," he offered.

Sarah knew she might be imagining it, but she thought she detected something a bit more than professional obligation in his offer. Before she could reply, they turned at the sound of approaching footsteps. Panting heavily, his face red from the cold, Michael burst into the room.

"Oh, good," he said, gasping for breath. "You're still here. Sorry 'bout taking off like that, but I went with Harry and Ed to—" He looked quizzically back and forth between Sarah and Elliott, then said to Sarah, "Hey, what's up?"

Sarah took a deep breath, then shook her head, trying to dispel the rush of fear, mistrust, and anger she had been feeling. "Ohh—nothing much," she said, moving over to Michael. Curling her fist, she gave him a light punch on the upper arm. "But thanks a ton for disappearing without telling me where you're going!" Turning to Elliott, she smiled sweetly and said, "Thanks again, Elliott." Then she and Michael left the room.

Before they were out the door, Elliott called out to her, "Just keep in mind what I said, okay, Sarah?"

— 4 —

"She didn't have long blond hair . . . like yours," Alan murmured. He was naked and on his knees behind the woman who knelt on his unmade bed. He lazily ran his fingers up her naked back and through her long, blond hair; then he wound up a fistful of hair and gripped it tightly.

"Who didn't?" the woman asked with a ditzy laugh as mild pain jolted her scalp.

Her name was Cheryl Jenkins. She worked at Harvey's, a bar in downtown Bangor, where Alan had gone after closing the Student Union. He bought a few drinks from her, chatted nonsense to her a bit, and ended up meeting her after her shift. Alan thought she was pretty close to what he was looking for—almost perfect, and everything had worked out exactly as he had hoped. After stopping for a drink on the way back to his apartment, they were naked and ready to have some fun . . . only Cheryl had no idea what kind of fun Alan wanted to have.

"Oh, she's just . . . someone I used to know," Alan said as he leaned forward and licked a wet line down her back. His free hand moved along her ribs and then forward to cup her dangling breasts as he pressed himself up against her.

"Well, I don't like it when fellas are thinking of someone else when they're with me," Cheryl said. She tried to turn around so she could look him squarely in the face, but he tightened his grip on her hair and pulled back hard enough to make her squeal with pain.

"I don't really care what the fuck you think," Alan said gruffly as he thrust into her, hard, and pulled back on her hair like a horse's reins. Another louder yelp of surprise and pain from Cheryl pleased him. His head filled with a slamming hot flow of blood.

"I can think about anyone I want to . . . even when I'm fucking a slut like you," Alan said with a snarl.

Cheryl's throat was stretched back, making it impossible for her to make a sound. Tears filled her eyes, and the entire top of her head felt like it was on fire. An undercurrent of rising fear made her body go limp and cold.

"Anyway," Alan continued, his voice nothing more than a heated, animal growl. "I wanted to have you because you're *blond.*" He pulled her head back even harder and pushed violently against her for emphasis. Cheryl's outstretched throat gleamed like white marble in the darkened room. Alan stared at her upturned face, positively enjoying the blank look of stark terror in her eyes. His hand cupping her breasts squeezed hard, just itching to feel the solid grip of his knife handle. He wanted more than anything right now to drag the blade ever so slowly across her throat. He wanted to feel the hot gush of her blood flowing down over his hands and her breasts.

"So don't tell me what I should be thinking. All right?" he rasped, pushing harder and faster as his climax built.

The only sounds coming from Cheryl were strangled, anguished grunts as pain inflamed her body. Many nights after work she ended up with men who used her body; that's how she made ends meet. Usually there was little if any pleasure in it for her, but this was something she had never reckoned with. The vague thought crossed her mind that this man just might be crazy enough even to kill her.

Alan's breathing came fast and raw, bellowing heatedly as he pushed faster and faster against Cheryl. Their sweat-slick flesh slapped with a rapidly increasing tempo. Alan grew dizzy as he looked down at her, all the while imagining the young, fresh-looking face of a college girl with pale blue eyes framed by thin blond hair. His free hand slid up the woman's back and gripped her neck with fingertips that squeezed like a steel trap. At last, his climax came on strong, exploding in his head like fireworks as his hips trembled violently. Both hands went to Cheryl's throat and squeezed tightly as wave after wave of relief swept through him. Satisfied, he released his grip and pushed himself away from her. Exhausted and used, Cheryl collapsed face-first onto the bed, where her breath came in hot, shallow gasps.

Alan was still shuddering as he rolled away from her. As he sprawled lengthwise on the bed, his body felt like a rubber band that had been twisted up and then suddenly unwound.

"Go on," he said. He swatted Cheryl on the backsides with the flat of his hand, making a loud *whack* as he pushed her toward the edge of the bed. "Get your ass moving! Get dressed and get the fuck out of here!"

Cheryl's body was inflamed with pain, but she was grateful to be alive as she scrambled off the bed and, staggering, felt around in the darkness for her clothes. She hurriedly dressed, all the while keeping a wary eye on the man on the bed. He lay there on his side, watching her through slitted eyes. The thin smile on his face spiked her with cold.

Taking a deep breath, she said in a trembling voice, "I— I live way on the other side of Bangor. Do you think I could have a—"

"You can walk home," Alan said with a snarl. "The exercise will do you good."

Chapter Fourteen

Haamu

—1—

"I'm so glad you could come and visit me . . . especially on my birthday," Ester Lahikainen said. She was sitting in the chair by her window, looking out at the distant snow-covered curve of the frozen Kennebec River. Bright December sunshine poured like honey onto her lap. Three vases of flowers lined the windowsill along with an unopened box of chocolates and five birthday cards. Sarah spotted the card and note she had sent a few days ago.

"And how about that, I'm only two days late," Sarah said, smiling as she walked over and gave the old woman a kiss on the cheek. The skin was dry and flaccid beneath her lips. "Anyway, how could I forget my mumu's birthday? I would have been here on your actual birthday, but my finals weren't over until late Wednesday afternoon."

Sarah was getting a ride home to Hilton for the Christmas break with Kathy Meserve's parents. They had told her they wouldn't mind stopping by Valley View so Sarah could visit her grandmother. She hadn't known what to expect when she walked into the bedroom, and was pleasantly surprised to see her grandmother looking chipper and alert. When she had told her father she was going to stop by the nursing home, he had said his mother was "failing fast." Either he was overreacting, or her grandmother was having an unusually good day.

Nervously rubbing her hands together, Sarah walked over to the window and looked out. The view was impressive. A wide field sloped down to the river. On the opposite bank, behind a thin stand of pines, were several houses. Farther along the river, toward Waterville, she could see larger buildings, either stores or apartments. Edging the sky in the distance was the blue-hazed skyline of Waterville. Sarah felt a twinge of sadness when she wondered how many people staying in Valley View weren't even aware enough to notice the beautiful view.

"It's hard to believe it's almost Christmas already," Sarah said, squinting from the glare. "And to think, I've already finished my first semester at college."

"That's right," Ester said, turning her gaze directly at Sarah. Her pale blue eyes sparkled with reflected sunlight. "Davy told me you were in college already."

Sarah nodded.

"And he's such a good boy," Ester went on. "I wish we could afford to send him to college, but—well, with the war on and all, I don't see how we can manage it."

A jolt went through Sarah when she looked into her grandmother's eyes and saw the clear, unfocused stare. As lucid as she had seemed at first, Sarah realized her grandmother was off in her own world.

"And it must be so very hard for the two of you . . . waiting to find out," Ester went on. Her pale lips made little smacking sounds whenever she spoke. Between words, her tongue would dart out like a snake's and flick her upper lip.

Sarah started to say something but then stopped herself, wondering if she should go along with whatever her mumu said, or if she should correct her. She decided just to smile and answer her as simply as she could and try not to confuse her.

"So, Mumu," Sarah began, "how do you like it here?"

Ester's face clouded over for a moment as her eyes danced maddeningly back and forth.

195

"The Christmas decorations downstairs are beautiful," Sarah added.

For a moment, Ester brightened and, smiling, said, "Oh, yes—they're beautiful, just beautiful . . . No, I don't mind it here, but I still think I'd rather go to America someday. Maybe someday soon." She leaned her head back, her eyes unfocused as she looked at the acoustic ceiling and took a deep, shuddering breath. "It's an easier life there, I hear. I think you'd like it there, too. Of course, they wouldn't let my mother in. She had that problem with her eyes. But I don't think you'd be so nervous if you lived in America."

Sarah sighed softly and shook her head, not knowing what in the world to say. Her grandmother's thoughts and memories were like a deck of cards, constantly being reshuffled. Ester suddenly stiffened and twisted around to look at her. The sunlight streaming in the window gave her pale blue eyes a milky cast. She was focused on something far, far away even as she turned and looked directly at Sarah.

"And you, dearie," she said, her voice low and cracked. Again, her tongue licked her upper lip. "I worry so about you. How many times do I have to tell you that you have *got* to stop being so nervous all the time."

"But I—"

"Oh, I know, I know—you say you have this and that to be worried about, especially the children, but you have *got* to have faith and believe that you're being watched over."

At a total loss for words, Sarah just stood there with her mouth gaping as she ran her hand through her hair. So, her father had been right after all. It broke her heart to see her grandmother, her Mumu, failing like this. She remembered those few good years, back when her mother and father were still married, back when visiting her grandmother was the way it was supposed to be—a cozy, nice-smelling house with cookies in the cookie jar and hugs and kisses whenever she needed them. All of that had ended soon after her parents' divorce. Once Sarah was in sixth grade, her mother told her she felt "uncomfortable" visiting her former mother-in-law. From time to time, Sarah had gone to visit her grandmother, but it just wasn't the same; and once she started high school, her visits had dropped off to only one or two times a year.

"You know what, though?" Ester said. Her body trembled from the effort as she leaned toward Sarah. Her eyes flicked back and forth from her granddaughter's face to a point just above her shoulder. "I think the two of you will do just fine. I have to keep telling myself that."

"Well," Sarah said, trying to choose her words carefully from the collision of thoughts in her mind. "You know, now that I'm in college, my father and I — "

"You have to promise me you won't push him away," Ester said, suddenly commanding. Her thin forefinger trembled as she pointed emphatically at Sarah. "Do you understand me?"

Sarah nodded that she did even though she didn't have the foggiest idea what her mumu was talking about. "Well . . . I mean, I realize that he has his own life to live, and I — Maybe I kind of dropped back into his life and really screwed up what he had going. It hasn't been easy . . . but now that I'm out of the house and at col — "

"*You* wanted *him!* Not the other way around," Ester said, her feeble voice crackling as she tried unsuccessfully to shout. "When you called him, he came." Again, she focused beyond Sarah, at a point on the wall behind her shoulder. "Now, if you tell him to go away, he will. But you must understand — our *huumu* has a life of his own. If you give in to your anger, there's no way you — or anyone else — will be able to stop him."

What the hell is she talking about? Sarah wondered. Her nervousness rapidly crested in a flood of fear. Her father sure had been right about his mother's condition. At first, her mumu had seemed fine, but it was obvious she was more than a little bit confused; she was right out of her mind.

"You both know what I'm talking about, don't you?" Ester asked, nodding her head up and down like a slack puppet.

Sarah nodded even as a shiver danced up her spine to the back of her head. "What do you mean — the *both* of us?" she asked as she glanced behind her at the bare wall.

"You know, my oldest brother, Jussi, told me he saw the

haamu. I think it was just last night," Ester said. Her voice lowered and her eyes darted back and forth, glazed with distant memory. Sarah had the impression her grandmother was seeing events happen, even now, right in front of her. "Ever since we first moved into this house. Every night, I can hear the same *tap-tap-tapping* sound in the corner of my bedroom. I've been thinking it must be one of my older brothers, trying to scare me because this is a new house. But Jussi says they aren't, and that the house must be haunted. He says it might be the *tonttu,* the house spirit, trapped in a floor board or something and clambering to get out. But one night — what, was it just last night?"

Ester's eyes glazed and widened with remembered fear.

"Yes. Yes, it was! Just last night! Jussi said he would wait up all night with me to see what was making the noise. I must have fallen asleep because of the pills they give me here, but Jussi told me this morning, just before you came, that he had seen something underneath my bed. It was curled up on the floor like a cat . . . a fat, black cat. We don't have a black cat, do we?" She looked earnestly at Sarah, then shook her head back and forth. "No, no — I didn't think so. But Jussi says there's something . . . something black underneath my bed. And then, just this morning, Jussi . . . oh, poor, dear Jussi! They found him in the gully along the side of the road outside town. He was dead. They say he must have just dropped in his tracks, as though his heart was just . . . just stopped, but I think it's because he saw the *haamu.*"

Tears glistened in Ester's eyes and spilled down over her sallow cheeks. Her hands, folded on her lap in front of her, made futile little motions as though she were trying to button her blouse.

"You'll be going to the funeral tomorrow, won't you? I know you both loved him so dearly," Ester said in a feeble, broken voice. "But not as dearly as I loved him! Poor Jussi!" She stared at Sarah with wide, teary eyes. "You are going, aren't you?"

Trembling inside, Sarah smiled grimly and nodded. "Of course I am," she said, her voice barely above a whisper.

"Well, then — let's get ready." With a look of pained determination on her face, Ester made as if to stand. Her hands gripped the chair arms and pushed. Her body trembled from the effort, but after a second or two, it proved to be too much. Sighing deeply, she collapsed back into her chair.

"Well, then — let's get ready! Poor Jussi!" she said as tears coursed down her face and deep sob wracked her body. "My dear, sweet Jussi."

Ester's eyes fluttered, blinking back her tears. She inhaled deeply as she struggled against her inability to move, then exhaled violently. Her eyes closed and she sagged back into her cushioned chair.

For a panicked instant, Sarah thought her grandmother had just died, right before her eyes. She was about to call for help, but she saw the shallow motion of Ester's chest, rising and falling with each thin, whistling breath. Her grandmother was fast asleep.

And she might just as well have been talking in her sleep, Sarah thought as she looked at her grandmother's wrinkled face. The skin look lifeless, as cold and unmoving as veined marble. Her cheeks were shiny with tears, and a line of bubbly drool ran from the corner of her mouth down her chin.

Why does it have to be like this? Sarah wondered, as an overpowering wave of pity for the old woman swept through her. After a long, active, and basically happy life, Ester Lahikainen was so far gone mentally she didn't even know where she was or what she was saying anymore. For all she knew, right now she was in her family home back in Finland and had to get ready in a hurry for her older brother's funeral.

And what did her grandmother mean by telling her about the death of her brother, Jussi? The story chilled Sarah because it reawakened some of her own buried emotions from when her brother, Brian, died . . .

"Choked on his rattle!"
"Suffocated!"

But it was deeper than that . . . something her grandmother had said was burrowing like a fat, black worm into her mind. She couldn't stop thinking about it even though it

199

didn't make any sense. She assumed her grandmother had meant her father, her own son, Devin, when she kept referring to both of them.

"The two of you will do just fine."

But it unnerved Sarah, remembering the way Ester had kept looking over her shoulder as though she were addressing someone else who stood behind her. She leaned against the wall, her legs—her entire body feeling unstrung and rubbery. Even with warm sunlight streaming in on her, she hugged herself and shivered as cold, strong fingers wrapped around her heart and squeezed ever tighter. All she could think about was what her grandmother had said:

"You wanted him! Not the other way around. When you called him, he came. Now, if you tell him to go away, he will. But you must understand—our haamu has a life of his own. If you give in to your anger, there's no way you or anyone else will be able to stop him."

"Our *haamu* . . ." Sarah whispered; then, trembling with sadness, she turned and left the room.

— 2 —

Click.

The cassette inside the tape recorder started to turn.

"Here we go again," Sarah whispered into the microphone. "The minute Kathy's parents left, I'm in the door, bringing my suitcases upstairs, and my father tells me he's got plans for the evening. Got *plans!*" She paused a moment, listening to the hiss of water running as her father took his shower. "He's getting ready now to go out to the movies—with Alice, of course. And he's in such a hurry to get going, he didn't even think to ask me how his own mother is doing."

Sarah sniffed, fighting back her tears as she looked around her bedroom, resentment growing like a dark flower in her chest. The room was exactly as she had left it: the yellow bedspread with her stuffed animals propped up by the pillows; the posters on the walls; all the trinkets on her desk and bureau she had decided to leave home rather than take to college. The furry gray skim of dust on the furniture told her

200

that her father hadn't even entered her room since she was gone, hadn't even bothered to come in here and clean up a bit before she came home.

"No, this isn't my room," she said, a deep rasp rattling her voice as anger and sadness warred inside her. "Not really. My bedroom is still in Westbrook although by now I'm sure someone else is living in it. This is someone else's bedroom."

She shivered as she looked at the blank, black rectangle of her window. She imagined the darkness was an animal, pressing against the glass, trying to get in at her. The bedside light reflected in the double panes of glass, looking for a moment like two gleaming eyes staring in at her with a steady, unblinking gaze. Her voice trembled when she spoke again.

"Sometimes I feel like this room belongs to someone else— someone who has died," she whispered. She held her hand up in front of her face and studied it, half expecting to be able to see right through it. "It's like this room is a memorial or something."

The sound of the shower stopped. Sarah listened to the sound of muffled activity in her father's bathroom. The rasping of the metal rings on the shower bar set her teeth on edge. Resentment and hurt twisted inside her, throbbing with a deep, dull ache.

"But I can't hate him," she said. "I can't get mad at him, and I don't need my grandmother to tell me not to let our differences come between us. What did she say?" Her eyelids fluttered as she looked up at the ceiling. "Something about our family *haamu* having a life of his own and that I was the one pushing him away. Does *haamu* mean *father?* But anyway, it isn't true! God knows I want to spend as much time as I can with my father. He's the one who never seems to have the time for me. What the heck am I supposed to do about it? I don't have any friends in this town. I guess there's Jennifer and Lisa, and maybe one or two others. They must be home on school break, too, but I don't feel like calling them. They probably pity me more than anything else because they know what happened to my mother—like everyone else in town does. And I—I . . ."

Her throat closed off, and tears flooded her eyes when the memory of her mother's brutal death came back with full force. Brilliant images from that rainy night flashed through her mind, jolting her with sharp pain. The memory was never far away, but every now and then the full intensity of that night would come rushing back like a dark whirlwind, sweeping her away in anguish and grief.

"I know they — my friends, I mean, and my dad, too — they try to be understanding, but I — damn it!" She punched the mattress as tears spilled down her cheeks. "God damn it! I don't know! I just don't know!"

The soft padding of feet in the hallway drew her attention. Then came a soft knock at her door. Sarah snapped off the recorder and slid it under her pillow. Quickly wiping her eyes, she called out, "Yeah?"

"Hey, baby. How you doing? You getting settled in here?" her father asked as he eased open the door and took a few tentative steps into the room. He was wearing a thick, terry cloth robe as he towel-dried his hair. Still dripping water, he left wet footprints on the rug as he moved closer toward Sarah.

Knowing her eyes were red-rimmed from crying, Sarah nodded, carefully averting her gaze. She stiffened when she caught sight again of the light reflecting in the windows. Again, it looked like two unblinking eyes, watching her from outside. She thought for a moment that it might be an animal, but then she remembered that her room was on the second floor.

"I am truly sorry about tonight," her father said, still standing by the door. "I forgot that you were coming home today. Honest to God, I thought for sure it wasn't until Friday. Otherwise I wouldn't have made plans with Alice."

"Oh sure; I know," Sarah said softly. It was a struggle to keep her voice from revealing the anger and hurt.

"Hey," Devin said, walking over and sitting on the edge of her bed. Sarah could smell the fresh scent of shampoo and soap as he placed his hand on her knee and gave her a little squeeze. "I can tell you've been crying. Come on, tell me;

what's wrong?"

Rubbing her nose with the heel of her hand, Sarah forced herself to look at him and smile. Still unable to speak, she simply shrugged.

"Is it kinda hard, coming home?"

Sarah nodded.

"I know. Adjusting to college life probably isn't as easy or as much fun as people make it out to be." His grip on her leg tightened a bit, transmitting a small measure of reassurance to her. "And I'll bet you're feeling pretty confused by it all."

Again, all Sarah could do was nod, even though what she wanted to do was burst out in tears and collapse into his arms. Let him hold her and hug her and protect her as if she were still a little girl while she cried it all out. It wasn't college or coming home or visiting her grandmother or missing her mother; it was everything combined . . . and more. She didn't know what to think about her relationship with Michael; she was still afraid of Alan Griffin; she even wondered how she felt about Elliott Clark being on campus because whenever she saw him, as friendly as he was to her, he reminded her of that horrible night nearly two years ago. Also, there was something in the way Elliott looked at her which, although not threatening, made her uncomfortable. Sarah fought against the powerful tide of emotions inside her, convinced that, if she opened the gate even a little bit, the flood would start and she would never be able to stop it.

"I promise you, princess," her father said, smiling warmly at her. "First thing tomorrow—well, first thing after work, anyway, we'll go out to eat at a nice restaurant and then maybe even drive into Lewiston and go shopping at the Mall or something."

"Yeah," Sarah said weakly.

"And I already told you, Saturday morning, we're heading out for some skiing. I already have a reservation for Saturday night at the Snow Bowl Inn at Lost Valley. They say the snow is great this year. So come on. Lighten up, will you?"

"Oh, I'll lighten up," Sarah said. She looked him straight in the eyes, horribly aware of the alienation she felt. He was her father, but she had absolutely no idea who he really was. The thought was numbing. She forced a smile, knowing she could pretend everything was all right. She was getting good at that. She'd had a lot of practice.

"All right, then," her father said, standing up and starting for the door. "You hold down the fort here tonight, and staring tomorrow, the weekend is just yours and mine."

"Okay, Dad," Sarah said, in no more than a whisper. Again, her gaze was caught by the double glowing reflection in her window. "Have fun tonight . . . and say hi to Alice for me."

"Oh," her father said just before leaving the room, "you'll be able to do that for yourself. She's coming skiing with us this weekend."

Chapter Fifteen

The Fifth Floor

—1—

Elliott and Sarah were sitting in a dark corner of the Bear's Den having coffee. Outside, it was a dreary January morning that threatened snow before noontime. Some of that gray wintry gloom imbued the Den. Elliott couldn't help wondering how much of it he and Sarah had brought in with them.

"So you had a decent semester break?" Elliott asked.

"Fair to middlin', as they say," Sarah replied, shrugging as she sipped her coffee.

"And how are things in Hilton? I haven't spoken to anyone back home in months," Elliott asked, trying his best to sound chipper and bright. He couldn't reasonably expect that Sarah would have heard anything about Carol—or even know who she was. Right now, he wasn't even sure he cared because whenever he looked at Sarah, he felt such a strong rush of mixed emotions.

Sarah smiled thinly and said, "I don't think I'll ever be able to think of Hilton as home. I dunno. I guess everything's about the same."

Elliott burst out laughing. "Now that's insightful. I think if there's any town in this state that doesn't change, Hilton's gotta be it. What did you do the past few weeks—

sit home and watch icicles form on the gutters?"

"Just about," Sarah replied with a tight smile. "I pretty much just hung around the house, except for one weekend. I went skiing at Lost Valley with my father and his girlfriend. That was about it."

"That's one thing I never tried—skiing," Elliott said. He hooked his thumbs through his belt loops and eased back in his chair, trying to appear relaxed. This wasn't the first time he and Sarah had sat together in the Den, chit-chatting about this and that. What bothered him was, whenever he was with her, his mind started along lines of thinking that made him uncomfortable. Was he really attracted to her? he wondered. Could he be? It was crazy. She was only eighteen, for Christ's sake! He was close to thirty-five.

"Ahh—it wasn't all that great," Sarah replied. She was about to start in on how her father had spent all his time with Alice when, glancing up, she saw Alan Griffin stroll into the Den. She froze for a moment, then looked down at the table.

"There he is," she whispered before taking another sip of coffee.

Elliott casually looked around, but Alan must have seen him first and ducked back out the door, out of sight.

Sarah's heart was racing. It had been like this throughout the first week of the new semester. Every time she came into the Student Union, it seemed as though Alan Griffin showed up. He never spoke to her or came up to her; he never even made eye contact with her; but it seemed as if whenever she'd turn and look—there he was. Whether she was with Michael or Elliott or a group of her friends—she never went to the Student Union alone—she knew he would be hanging around. And she was *positive* he was just waiting for his chance to catch her alone. The few times she had looked straight at him and been ready to challenge him, he turned his back and acted as if he hadn't even seen her.

But Sarah knew he was watching her. She could feel his eyes boring into her back almost all the time now, no matter where she was.

"Hey, you know, I heard a rumor that Henry closed the White Crane and moved to Florida," Elliott said, trying to pick up the conversation. "Is that true?"

Still distracted, Sarah nodded and said, "Yeah—I think so."

"Can't say as I blame him, after what happened and all."

"Look, uhh-Elliott, I have to get to my class," Sarah said, glancing at her watch. She scrambled to her feet, leaving her half-finished coffee on the table, and said, "I'll catch you later, okay?"

"Yeah, sure," he replied as he stood up and slid his chair up to the table. His eyes flicked over toward the door again, but he knew Alan wouldn't be stupid enough to still be hanging around. "Actually, I should get back to work, too. How 'bout I walk you to the door?"

Standing behind Sarah, he helped her on with her coat before putting on his own. Standing so close to her, he caught a whiff of her perfume, and for one spinning moment he had to fight the spontaneous impulse to put his arm around her as they started toward the door.

What the hell's the matter with me? he chided himself as they wended their way between the booths. *She's just a kid, for Christ's sake!*

When they were almost to the door, Elliott saw her smile widen. Looking up, he saw Michael Shulkin walking into the Den with several of his fraternity brothers.

"Up and about kind of early, aren't you?" Sarah asked with a giggle as she went over to him and gave him a little hug and a kiss on the mouth. Elliott followed a few steps behind. The guys with Michael, all wearing the same fraternity jacket, pushed past the three of them and went over to the unofficial Sig Ep table, where the brothers usually congregated.

Michael smiled at Sarah, but his expression hardened

207

when he noticed Elliott standing a short distance behind her. Elliott and Michael silently nodded greetings at each other as Michael slid his arm protectively around Sarah's waist.

"Come on over and sit with us," Michael said, pulling her in the direction of his friends' table.

Clutching her books tightly to her chest, Sarah shook her head. "Gotta get to class. Will you still be here around eleven o'clock?"

Eyeing Elliott suspiciously, Michael shrugged. "I dunno. Probably."

"I'll look for you then," Sarah said. She gave him another kiss, this time on the cheek, and started toward the door. Glancing over her shoulder at Elliott, she waved her hand and said, "Come on! Hurry up or I'll be late for class!"

Elliott looked at Michael but said nothing.

"See you then," Michael said to Sarah. Turning to Elliott, he pointed a finger threateningly at him and seemed about to say something, but then let it drop. Although this was the first time he had been on the receiving end of things, Elliott had seen it played out plenty of times before; Michael was bristling with jealousy and anger at catching him with his girlfriend. Given the right—or wrong—circumstances, he probably would have picked a fight with Elliott right there on the spot.

"Later," Elliott said, cocking and pointing his finger like a gun at Michael before following Sarah out the door and up the stairs to the front entrance. While she wrapped her scarf around her neck and slipped her gloves on, Elliott swung the door open for her. Side by side, they went out into the frigid blast of air.

"Where are you headed?" he asked.

"Psych class—in Little Hall," Sarah replied, panting as the freezing wind whipped her words away.

Elliott nodded and strode silently beside her down the sloping walkway. Again, he had to fight the impulse to put his arm around her. He couldn't stop thinking about Mi-

208

chael Shulkin's suspicious reaction when he had seen them together. And the truth was, what Michael might have suspected was exactly what was bothering Elliott so damned much; he did want it to be the way it had looked; he wished to hell it was the way it had looked. He couldn't get Sarah out of his mind. He knew his deep feelings for her must have started back in Hilton on that horror-filled night when she had shown up at the police station, her hair soaking wet from the rain, her clothes smeared with mud, twigs, and leaves, and her face an absolute mask of terror.

But it hadn't ended that night. Not by a long shot.

Whatever Elliott had felt for her then—as crazy as it was—had steadily grown throughout his involvement with the investigation to find her mother's murderer. More times than he cared to consider, he had to resist the overpowering urge to take her in his arms and hug her. But being with her now at college, seeing her blossoming into adult life, was only making matters worse.

Before he told her to have a nice day and turned off toward the parking lot beside the Performing Arts Center, Elliott finally admitted to himself for the first time that he was falling in love—that he already had fallen in love with Sarah Lahikainen.

— 2 —

By now, his beer was warm and flat, but Alan hardly noticed as he sat slouched on the couch in his apartment on Water Street in Orono. Ghostly figures tracked across the TV. The sound was turned way down, and Alan's eyes barely focused on the screen as he sat staring blankly ahead. He had gotten home from work a little after midnight and had been sitting like this for nearly an hour, seething with anger as he thought about and planned what he was going to do next.

"One thing for sure," he whispered. "She *knows.*"

He gritted his teeth and let his voice hiss like a snake on

the last syllable. "She has to know." His gaze shifted slowly to his right hand as he clenched his fist and squeezed it tightly until his knuckles went white and his whole arm started to vibrate. "She must have known all along, and so does that asshole, Elliott Clark."

He took a swallow of beer, unmindful of the liquid that spilled from his mouth and ran down his chin. His chest felt as if it were bound by steadily tightening steel bands; his breath was shallow and hot.

All day at work, all he could think about was that he had to do something . . . something soon. But work had too many distractions, and after running through far too many contingencies, he was starting to get confused. He had hoped that once he was back at his place, he could sit down, relax, enjoy a beer, and start making some definite plans.

There was equipment he had to get. Should he buy some handcuffs, or would rope and something for a gag be enough? He would need weapons, of course, and maybe a supply of food and possibly a couple of sleeping bags and extra clothes if he decided not to chance bringing her to a motel. But where could he take her, and for how long? He needed to find someplace that was isolated so he could do whatever he wanted to her, as long as he wanted to . . . until he decided to dispose of her.

But even after he got home and plopped down on the couch with his beer in hand, whenever he tried to concentrate on what he had to do next, he would be filled with blinding rage at Sarah Lahikainen. The bitch was lying to him, leading him on! She was taunting him because she knew he was the one who had raped and killed her mother, and Alan was willing to bet his left nut that both she and Elliott Clark were in on this together, plotting and planning to wear him down until they finally nailed him for what he had done.

"Only *you* don't know that I'm on to you, do you?" he whispered, followed by deep, malicious laughter. "If you

210

want to play cat and mouse, two can play that game. You may be the pussy, but I sure as hell ain't no mouse."

When he noticed a blond woman on the screen — young, attractive, but certainly not college age, he reached blindly down to his leg sheath and withdrew his knife. He held the blade up between him and the TV screen and, with a quick flick of his wrist, pretended to cut an angled line across the actress's face as she mouthed words he couldn't hear.

"There!" he said, lowering his voice to a mean snarl. "How did that feel?"

The scene shifted to an older man talking earnestly to the woman; then it cut back to the close-up of the blond woman. In rapid succession, Alan sliced the air three times with his knife before the scene cut away again.

"There, did you feel that, you bitch?" Alan said, his voice rising in anger as he shook the knife at the TV. "Huh? Did you feel it?"

He snorted loudly and almost spilled his beer when he wiped his nose with the back of his hand. "Well, you will, goddamnit!" He placed the knife on the couch beside him and took another sip of beer. Then, with a suppressed shout, he wound up and threw the half-full can across the living room. A fantail of beer spewed out before the can bounced off the TV, leaving a foamy wet splotch on the screen.

"But the only thing I need right now is time . . . time to think and make sure I don't miss a thing. Sooner or later, though, you sure as shit will feel it! You can count on that!"

—3—

"Oh, you think you're so funny," Sarah said. Laughing softly, she nudged Michael, who was sitting beside her at one of the tables in the Fogler Library reference room. It was a Friday night, and the room was nearly deserted; but

211

Michael had a report on Buddhism due on Monday for his Religions of the World class, so they were having a weekend study date. He was so absorbed by what he was writing that he merely grunted and, without looking up, whispered, "What? What's so funny?"

"This," Sarah said, rapidly tapping the page of her opened notebook with her pen.

Michael frowned as he looked up at her, then at the large block letters scrawled across the page.

YOU KNOW YOU WANT ME.

Shaking his head, he turned back to his own work and whispered, "Well, it may be true, but I didn't write it."

"Yeah, as if," Sarah said. Sighing deeply, she tore the page out, crumpled it into a ball, and threw it onto the table; then she leaned back in her seat and vigorously rubbed her eyes. No matter how hard she tried to concentrate on her work, she couldn't stop her mind from wandering. Ever since visiting her grandmother at Valley View, she had been wondering from time to time what those Finnish words she had used meant.

"Tonttu . . . haamu," she whispered, but Michael didn't respond.

Tonight, before he had joined her at the library, she had found a Finnish-English dictionary listed in the card catalog and had jotted down the section number. Now was as good a time as any to find the book and get an answer. Sighing deeply, she stood up, gave Michael a light tap on the shoulder, and whispered, "Don't go anywhere. I'll be right back." She clutched her notebook to her side and left.

Michael nodded but didn't look up from his work as Sarah walked out into the foyer and headed straight for the stairway leading up into the library stacks. She never liked going up there—especially alone. No matter how many students were gathered in the downstairs study lounges, the upstairs study carrels always seemed deserted. The higher up she went, climbing the narrow, enclosed stairway, the quieter and darker the library got. She imagined that on the top floor there was nothing but a twenty-five-watt light bulb illuminating an inches-thick coating of dust on shelf after shelf of unused, long-forgotten books.

"Damned high enough," she whispered between heavy, panting breaths once she reached the landing at the fifth floor.

She hadn't told Michael where she was going or what she intended to do. She wasn't sure she wanted to explain it all; but now, alone in the dusty silence of the fifth-level stacks, she wished she had asked him to come along. The only sound, other than her labored breathing and the *click-click* of her heels on the worn linoleum, was the chattering rattle of a heater from somewhere behind the rows of books.

She moved slowly along the stacks, glancing up from time to time at the signs that listed the call numbers of the books. The narrow aisle seemed to telescope outward as she walked down the line. On either side of her, the military green metal shelving seemed to lean inward, making the aisle feel narrower and narrower.

Ever since she got back to school from semester break, she had been curious as hell to find out the meaning of those two Finnish words—*haamu* and *tonttu.* The way her grandmother had used the word *haamu,* Sarah guessed it meant either "elder" or "parent," maybe "father." She had told Sarah that the family *haamu* had a life of its own. *Tonttu,* on the other hand, could mean anything. Sarah didn't see what any of it had to do with the story about what her older brother, Jussi, had seen under her bed or how he had died.

Her throat was as dust-dry as the books surrounding her as she moved slowly along, scanning shelf after shelf and listening to the *click-click* of her heels on the floor. Her breathing slowed, but she could still hear the rapid whisper of her pulse in her ears. The notebook in her hand was slippery in her sweaty grip. The cataloging numbers seemed to go on forever. Realizing she had been holding her breath, Sarah stopped abruptly. In that instant, she was positive she heard someone else take two more quick steps behind her before stopping.

Was that her own footsteps, echoing in the stacks? she wondered. Or was someone up here following her?

Her heartbeat sped up as she looked frantically around. Anyone could easily be trailing her, hiding behind the barricades of bookshelves. Her first panicked thought was that Alan Griffin knew somehow that she was up here. He was stalking her.

"Cut the crap, all right?" she told herself, clutching her notebook protectively to her chest. After all, it was reasonable that someone else would be up here. It was just someone looking for a book, as she was. Why instantly assume there was someone following her?

Why, indeed? she thought as a chill raced up her back. Because she knew damned well that Alan Griffin *was* watching her! It wasn't just her imagination. She would see him just about every time she went into the Student Union. And he would look at her and smile that thin, cruel smile of his. The problem was, he never did anything overtly threatening, so she would have felt foolish complaining to the police about him.

She peered earnestly up at the section signs, then took two quick steps toward the nearest bookshelf and waited there, listening tensely. She scanned the dusty titles so she wouldn't feel completely foolish if someone saw her. Her ears tingled as she waited to detect the soft shuffle of footsteps behind her, but except for the distant rattle of the heater vent, the fifth-floor stacks were as silent as a tomb.

Sarah sucked in a breath and held it as her eyes darted back and forth across the faded book spines. The noisy heater vent could easily be masking the sound of someone approaching—especially if that someone was intent on sneaking up on her.

Panic seethed in her stomach, and she bit down hard on her lower lip, desperately trying not to let her imagination run rampant. But her mind was filled with the image of

Alan Griffin, his pale face set in a harsh, humorless smile as he approached her, step by heart-stopping step, with a gleaming knife in his hand.

The image sent a strong ripple of fear through Sarah. Why would she imagine Alan Griffin coming after her with a knife? The thought entered her mind seemingly against her will, like a projection from someone else's mind. As clearly as if she were watching a scene in a movie, she saw herself, threatened by a flashing blade as she backed up between two tall shelves of books until the cement wall stopped her. A scream caught inside her throat as she vividly imagined Alan raising his knife, stepping up close to her, nothing more than a towering black shadow as he slashed and slashed at her.

"Jesus Christ!" Sarah hissed, wishing more than ever that she had asked Michael to come along with her. Her eyes were wide with fear as she took a deep, shuddering breath and tried to dispel the horrifying flood of images. She raised her hand to her throat and rubbed her smooth skin, all the while clearly imagining hot blood gushing down over her chest as Alan's knife laid her throat wide open.

"*Stop* it!" she commanded herself, but the image was too stark, too real to be ignored. Bracing herself, and ready to scream as loud as she could if she had to, she started again down the aisle toward the section she wanted to find; but she was so wound up, she walked right past the section without even noticing it. Once she saw the numbers were higher than she needed, she spun around on her heel to turn back. As soon as she did, she caught a flicker of motion at the far end of the stacks. This time, for a fleeting instant, she was positive she saw someone—a man—duck behind one of the distant shelves.

A low, strangled whimper escaped her as she stared down the long aisle, all the while wondering if she had truly seen someone or if she was imagining all of this. Could that have been Alan Griffin? Or was it someone else? Even now she imagined that he was coming toward

215

her. Her pulse sounded like tinny hammer strikes in her ears as she waited to hear or see something.

At last, convinced that she was overreacting, she wedged her notebook under one arm and quickly ran her finger down the spines of the books until she found the volume she was after. She wasn't sure how to spell the words she needed to look up, but it didn't take her long to find *haamu*. A shiver ran up her spine when she read the definition aloud.

"*Haamu* . . . ghost or apparition. Oh, boy," she said. She blew out a thin stream of air and looked fearfully around her.

"Now *tonttu* . . . *tonttu*." Her fingers were trembling as she flipped the yellowed pages to the *t*'s. At first she thought the second letter of *tonttu* was an *a* because of the way her grandmother had pronounced it; but when she didn't find the word there, she skipped ahead to *to-* and ran her finger down the page until, at last, she found it. She frowned with confusion as she read the definition aloud to herself.

"*Tonttu* . . . a brownie or pixie," she whispered. She closed her eyes for a moment, searching her memory for exactly what her grandmother had said. "Now what in the hell do *brownies* have to do with my grandmother's brother dying? It just doesn't make any sense at all!"

Was her mumu completely crazy? What did she mean, saying the black shape under her bed that looked like a cat might have been the house *brownie?* And what was this about the family *ghost* having a life of its own? A ghost was the soul of someone already dead. How could it have a *life?*

Sarah slammed the dictionary shut and slid it back into place on the shelf. If anything, she had only created more confusion for herself.

Shaking her head, she took her notebook in hand and started back down the aisle toward the stairway. She walked briskly, unable to stop feeling as though someone else was still up here with her . . . someone who was following her, watching her. Tension wound up inside her like a coiled

216

spring, and before she realized it, she was running toward the stairway. Her shoes clicked loudly on the floor with a steadily increasing beat that slowed only slightly as she neared the turn onto the stairs. She was just starting to think she had made it, that she could run down to the ground floor and be safe with Michael, when she collided full force into someone who was coming up the stairs. Her scream echoed in the stairwell as her notebook flew from her hands and went skittering down the stairs to the landing. Sarah bounced backward from the impact, staggered, and almost fell.

Dizzying fear choked her, momentarily blurring her vision. She expected to look up and see Alan Griffin, looming in the doorway, smiling cruelly as he reached for her with one hand while the other hand held a gleaming knife high above his head.

"Christ — you scared the shit out of me!" Michael shouted. He put one hand to his forehead and shook his head to clear it from the impact.

"I scared you?" Sarah shrieked, still not quite able to believe it was him and not Alan. "What the hell are you doing up here anyway?"

"I could ask you the same question," Michael said, still looking dazed as he came the rest of the way up the stairs. "I came up here to find you. Some of the guys said they saw you heading up into the stacks. I thought you went over to the Den for a soda or something. Are you all right?"

Sarah nodded and dodged past him so she could retrieve her notebook. Dusting it off, she held it tightly against her chest as she looked up at him standing on the top flight.

"Yeah," she said shakily, "I — uh, I'm okay. I just needed to find a book." Her face felt feverish, and her throat was parched. "A soda sounds like a good idea."

"Why were you running so fast?" Michael asked. He leaned his head out of the stairwell and glanced up and down the aisle as though he expected to see someone else.

217

There was a suspicious look on his face, and Sarah wondered if he suspected she had met someone up here.

"I just got a little spooked. It's so quiet," she said, looking at him with fear-widened eyes.

"Yeah, well, let's get out of here," Michael said, holding out his hand. "This place gives me the creeps, too."

Chapter Sixteen

Watching and Waiting

—1—

"So what is it with you anyway?" Michael said. "What's wrong with you?"

"With *me?*" Sarah snapped. "What do you mean? Nothing's wrong with me!"

"Oh yes there is. You act so . . . I don't know! It seems like you're still holding out on me."

Sarah snorted and shook her head. "Don't start in on *that* again, okay?" There was a low tremor of hostility in her voice.

"No! No! No!" Michael said, trying hard not to shout. "I'm not talking about sex! For Christ's sake! I'm talking about you and me! I don't know what it is, but you always seem so . . . so distant from me. Like you're holding something back."

Sarah scowled as she took a sip of her whiskey sour and eyed Michael over the rim of the glass. They were sitting side by side on the couch, in the relative quiet of Michael's fraternity room. From downstairs, the heavy thump of the bass drum and a screeching guitar made the walls vibrate. The hallways were packed with hooting, dancing, mostly drunk or stoned couples. It was Sig Ep's annual February "Klondike Night" party. "Spring Fever

Bash" would have been a more apt description.

"But you're not having any fun," Michael said. He was fighting an impulse to take her drink from her, wrap his arms around her, and hug and kiss her without stopping. They had been dating since early fall, and he was beginning to think it was time they went a little farther than a goodnight hug and a kiss at the door when he dropped her off at the dorm.

Sarah bristled. "And how do you know I'm not having any fun?" she asked snidely.

"Well, for one thing, you've been gnawing your lower lip pretty much since I picked you up," Michael said. "And earlier tonight, when we were dancing downstairs, you moved like a—like a robot—"

"Well, you're no Fred Astaire yourself," Sarah said as a wave of anger swelled inside her.

Michael sighed. "Yeah, well—and then Eddie and Guy asked us up to their room for a drink, and what do you say? You blurted out *no* as if they had asked you to take your clothes off or something."

Sarah shrugged and took another sip of her drink. "I didn't feel very much like socializing."

"Sure. No problem. I mean, who would want to do anything like socialize at a fraternity party or anything!"

"That's not what I meant, and you know it. I just didn't want to go up to their room, if that's all right with you."

"Sure, Sarah. That's fine with me," Michael said, his voice vibrating with repressed anger. "I mean, they're only my two best friends in the house. What does a little drink among friends mean?"

"Well, sometimes, the way some of the guys around here look at me, I think they do want me to take my clothes off."

"Jesus Christ, Sarah! Maybe you don't realize it, but guys are horny pretty much all of the time," Michael sputtered as he stood up and walked over to the window. Leaning his elbow against the window frame, he sighed deeply as he stared out on the snow-covered night. The curved front driveway of the fraternity house was lined on both sides with candles burning inside brown paper bags. An eerie, orange glow reflected off the snow.

"You don't have to swear," Sarah said softly as she stared at the drink in her folded hands. She felt torn. As much as she wanted to go to Michael, hug him, and tell him everything truly was okay, she couldn't deny that what he said—just about everything he said tonight— filled the pit of her stomach with hot, twisting anger.

Michael snorted and shook his head in disgust.

"Come on," Sarah said, with an edge of pleading in her voice. "Who's being the downer now?"

Michael turned and looked at her. Sitting on the couch in the faint, blue glow of his "mood" light, she seemed somehow insubstantial, ethereal. Her pale face hovered in the darkness, an illusion that would vanish the instant he blinked his eyes.

"But what *is* it with you?" he asked, aware that his voice sounded raw with desperate pleading. "Why are you being so distant with me, like you're holding back all these secrets?" Michael said. "I'm not talking about to-night. I mean all the time. You seem to be—"

"I haven't been anything," she said, cutting herself off when she saw him shake his head.

Don't get mad at him! Don't get mad at him! she commanded herself.

"Don't you realize how much I—I love you?"

"Of course I do," Sarah replied. "And I love you, too."

"Oh, sure. You *say* the words, but you don't *act* like you really mean it."

"And exactly how am I supposed to prove it," Sarah asked tightly. "By jumping into bed with you because— like all men—you're horny?"

221

"Look, I don't want to pressure you," Michael said, "but—yeah. I think sometimes sex isn't such a bad way to show how much you care about someone. Maybe women are different, but I think it's good; it's natural."

"Well, I would think—or hope, at least—that sex isn't the only way we can demonstrate our love."

Michael was silent a moment. Then he sighed heavily and shook his head. "You still haven't forgiven me for that night, have you?"

Sarah's mind flooded with things she could and should say, but she remained silent.

"That's it, isn't it? You don't . . ." He swallowed noisily. "You don't love me anymore?" His voice broke, and before Sarah could respond, he added, "I mean, if you want to, you can call it all off, you know. Hey, it wouldn't be the first time. You're free to do whatever you like."

Sarah took a deep, shuddering breath as she leaned back against the couch and brought her knees up in front of her. Closing her eyes tightly, she hugged her legs tightly against her chest. Behind her eyes, she saw nothing but a shifting curtain of bright, flickering red light.

Don't get mad at him! Don't get mad at him! she mentally chanted.

"No. It's not that," she finally said, her voice barely above a whisper, her eyes still tightly shut.

"Then what *is* it?" Michael said, turning to her and clenching both hands in frustration. "Why are you so damned cold to me all the time?"

Sarah opened her eyes to mere slits and let her breath out in a loud *whoosh*. "And why are you being so mean to me?"

"I'm not trying to be mean," Michael said. "Honest, but after a while—I mean, my God!"

"I just have a lot on my mind," Sarah said. "That's all."

"Yeah, like what? Like maybe Elliott Clark?"

222

Michael's words hit her ears like a solid one-two punch. A cold shock jolted her as she looked at him, a dark silhouette against the orange glow outside the window. Her anger blossomed.

"Elliott's a . . . a friend of mine," she stammered, her voice low and trembling. "We're from the same town, in case you didn't know, and he . . ." She took a deep, shuddering breath, wondering how much she could reveal about that horrible night nearly two years ago. "Elliott helped me out once when I . . . when I really needed help." With the last few words, tears filled her eyes.

"Yeah, well—if you ask me, I think maybe you're getting a little bit *too* friendly with him," Michael said. Now that he had broached the topic, he was unable to keep the sour jealousy out of his voice. "Why are you pushing me away, Sarah? Don't you want me anymore?"

His words came at her like gunshots out of the darkness. For a fear-filled instant, it didn't even sound like Michael talking; the cold, heartless voice sounded more like . . .

Tully!

"Oh, shit," Sarah said in a flat, broken whisper.

"What?" Michael asked. "Are you surprised I figured it out?"

"No, it's not that. I—"

"I suspected quite a while ago that you were seeing him."

"I am not seeing Elliott!" Sarah shouted as a rush of terror gripped her. She couldn't shake the horrifying feeling that she was talking to Tully, not Michael. "We . . . we have coffee together in the Bear's Den a couple of mornings a week and talk. That's *all!*"

"Sure it is . . . if you don't count the times he's walked you to class afterwards." Michael's voice sounded colder, meaner.

Sarah had the terrifying sense that someone else—

maybe Tully—was using Michael's voice to pour out his bitterness and anger.

"Elliott usually leaves for work when I do," she whispered. "And yeah—sometimes we head in the same direction. So what?"

The silhouette by the window snorted derisively, unaware—or uncaring—of the warm tears carving tracks down Sarah's cheeks. A hard, burning lump formed in her throat.

"Yeah, well, to tell you the truth, I don't really believe you. If you want to know what I think, I think you have been seeing him—plenty!"

Sarah could hear the sneer in his voice. She still couldn't get the idea out of her mind that this wasn't Michael speaking at all; it was Tully. He had already done to Michael what he had done to Myrtle and Brian and Rosalie and maybe her mother, and now he was going to do it to *her!* She trembled as she stared through her tears at the silhouette by the window, expecting at any second to see Tully's pale face and unblinking blue eyes leer at her out of the darkness.

"You know, I even think sometimes you might be *screwing* him," the voice out of the darkness said snidely. "You won't do it for *me,* but you will for *him!* Is that it? Is that why you act like you don't even want me around anymore? Huh? Because you're screwing Elliott Clark?"

"I am *not!*" Sarah said, her voice tight and dry. To her fear-heightened senses, all she could hear was Tully's voice. This wasn't Michael! This couldn't be Michael!

"Yeah, well," the silhouette said with a disgusted grunt, "I don't believe you. I think maybe you got a thing for older men. Hell, how many times have you told me how you and your father don't get along, huh? You're probably screwing Elliott because, deep down inside, you want to be screwing your own father!"

"Why, you lousy son of a bitch!" Sarah shrieked. With

224

a sudden jerk, she propelled herself off the couch and darted for the door. She frantically twisted the door knob and flung the door wide open, all the while fearing the strong, cold grip that might take her from behind. As the door swung open, the blast of music from downstairs was deafening. In the suddenly bright light, Sarah turned and caught a glimpse of Michael's face.

Yes. It's really Michael.

His mouth was nothing more than a cold, expression line as he stood there, glaring at her, his arms across his chest.

"Go ahead," he whispered in a low, defeated voice. "You're free to go. I can't make you stay."

Trembling with relief, Sarah bit down hard on her lower lip. Her breath burned in her lungs. She couldn't stop the red rush of hatred directed at him.

"Go on," he said more forcefully. "I *said* you can *leave!*"

"But aren't you . . ."

She was going to ask for a ride back to the dorm but then stopped herself. This was his fault! All of it! She hadn't wanted or even suspected a rift was growing between them. It was all his doing. *He* was driving the wedge between them by being so jealous of her and Elliott, and by not even trying to understand what might be making her feel so upset and nervous.

Fine, she told herself. *If that's the way you want it, then that's the way it's going to be. And it's going to be up to you to make things good again.*

"Well . . . maybe I'll see you around," Sarah said. Her voice was barely audible above the blaring music from downstairs as she stepped out into the corridor. She started down the hallway, her shoulders hunched, the back of her neck burning as she waited . . . hoping against hope to hear him call her back. As she walked down the stairs toward the front door, the music blocked out everything else; but as she snagged her coat from the heap in the coat closet and pulled it on, she was positive she heard a burst of high, derisive laughter that seemed to come from Michael's room. Without another word, she walked out into the cold night . . . alone.

— 2 —

It was bitterly cold, waiting in the car outside the Sig Ep fraternity house. Maybe even more than he wanted to make Sarah Lahikainen suffer for what she was trying to do to him, Alan wanted to start the engine and get the heater going. But he didn't dare chance it. One of those fraternity assholes might notice him parked outside their house. Besides, the campus police had driven by twice already. Alan figured they were just keeping a watchful eye to make sure the party didn't get out of hand, but it wouldn't pay to make any stupid mistakes, not at this point.

Alan also wanted to light a cigarette, but he didn't think that would be very wise either, so he contented himself watching the steam of his frozen breath blow like pale smoke out of his mouth. Pursing his lips and snapping his jaw, he blew wispy air rings.

What he needed right now, he thought, was that blond bimbo waitress he'd picked up at Harvey's that night after work. What was her name? Shirley or Cheryl? If she was down on her knees on the car floor with her mouth open and her head bobbing up and down, this waiting around to see when Sarah and her dickweed boyfriend left the party might not be so miserable. He'd been there almost two hours, and every lousy, teeth-chattering second merely increased his anger at Sarah and did nothing for his rock-hard erection.

"But when I get you . . . oh when I *get* you!" he hissed in the darkness as he scanned the front yard of the fraternity.

226

Even with the car windows closed, Alan could hear every thumping note of the band in the fraternity's party room. The throbbing rhythm of the drum never seemed to vary from the heart-thumping *whomp-whomp-whomp*. He got a slice of the singer's tuneless voice whenever the front door opened and a couple either came or left.

At one point, several couples, obviously drunk, came outside and started an impromptu snowball fight. The jerks weren't even wearing jackets while the girls — silly little bitches that they were — squealed with mock terror as their big, rugged boyfriends pelted them with handfuls of snow. When the snowball fight spread out across the front lawn, closer to his car, Alan slouched down behind the wheel, hoping to hell one of those jerks wouldn't notice him.

"Take 'em inside and slam some ham to 'em, why don't yah?" he muttered. "That's what they really want anyway." He shook his head approvingly when he caught a glimpse of one of the girl's decently shaped body. "No matter what they tell you or how they act, that's what they all want."

As the snowball fight continued, Alan caught sight of the campus police cruiser coming up the road for a third pass. Tucking down deeply into the collar of his coat, he slid down even farther behind the wheel, holding his breath as the cruiser slowly approached.

"Got to be that asshole Elliott Clark, too," Alan whispered, his fists clenching as his scowl deepened. Alan sure as hell hadn't forgiven Elliott for arresting him back in Hilton and sending him off for a fun-filled year at the State Prison in Thomaston. At first he had been surprised to find Elliott working as a campus cop, but it didn't take Alan long — especially once he saw through that lying bitch Sarah — to figure out that Elliott was working undercover with her to nail his ass for what he had done to Sarah's mother.

227

The police cruiser stopped at the head of the driveway four cars away from where Alan was parked. One of the snowball fighters saw it, signaled to the others, and they all scurried like scared rabbits back into the fraternity house.

"Fuckin' wimps," Alan said, snickering under his breath.

A thick tornado-shaped cloud of exhaust spewed into the cold night air from the cruiser's tailpipe as it idled there. Peeking up over the rim of his steering wheel, Alan tried to see who was driving, but all he could make out was a dark silhouette. It could have been anyone, but he watched it with an angry scowl, convinced that he saw Elliott's Clark's ugly profile.

Alan's breath came out in a long, slow whistle when the cruiser began to move slowly forward. He was positive the driver almost stopped when he was beside his car. Alan froze, not even blinking until the cruiser crept past him. Wiggling up in his seat, he watched the taillights recede in the rearview mirror.

"And fuck you, you dickhead!" he muttered.

He reached down and patted the reassuring bulge of the sheathed knife strapped to his left leg as his eyes shifted back to the fraternity house. Although he was still formulating the details of what he would do once he had her, he was content to wait out here all night if he had to. He felt confident that, if he did get her tonight, he would be able to handle everything. And his bottom line was, he didn't really care because if worse came to worst, he'd simply slit her throat and dump her body on the roadside like he'd done to her mother . . . after fucking her real good, of course.

The front door of the fraternity house had been opening and closing all night as couples arrived and left and came back again. It was getting late now, almost midnight, and the activity had finally slowed down a bit.

Three or four of the "bag" candles had burned out. Fewer cars pulled into and out of the parking lot behind the house. Alan started to wonder if maybe Sarah and her jerkoff boyfriend had given him the slip. Maybe they had left by the back door, or maybe he hadn't seen jerkoff's blue Toyota leave. Tension filled Alan's stomach like a poisonous snake, coiled and ready to strike.

As he casually watched the front door, he saw it swing wide and a solitary figure emerged. Alan immediately recognized Sarah. He knew her well enough to know just by the way she stomped up the walkway that she was angry. And she was *alone*. She jabbed one arm into her coat sleeve, then the other, and pulled the collar tightly around her neck.

"Oh, what's the matter?" Alan muttered as he sat up straight and reached for the key in the ignition. "Is my little bitch upset about something?" He laughed softly. "Maybe you finally got a glimpse of jerkoff's dick and were disappointed by its dimensions. Is that the problem?" He sniffed laughter that came out of his nose as thin frozen vapor.

"Maybe now's the time," he whispered, his dark eyes tracking every step as she started down College Avenue toward campus. "Maybe now . . ."

Feeling a heady rush of excitement, he turned the key. The car growled once, then started up, sputtering in the cold. Just as his hand was reaching for the shift, though, he was startled by a quick tapping on the driver's window. Cold pinpricks ran up his neck when he turned and saw Elliott Clark, leaning close to the window. He made a motion with his hand to indicate that he wanted Alan to roll his window down.

"Nice night, isn't it?" Elliott said, smiling widely.

Alan's teeth chattered when a cold blast of night air entered the car. He opened his mouth, but before he could say anything. Elliott wagged his forefinger in front

229

of Alan's face and said, "Ut-ut. Don't tell me. I know what you're going to say."

"Fuck you!"

"Damn! I knew it!" Elliott said, slapping his gloved fist into his hand. He frowned like someone who had just missed the bonus question on "Double Jeopardy."

"What, is there some kind of law against sitting in your car?" Alan asked with a sneer.

Glancing into his rearview, he saw the cruiser parked right behind him. He cursed himself, wondering how in the hell Elliott had pulled up so close without him noticing. Probably, he'd been too involved watching Sarah walk away from the fraternity house. Had they timed it all to happen this way? Alan wondered. He scanned the darkened stretch of College Avenue but couldn't spot Sarah. She was out of sight . . . gone.

Elliott shook his head with feigned disappointment. "No—there's no law against it. But I'm kind of curious about what you're doing parked out here."

"I was just checking out the action at the party here," Alan said, trying to sweeten his voice. "See, I was just driving by, and I saw the way they had these candles inside grocery bags. I pulled over to admire them a bit. Kinda pretty, don't you think?"

"It takes you two and a half hours to admire something like that?" Elliott asked. He shook his head as though completely astounded. "I mean, I realize that you have a limited brain capacity, but I wouldn't guess it'd take even you that long."

"What do you mean? I just pulled up. I just got out of work five minutes ago."

Elliott shook his head as though he was trying to reason with a two-year-old. "You've had your ass parked out here for the past two hours plus," he said. "What, you don't think I'd recognize this piece of shit you're driving? Lord knows you were driving this hunk o' junk when I

230

gave you plenty of speeding tickets back in Hilton."

"Don't insult my car, man," Alan said, his voice low and tight as he curled his fists into hard knots around the steering wheel. In a hot rush of anger, he considered getting out of the car and beating the shit out of Elliott, but he checked himself, knowing that was probably exactly what this creep was after—any excuse to send him back to the slammer.

"You know," Elliott said, chuckling as he leaned his elbow on the opened car window, "if the chicks you score with are anything like your car, you must be thinking you have another use for grocery bags, other than burning candles, I mean. You might want to put one over the head of that woman I saw you with a few nights ago down at Pat's."

"Fuck off!" Alan said. He stepped down hard on the accelerator, making the engine whine loudly.

"A word of advice—forget it with these college girls. They're way out of your class," Elliott said, adopting a irritating fatherly tone. "Or maybe . . ." He snapped his gloved fingers and pointed at Alan. "Maybe you've got a hankering for one of these fraternity guys." Elliott glanced up at the house. "Is *that* what you learned in Thomaston?"

"I swear to Christ, man. If you keep this shit up, you're gonna be sorry."

"Is that a threat?" Elliott asked, a look of astonishment spreading across his face.

"You fuck with me, man, and it's a promise!" Alan snapped as he jabbed a finger at Elliott, who didn't budge back an inch.

"Come on! You can be more original than that!" Elliott said. He stood back from the car and gave the roof a resounding slap before adding, "Now why don't you get your sorry ass out of here. And if I ever see you hanging around places I think you're not supposed to be, I'll drop

231

on you so hard they'll carry you to Thomaston in three separate boxes. And *that*, my man, is my promise to you."

Seething with anger, Alan rolled up the window and reached for the gear shift. For a flickering moment, he considered popping it into *reverse*, stepping down hard on the accelerator, and ramming that mother-fucker's cruiser into scrap metal. But he held his fury in check as he rolled up his window and eased out of his parking spot onto the road. Anger like this, he told himself, was good to save and store up so once he got her, he'd have plenty to unleash.

Elliott stood back, his hands on his hips as he watched Alan pull out onto the road. When he was right beside the cop, Alan raised his middle finger and waved it at him through the closed window. He resisted the temptation to lay down a stretch of rubber on the road and drove slowly down College Avenue instead.

As he drove away, Alan knew one thing for certain: without a doubt, Elliott Clark was going to be one sorry, *dead* campus cop before all of this was over.

Chapter Seventeen

The Tulpa

—1—

It was Friday night. Michael and Sarah were sitting in the movie theater of Nutting Hall, waiting for the late showing of *Annie Hall*, part of the Woody Allen film festival. Michael had his arm around Sarah's shoulder, but there was something tentative in his touch, as though he was still holding back.

"I don't know. I just felt like such a jerk all week, you know?" Michael said. "I should never have talked to you like that."

"Yeah, I know. I felt kind of stupid, too," Sarah said, keeping her voice down to a whisper. "I mean, every time I'd see you on campus, I wanted to run away and hide somewhere. I'm so embarrassed. I was acting like such a spoiled, little kid."

Michael took a deep breath and let it out slowly. Then, with an embarrassed laugh, he said, "I knew I was being a jerk—even when I was giving you such a hard time. But I . . ." He shook his head. "I dunno what got into me. I was just in this . . . this mood where everything either one of us said just made me get madder and madder."

"Well I'm glad you finally got out of that mood and called me," Sarah said, smiling as she leaned into his hug.

"For a while there, I thought there were going to be two people on campus I'd have to avoid like the plague." The words were out of her mouth before she could stop them.

"Two? Who else?" Michael asked.

By the hopeful tone in Michael's voice, Sarah knew he thought she meant Elliott Clark, but she was swept by a cold, dull ache as the memory of Alan Griffin filled her mind.

"Uh, nothing." When he remained silent, she continued, "It's just there's this other guy who's kinda been bugging me." She glanced over her shoulder at the nearly full room, half-expecting to see Alan sitting a few rows behind them, watching her. "I think he's been wanting to ask me out."

"Tell me who he is," Michael said, turning to follow her gaze. "I'll beat the shit out of him."

"Come on. Don't worry," Sarah said, wishing she could stop worrying herself. For weeks now, she had been trying to convince herself that she was overreacting, but she couldn't dispel the feeling that Alan was following her around.

Michael looked at her expectantly, waiting for her to say more, but before she could, the lights dimmed and the movie began. The audience settled down in their seats and spent the next hour and a half roaring with laughter. But it was laughter Sarah couldn't share because, even with the security of Michael's arm around her, she felt vulnerable and exposed, constantly under surveillance. She couldn't shake the feeling that there was at least one person in the darkened room with them who wasn't watching the movie at all. He was sitting in the darkness, staring at her with cold, intense eyes filled with . . .

With what? Sarah wondered. *Anger and hatred? . . . Or loneliness and longing?*

As the movie played, the sensation intensified, a palpable presence in the dark room that had its sharp edge directed at her. Several times during the movie, she squirmed in her seat and turned to scan the audience. Dozens of smiling, pale faces stared up blankly at the moving images on the screen, but nowhere did she see anyone staring at her.

But he was there . . . somewhere. She *knew* it.

Michael picked up on her nervousness and once or twice asked if she would just as soon leave. Sarah told him she was enjoying the movie, but in fact, she had no idea what was happening on screen; her mind was overwhelmed with worry, questions, doubts, and nameless fears. She realized that she had been living with this tension for so long now that she was almost resigned to it.

Paranoia, she thought even as she wiggled under the steady stare of the unseen person watching her. All of this had to be in her mind. This was the University of Maine in Orono, for Christ's sake. There certainly were dozens of reasons to be nervous and wary these days, but people didn't go around following other people — stalking them — for no reason, did they?

But even as she asked herself that, another question came to mind: *Do people rape and kill women in little hick towns like Hilton, Maine?*

She knew the answer to that question all too well.

A scream was building up inside her, coiling like a shifting, black mass of storm clouds. Every nerve in her body was raw and jumpy, tingling with expectation. She wondered why she hadn't dared tell Michael more about herself. He was always accusing her of holding back from him, and it was true. There were things about her, things from her past that she still felt she couldn't reveal to him. Not yet. She wondered if she should try to find someone she could talk to about all of this — a therapist, like she'd had right after Brian died. Maybe the university had a campus shrink she could talk to.

Sarah was caught by surprise when the movie ended. As the credits rolled and the lights came on, the audience shuffled toward the doors, filling the room with laughter and noisy conversation. Michael helped Sarah on with her

235

coat before they walked out into the press of the crowd. They went up the aisle side by side, jostled in the crowd. Just before they exited the door into the hallway, Sarah glanced to her left and caught a fleeting glimpse of a familiar face. In less than a second, the face was lost in the swirl of people, but it left a burning afterimage in her mind.

"Oh, shit. Make that *three* people," she whispered as cold pinpricks danced lightly up the back of her neck.

"Huh?" Michael said.

Sarah glanced over at him and shook her head. "Oh, no—nothing," she stammered. "I just thought I saw a . . . a friend of mine." Her mouth felt bone dry as it twisted into a tight smile. "A guy I used to know . . . back home."

"What? Not that campus cop Elliott Clark, I hope," Michael said, craning his neck to see above the crowd as they made their way through the foyer toward the front door of the building.

"No, not Elliott," Sarah said. The icy chill tickling the back of her neck wouldn't stop. "His name's . . . Tully, but I guess it wasn't . . ." She shook her head vigorously and bit her lower lip. "No! It couldn't have been him!"

—2—

Shit. *She saw me.*

Sitting in the far back corner of the room, Alan had been positive Sarah wouldn't spot him; but at least fifteen, maybe twenty times during the movie, she had twisted around and looked right where he was sitting. That jerk-off boyfriend of hers had kept his arm around her shoulder throughout the whole movie, but Alan couldn't stop wondering if she was looking at him—maybe even wishing *he* was the one sitting there beside her, not that wimp fraternity guy.

That's what you're looking for, babe, ain't it? he thought.

He barely paid any attention to the ridiculous antics on the screen. His gaze and his attention were focused on the back of Sarah's head, on her beautiful blond hair. His erection hardened and stayed that way as he thought about what he would like to do to her. He'd do all the laughing he needed to do once he got that lying bitch where he wanted her and made her pay for what she had done—for getting away from him that night two years ago.

The movie dragged on. After sitting in the dark for nearly an hour, all the time watching Sarah squirm in her seat and keep glancing back at him, Alan got up and left the theater, figuring he would much rather wait outside than sit through such a moronic waste of time. As he pushed open the metal door, a light touch brushed against his shoulder, as if someone standing behind him was trying to nudge past him.

"Hey! Watch it, assho—" he said, turning around with clenched fists. He fell silent when he saw no one there. Confused for a moment, he looked back and forth, then concluded that the door must have grazed his shoulder as it closed behind him. He put on his gloves and, moving quickly, just in case anyone spotted him and might be able to identify him later, pulled his coat collar up around his face, shouldered the door open, and stepped out into the frigid night. His boots crunched on the icy walkway as he made his way down to the parking lot, where he had left his car.

Earlier that evening, he had waited outside Sarah's dormitory. Boiling with anger, he had watched when her boyfriend came to pick her up. They had looked oh-so-cute and happy as they hugged on the dorm steps and then got into jerk-off's car. Keeping a safe distance behind, Alan had followed them over to the Performing Arts Center parking lot.

"I'd bet the *first* six inches of my pecker that jerk-off doesn't have a faculty parking sticker," Alan had muttered when he saw Michael pull into a slot marked for faculty. Shaking his head with disgust, Alan had looked all around the parking lot. "Christ! Where are the campus cops when you really *need* them? Come on! Give this guy a ticket!"

As Sarah and jerk-off got out and started up the walkway behind the Arts Center, heading toward Nutting Hall, Alan had circled the parking lot. The important thing had been to find an empty space that afforded a clear view of jerk-off's Saab so, if he lost track of them, he'd be able to come back to his car and wait. Now, as he walked away from Nutting Hall, he was glad that he had done just that. Who gave a shit if he missed some or all of the dumb-ass movie? He should have saved his money. So what if he ended up sitting out here in the cold like he had last week in front of the Sig Ep house and on so many other nights? He wasn't about to lose track of her now.

Alan shivered with anticipation as he unlocked his car door and slid onto the cold, plastic seat. He was grateful he had planned ahead. Earlier that day, he had unscrewed the dome light bulb so it wouldn't shine on him whenever he opened the car door. Not wanting a repeat of what had happened in front of the fraternity house, he angled the rearview mirror so he could see jerk-off's Saab while lying down flat on the front seat. Pressing his hands between his legs and scrunching up his shoulders to try to stay a bit warm, Alan lay down to wait.

Time moves so fucking slow when you're freezing your ass off, Alan thought as he checked his watch for the hundredth time. The movie must have ended by now; it had been long and boring, but it wasn't *this* long. Cars came and went from the parking lot. Couples and small groups passed by, some much too close to Alan's car for comfort. Their laughter and conversation carried clearly in the cold night air. Every so often, headlights would sweep across Alan's windshield. He tensed every time, expecting a harsh blast of light to shine onto his car and stay fixed there as a campus cop—no doubt that asshole, Elliott Clark—came over and asked him what he was doing here, sleeping on his car seat.

Again, Alan checked his watch. He had been waiting

238

more than forty-five minutes. He was starting to lose his patience, but he told himself to stay calm, don't get upset; he would be able to use this frustration and anger later.

But maybe they were on to him? he thought. Maybe jerk-off was in cahoots with Elliott and Sarah and the fucking state police; maybe they were all setting him up.

He pushed such thoughts out of his mind, focusing instead on doing what he had to do. They hadn't nailed him yet; and before they did, someone else would pay the price.

Another fifteen minutes passed. Alan's teeth were chattering as he curled up into a tight ball on his car seat and stared at jerk-off's Saab. It was still there, so unless that was one mother-fucking long movie or they were showing a second feature, Sarah and jerk-off must have gone someplace else. They were probably at the Bear's Den with a bunch of his fraternity asshole friends. But as cold and as miserable as he was, Alan knew he could be patient. He could watch and wait all night if he had to because he knew, if not tonight, *eventually* his patience was going to pay off.

— 3 —

"You still seem kind of quiet," Michael said, leaning close to Sarah as he sat with her in one of the booths in the Bear's Den.

"Don't start, all right?" Sarah said tightly. She was clutching a large Coke but had barely taken a sip of it since they sat down nearly half an hour ago. Michael was finishing his second coffee. From the far end of the room, where students of legal age could drink—in what many students referred to as the Bear's Hole—came blasting rock music and waves of raucous conversation and laughter.

"No, I just mean I'm concerned."

"Well, I . . ." she started to say but then simply shrugged.

"Still feel a little uptight, right?" Michael finished for her.

239

He reached across the table, took hold of her hand, and gave it a firm squeeze. It was cold and stiff in his grip. Every time he tried to make eye contact with her, she would either look down at the floor or at the wall behind him.

"Did you enjoy the movie?" Michael asked earnestly.

Sarah shrugged again. "It was okay."

"Then what's bugging you?"

Sarah pressed the flat of her hand against her cheek as she took a deep breath and then raised the Coke to her mouth and sipped. The cold liquid tingled the back of her throat.

"You're not still mad at me from the other night, are you?"

Biting her lower lip, Sarah shook her head. "No," she whispered.

"Then what *is* it?" Michael asked. His voice was tight with pleading as he squeezed her hand and pulled her toward him.

"I don't know. I just don't feel all that . . ."

Comfortable was the first word that came to mind, but that wasn't the right word; the feeling was deeper than discomfort, more disturbing. After their argument at the Klondike Night party, she still wondered if she could ever fully trust Michael again. Was he just like other guys, simply out for sex? She remembered the old saying: "Women give and forgive; men get and forget." But even if he wasn't just a jerk whose awareness was primarily below his belt, wouldn't he end up deserting her—*abandoning* her—like everyone else she had ever loved?

"But you have to trust me," Michael said, as if reading her mind. "You know what I feel for you."

Sarah nodded, still unable to meet his steady, earnest gaze. In the center of her heart, she felt a fragile blossom of warmth; but she couldn't stop thinking that, no matter how much she might love Michael and he might love her, that love would eventually be lost, smothered by the darkness inside — and all around her.

Like always, I'm ruining it, she thought guiltily. *Why did I ever think this time might be different?*

"You know you can talk to me about it," Michael continued, lowering his voice and leaning toward her across the table. "You can tell me anything and everything that's bothering you."

Sarah chuckled and, raising her eyes, asked, "Do you have ten or twenty years?"

"If that's how long it takes," Michael replied with a high tremor in his voice.

Heaving a deep sigh, Sarah pulled her hand away from his and leaned back in the padded booth. She realized that, with the high-backed booth behind her, for the first time in a long time she felt secure, positive there was no one lurking behind her, watching her.

"You know that guy I mentioned at the movies . . ." she began.

"Yeah, you mean — well, you never told me his name. But you mean that guy you said was from your hometown?"

"Yeah," Sarah said, biting her lower lip. "His name's Tully."

Hearing herself say his name aloud sent a wave of chills racing through her. She shifted uneasily on the seat, pressing hard against the cushioned back of the booth but knowing she had to go through with this; now or never, she had to confide in Michael.

"What about him?" Michael asked, his body tensing as if getting ready for a fight. "Is he the guy you say has been bugging you?"

Sarah sniffed with nervous laughter. "Not quite," she said, almost laughing aloud at how foreign her voice sounded to her own ears. "You see, this guy Tully . . . he doesn't even *exist.*"

"What?" Michael said. He looked at her with a mixture of confusion and humor on his face. "I — I'm not quite fol-

241

lowing you here."

Sarah squinched her eyes tightly shut, focusing her awareness on the spinning darkness behind her closed eyelids.

"I don't think I quite follow it either," she said. She wished her voice would stop sounding like there was someone else using her mouth. "It really goes back a long way— back to when I was a kid."

"You've known him that long?" Michael said.

Sarah shook her head. "No, no. I told you; he isn't even real. He's something I made up."

Michael was silent for a moment; then his eyes brightened. "Oh, wait a minute—I get it. You're talking about, like, an imaginary friend or something you had when you were little, right?"

"Sort of," Sarah replied as she sank down in the booth and looked at Michael with a furtive glance. "I mean— you're going to think I'm crazy or something."

She was very close to tears as she finally looked straight at Michael and acknowledged the strong wave of affection she felt for him. Maybe it was even love, although she wasn't sure she knew what love was anymore—at least not until she lost it. She could see—now—that she had loved her baby brother Brian, and Myrtle, her cat; she had honestly been trying to get to know Rosalie, and she had absolutely no doubt that she had deeply loved her mother. And still did! She loved her father and grandmother, too, but both of them were slipping away from her, each in their own way. She wasn't sure if what she felt for Michael was the kind of love she could revel in and build a life around. Even though she had been so hopeful about starting a new life for herself at college, romantic love no longer seemed like a valid possibility for her.

"The only thing that makes me wonder if you're crazy or not," Michael said, "is that you still want to go out with me, even after I proved to you what a jerk I can be sometimes."

"Sometimes?" Sarah said. She didn't come close to cracking a smile as she lowered her gaze to her hands, which were folded in front of her on the table. "*Sometimes* is okay. What I'm talking about is permanent crazy."

"And what exactly do you mean by that?"

"I mean," Sarah said, her lower lip trembling, "that sometimes I wonder if I might be mentally ill."

Michael tried to say something, but she cut him off with a quick wave of her hand. "I mean it. This . . . this—God, I can't really call him a *person* because I don't think he really exists, except in my mind."

Michael frowned as he leaned back in his seat and looked at her with a mixture of perplexity and concern. She stared back at him with a desperate pleading in her eyes; but as hard as he tried, he honestly couldn't think of anything to say.

She took a deep breath. "I started seeing a shrink back when I was a kid, right after my baby brother died . . ."

"You never told me you had a brother who died," Michael said.

"There's plenty of things about me you don't know," Sarah said with a weak smile. "Yeah, my baby brother Brian. He died before he was even two. I was eight years old."

"Gee," Michael said as he ran his fingers through his hair. "That must've been pretty tough."

Sarah looked at him with a harsh glare and said, "Yeah, especially because I was convinced I had killed him." Her voice was trembling with barely contained panic. "And it wasn't the first time that I . . ." She pounded the table with her clenched fist, almost knocking over her drink. "There, see? I almost said it wasn't the first time *I* did something like that. That's partly what I was seeing the shrink about—this feeling I had that *I* had caused Brian's death."

Michael's expression never wavered as he asked, "Well, you didn't, right?"

"I wasn't even in the same room when he died!" Sarah's

243

voice rose a pitch higher. "The therapist called it—I think the term he used was 'magical connection'—something like that. It's when a child think they're responsible for everything bad that happens, like when someone in the family dies or there's a divorce or something. He said all kids do it to some degree or other. When it really started for me was a year or so before that, when my mom and dad weren't getting along all that well. That's when I made up Tully."

"Your invisible friend?"

Sarah nodded. "I can't remember everything from back then, how it started and all. In some ways I feel as though Tully was always there, and it was just a matter of time until I met him. I think what I did at first was make him up, sort of like an older brother, so I could have someone to talk to, someone who was older and smarter than I was, someone who could help me cope with what was happening."

"Because you thought you were to blame for your parents' divorce, right?"

"What kid in that kind of situation wouldn't feel like that?" Sarah said, her voice bordering on a shout. She knew she was being defensive, but she couldn't stop it. "As far as I knew, I was the only thing that could have come between, so—yeah, sure. I felt plenty responsible."

"But you weren't," Michael said in a low, kind voice. "I mean, you must realize that by now."

Sarah's eyes brimmed with tears as she looked straight at Michael. She wanted to trust him, to love him, but she still sensed a chasm widening between them.

"I know I wasn't, just like I know I didn't really kill Brian, but—" Her eyes went unfocused for a moment. "I never wanted my parents to split up, but with Brian—well, what kid *isn't* jealous when a new baby comes home?"

"You keep saying things like that," Michael said, interrupting her before she could go on. "You keep saying 'of *course* all kids do this and think that.' Seems to me you know these things intellectually, but you're not letting yourself feel them. I mean *really* feel them, in your heart. You're not accepting—"

"But don't you see?" Sarah snapped. Her voice threatened to shatter into a million pieces. "That's just it! I think I must be crazy because I'm convinced Tully killed Brian."

"Whoa! Wait a minute there," Michael said, but when Sarah looked expectantly at him, he found himself at a complete loss for words.

"Almost all my life," Sarah said in a trembling whisper, "and I mean right up until last year, and maybe even tonight at the movies, I think I *saw* Tully."

As much as she wanted to, she couldn't quite bring herself to tell Michael that she had also seen Tully that night in his fraternity room, the night when he had been, as he later told her, maybe a little bit crazy from horniness and too much to drink, and had pushed a little too hard to make love to her . . . the night she, too, under different circumstances, might have given in to his desires except for her nervousness and fear at how strong he was coming on to her. And then, any possibility of feeling romantic and loving had instantly evaporated the moment she saw Tully, standing there in the corner, watching them with a dangerous look of disapproval.

"You say you *saw* him," Michael asked. His voice was strained and raw. "Do you mean as in right there in front of your eyes? Like you're seeing me?" He shook his head when Sarah nodded agreement. "I just can't quite swallow that. I mean, that's . . . that's—"

"*Crazy!*" Sarah said with a helpless shrug. "See! I told you you'd think I was crazy. And what it all comes down to is, either Tully's real, and he can do things like kill my baby brother, or else he's a . . . a figment of my imagination that I blame for the horrible things *I* do."

"You know, this reminds me of the concept of the Tulpa. Have you ever heard about that?"

Sarah shook her head.

"Well, supposedly these Tibetan Buddhist monks who

245

live high up in the Himalayas can produce physical beings from their mental energy. Not imaginary stuff. We're talking real, physical beings. As far as anyone else is concerned, they see an actual human being, and there is some physical evidence that they exist, but they reputedly come from the monks' pure mental energy."

Sarah snorted with laughter and looked down at her hands. "Come on! You're making that up. Where'd you ever hear about something like that?"

"In Introduction to Eastern Religion, the professor mentioned it."

"Well, whatever, I'm certainly not a Buddhist monk," Sarah said, her smile twisting tight. As she looked at Michael, she felt torn between laughter and a scream.

"No, but what if something like that is really possible?" Michael continued, excited by the idea. "What if there's something about you, a talent you were born with, that gives you the ability to do what these guys in Tibet have to meditate and fast and study to do? Think about it! Maybe it's more than mere coincidence that you nicknamed this imaginary friend of yours *Tully?*"

"Tully . . . Tulpa," Sarah whispered softly, shivering as the idea sank deep into her mind. Suddenly she looked at Michael with panic-stricken eyes. "You know, that's kind of scary." Her voice barely rose above a whisper. "I mean, all my life, I thought Tully was—that he *had* to be just a product of my imagination. To think that he might actually be *real* somehow . . ."

"And can act in the real world as if he has a life of his own," Michael said.

His words hit Sarah like a jolt of electricity. Her peripheral vision began to vibrate with blinking dots of white light. Looking at Michael, she almost screamed aloud when she saw that he, too, was shimmering, as though she were looking at him through a depth of rippling, sunlit water.

"A life of his own," she whispered, barely aware of the

246

rapid-fire hammering of her heartbeat. Those were the exact words her grandmother had used to describe the family *haamu* — the family *ghost* or *apparition!*

"Oh, Jesus," she said, covering her mouth with both hands as the blood drained from her face.

"What is it?" Michael asked, again reaching for her across the table.

Sarah pulled back from him as terror sliced through her.

What if it was never just in my mind?

What if Tully really does exist?

What if he did kill Brian and Myrtle and Rosalie? And Mom?

What if he had meant it when he told me he was going to take care of me whether I liked it or not?

"Maybe that's what my grandmother meant," Sarah whispered. Her voice was so soft Michael almost missed it. Her vision went unfocused as she stared past Michael at the distant wall. For a fleeting, panicked instant, she had the impression that she could see clear through him. The music coming from the bar, the conversations around her, everything receded into a loud, meaningless buzz as her grandmother's voice rang in her memory . . .

"You have to promise me you won't push him away. You wanted him! Not the other way around. When you called him, he came. Now, if you tell him to go away, he will. But you must understand — our haamu has a life of his own. If you give in to your anger, there's no way you — or anyone else — will be able to stop him."

"Jesus, Sarah, are you feeling all right?" Michael asked. He got up and came over to her, wondering what the hell was happening to her. Her face was sheet white, and her eyes twitched back and forth as though she had no control over them. A thin line of drool ran from one corner of her mouth. Her hands clenched into tight fists on the table and trembled as though she was about to explode with rage.

"No, I . . ." But that was all she could manage as a flood of terrifying thoughts filled her mind.

He was there in the woods the night my mother was killed. He

247

told me he was! And he must have had something to do with Rosa-lie's death! Didn't he tell me he was going to take care of me whether I wanted him to or not? What else has he done for me, thinking he was helping instead of harming me and those I love?

Her body shook violently as she swung her legs out of the booth and stood up. Her hands looked like someone else's to her as she reached for her coat and slipped her arms into the sleeves. When she wiped her forehead with the flat of her hand, she was surprised by the icy dryness of her skin. She had expected her face to feel flaming hot and sweaty.

"Maybe you're coming down with the flu or something," Michael offered. His voice came from far, far away as he eased his arm around her to support her. He grabbed his coat from the booth, and side by side, they started slowly to the door.

"Yeah, maybe," Sarah said, taking slow, careful steps as though she were walking on sheer ice. "I probably better get back to the dorm and get some sleep. I'm sorry. It's just that—" Her voice caught in the back of her throat but she forced herself to continue. "Tully's ruined my life up until now, and I just don't want him to ruin it anymore! I want to get rid of him—*forever.*"

The muscles in her legs felt unstrung as she and Michael made their way out of the Student Union and down to the parking lot. The cold, fresh air helped restore her some, but Sarah was grateful that she didn't have to walk back to the dorm alone. When they got to his car, Michael opened the door for her and helped her onto the seat. For just an instant, as he went around the car to the driver's side, he caught a shifting of motion in one of the cars parked close by, but he was so concerned about Sarah, he never gave it a second thought as he started up the car and headed back to Hancock Hall.

Part Three

The Darkness Falls

Kylla kissa kyntensä loytää kun puuhun pitää. ("The cat can find his claws when he needs to climb the tree.")
— A Finnish proverb

Chapter Eighteen

Nabbed

—1—

It was late, well past midnight, by the time Michael dropped Sarah off at Hancock Hall. After a kiss good night, which Sarah felt very easily could have led to a lot more if she didn't mistrust things so much, she got out of the car. Standing at the bottom of the steps leading up to the front door, she watched as Michael's car slowly pulled away. He tooted his horn once for her as he rounded the corner by Wingate Hall. The sound carried well in the chilled night air. Sarah waved, even though she knew he couldn't see her. Then, closing her eyes, she smiled to herself and listened to the receding whine of the car's engine. She tried to imagine every turn in the road on the way back to the Sig Ep fraternity house. Once the sound of the car had faded, Sarah opened her eyes and looked around at the peacefully quiet campus.

She was alone except for one couple walking hand in hand down the sidewalk across the street in front of Oak Hall. Huddling into the warmth of her coat, she stepped out of the light in front of the dorm and went quickly around the side of the building, hoping to catch a glimpse of Michael's car as he headed down College Avenue. The street was empty; she had missed him. Looking longingly at the dark strip of road, she was filled with a feeling of sadness, of desertion.

Her gaze shifted beyond the parking lot to the tree-lined edge of the Stillwater River, no more than a jagged gray line meandering among the trees. Moonlight cast the snow-covered landscape in an eerie, blue glow. Steam from the heating plant rose into the night sky like a threatening tornado. Tilting her head back, Sarah looked up at the star-splashed sky, took a deep breath, and let it out slowly, a stream of thick vapor in the frozen air. Although she knew she should head up to her room and go straight to bed, she didn't feel the least bit tired. After revealing so much to Michael, she was both nervous and exhilarated, filled with conflicting thoughts and emotions.

It's all right to tell people things, even private things, she told herself. *Especially if they love you . . . and you love them.*

She resisted the thought that she was trying to convince herself of this, but there was no denying that Michael had been wonderfully understanding with her tonight. With remarkable openness, he had accepted everything she had to say—even when she finally revealed to him the horrible events of less than two years ago, when her mother had been murdered. He had hugged and kissed her, reassuring her that he understood how deeply and permanently something like that would affect someone. And he had made it clear that he didn't think she was the least bit crazy or even foolish; he had been compassionate, helpful, and caring; he had listened to her and responded as though . . . "As though he loves me," Sarah whispered to the night with a tremor of excitement in her voice. "As though he *really* loves me."

But as happy as she felt, she still was unwilling or unable to accept this feeling. In some ways, it was too scary. She had never in her life felt so connected and so vulnerable at the same time, but maybe . . . just maybe there was hope for her, and being with Michael was going to give her a

252

new start, a chance for a happy life. The hope was as fragile and delicate as an eggshell in her hands.

Her feet crunched in the snow as she walked down the length of the dormitory to the back of the building. Her teeth chattered from the cold, but she wanted—she needed—time alone to think her feelings through. If she went up to her room now, Martha would probably be awake and full of questions as soon as she saw the look on her face.

But what would that "look" be? Sarah wondered.

She had always believed that, when people were in love, they felt happy, smiling and giddy all the time, showing the world the joy they felt in their hearts. But that wasn't how she felt—not entirely, anyway. As much as thinking about Michael gave her a good feeling, there was still a cold, dark dread at the core of her heart that maybe all of this was a fool's dream. Doubts and fears plagued her, nagging at her mind like a sludgy, backward pull. What if, as soon as she surrendered herself completely to Michael, as soon as she said the words "I love you," she lost him? Would she be able to handle the rejection and hurt?

"That's exactly what I'm afraid of," she whispered. Her voice was no more than a low hiss in the still night. Her footsteps crunched like grinding teeth in the crusty snow as she walked behind the dormitory and then started back up toward the road. If it hadn't been so damned cold, she might even have cried as the conflict raged inside her.

"Tully!"

Sarah stopped abruptly in her tracks and turned around when the name suddenly popped unbidden into her mind. Or had she spoken it aloud? Whatever the case, *that* was the true source of her fear—that Tully wasn't gone from her life; that he was still nearby and would do something horrible to mess things up simply because he was jealous of her . . . because he wanted her all to himself.

For a panicked instant, Sarah tensed, positive someone had followed her out behind the dorm. Had *she* spoken his

253

name aloud, or had someone else?

A wave of shivers that had nothing to do with the cold night air raced through her. Holding her breath and straining to hear, she scanned the darkness around her, convinced there was someone nearby, watching her . . . stalking her.

"Is that you, Tully?" she whispered, peering into the ink black shadows under the pine trees. "Are you out here?"

Her voice was faint and trembling even to her own ears. Her eyes widened as she looked around and behind her but could see no one. There were no sounds except for the high whine of tires as a car passed by on College Avenue and the low hiss of wind in the pines. Sarah looked back at the wavering line of her footprints in the snow—dark oval wells on the blue-glazed icing.

"Tully!" she said, her voice gaining strength. "If you're here, I want you to come out right now. I want to talk to you one last time. Do you hear me?"

For an instant, the hissing of the wind intensified. The shadows pooling under the pines thickened, and faintly, just at the threshold of hearing, Sarah thought she heard the soft sound of whimpering coming from the surrounding darkness. Her heart gave a cold, tight squeeze in her chest when she thought she detected a human figure crouching deep within the shadows of the trees. She tried to call again, but her voice caught in her throat when she recalled her grandmother's words:

"Our haamu has a life of his own . . . You can try to get rid of him . . ."

"Tully, I want you to know that I mean it. I don't want you around anymore," Sarah whispered as she closed her eyes and clenched her fists tightly.

Her grandmother's voice spoke in clear, precise tones in her memory:

"If you tell him to go away, he will . . ."

The dense shadows under the trees absorbed the dull echo of her voice. Icy tension gripped her, twisting in her

254

gut like strong fingers.

"I don't *need* you anymore, Tully. I want you to go away," she said, forcing strength and command into her voice.

A frigid gust of wind blew snow into her face, swirling in a haze around her. The lurking shadow under the pines deepened and seemed to shift forward among the twisted branches. Another car sped by on the road, but the sound of its passing was muted by the whooshing rush of blood in Sarah's ears.

"I hope you believe me," she said, lowering her voice to a harsh whisper. "I mean it."

She turned and started up the slight slope, moving slowly in the shadow of the building. As she approached the yew bushes that lined both sides of the front steps, an instant before she saw it, she sensed motion in the darkness to her right. A cry was bottled up inside her chest as she spun away from the dark figure that leaped up in front of her. Gloved hands caught her, and thick arms tightly enfolded her, squeezing the air from her lungs in a *whoosh*. One hand rose high above her, then crashed down on the side of her head. Circling pinpoints of light exploded across her vision. Her legs gave out beneath her, but the strong arms caught her before she hit the snowy ground.

"Well, well, well," a deep voice said, speaking in a harsh, laughing whisper close to her ear.

– 2 –

"Patience . . . patience always pays off eventually," Alan Griffin whispered as he huddled with Sarah in the darkness beside the dormitory. He cradled her in his arms, surprised by how light she was. His breath was ragged in his throat as he looked excitedly at her face. More than anything, he wanted to whoop with excitement, but he knew he had to stay quiet. There would be time enough for *whooping* and a whole lot more later.

He hadn't seen anyone in the area, but he didn't dare to

255

chance making a mistake now. As much as he had waited and hoped for an opportunity like this, he'd had his doubts that it would ever actually come. Now that it had, he was so giddy with elation that he wasn't sure what to do next. But he would have to think of something—fast—because this was it; he was committed.

The cold air nipped at his face as he lowered Sarah to the frozen ground; then he stood up and looked down at her. Her eyes were closed, and her face looked remarkable reposed, peaceful. For an panicky instant he thought he might have killed her, but when he leaned close, he would feel the warm flutter of her breath on his ear.

His car was parked at the far end of the Hancock Hall parking lot where he had waited after following jerk-off's car out of the Arts Center parking lot. Again, for much longer than he thought necessary, he had waited while jerk-off and Sarah talked in the car out in front of the dormitory. No doubt jerk-off was trying to coax her back to his fraternity room for the night. He probably had his hand inside her sweater and up her skirt the whole time they were out there.

While Alan had been stalking Sarah for the past few months, he had developed several options as to what he would do once he got her. He had actually been surprised—and ecstatic—when he saw jerk-off drive away and Sarah hesitate outside the dorm. When she had turned and started to walk around behind the dorm, he knew—no matter what—this was it, the moment he was waiting for. The show was on.

Suspecting that she would make a circuit of the building, he had gotten out of his car and walked quickly over to the dorm, staying on the shoveled sidewalk as much as possible so he wouldn't leave any footprints in the snow. His heart pounding with anticipation, he had waited until that one dipshit couple disappeared down the street and then had hidden behind one of the bushes to the right side of the granite steps. He had been barely able to contain his excitement as he waited . . . and waited, nearly freezing his ass off, for the third time tonight. And then she came around the corner, walking slowly and talking to herself. She came steadily closer to where he hid, and when he had heard her say, "I really mean it," he made his move. With one quick punch, he silenced her and then dragged her back into the cover of the shrubbery.

And now, there she was! He couldn't believe it! He'd done it! She was unconscious on the ground in front of him. *He had her.*

But crouching in the darkness, he was unsure what to do. The easiest thing would be to slit her throat with his knife while she was out cold. But as much as that idea appealed to him, he could think of a few commanding reasons why he shouldn't. Besides the incredible uproar and police investigation that would follow the murder of a college student on campus, he wanted to keep her for a while, he *had* to keep her alive so he could make her suffer for everything she had done to him.

No, before she died she had a *lot* to answer for!

"First things first," Alan muttered as he bent down and lifted Sarah to her feet. She moaned softly, and her head lolled back and forth as he slung her arm up over his shoulder. Grabbing her by the hip, he held her body tightly against his. Again, he was surprised by how tiny she seemed in his arms. He hoped they would look like lovers who maybe had had a bit too much to drink and were out for a late-night stroll to walk it off. Not wanting to leave any more tracks in the snow than he had already, he lugged her up to the sidewalk and then headed toward the parking lot. The few tracks in the snow under the yew bush were unavoidable. Maybe he'd have time to get back and smooth them over once he had her safely secured in his car, but his intention was to get her as far away from campus as possible.

Tension surged in him as he made his way slowly toward his car in the parking lot. He had to fight the urge to

257

hurry, but he knew he had to make this look as casual as possible, just in case anyone noticed them and reported it later. Sarah's boots dragged toe-first on the cleared walkway, making a long, harsh tearing sound that set Alan's teeth on edge. He kept his face lowered, all the while shifting his eyes back and forth, tensed and waiting to see the flickering blue light of a cop car.

Alan's car was parked way out back, out of the direct light of any streetlights. It looked to him as if it were at least fifty miles away. Step by staggering step seemed to bring it no closer. All around him, the gentle night wind hissed over the snow, sending shivers up his back. The pine trees that lined the back edge of the parking lot swayed gently, casting long shadows over the ground. The urge to run, dragging her along behind him, became almost overpowering, and it was with an incredible rush of relief that he got to his car. He flopped Sarah over the front fender as he unlocked the passenger's door, swung it open, and eased her into the car. Again, he was glad that he had taken the bulb out of his dome light so it didn't blind him as he settled Sarah into position on the cold seat.

"There you go, sweetie," he said, leaning close to her face. "You all nice and comfy now?"

Once he was positive she was still unconscious, and not faking it so she could make a break for it as soon as he was away from her, he went around to the driver's door, opened it, and slid in behind the steering wheel. He rolled up his pant leg and withdrew his hunting knife. Placing the knife on the dashboard, he smiled, recalling that this was the same knife with which he had silenced the lying bitch's mother two years ago. His hands were trembling as he slipped his gloves off and reached under the car seat to produce a roll of duct tape. He ripped out a six-inch length of tape and cut it by tearing it with his teeth.

"This'll keep you nice 'n' quiet for the time being," he said as he positioned the tape over Sarah's mouth then pushed down hard. The pressure made her face look

258

pinched and distorted. Alan chuckled to himself, thinking of the wide smile she must have underneath that thick strip of tape.

"Keep smilin' while you can, sweetie. There isn't much time left for you, you lousy, lying little bitch."

— 3 —

"Who the hell're you?" Elliott asked, freezing in midstep. Through the alcohol haze that dulled his senses, he barely felt the shock of surprise at seeing someone sitting on the landing in the darkened stairway of his apartment building. His hand automatically went to his side where, if he was still a *real* policeman, he would be wearing his gun. When his hand came up empty, his stomach did a sour little flip.

The person looked at Elliott with a blank, expressionless stare. Blond hair fell down over his brow, shielding eyes that hovered in the white blur of his face. The mouth was a thin, dark slash, a bloodless knife wound on the pale, thin face. For an instant, Elliott thought it was Sarah, but then he saw that it was a boy, leaning his head against the peeling wallpaper on the hallway wall. His arms were wrapped tightly around his legs, which were pressed up against his chest.

Elliott tensed even though he knew the boy couldn't easily spring into an attack from that position. His right hand curled up into a fist and dropped low to his hip, ready.

"I don't make a habit of askin' questions twice," Elliott said, his voice slurred from the beer he'd had at Murray's Bar.

The boy looked at him with an unblinking intensity. His mouth twitched as though he was trying to speak but couldn't form the words or force any air out of his lungs.

Christ! Elliott thought. *He's just a kid . . . a scared, little kid!*

"Are yah hurt?" Elliott asked, feeling a strong tug of drunken dizziness. "D'you need help or somethin'?"

259

His left hand, gripping the railing, tightened so he wouldn't fall down. He knew he should have stopped drinking after his fourth beer, but—hell, it was Friday night; he didn't have to work in the morning, and he didn't have anyone to come home to, so what the hell did it matter, tonight or *any* night?

"I asked if yah need help?" Elliott said, for some reason not daring to come any closer to the boy, who just sat there, huddled in the darkness, staring up at him. There was something really odd about this kid—something that set off the old cop's warning bell in Elliott's brain in spite of booze.

"Look, kid—uh, if you're looking for—"

"Help . . . her," the boy said. His breath was no stronger than a light breeze blowing through an opened window. Elliott wasn't even sure the boy had spoken; his mouth barely moved, and the words flitted away like dust in the wind, coming at him from several directions at once.

"Lookie-here, son," Elliott said, taking one step closer. His fist was still clenched, ready to swing the instant the boy made a hostile move. "I don't know what you want here, but I—"

"Help *her!*" the boy said again. This time Elliott was looking straight at him, and he was positive the boy's lips hadn't move.

"What the hell you talkin' 'bout?" Elliott asked. It was obvious this boy—or someone he knew—was in serious trouble, but he still didn't dare let his guard down.

The boy's pale, round face loomed closer to Elliott, seeming to float toward him out of the darkness like a helium balloon. His blank eyes widened into perfect twin circles that held Elliott in their hypnotic glaze.

"You *must* . . . help her. I . . . *can't* anymore," he said. His voice was strained and weak, yet still, the illusion in the darkened stairway was that his lips weren't moving at all.

"Yah know, if you're in any kind of trouble, you should

contact the police," Elliott said mildly.

"You were there . . . that night," the boy whispered, still staring blankly at Elliott. "I *saw* you there!"

"What? What the hell you talkin' about? Look, d'you want me to call the police for yah?" Even as he asked the question, Elliott wondered how — or if — he would even dare walk past this boy to get up to his apartment. He couldn't dispel the tightening fear that, as soon as he was up close to him, the boy would suddenly leap up and attack him.

"She . . . doesn't *want* . . . me," the boy said, his whispering voice no more than a raw, scratching sound. It reminded Elliott of metal scraping against stone.

"Who?" Elliott asked as tingling fear flooded through him, intensifying. "What the hell?" He took another tentative step up the stairs, frantically willing the muffled buzzing in his head to stop. The back of his throat was dry. His lungs felt as if they were being compressed inward, and he couldn't for the life of him take a deep enough breath.

"She . . ."

That was all he said. In a flicker of dull light, his pale face and huddled form winked out as though sucked back into the dark, stained wallpaper. A muffled *pop* sounded deep inside Elliott's ears before he staggered backward a step or two. He pivoted around on the tight grip he still maintained on the railing and slammed against the wall. Hundreds of tiny yellow lights exploded across his vision with a loud crash of cymbals. The curved edge of the handrail dug painfully into his kidneys, then slid slowly up the knobs of his spine, like a xylophone as he sank to the floor. Deep inside his brain, he heard the dull echo of an explosive concussion, as though something unseen and silent had shot past his head close to his ear. The echo faded with a weird warble, and Elliott followed it down . . . down . . . and down until it — and he — were lost in darkness.

"Help her!" was the last thing he heard before losing consciousness.

Sarah's eyes snapped open. Blinking rapidly, she stared in terror up at the face leaning over her. She tried to think through the buzzing blur of pain centered inside of her head, but for several heartbeats, she had no idea whom she was looking at or where she was. She was lying on her side with her body squashed against something hard. Her legs were raised so her knees pressed against her chest, making it impossible for her to take a deep breath. Something sticky and tight squeezed her face as though cruel fingers were trying to force her to smile. The left side of her head throbbed with pain that radiated behind her ear and down into her neck and shoulders.

In bright, fragmented bits, the night started to come back to her.

Michael dropped me off at the dorm after the movie . . . sort of a funny movie . . . he had tried to get me to go back to the fraternity house . . . but I didn't go . . . I knew what he wanted . . . I told him I was tired and wanted to get to bed . . . I was still feeling drained, out of it . . . then I watched him drive away . . . but I didn't go straight up to my room . . . I took a walk out behind the dorm . . . I wanted to feel good about us, but I felt . . . sort of creepy . . . like there was someone following me . . . watching me . . . maybe Tully . . . and then— and then . . .

Pain! Crashing pain and darkness . . .

"Ah-hah, you're waking up, are you?" an unfamiliar voice asked.

Sarah groaned when she realized she was staring at the ceiling of a car. It was the door handle, pressing painfully against the side of her head. The dim blue wash of a streetlight filtered through the dirty windows, casting a speckled haze over everything. The driver turned and looked at her. His face was lost in the hazy shadows and her swirling vision. He turned the key, starting the car, and stepped down hard on the accelerator. The engine rumbled low like an angry beast ready to run; but before he shifted into gear and drove away, he leaned down close to her. A cold shock ripped through Sarah when she recognized him. Alan Griffin! His eyes sparkled wickedly in the gloom of the car. With his right hand, he gently smoothed the tape that stifled whatever feeble sounds she was making in the back of her throat. Then his fingers trailed down her neck to her shoulder, then down around the rounded curve of her breast and squeezed—hard. Without a word, he cocked back his hand and slapped her hard on the bruised cheek. The impact startled her and brought tears to her eyes.

"Well, well, well," he said, chuckling softly as his hot, sour breath washed over her face. "If you *were* feeling comfortable, it sure as shit ain't gonna last long."

Chapter Nineteen

The Storage Closet

— 1 —

When Elliott finally came to, he was sitting on the bottom step with his legs splayed out in front of him. He had no way of knowing how long he had been out cold in the dark stairway. A sharp pain shot out from the small of his back, numbing him from the waist down. For a panicky instant, he thought he might have broken his back and become paralyzed; but he could wiggle his feet, and soon enough the numbness faded to be replaced by burning pins and needles. The prickling stiffness quickly spread up his back to a point between his shoulders. The alcohol haze thinned a bit as he grabbed hold of the railing and struggled to pull himself up. Once he was on his feet, he straightened up stiffly, blinked his eyes to clear his vision, and then stepped shakily on the first step leading up to the landing.

The pale-faced boy was gone.

"Christ!" Elliott muttered as he painfully pulled himself along the railing like a mountain climber on a rope. After every three or four steps, he hunched over, panting from the effort. His knees felt as if they were strung with fraying rubber bands; his whole body trembled as he leaned back against the wall and took a deep, shuddering breath. The thin *whoosh* of his pulse in his ears masked all other sounds as he carefully placed one foot on the next higher step and, gritting his teeth, continued slowly up the stairs. He moved like an old man, dimly thankful that the movement was making the burning pins and needles go away.

He couldn't repress a shiver as he focused on the landing above him where . . .

How long ago? A few minutes ago? A couple of hours ago?

. . . a thin, blond boy had been sitting, staring at him, whispering to him in the dark. Why had he been there? He seemed to be waiting so he could ask Elliott or someone for help. Why hadn't he stayed around after Elliott fell? Where had he gone?

"Help *her*," Elliott whispered. His voice was no more than a raw grating in his throat and sounded like someone else's.

Another, stronger wave of chills danced up his back. Every muscle, every nerve screamed in agony, but he forced himself to hurry up the stairs, turn quickly on the landing, and race down the hallway to his apartment door. His hand shook uncontrollably as he fished his key ring from his pocket and, looking back over his shoulder down toward the stairway, fumbled to fit the right key into the slot. He couldn't stop the frantic fear winding up inside him; he expected at any moment to see the thin boy sitting in the hallway, staring at him with eyes like laser beams as his motionless mouth whispered . . . *"Help her! . . . You must help her! . . . I can't!"*

The words echoed like hollow thunder in Elliott's mind.

"You were there that night. I saw you there!"

The key turned, and the lock clicked. Elliott spun the doorknob and leaned his weight hard against the door. It swung inward surprisingly fast. He flailed his arms to keep his balance as he staggered into the dark living room. He was just starting to congratulate himself, thinking he could flop onto the couch and sleep this sucker of a drunk off, when his knee caught on the edge of the end table. Yelping with pain, he pitched forward onto the floor. A blinding bolt of light streaked across his vision when he hit the floor face-first.

You gotta stop doing this, he thought through the confusion raging in his mind. *It's gonna end up killing you.*

After resting on the floor for a moment, keeping his eyes tightly closed, he sucked in a deep breath, willing his whirling brain to clear. Then, with a deep-gut groan, he positioned his hands under his chest, preparing to push up off the floor. He wanted to open his eyes, but the best he could manage was narrow slits as a hot lance of pain jabbed the back of his head.

"Can you . . . can you *do* it?"

The faint voice rang in his ears like the tolling of a distant bell. He couldn't tell if he or someone else had spoken. Every muscle in his body seized up as cramps paralyzed him like jolts of electricity. He couldn't force himself to move as the darkness in his apartment and the darkness inside his mind collided like tidal waves, engulfing him in blackness so cold he thought it must be the icy touch of death.

"You have to . . ."

The voice was fainter, muffled like the distorted sound of a radio heard through thin apartment walls.

He's out in the hallway, on the landing, Elliott thought as he struggled against the cold waves that threatened to pull him under.

"Help . . . her!"

The image of the pale blond boy in the hallway filled his mind, almost choking him with panic.

I have to be imagining all of this! he told himself even as he admitted that the boy had seemed too real to be dismissed as mere hallucination.

From behind him, all around him, he felt as if he was being watched by cold, unblinking eyes. The darkness of the living room twisted with shadowy figures that weaved and danced around him like roiling storm clouds. Hands formed within the swirling blackness and reached out to him, trying to touch him, but they passed around him like puffs of smoke and then vanished.

"No, I—" was all Elliott could say before hot, sour vomit gushed from his mouth and splashed onto the floor in front of him. It splattered over his hands and soaked into the cheap carpet. Burning liquid filled the back of his throat and nose.

266

He snorted back quickly before the next wave came, got up onto his hands and knees, and started crawling toward the bathroom. After only a few feet, he collapsed face-first onto the floor again. His body twisted as though caught in a huge vise that squeezed in time with the violent contractions of his stomach.

"*Can you? . . . Please?*" a faint voice asked, fading with a distorted echo. "*Please? . . .*"

That was the last thing Elliott heard before he passed out with his cheek resting in the warm puddle of his vomit.

— 2 —

Alan knew he had to hurry, but more than that, he had to be cautious. The last thing he needed right now was to get picked up for speeding off campus this late at night. Gripping the steering wheel tightly with both hands, he drove slowly down Munson Road and took a right-hand turn at Fernald Hall, heading for College Avenue. He sucked in a sharp breath and held it when he looked out across the field toward the steam plant parking lot and saw a police car, parked along the side of the road.

"Shit, they're already on to me," he whispered as tension coiled up inside him. He slowed almost to a stop before turning left onto Schoodic Road. Sarah sat quietly on the seat beside him, but he knew she was conscious; her eyes stared at him, wide and glistening, above the top edge of the duct tape.

"Hey! Stop looking at me like that, or else I'll tape your goddamned eyes shut, too," he hissed.

Sarah looked away, but only for a moment.

Alan turned right at Winslow Hall, then left onto Sebago Road. Past Merrill Hall, he turned right onto Grove Street Extension, figuring he could leave campus out the back way, by the University Cabins, but as he drove past Nutting Hall, he couldn't dispel the gnawing fear that he would see a cop parked and waiting for him out there, too. He became suddenly convinced that he would find every exit from campus

267

blocked by campus police. Maybe the state cops from the barracks in Orono were on their way, too.

If that was the case, if someone had seen him and already reported what had happened, then he had to come up with an alternative — at least until he could check things out and see if there was anything going on.

"All right, all right," he muttered grimly as he considered an idea that had just hit him. Finally, he made up his mind that it was the best option for now. He turned around in the York Hall parking lot and headed back toward the center of campus. "We'll just have to find someplace else to stash you until I can see what the fuck's going on around here," he said.

Sarah looked at him, her eyes silently pleading.

Alan chuckled as he drove back to where tonight's adventure had all begun — the parking lot beside the Performing Arts Center. He doused his lights as he pulled to a stop close to the side entrance door to the Student Union, the one he used every afternoon to go to work. After scanning the area to make sure no one was in sight, he smoothed the tape across Sarah's mouth, got out of the car, and walked quickly to the door. His breath came in hot, rapid gulps in spite of the freezing night air. His hand was shaking as he slipped the pass key into the lock and turned it. Easing the door open as quietly as possible, he stuck his head inside.

Herb Snyder, the night watchman, had to be somewhere in the building, but Alan was counting on Herb to be either watching TV or — more likely, from what Herb had told Alan — sleeping on a couch in one of the study lounges. When he saw that the corridor was dark and empty, he left the door ajar and ran back out to the car.

Crouching low to stay out of sight, he swung open Sarah's door. She made strangled, muffled sounds that he took to be pleas for him to let her go, but Alan smiled wickedly, actually enjoying the hollow fear he knew she felt.

"Now you're gonna come along nice and quiet with me, aren't you?" he said. Before helping her out of the car to her feet, he took his knife and, holding it up close to Sarah's face, twisted it back and forth so the dull light of the streetlight

268

reflected from the honed blade. "You're gonna be real quiet. so I won't have to use this—"

Yet, he finished in his mind, but he didn't see any point in letting her know she wasn't going to survive this. Half the fun, besides finally getting even with her for getting away from him that night, was going to be watching the terror in her eyes, the constant grinding fear that she would have no idea if she would be alive the next minute. Goddamn, this was going to be *fun!*

"You're gonna behave, right?"

. Sarah nodded her head stiffly. Her legs nearly collapsed when she stood up. The cold air was a slap-in-the-face shock after sweating in Alan's warm car. Before she had her balance, he grabbed her around the waist and directed her toward the side entrance. Again, he eased the door open, checked the corridor, then quickly pulled her inside with him. As soon as they were through the door, he quietly shut it, making sure it was locked.

The corridor was illuminated only by the single red EXIT sign above the door as they started down the hallway. Sarah's mind flooded with fear as she wondered what—if anything— she should do. If Alan had gone this far to kidnap her and gag her, he wouldn't hesitate to use that knife on her. So for now, as frightened as she was, she had to cooperate with him, bide her time until she saw an opportunity to make a break.

Halfway down the corridor, Alan pulled her roughly to a stop and turned her to face a closed door. He searched his key ring until he found the right key, unlocked the door, and pulled the door open. Inside was as black as pitch.

"After you," Alan said, chuckling meanly as he pushed her into the dark room. She stumbled and fell to the floor. He came in right behind her and shut the door before snapping on the overhead light to reveal a large storage closet filled with mops, brooms, and buckets. A tall, metal utility shelf loaded with assorted equipment and bottles of cleaners divided the room roughly in half. The smell of industrial cleaners was almost overpowering.

Sarah lay there, unmoving as Alan went over to the utility

shelf and picked up a length of rope. Without a word, he came to her, lifted her to her feet, and jerked her hands behind her back. With a few deft loops and knots, he bound her wrists together, pulling the rope so hard bright jabs of pain shot up her shoulders. Once her hands were secure, he guided her over to a spot behind the shelving where there were three large wastebaskets. Without warning, he kicked her feet out from under her, catching her just before she hit the floor.

"You gotta understand—I have to take precautions," he whispered as he eased her onto her side. He looped the rope around her ankles and then pulled it up behind her back and tied it off around the rope binding her wrists. Trussed up like a rodeo calf with her back arched painfully and her shoulder joints burning from the backward pressure, Sarah wanted to scream, but the tape muffled any sound she made, pushing it back down her throat. Alan ignored her faint whimpers as he jerked the rope several more times to make sure she wouldn't be able to work the knots loose.

When the job was done, he stepped back and looked down at her with a mean smile twitching the corners of his mouth.

"There, you look nice and secure," he said softly. "Do you think you can be a nice girl and keep quiet for me? Huh?"

Sarah twitched her head back and forth, but no matter what he took it to mean, Alan shook his head with dissatisfaction.

"I didn't think so," Alan said.

Sitting down beside her, he placed one hand almost lovingly on her shoulder. With her back arched, her breasts stuck out temptingly; he couldn't resist the urge to run his hands over them, squeezing and mauling her. He closed his eyes and moaned with pleasure as his erection hardened.

"Oh, no nice . . . so firm . . ." he whispered.

He almost added, *Just like your mother's,* but didn't. After a while, he forced himself to stop before things went further. Before he could begin, he had to know if the cops were staked out to catch him. Maybe it had been coincidence that they had been out there. He told himself there would be plenty of time for whatever he wanted to do, later. For now he had to make absolutely sure she couldn't do anything to alert anyone who might pass by the janitor's closet before he got back.

"You know, I think you're right," he said as his frown deepened. "I can't trust you!" A horrible smile tightened his mouth. "You know exactly what this is all about, and I can't trust anything you say!"

Sarah's eyes widened with terror as she shook her head in vigorous, silent denial. This man was crazy! What he was doing to her was crazy! Why hadn't she trusted her instincts and listened to Elliott's advice? She should have had the cops watching this guy long before this could have happened!

Alan sneered as he slapped his fist several times into the flat of his hand, making a wet smacking sound. "But you ought to know by now that I can't trust a single thing you say. After all, you are one lying little bitch, aren't yah? Pretending you don't know who I am!" He snorted with laughter but then cut it off abruptly.

"You should be all right here for a little while," he said. He bent down and checked the ropes holding her before moving toward the door. Before he left, he turned to her again and said, "And don't worry. I'll be back before you know it. Don't try to get loose. You'll just exhaust yourself. And I don't think anyone would hear you even if you *could* scream."

He snapped off the light, plunging the room into thick darkness, then opened the door and went out. Sarah's heart did a cold flip in her chest when she heard the door lock click. She listened in agonized silence as Alan's footsteps receded. Once she was alone, with pain blazing along every nerve of her body, she cried. Tears flooded from her eyes, but the duct tape muffled every agonized sound she made.

— 3 —

The darkness was total, vibrating with shifting curtains of dark against dark. Not even a tiny sliver of light shined in under the edge of the closed door. Time and pain became an eternally long, dark tunnel for Sarah who, lost in a morass of agony and despair, lay still on the floor in the storage closet. Her bruised cheek was mashed against the linoleum floor, which was sticky with her tears and mucous. Her stomach muscles contracted painfully from her violent sobbing. The stinging smell of cleansers and other janitorial supplies along with her tears clogged her nose and throat. Unable to take a deep enough breath, she was terrified that she might suffocate or drown in her own fluids, but that fear was mitigated by the pure, stark terror of wondering when Alan would return and what he would do next. Lying in total darkness, she had no doubt that he would be back before anyone else could find her.

Why me? Why is he doing this to me?

The thought repeated in her mind until it became a terrifying endless echo in the night-black room. Several times she tried to loosen the ropes binding her, but as Alan had said, it was useless effort. And now . . .

How much later? she wondered. Every passing second felt like an hour . . . an eternity.

Her muscles trembled and burned with exhaustion; every nerve was on fire. One moment she felt as though she was dissolving in raging flames; the next moment, wave after crashing wave of arctic cold wracked her body.

Why me? Why is he doing this to me?

When she wasn't whimpering with fear, when her mind wasn't overloaded with horrifying certainties of what Alan intended to do to her, she tried to sort through her thoughts and figure out as calmly as possibly why this was happening. She racked her brain, trying to recall every detail of the two times they had spoken. That was all it had been, right? Just twice? What could she have said or done to set him off like this? If she could remember their conversations, she might find a clue that would explain it all, but she was so lost in terror that she couldn't focus on a single thought for long.

This couldn't all be happening simply because she had snubbed his advances, could it? No one — not even someone as obviously off-balance as Alan Griffin — could be crazy enough to take things to this extreme just because she wouldn't talk to him or go out on a date with him.

Alan Griffin did seem absolutely insane. She had seen that wild, crazy spark in his eyes, that twisted smile. And he was stark, raving mad to think he could kidnap her like this, bind and gag her, and keep her in a storage closet until he . . .

Until he . . . what? What does he plan to do with me?

From far away, so faintly, in fact, that it took a while for Sarah to realize she had heard it, a door opened and then slammed shut. The sound echoed in the hallway like rolling thunder; it made Sarah's ears ring as the receding echo dragged her back to awareness. She strained to lift her head and listen for the sound of approaching footsteps. At first, she heard nothing, then there came the soft *click-click* of shoes on linoleum. The sound rebounded down the corridor outside the closet.

Sucking air noisily in through her nose, she tried to make a sound—any sound that would reveal her presence here in the storage closet. The footsteps were steadily approaching the door. Was it another janitor? she wondered. Or maybe a night watchman? Or maybe it was . . .

Tully!

Oh, sweet Jesus, please be Tully! she thought, wishing her mouth was free so she could say his name out loud—just once.

Tully! Can you come to me now, Tully?

She tried desperately to remember how she was oriented in the room. What was there around her, unseen in the dark? Was there something she could knock over to draw attention to her? Maybe one of those three waste cans was close enough.

What if it isn't Tully? Sarah wondered as cold fear compressed her stomach. *What if he can't come to me anymore? What if it's Alan?*

Sarah doubled up and then, arching her back, kicked out as hard as she could against the restraints of the rope. She imagined herself an inchworm, twitching in agony on the linoleum, but all she accomplished was a painful bang of her head against the floor. Bright white stars exploded across her vision and then sucked back down into the total black of the storage closet. Without waiting for the bolt of pain to lessen, she tried again, thrashing her body back and forth, all the while listening for the moment the approaching footsteps were directly outside the storage room door.

Please . . . please hear me! she pleaded in her mind. Desperate words formed in her throat but were blocked by the strips of tape over her mouth. She twisted this way and that on the floor. Whenever she made contact with something—either the wall or the base of the storage shelves—she knew she didn't hit with enough force to make a loud enough noise. She knew, with a cold, dead certainty that no one was going to hear the soft scuffing sounds she was making, not through the closed, heavy door.

The footsteps paused outside in the hallway for a moment, then started again, coming closer. Sarah's mind filled with silent, shrill screams for help.

Tully or anyone! Please! Help me!

Tears sprang from her eyes and sweat bathed her face. The footsteps got closer, then stopped again, right outside the storage room door. Her breath was like acid in her lungs, longing to escape in a long, loud cry for help when she heard the doorknob jiggle from the outside. For an instant, a line of light appeared at the bottom of the door edge, but then, apparently satisfied that all was secure, the person outside continued moving down the hallway. The sound of footsteps receded and then was lost when another door opened and then slammed shut.

Sarah was certain her head was going to explode from the steadily building pressure of tension and agony. Someone—it had to have been the night watchman—had been out there, so close . . . so *close.* And now he was gone without even an inkling that, had he unlocked the closet door and looked inside, he would have found her.

He could have saved my life!

Deep muscle tremors rippled through her body after she ceased her efforts and lay still on the floor. Her shoulder joints and neck screamed with fiery pain, and the pressure at the small of her back felt as though her spine was about to snap.

If you're not going to come, Tully, then let me die, she pleaded. As hot tears ran down her face and into her mouth, her voice was a ragged scream inside her brain. *Please, Tully, come to me . . . And if you're not going to come, then just let me die! Right here! Right now!*

But Tully didn't come. As much as she willed him to be there with her, she knew she was alone in the room. She wanted to die rather than endure another minute of this torment, but the blackness didn't swallow her, not entirely. The darkness of the room shifted subtly, pulsating with hammering flashes of dull red light that kept time with her surging pulse, but neither Tully nor the relief of death would come.

What came, some indeterminate time later, was Alan Griffin.

Chapter Twenty

Gone Missing

— 1 —

The light blinded Sarah when Alan switched it on after locking the closet door behind him. She cringed, listening to him approach her, but couldn't open her eyes even after she knew he was kneeling down beside her. Her body twitched when one hand clasped her roughly by the shoulder. There was a rough jerking motion and a painful backward pull on her arms for a few moments; then a sudden release as the rope binding her hands to her feet let go. She stretched out, feeling the fiery rush of blood into her legs and arms. Her hands and feet were still tied, but at least she wasn't trussed up like a hog waiting for the slaughter.

"Hope you weren't too uncomfortable waiting for me here," Alan said, smiling grimly as he rolled her onto her back. Sarah narrowed her eyes open and looked at him but saw nothing more than a gauzy blur against the bright light.

"Didn't mean to take so long, but after I checked out what the cops were up to, I figured I'd better get back to my place and make sure I have everything we need. Picked up a little extra food." He leaned close to her, his sour breath cascading over her like water. "And don't get your hopes up. I drove right past two cop cars and they didn't even look at me, so I don't think they realize you're missing yet. So okay, are you ready for a little trip, or do you want to—"

His cut himself off as his eyes shifted down the length of her body. Stifled screams pressed against the tape across her mouth when he started tugging at her clothes. Before long, he had her coat and blouse open and her bra pushed up to her neck. He spent some time fondling her breasts, kneading them and licking the nipples until they were erect. Then he started to work to get her pants down. When it was obvious he wasn't going to get any farther with her feet tied, he quickly cut through the rope around her ankles, yanked off her pants and underwear, and sat back, letting his hands run lightly up and down her stomach and thighs.

"Umm, so pretty . . . so pretty," he said as he rubbed his hand over her crotch. "Nice . . . nice."

Sarah closed her eyes, silently begging for the darkness to return.

Alan made soft moaning sounds as his hand vigorously rubbed her. Then, without warning, he rolled her over, raised her onto her hands and knees, held her legs spread wide with his own knees, and thrust into her.

"Well what do you know!" he bellowed when he met some initial resistance. "A fuckin' virgin!" He snorted laughter as he thrust all the harder. "Been a while since I popped a cherry."

The pain was sudden and intense. Blood ran down her inner thighs, but Sarah was so far gone in misery that she barely noticed. She willed herself to sink deeper and deeper into the darkness of her mind, blocking out as much of this as she could while Alan pushed harder and harder against her, grunting with deep animal pleasure. By the time he shuddered and spent himself, Sarah was unconscious. She came to when she gradually became aware of him rolling her roughly from side to side as he tugged her clothes back on.

It was still dark when Alan dragged her back outside into the cold, predawn silence. Supporting her with his arm held tightly around her back, his hand snuggled into her armpit, he hustled her over to his parked car. She could see that it was a Mustang, but in the faint blue glow of streetlights along Flagstaff Road, she couldn't make out what color it was. The faint glow of dawn lined the trees with white light. The sight filled her with a dull ache of melancholy beneath her frenzy of fear.

"Took a little more time in there than I wanted to," Alan said with a frown. He glanced at his watch before he opened the passenger's door, swung the front seat forward, and pushed her, face first, onto the humped backseat. "Actually — I think I must've dozed off there a bit." He snickered softly and shook his head. "Too bad you passed out. You might have been able to get my knife and get loose while I was asleep." He sighed deeply and slapped his thighs. "Oh, well — you had your chance."

Sarah was still wearing her coat, but that didn't stop the wave of shivers that raced through her as she twisted her head around and looked up at him. Her face was crusty with dried tears and mucous, and it was difficult to breathe with her face squashed against the cold plastic seat.

"Well, I guess we're gonna take ourselves a little ride," Alan said almost cheerfully as he got into the car and started it up. He turned and smiled at Sarah, lying on the backseat. In an instant, his face hardened, and with a quick motion, he raised his knife up over the edge of the car seat.

"You must remember *this*," he said. His voice was as hard as the blade that reflected the dull light of the sky in the dark interior of the car. "And you're gonna behave so I won't have to use it, right?"

Sarah made a gagging noise in the back of her throat and twitched her head up and down in agreement.

"So you just lie there nice and quiet," Alan said. " 'Cause if you give me any trouble, I'll do to you what I did to —"

He stopped himself and let his grin widen all the more as he chuckled softly. He finished by simply saying, "Well, you know damned well what I'm talking about."

He lowered the knife out of sight before reaching into the backseat and lifting a dirty woolen blanket off the car floor. With one hand, he shook it out and spread it over her, covering her face. The smell of rotting fabric gagged Sarah as he rumpled the blanket so it wouldn't look quite so much like there was someone underneath it.

In the close darkness beneath the blanket, Sarah's silent screams filled her mind. Alan stepped down hard on the gas, revving the engine a few times before backing up. When he hit the brakes before shifting gears and starting forward, the force squashed Sarah hard against the backseat. As much as it hurt to do so, though, she wiggled onto her side and twisted her head so it poked out from under the blanket. Besides needing to catch a breath of fresh air, she wanted to try to get a glimpse out of the rear window, just in case she saw something that would help her figure out where he was headed.

Brightening gray sky, pine trees, and the sides of brick buildings all spun crazily around her as Alan negotiated several sharp curves in the road. The engine rumbled with a low droning sound as the car swayed back and forth. Before long, Sarah's sense of direction was totally confused. Nearly fainting from terror, she eased her head back down onto the seat and tried her best to hold back the tears.

Where is he taking me? What's he planning to do? And why—why didn't Tully come to me when I called him?

—2—

"Martha will be right down," the girl at the reception desk in Hancock Hall said, smiling as she looked at Michael over the top of her glasses. There was nothing in her expression to indicate that she thought anything was out of the ordinary, but Michael's first thought was — *Something's wrong.*

"Uh — yeah. Okay. Thanks," he said, feeling both confused and concerned as he walked over to the waiting area and sat down in one of the overstuffed chairs. He started idly flipping through an issue of *Rolling Stone,* but his brain didn't register anything he saw because of the dozens of panicked thoughts that were crowding his mind.

Had he been too forward with Sarah last night? He had tried his damndest simply to listen to her, to let her tell him whatever was bothering her; but it had taken immense effort to hold himself back, not to respond to Sarah as physically as he had wanted to. It was especially difficult in his car once they got back the dorm. He had desperately wanted her to come back to the fraternity with him. They had been dating each other exclusively for several months now, and he was feeling increasingly anxious — and disappointed — about their lack of physical relations. He thought he had restrained himself quite well, but maybe she had picked up on — and been scared off by — his obvious sexual needs.

Or maybe Sarah's psychological state was even more seriously off-balance than he realized. After telling him all about this invisible friend of hers — whom she honestly seemed to think was somehow real — maybe she had suffered some kind of nervous breakdown or something once she got back to her room. What if she was up there right now, crouching on the floor and whimpering, unable to say anything coherent? Or worse — what if her mind had completely snapped? What if she had *really* lost it and had to be hospitalized late last night?

As a light tingle of chills danced up the back of his neck, Michael thought that maybe he was right about Sarah wanting to break up with him. After some of the garbage he'd pulled lately, he couldn't really blame her. Maybe for the past few weeks, she had simply been trying to get her courage up to drop the bombshell today that she didn't want to go out with him anymore. Maybe she didn't dare face him just yet and was sending Martha down to do the dirty work. Would he be able to handle it if she admitted that she had the hots for someone else? What if it was Elliott Clark?

The sound of approaching footsteps drew Michael's attention. Looking up, he saw Martha, still dressed in her bathrobe and pajamas, walking toward him. When he saw the tight worry in her expression, a cold knot settled in his stomach as he stood up. He was expecting Martha to tell him Sarah didn't want to see him right now, but he forced a wide smile and friendly greeting.

"Hi, Marth—"

"Sarah didn't spend last night with you?" Martha asked. Her voice was high and thin, sharp with agitation.

Michael shrugged, letting the flats of his hands whack against his thighs. "I . . . well, no. She didn't. I dropped her off in front of the dorm a little after midnight," he replied. The cold tension inside him was growing steadily worse.

Martha glanced nervously over her shoulder and then shook her head with downcast eyes. "I haven't seen her since yesterday afternoon. She never came back to the room last night."

Michael took a deep breath, held it, then let it out in a shuddering burst. He was at a complete loss for words as the winding tension gripped him even tighter. *Where the hell is Sarah?*

"Did you see her come into the dorm?" Martha asked.

Michael shrugged, feeling like a specimen underneath Martha's steady, suspicious gaze. "Not really. I . . . I let her out of the car and—"

"You didn't walk her up to the door? You didn't make sure she went inside? Why's that? Did you two have an argument?"

Again, Michael shrugged helplessly. "No—we, uh, we had a pretty intense talk, and I think she wanted to be alone."

"Are you sure you didn't have an argument or something?" Martha asked. Each question was direct and pointed.

Michael stiffened, feeling a rush of anger as he looked steadily at Martha. Barely able to contain his hostility, he asked, "What the hell are you, the cops or something? I don't have to explain myself to you." It took an immense effort not to shout. "We didn't have a fight or anything, okay?"

Martha's mouth twisted with unspoken words as her eyes flickered back and forth, filling with tears. Her voice was broken when she said, "Jesus Christ, Michael—I'm really afraid something's happened to her!"

"Don't be ridiculous," Michael said, although he noticed that his own voice was trembling. "She just . . ." But he stopped because he honestly didn't know what else to say.

"Just didn't come home last night," Martha finished for him as tears tracked down her cheeks. Michael rushed over to her and enfolded her in his arms. Her body shook with sobs as he patted her reassuringly on the shoulder, but all the while he couldn't stop wondering—*Where in the name of Christ is Sarah?*

— 3 —

Elliott was dreaming. He was lying in the sun, facedown on a sandy beach. Although he had never been there, he had the vague idea he was in Jamaica. The sound of waves washing over the sand close to his ear sounded like ripping paper . . . or a snake, hissing. When the telephone rang, it came from far away with a tormented, bubbling sound as though it were ringing underwater. After several rings, the dream evaporated, and Elliott rolled over in his rumpled bed, fumbling blindly for the receiver.

"Yeah—hello," he said. His voice sounded as though his throat was still full of beach sand as he held the phone to his ear with one hand and ran the other hand over his eyes.

The mere touch of his hand to his head sent a spike of pain shooting through his forehead. He glanced around his bedroom, wondering when and how the hell he'd got into bed. He was still wearing the clothes he had on last night; they was stiff with dried vomit.

"Elliott—this is Phil Hunter."

It took a few seconds for the name to register, but then Elliott recalled that Phil was one of the part-time campus cops who worked the weekend shift.

"Uhh—yeah, Phil," Elliott said, his voice still sounding crusty. "What can I do for you?"

"I just got a call from someone who says he has to talk to you."

"He?" Elliott asked. He hiked himself up onto one elbow and opened his eyes a little bit more, allowing a dim view of his gloomy bedroom in spite of the pounding pain. Bright morning sunlight lined his windowsill. "Who is *he?*"

"Some college kid. Name of Michael Shulkin," Phil continued. "He insists he has to talk—"

"Shulkin?" Elliott said as he tried to sit up. The motion sent an even stronger wave of pain through his head. The sour churning in his stomach and the rotten aftertaste of vomit in the back of his throat brought back last night all too clearly. Before he could reprimand himself for drinking too much, though, the image of that thin, blond boy, sitting on the landing in the hallway, returned with striking clarity.

"Wha—what's this all about?" Elliott asked. His eyes shifted away from the window. Thick, black shadows still clung to the corners of his bedroom. His vision was still too unfocused to make out the digital readout on his alarm clock.

"He says his girlfriend—Sarah Lahikainen—is missing."

Phil's words were like a solidly placed punch in the gut as he sat bolt upright in bed.

"Missing?" he rasped.

"That's what he says."

"When did this all happen?" Elliott asked sharply. He was trying like hell to pull his attention to the surface, but the hangover was tenacious and kept trying to drag him under.

"He says he dropped her off at Hancock Hall last night, sometime after midnight. Her roommate . . ." The sound of rustling paper came over the telephone like a blazing fire. "Her name's Martha Lewis. She says she didn't see her roommate last night or this morning. I haven't notified the Orono police yet because—well, you know how these things can go. She may have gotten in after her roommate was asleep and then took off first thing this morning without telling anyone. I told him not to get so worked up, but he insisted on talking to you. What—do you know this guy or something?"

"No—the girl, Sarah. She's a friend of mine from back home."

"Oh," Phil replied, and left it at that.

"You got a number I can reach this guy at?" Elliott asked as he fumbled in the bed stand drawer for paper and pen. The pen he found didn't work, but he bore down hard enough on the paper to leave a deep impression of the number Phil gave him.

"You sound kind of out of it, Elliott. Is there something about this that you know and ought to be telling me?" Phil asked.

Before Elliott could answer, the memory of the blond boy on the landing last night, staring at him with those blank, lifeless eyes, filled him with a numbing tension.

What had he said? Elliott wondered as he fought back a gray rush of worry and mounting fear. He desperately wanted to believe that he had imagined seeing the boy there last night. There had been something so . . . so *odd*, so damn *spooky* about the kid that Elliott wanted desperately to convince himself that he couldn't have been there at all. But the boy's toneless voice, as though fading with the effort of each word, filled his memory—

284

"*Help her!* . . . *You must help her!* . . . *I can't! You were there that night. You have to help her. Can you . . . do it? Can you help her? . . . Please?*"

He shook his head vigorously and focused his attention on his conversation with Phil.

"No, I—uh, I just know Sarah, and something like this makes me a little worried. I want to make sure she's all right. Let me give this Shulkin guy a buzz, and I'll get back to you," he said.

"Probably just overreacting," Phil offered.

"Yeah—no doubt," Elliott said, but that didn't stop his hand from trembling as he hung up the phone and dialed the number for Michael Shulkin.

— 4 —

"You've got to tell me everything you remember from last night," Elliott said.

He and Michael were standing along the north side of Hancock Hall, between the dorm and the parking lot while Martha was upstairs, getting dressed. Sunlight reflected harshly off the snowy slope beside the dorm. It sent splinters of pain shooting through Elliott's head as he forced himself to ignore his hangover and write down everything Michael was telling him.

"I told you everything a dozen times already," Michael said. His voice was edged with frustration as he stood hunched against the cold in his gray and black fraternity jacket. He kept punching his gloved hands together in an attempt to keep warm. "Sarah and I went to the movies in Nutting Hall. After that, we spent an hour or so just talking in the Bear's Den. Then we drove back to the dorm, and I dropped her off." He paused long enough to rub the flat of his hand against his forehead. "But look at these tracks in the snow. Doesn't it look to you as though there were two people out here, and that . . . that *something* happened?"

285

For the dozenth time this morning, Elliott looked down at the marks in the snow. Most definitely, there was a clear impression where someone had obviously fallen down. The marks in the snow looked a bit like the snow angels he used to make as a child. Cutting down the sloping ground from the sidewalk to the side of the building was a trail that had obviously been made by a man's thick-soled boots. Right beside the yew bush, where someone could easily have been hiding, the tracks intersected the wandering line of smaller footprints that came around from behind the dormitory. The trail leading back to the sidewalk was marred by two lines that sure as hell looked as though someone had been dragging their feet—or been dragged. Elliott was no expert, but the imprints in the snow certainly indicated that there had been some kind of struggle out here.

"Yeah—so what? What makes you think this has anything to do with Sarah?" Elliott asked, finding it difficult to keep himself from overreacting.

Michael was silent, and his expression hardened as he stared blankly at the footprints in the snow.

"You say you didn't walk her up to the front door, is that right?" Elliott asked.

"Yes—for the tenth time, I didn't walk her up to the door. After we said good night, she got out and went up to the dorm by herself and I drove off."

"Why didn't you escort her to the door, though?" Elliott asked. "Did you have an argument or something?"

Michael bit down on his lower lip and shook his head tightly. "No! We didn't have any argument! Why does everyone think we had an argument?"

"What—did someone else ask you that same question?"

Michael exhaled heavily. "Yeah—Martha, Sarah's roommate asked me if we'd argued."

Elliott nodded as he jotted down a note. "Why would she suspect you and Sarah had argued?"

Michael blew his breath out in a *whoosh*. "Because we hadn't been . . . getting along all that great lately. Kind of

286

a little misunderstanding. That's all."

Don't let yourself hope, Elliott thought as he struggled to bring his attention fully to bear on the current situation.

"So what did you two talk about—you know, throughout the evening?"

"Oh, just stuff," Michael said with a tight shrug.

Elliott had the definite impression Michael was hiding something—something had happened last night that he didn't want to talk about. He stared at the boy until it was obvious he was getting uncomfortable.

"It was nothing important—nothing heavy, you know? Just small talk."

Elliott nodded slightly. "And when you dropped her off, did you just drop her off and leave, or did you sit out here awhile and talk awhile longer?"

Michael shrugged tensely. "I already told you that, too. We parked out in front of the dorm for a little while. Not long."

"How long?"

"Jesus Christ! An hour, tops, okay?" Michael said tightly.

"Did you say anything or do anything that might have upset her?"

Michael silently shook his head in denial as he took a shuddering breath.

"I mean," Elliott went on, pressing the point, "you didn't come on strong to her or anything, did you? You know, something like that might have scared her."

"I don't see where that's any of your goddamned business, all right?" Michael shouted. His face infused with blood, and his hands curled into fists.

Elliott gritted his teeth and smiled in spite of his throbbing headache. It took effort not to let his true feelings for Sarah show. Jabbing the tip of his pen at Michael, he said, "Look here, pal, *you* called *me* into this, all right? I'm not even on duty today, much less a fucking detective. I'd just as soon be back home sleeping late. If you're so damned positive something's happened to Sarah, why don't you get

287

your ass over to the Orono police station and file a missing persons report?"

Michael's shoulders dropped a bit, and his tense expression softened.

"I called you," he said, "because I know you and Sarah are friends." For an instant, he considered asking Elliott just exactly how *friendly* they might be, but he quickly realized that this was neither the time nor the place.

"Yeah," Elliott said, nodding. "Sarah and I are friends." Even as he said her name, he tried to deny the warm feeling that welled up inside of him.

"You must help her! I can't!"

The blond boy's voice echoed faintly in Elliott's memory, sending a rush of chills up his spine.

Maybe he just wasn't thinking straight, standing out here in the glaring winter sun after drinking so much last night. He was still too hung over to think clearly.

"You were there that night. You have to help her!"

He was about to ask Michael something when Martha came outside and joined them. Her expression was strained and tense as she looked back and forth between Michael and Elliott. She opened her mouth, as if about to say something, but then remained quiet.

"Look," Elliott said, lowering his voice as he glanced back and forth between them. "I think you're both probably overreacting to this. I honestly do. Sarah's no child. She probably just took off early this morning to go do something with a friend or whatever."

"She never mentioned anything to me," Martha said, shaking her head.

"Me neither," Michael added quickly. "That's why I came by this morning; we had plans to go out for lunch and then go to the Bangor Mall this afternoon."

Elliott took a deep breath and let it out slowly. It misted in the frigid air and wreathed his head like thin cigarette smoke. His gaze shifted over to the rounded impression in the snow beside the yew bush and the double trail that went up to the sidewalk. He wanted to believe this had absolutely nothing to do with Sarah, but a faint, echoing voice in his mind said otherwise.

"You have to help her. Can you . . . do it?" He was about to say something, but then another thought hit him, so hard he winced and had to press both hands against his forehead.

Alan . . . Alan Griffin! Sarah said that asshole had been bugging her. What if he's . . . done something?

"Uh—yeah, okay," Elliott said, straightening his shoulders and hoping to hell his voice didn't betray how nervous that thought made him. "Let's say we all go to the office and fill out a report on this. We can have a File 6 out on the teletype within twenty-four hours."

"That long?" Michael asked.

"That's the way it has to go," Elliott said. "If she turns up before then, all well and good. What I'm going to need from you is a complete description of what she was wearing last night. And do either of you have a photograph of her?"

Michael shook his head, but Martha said she probably could find one in Sarah's things in their room.

"I hope you're wrong about this," Elliott said as the three of them started over to his car, which he had left parked in the circle driveway in front of the dorm. He was hoping that nothing had happened to Sarah, but that didn't silence the faint voice whispering in his mind.

"Can you help her? . . . Please?"

Chapter Twenty-one

Pushaw

— 1 —

All Sarah knew was shame, humiliation, and the suffocating terror of being bound and gagged, lying on her side under a smelly woolen blanket in the backseat of Alan's car. Drifting in and out of consciousness after her ordeal in the storage closet, she had no idea how long they had been driving—it could have been ten minutes or ten hours. Soon enough, she gave up trying to figure out where Alan was taking her. What did it matter? After what he had done to her, she might just as well die. Whenever the word *rape* came to mind, she tried desperately to block it out, but tears poured from her eyes anyway. She now knew what her mother had gone through, and she *wanted* to die.

Early morning sunlight, surprisingly warm, poured in through the rear window and soon turned the backseat into an inferno. She realized that since the sun was behind them this early in the morning, then they must be traveling roughly due west. But she had no idea where they were in relation to Orono or Bangor; Alan could be driving around in circles for all she knew.

The bruise on her left cheek chaffed against the seat. The wool blanket made her skin itch maddeningly. After having the duct tape across her mouth for so long and not suffocating, Sarah's fear of dying that way began to subside. Her shoulders and arms were numb from having her hands tied behind her back for so long, but she was resigned. Through wave after wave of terrifying thoughts that filled her mind, it was clear that Alan was bringing her somewhere so he could abuse her again . . . or else get rid of her.

He's going to kill me! she kept thinking. *No matter what else he has in mind, eventually he's going to have to kill me; so please — just make sure it's quick and painless. I don't want to have to go through what Mom went through.*

The possibility of escape seemed so distant, so vague; what was the point of even wanting to live if Alan was going to do to her over and over again what he had done to her last night? She knew she should try to clear her mind as much as possible so she could see — and take — whatever opportunity to escape presented itself, no matter how slim, but in body and mind, she was already defeated.

From time to time as he drove, Alan looked back at her, making sure her face was still covered by the blanket. Whenever he saw that she had poked her head out, he would quickly cover her back up, muttering angry threats about what he would do to her the instant he was pulled over by the cops. He played the radio at full volume, blasting an endless string of rock 'n' roll from WOOZ. On some songs, he sang along with a raw croak in his voice. He chain-smoked cigarettes, filling the car with a choking blue cloud, but Sarah was too far gone in misery to notice or care.

The heat of the sun bearing down on her constantly shifted from one window to another as he took far too many left and right turns to count. After a while, the road got rougher and more curving. Sarah was tossed about back and forth on the car seat and almost rolled onto the floor several times as Alan drove a bit too fast for the terrible condition of whatever road they were on. The exhaust pipe rattled on the chassis underneath her ear with each teeth-crunching bump the car took.

"We'll find someplace to stop soon enough," Alan said. His voice sounded chipper and bright, as if he were out on a joyride with a friend and had the entire day planned out. "You must have to go to the bathroom *real* bad by now, huh? You ain't wet yourself or anything, have you?" He chuckled softly under his breath, and Sarah was completely confused when he added, " 'Cause in a way, that's how this whole damned thing got started, isn't it, with you having to go the bathroom?"

His mean-sounding laughter rose higher, taking hold of Sarah's nerves and twisting them unrelentingly. But the truth was, she felt numbed, as though she didn't have any nerves or muscles left. Alan had kidnapped her a little after midnight so, although in ways it felt like so much longer, they couldn't have been driving more than a hour or so. It was probably eight or nine o'clock in the morning, so she had been with him no more than eight hours. And in all that time, she hadn't felt the slightest urge to go to the bathroom or even the least bit hungry. She wondered if this meant her subconscious mind had already given up any hope of her ever getting out of this alive. Was her body already shutting down? Was her brain instructing her body not to waste any more energy with simple daily routines? Was she getting ready to die? The thought sent a subtle chill through her, but maybe she was already as good as dead.

"We can find ourselves a place out here where we can stay for a day or two," Alan said as the car thumped down a rutted dirt road. "At least until we figure out where to go from here. We've got so many options."

In spite of her terror and exhaustion, what he had just said gave Sarah a faint spark of hope. Either he was too tired to guard his words, or else he was just plain stupid. He had just let slip that he *didn't* have a detailed plan; he wasn't sure what he was going to do next. However he had gotten to this point, she knew now that he was winging it from here on out. As long as Alan didn't flip out and kill her right off, that meant there might be an opportunity to do something to get away.

As frightened as she was, she would have to stay sharp and alert so she could take the advantage of any opportunity that came. So even as she sweated and cried in the smothering darkness of the blanket, Sarah began to see the faintest glimmer of hope in the dark recesses of her mind. At some point, that hope turned into a name . . .

Tully.

— 2 —

The car jolted to a stop. Alan cut the engine and got out, slamming the door hard behind him. Trembling, Sarah listened to the *crunch-crunch* of his feet on packed snow as he walked around to the back of the car and opened the trunk. Faintly, like the sizzle of distant fire, she heard the crinkling of paper and realized he was taking several paper bags out of the trunk. After he shut the trunk lid, she heard his footsteps move away from the car. She was alone in the cold, dead silence.

As soon as Alan's footsteps had faded, Sarah started to struggle with the ropes binding her hands behind her back. The cuffs of her winter coat were peeled back, no protection at all from rope burn on her bare wrists. Fighting to ignore the pain, she wiggled and twisted her hands to free them; but the pressure of her body wedged against the backseat impeded even the smallest movements. The heat beneath the blanket was stultifying. Sweat broke out over her face and dripped down, stinging her eyes and the abrasion on her cheek.

Like a contortionist, Sarah tried every possible movement. Gritting her teeth, she arched her back and raised her knees to her chest in an attempt to work her hands under her butt so she could bring her arms around to the front. But she knew, even if she managed to do that, her mouth was covered with tape, so she wouldn't have been able to undo the knots with her teeth. She grunted and strained with the effort until her shoulders felt as if they were going to pop out of their sockets and the small of her back was going to crack, but she couldn't get her hands past her butt. Her fingertips clawed frantically against the thick knots at her wrists, but she couldn't find the end of the rope even to begin working it loose. She rubbed her face against the car seat, trying to roll the duct tape down off her mouth so she could at least take one clean, deep breath of air, but even that was futile. All she managed to do was exhaust herself. The sticky tape pulled back hard on her hair, bringing fresh tears of pain to her eyes.

Every joint and muscle in her body was screaming from her efforts; but just like the time she had spent in the storage closet, it was all for nothing. Finally, she collapsed back onto the seat, panting heavily and bathed with sweat as she focused on the sunlight, shining through the worn blanket.

"Hey, don't stop now! It looks like you're having one *hell* of a time."

The suddenness of Alan's voice made Sarah grunt with surprise. Lint from the blanket scratched her eyes as she looked frantically around for some sign of him. She heard the car door open and the backseat click as Alan pushed it forward. Lifting a corner of the blanket, he looked down at her and roared with cruel laughter.

"Come on! Don't stop for me! Go ahead. See if you can get loose."

The sudden blast of direct sunlight burned Sarah's eyes. Alan was nothing more that a watery, black blur, looming over her like a huge, gaping mouth about to swallow her whole.

"Well," Alan said with a quick glance over his shoulder. "I guess there's no one around. What say we take ourselves a little walk?"

He grunted as he lifted her from the backseat and swung her bound feet down to the car floor before dragging her

294

out into the cold morning air. After getting so hot under the blanket for so long, Sarah shivered wildly from the chill. Her nostrils flared as she greedily sucked in the numbingly cold air.

"You know, you were really cracking me up there in the car," Alan said, shaking his head as he chuckled softly. "The way you were twisting under that blanket, you looked like a bunch of kittens in a sack." He eased his arm around her waist and guided her backward until she was leaning against the side of the car. Then, with a rough shove, he pushed her so she was lying flat across the car hood.

Sarah blinked rapidly, trying to stop the shooting pain of the dazzling sunlight in her eyes. Everything was blinding white with indistinct moving black shadows. She heard as much as saw Alan take his knife and start sawing through the ropes that bound her feet. Even before she felt the restraint around her legs loosen, she considered rearing back, kicking him in the face, and making a run for it. But she knew — with her hands still tied — she wouldn't get far unless she knocked him out or killed him. He'd run her down and kill her on the spot.

Could I do that? she wondered as she looked down at him, kneeling in front of her. *When the time comes, and I have to do it, will I be able to kill him?*

Right now, she knew she wouldn't accomplish anything more than getting him angry as hell at her, so she just lay back until he was done. Once her legs were free, he yanked her back to her feet. He picked up the rope from the snow and tossed it into the car, swung the car door shut, and then, gripping her tightly by the upper arm, guided her down a narrow, shoveled pathway. Her leg buckled beneath her, and she almost fell.

"Jesus Christ, walk! I sure as hell ain't gonna carry you!"

As Sarah moved slowly along beside him, her vision adjusted to the daylight. She looked around, trying to figure out where they were. Alan's car was parked in a short driveway alongside a single-lane dirt road. Snow was piled up head-high on both sides of the road, and the car was positioned behind the plow ridge so it couldn't be spotted from the road. Sarah was surprised by the amount of snow; there was a lot more here than there was back on campus. She wondered how much farther north they could have gotten in the short time they were on the road.

As her vision cleared, she saw that they were in the forest. Tall pine trees, harsh black lines towering against the brilliant blue of the sky, surrounded them. A gentle breeze hissed high up in the branches. A hundred yards or so down a steep slope was a small snow-covered cabin — someone's summer camp, no doubt, now boarded-up for the winter. Beyond the camp was the wide, white expanse of a frozen lake or pond. There were no other buildings in sight except far out on the lake, where Sarah could see several small dark rectangles — ice-fishing houses.

As they made their own path through the snow down to the camp, Alan glanced at her and said, "Pretty out here, ain't it? Nice and peaceful." His face was horrifyingly close, and his breath had a sickly sour smell that washed warmly over Sarah. "And you know, if you're a good girl, I may even take that tape off your mouth later 'cause sure as shit ain't no one gonna hear you if you scream."

We'll just have to see about that, Sarah thought, trying to guess how far a shout would carry in such quiet isolation. Maybe all the way out to those fishing houses, and maybe there'd be someone out there to hear her, too, if she was lucky.

For now, she kept her eyes completely blank and expressionless, her body limp and cooperative as Alan directed her down to the cabin. As defeated and intimidated as she was, she wanted to give him the impression that she had given up completely, that she wasn't going to be any trouble to him at all. The whole time, though, she was studying her surroundings, hoping to see a possible escape route.

At least three feet of snow covered the camp's roof. The

296

snow on the ground looked deeper, maybe four or five feet deep. The walkway leading to the door was nothing more than an indistinct indentation in the snow. It was obvious no one had been out here, at least not since the most recent blizzard. The owners must have come out to clear a path and shovel off the roof so the weight wouldn't cave it in.

When would that have been? Sarah wondered, trying to remember the last time it had snowed. At least three weeks ago. She remembered Michael and some of the other Sig Eps complaining about not being able to go skiing since semester break.

Once they were at the door, Alan pushed Sarah to one side. Leaning close to the door window, he peered inside, his breath fogging the icy glass.

"Looks nice and homey," he said, glancing at her over his shoulder. Without another word, he raised his gloved fist and punched the window with a single, quick jab. The cold glass broke cleanly and fell to the floor inside, leaving a fist-sized hole through which Alan reached inside, clicked the lock, and swung the door open.

"Ladies first," he said. Without warning, he grabbed her arm, spun her around, and pushed her into the entryway. Her legs, still numb from being tied up, wouldn't work right, and she tripped. Without her arms free to help keep her balance, she couldn't stop herself from falling. She landed on her side on the cold linoleum floor. The impact knocked the wind out of her and sent a flash of white light across her vision.

"Clumsy little bitch, ain't you?" Alan said, laughing as he entered the camp behind her and bent to help her to her feet. Still dazed, Sarah shook her head as she stood up on legs that felt like soggy spaghetti.

Thick, dark gloom filled the silent camp, an atmosphere heavy with the nostalgia of long-gone summers and summer fun. Alan directed Sarah through the crude kitchen into what passed for a living room. Their snow-covered

297

boots made soft crunching sounds on the threadbare carpet. In the center of the small room, a large, overstuffed couch and two upholstered chairs circled a battered wagon wheel coffee table covered with an array of outdated magazines and an ashtray, still full of last summer's cigarette butts. On the wall above the stone fireplace, the dull-eyed gaze of a dust-covered stuffed moose head stared down at them. Everything—the floor, the furniture, and the walls— had a coat of dust. Whoever owned this place certainly didn't spend much time doing housekeeping. The only brightness was the view from the front picture window of the flat expanse of snow out on the lake.

"Yeah, this will do just fine for a bit," Alan said, placing his hands on his hips and nodding with satisfaction as he surveyed the place. "What do you think?"

He looked at Sarah expectantly, then scowled when he saw her regarding him with a steady, emotionless stare. She wanted to scream at him, pour a string of curses out onto him, but the tightly wrapped duct tape forced her words back into her throat.

"Well, I've got to get a few more things from the car," Alan said. "Why don't you make yourself comfortable right here." Again, without warning, he gave her a quick push. Sarah tried to scream but couldn't as she fell backward. She bounced off the couch cushions and then fell forward, banging her bruised cheek against the edge of the coffee table before hitting the floor. Alan regarded her with a twisted smirk as he came over to her. Holding his knife loosely in his right hand, he knelt down beside her, cupped the back of her head with one hand, his fingers twining in her hair as he lifted her head, exposing her bare throat.

He's going to do it! Sarah's mind screamed as she stared in horror at the razor-sharp blade. *Go ahead! Do it! Kill me now!*

Holding her hair tightly and pinning her to the floor with one knee, Alan brought the tip of the knife up close to Sarah's face. She watched him, wide-eyed and unblinking,

298

as the point lowered and nicked her lightly on the neck, just below her jaw. The blade touched her skin like a hot spark. She snorted a breath in through her nose and held it, whimpering softly as she closed her eyes and waited for him to lay her throat wide open.

But the pain never came. The edge of the knife rubbed against her skin as Alan worked it up underneath the layer of duct tape. Once he had a corner of it, he ripped it viciously aside, taking a layer of skin with it. Relief and fiery pain flooded Sarah when she realized that her mouth was free, and she took a deep, roaring breath.

"I don't want to have to use this shit again," he said, dangling the strip of tape in front of her face, "but I will if I have to." Still supporting her head, he brought his face so close to hers their noses almost touched. Sarah was terrified that he was going to kiss her. "But you're gonna stay nice and quiet, aren't you?"

Sarah's lips tingled with the fresh flow of blood rushing into them. She licked them and managed to croak, "Yeah."

"That's good," Alan said, nodding. "That's real fucking good." He let go of her so suddenly her head fell back, bumping hard against the floor. Bright sparks shot across her vision in a dizzying swirl.

Alan stood up, crumpled the duct tape into a tight ball, and tossed it onto the floor beside her where she lay. Without another word, he snorted with laughter, turned, and left the cabin.

—3—

Completely drained, Sarah was incapable of processing the black fear that crashed inside her. Still dazed by the blow to the back of her head and the sudden freedom of having the tape removed from her mouth, she just lay there, looking up dimly at the cabin walls. She wasn't even sure if she remained conscious. Feeble sunlight managed to enter the camp, but it was about the same intensity as when they had entered; so if she had passed out, it couldn't have been for long. The bottom line was, it really didn't matter — nothing mattered. Alan was gone right now, but he would be back. Her heart went cold when she thought about what he might do to her then.

Scorching waves of pain swept through her as she rolled her head from side to side, glorying in her ability to open her mouth and take a breath unhindered. She had a vague interest in what was around her, but from the floor, the best view she had was of the clots of dust, cigarette ashes and butts, and the other traces of garbage that littered the floor under the couch and coffee table. A stale, moldy aroma from either the couch or the rug nearly choked her, but she didn't mind because she was so grateful that her mouth was free.

Whimpering deep in her throat and licking her lips to moisten them, she rolled over from her back to her side and then hiked herself up on her elbows. Every joint and muscle screamed in agony as she tried to sit up and look around the silent cabin. A distant, dull ache in the pit of her stomach told her she needed food. Judging by the slanting sunlight, she guessed it was either late morning or early afternoon, which meant it had been at least twelve hours since she had that Coke with Michael in the Bear's Den. All of that seemed so long ago now, as if it had been another lifetime.

And where is Michael now? Sarah wondered. Did he realize she was missing? Would he even guess that she had been kidnapped? Or would he assume, reasonably enough, that she had forgotten about their plans and had gone off somewhere else for the day.

When would he — or someone — first miss her? When would Michael or Martha or anyone else realize that she was gone and she wasn't coming back? When would someone guess that she was in trouble? How would anyone know? How about her father? He was so busy with his own life, it would be days or weeks before he suspected some-

300

thing was wrong.

Tully.

The name sprang into her mind as clearly as if someone had spoken it close to her ear. Sarah's eyes widened with shock as she struggled to get up off the floor. By hitching her still numb legs to one side and levering her weight with her shoulder, she finally managed to get into a sitting position with her back against the couch. Her breathing came in hot, ragged gulps through her open mouth as she looked frantically around the cabin, desperately hoping to see his smiling face, watching her.

"Jesus Christ, Tully," she whispered, closing her eyes and letting her head drop back in complete exhaustion. Shivers raced through her body the instant she said his name aloud. A moment later, her eyes snapped open and she sat up stiffly. She had the uncanny sensation that someone was behind her, watching her. She turned to the doorway, thoroughly expecting to see Tully standing there . . . or else Alan, watching her with a hate-filled stare.

But she saw no one.

She tried to convince herself that she was alone in the cabin, but the feeling wouldn't go away. No matter where she turned, she felt as though the unseen presence shifted out of sight.

"Tully, is that . . ." she said, her voice cracking with desperate pleading. "Come on, Tully! If I ever needed you, it's now! Help me!"

". . . can't . . ."

The word entered her mind with the silence of a thought.

"Tully . . . *please*," she whispered.

". . . don't . . . want me . . ."

Was that really a voice, Sarah wondered, or was she imagining things? She turned around expectantly, but what she had been about to say faded away when she saw no one there, nothing except for a shifting, gauzy shadow on the wall above the couch. Light reflecting off the snow outside

301

was throwing a dark shadow that rippled like thin smoke. Sarah stared at the blot of darkness for a moment, then looked away. As soon as she let her focus shift, the shadow disappeared entirely. As if for the first time, she noticed the framed map, hanging on the wall above the couch. Beneath the glass, the paper was yellowed with age, but she could clearly read the antique scroll legend at the bottom of the map. The owner of the camp had put a small red X on the map at the north end of the lake near the end of a road marked Hudson Landing Road.

"Pushaw Lake," Sarah said, smiling as she said the name aloud. "Okay. All right. At least I know where I am." She had never heard of the lake before, but the map showed that it was on the western edge of Old Town, near an area designated as Caribou Bog. She couldn't tell the scale, but it looked like she was only a short distance from campus, certainly no more than a few miles.

Why, she wondered, would Alan take her here, so close to where she had been kidnapped? Wouldn't it make more sense to hightail it as far away from Orono as possible? But at least she had some idea where she was. That was a start.

She looked around the camp, not daring to hope that there was a telephone. Even if there was one, she was positive it would have been disconnected for the winter. No one would want anyone breaking into their summer camp and racking up hundreds of dollars' worth of long-distance phone calls along with trashing the place.

Sarah's eyes darted back and forth around the room, seeking something — *anything* that might provide her with a means of escape. At last, her gaze landed on the dirty ashtray on the coffee table. It was made of thick, green glass. If she could get a hold on it and break it on the table leg or something, maybe she could use a sharp edge to cut through the ropes binding her hands before Alan came back.

Without waiting to consider it further, she leaned back, placed her feet on the underside of the table, and kicked upward. A few magazines shifted and slid onto the floor, and the motion made the ashtray jump, but it didn't fall. Gritting her teeth with the effort, she kicked the table a second time, harder. She smiled triumphantly when the ashtray hit the carpeted floor with a heavy *thump*.

"All right, now," she whispered as she twisted around and, moving like an inch worm, wiggled across the floor to retrieve the ashtray. When she was up close to it, she twisted around and felt for it blindly with her tied hands. Her heart leapt up into her throat when her fingers curled around the smooth glass edge.

"Careful now," she cautioned herself. "Take it easy now."

Gripping the ashtray with both hands, she got up onto her knees, turned her back to the table, and started banging the ashtray as hard as she could against the table edge. Her fingers were slippery with sweat, and she almost lost her grip as the heavy glass rebounded time and again with a dull *clunk* against the wood. Every joint in her fingers was aching from the tight grip she had to maintain, but she repositioned her back toward the table and again started whamming the ashtray as hard as she could against the table top. But try as she might, with her hands bound, she couldn't generate enough force to break the glass. Finally, exhausted, she released the tension in her shoulders, slouched forward, and let the ashtray drop to the floor.

She looked frantically around the camp and out all the windows to see if Alan had heard the commotion she was making. He was nowhere in sight, but instead of feeling relieved, she began to wonder if something had happened to him. Where could he be? Shouldn't he have come back by now? He'd been gone at least half an hour, maybe longer. She tried to resist the hope that someone had already discovered that they had broken into the camp . . . or that he had slipped on some ice and been knocked unconscious.

With renewed hope, Sarah picked up the ashtray again. It took immense effort, but she finally managed to slide her legs under her butt and shift her weight forward up onto her knees. If she could stand up and drop the ashtray onto the table, it might break. Just as she was pitching her weight forward, though, she heard the camp door open. With a rush of fear, she looked over her shoulder toward the doorway.

"So how you doin' in—"

Alan let his voice drop off the instant he saw her poised halfway to her feet, the ashtray in her hands behind her back. He dropped the two rolled-up sleeping bags and overnight bag he was carrying as he stared at her in amazement. Then his face clouded over with a dark scowl, and he started toward her with clenched fists.

"And just what the *fuck* do you think you're doing?" he shouted, his face turning a deep red.

"I was . . . was just . . ." Sarah stammered, but she fell silent, knowing she had no reasonable excuse.

"You were just trying to what? Cut the rope, perhaps? Get loose, maybe?"

A cold tightening gripped Sarah's stomach. Again, she had the unnerving sensation of being watched from behind, but she didn't dare look away as Alan came up to her. Reaching behind her back, he took the ashtray out of her numbed hands.

"How fucking *stupid* do you think I am?" he shouted. Spittle flew from his mouth, and his eyes widened with anger. He raised one hand threateningly, but then let it drop. Sarah shied away from him, but before she could say anything, he spun around on his heel and flung the ashtray at the fireplace. It hit inside the hearth and exploded into hundreds of tiny green fragments.

"There! Are you satisfied?" he shrieked as he clenched his fists and shook them dangerously close to her face.

"These ropes are cutting off the circulation to my hands. It really hurts," Sarah said. She found it unnecessary to keep the panicky edge out of her voice as she looked past him and stared almost wistfully at the sharp fragments of glass scattered inside the fireplace. Tears filled her eyes, and she took a deep, hitching breath. "You—you don't have to keep me tied up like this," she went on, lowering her voice. "Where do you think I'm going to go anyway? I—I don't even know where we are, other than in the middle of nowhere. Take these ropes off so I won't hurt as much and I'll—" Her throat caught and she had to swallow hard before continuing with a husky rasp in her voice. "I'll do whatever you want me to do," she finished, casting her eyes to the floor.

"You'll do whatever I want you to no matter *what!*" Alan shouted. "And don't talk to me about your hands hurting!" He clenched his fists and shook them close to her face. "I'll tell you about hurt!" He looked at her coldly and shook his head, his upper lip curling with disgust. "It's obvious I can't trust you, but I guess it figures! You're nothing but a sneaky, lying little bitch! But I'll tell you this! You're not gonna get away from me . . . oh no. Not *this* time."

Before Sarah could react, he cocked his arm back and threw a punch at her face. In the split second she saw his fist rushing toward her, she tried to scream but was cut off by a bright explosion of pain. She was only half-conscious as she fell and hit the floor. She feverishly prayed for total unconsciousness when she felt him pin her down to the floor, hastily work her pants down to her ankles, and then unbuckle his own jeans.

Chapter Twenty-two

The Bean Can

— 1 —

"I don't know what the hell else you expect me to do," Elliott said, sighing deeply. It was early afternoon, and he and Michael were seated across from each other in a booth upstairs at Pat's Pizza. Elliott was almost finished with his second beer while Michael's first one sat in front of him, barely tasted and going flat. From downstairs, the noise of a rowdy Saturday afternoon crowd watching a hockey game thumped and echoed through the floor.

"I don't know what I expect you to do either," Michael said. His voice trembled with fear and frustration. Squeezing his eyes shut for a moment, he flopped back in his seat and gripped his forehead with both hands as if his head were about to explode. "You're the cop. I don't know how you guys handle these things."

Elliott sighed again. His own sense of increasing frustration gripped his heart like a cold hand squeezing ever tighter.

"Look, Mike," Elliott said softly, "as far as I know, every law officer in the area is doing everything they can — at least up to this point." He paused and took a deep gulp of beer, deciding not to mention that earlier that day, he had

306

spoken with the captain of the Orono police and had given him Alan Griffin's name as a possible suspect. "Until we know — for certain — that she's been hurt or kidnapped, they're assuming she just took off somewhere without telling anyone where she was going."

"But that isn't like her," Michael said, narrowing his gaze at Elliott. "She isn't going to just take off like that. Where's she going to go? Have the police checked to see if she went home?"

Elliott shrugged. "Sorry, they haven't filled me in on what — if anything — they're doing. Do you think it'd be a smart idea to call her father and ask if she's shown up?"

It was Michael's turn to shrug.

"Well, I don't see any point in getting him worried if, in fact, nothing's happened."

Michael shook his fists in frustration. "But that's just it! I *know* someone's done something to her."

"And how do you know that for sure?" Elliott asked, watching Michael's reaction closely and all the while thinking that he, too, knew it. He was willing to lay a sizable wager that Alan Griffin was somehow mixed up in all of this. Of course, when he had given Alan's name to the authorities, they had reacted just as he would have if he were on the police force: he had to admit to them that he had no basis for suspecting Alan other than a hunch. His experience in police work told him just how damned feeble a *hunch* was at initiating an official investigation.

"I just know it." Michael said.

Elliott's police instincts told him that Michael probably didn't have anything to do with Sarah's disappearance, but he also knew from personal experience that you never eliminated anyone from suspicion. If Sarah didn't show up in a day or two, and the police became convinced there had been some kind of foul play, Michael was going end up as the prime suspect.

"I *know* Sarah, all right?" Michael said sharply. He banged a fist onto the table, almost knocking over the

307

glasses of beer. "I know she wouldn't do something like this, all right?"

Elliott ran his fingers through his hair and considered. As little as he knew Sarah, he guessed that what Michael was saying was true. The faint voice of that blond kid whispered in the back of his mind, convincing him that something bad had happened to Sarah.

"Help her! You must help her!"

"Look, Mike, there's a File Six out on the wires now with a complete description of her," Elliott said. It took effort for him to keep his voice steady. "Every police unit in the state—in New England—has been notified. And if no one else follows up on this, I'll get on the phone myself to the FBI."

"And exactly how much attention is something like this going to get?" Michael snapped.

Elliott smirked. "You know damned well it won't get much because we haven't clearly established that there's been any kind of trouble."

"Bullshit! You don't think those footprints in the snow out beside the dorm looked suspicious?"

Elliott shrugged. "There are experts who are checking those out. Those tracks probably have nothing to do with Sarah. And anyway, you seem to be forgetting that I can't do a whole hell of a lot as it is. I'm just a campus cop, for Christ's sake, not the God-all-mighty FBI!"

"You mean to tell me you aren't worried about what might have happened to Sarah?" Michael asked.

His steady gaze unnerved Elliott, who was forced to look down at his own hands folded around his beer glass. Through his concern and worry for Sarah, the memory of that blond boy, staring at him with unblinking eyes, wouldn't stop playing in his mind. The boy's thin, bloodless lips formed words . . . words that seemed to come, not from his mouth, but from the surrounding darkness that filled the stairwell.

"I can't! . . . She doesn't want me! . . . You must help her!"

After taking a deep breath and holding it, Elliott said softly, "Of course I'm concerned." Sweat broke out on his brow in spite of the cool breeze that wafted over their table whenever someone came or went by the restaurant's back door. He wanted to take another sip of beer, but the sour twisting in his stomach was getting steadily worse. "But my hands are tied."

"Bullshit!"

"Is there anyone else on campus that Sarah knows?" Elliott asked. "Anyone she might contact if something was wrong?" The question didn't sound at all casual; his voice was wire-tight.

Michael looked at him and shrugged. "She hasn't made all that many friends, if that's what you mean. She's pretty withdrawn most of the time, you know. I think a lot of it has to do with— well, you know all about what happened to her mother and all."

The blond boy's voice whispered in Elliott's mind— *"You were there that night . . . I saw you there!"* The voice was so clear, Elliott was positive the boy must be sitting in the booth behind him, leaning over the back of the chair and whispering into his ear. He shifted uncomfortably in his seat and glanced over his shoulder.

"Yeah, I know what happened. I was there that night." Elliott said, unable to stop himself from echoing the blond boy's words. A shiver raced through him and again he glanced nervously over his shoulder.

"Well," Michael went on, "I know there's one friend of hers from Westbrook on campus, but—I can't remember her name. Sarah got a ride home with her during semester break." He scratched his chin and shook his head. "Kathy . . . something-or-other."

"Kathy Meserve," Elliott said. "The police told me that they've already questioned her."

Michael looked at him with mild surprise. "I thought you said they weren't letting you in on the investigation."

Elliott smirked and said, "It was something I sort of

309

overheard. Did Sarah spend much time with Kathy? Did she talk about her?"

Michael shook his head. "I don't think so. Not that I ever saw, anyway. I know Sarah complained a bit how Kathy was getting into the whole sorority thing. I'd say, when Sarah wasn't studying at the Union or out with me, she was pretty much a loner."

Elliott nodded stiffly, still unable to get rid of the creepy feeling that someone was sitting in the booth behind him, staying out of sight by ducking or shifting to the side every time he turned to look. Goosebumps sprinkled his arms, but he knew he couldn't let his guard down in front of Michael. Still, he was filled with the compulsion to get up from the booth and start pacing or something—do anything to get rid of the eerie feeling that he was being watched.

"Well then—one thing I can tell you from years of experience," Elliott said. It took effort to keep his voice from breaking. "It's exactly these 'loner' types who do crap like this. They up and take off for a few days or weeks at a time without telling anyone. As concerned as I know both you and I are, I think we just have to trust that the police will follow up every lead they—"

Michael cut him off with a burst of mocking laughter. "Oh, yeah. Sure," he said.

"You got any better ideas?" Elliott asked. "What more do you think we can do?"

"You're the cop. You tell me!" Michael shouted with startling hostility.

"I already told you," Elliott said softly. "There's nothing more we can do except wait . . . and hope."

Michael looked at Elliott, feeling his anger and frustration boiling up inside him. As worried as he was for Sarah's safety, he couldn't stop wondering if his suspicions might be true. Maybe Elliott and Sarah were involved after all. Wouldn't someone who claimed to know her, to be her friend, who might be her secret *lover* want to get more actively involved in finding her? Why the hell was Elliott telling him just to sit back and wait? Why, unless there was something going on that he didn't want Michael to know about?

"Well, you can sit around all day on your lard ass, sucking up beer if you want to," Michael said. "I'm not going to wait for her to show up. I'm going out there to find her."

"You don't even know where to start."

"Fuck you!" Michael pushed himself out of the booth and rose to his feet. His hands were trembling as he looked down at Elliott, their eyes locked.

"Good luck," Elliott said smoothly. It took concentration and effort to keep his voice from shaking. He watched with a steely coldness in his eyes as Michael turned and strode out of the restaurant. As the door whooshed shut behind Michael, Elliott looked down at his near empty glass of beer and whispered softly, "But Michael old buddy, I *do* know where to start."

— 2 —

Sarah was drifting . . . floating like a dandelion puff on a warm, gentle breeze. Every time she started to spiral upward, the sludgy darkness below her would tug at her, dragging her back down. Warm, throbbing currents of life tingled like red fire all around and inside her, but all she knew was that she felt safe and warm, as if wrapped in a cozy, dark blanket. But now — even against her will — she was being forced to peek out from under the edge of that secure, black blanket.

And with returning consciousness came pain. When she first opened her eyes and looked around the dimly lit room, for several panic-filled seconds she didn't know where she was. Back at the dorm? Or was this her bedroom in her father's house in Hilton? Someplace else?

It was impossible to tell. The only thing she knew for sure was the room was cold . . . frigid.

311

Sarah tried to sit up to get a better view, but something was pinning her hands behind her back. The effort sent a jolt of pain slamming through her. A faint whimper came from deep inside her chest as she shook her head and tried to push aside the horrifying nightmare she had just escaped. In the dream, that janitor, Alan Griffin, had kidnapped her and, after raping her and tying her up in a storage closet on campus for what seemed like forever, had taken her out to an unoccupied summer camp on a lake.

". . . Pushaw . . ."

The single whispered word hung suspended like a cartoon bubble in the frozen air around her. Staring into the darness, Sarah was unable to tell if her eyes were opened or closed. Her lips and throat were parched. She watched breathlessly as that single word — *Pushaw* — drifted away like dust caught in the breeze that swirled inside her head.

"How'd you know that?"

The harsh voice hit her ears like a bullet out of the darkness. Grunting with surprise, Sarah widened her eyes and frantically scanned the surrounding gloom. She shifted again to sit up and see exactly where she was and who had spoken. It had sounded almost like . . .

"*Tully?* Is that you?" she croaked. The ropes binding her hands cut into her wrists, bringing fresh tears to her eyes.

"How the hell do you know where we are?"

The voice came again, harsher, lower, an angry growl . . . not at all like Tully's, but someone frighteningly familiar.

"You ever been out here before?" the voice asked, grating on Sarah's nerves like the whine of a power saw.

"Where am—" That was all she managed to say as the memory came crashing back. It hadn't been a nightmare. She was here, tied up, lying on the grimy floor of the unheated summer camp Alan had broken into—when? Just this morning . . . or days ago? How could she tell?

It couldn't have been just this morning, Sarah thought as she resisted the cresting waves of panic raging inside her.

She must have been here—unconscious—for days . . . or weeks?

"You just said the name of the lake where we are," Alan said. His voice sounded like a hungry tiger, prowling in the dark, ready to pounce.

"I don't . . . I'm not . . . sure," Sarah said. She licked her lips after every other word, but it was like scraping her mouth with sandpaper.

"Fuck you, you don't know! How did you find out?"

"No! Really, I—" Sarah whispered. Again, she tried to sit up, but pain exploded like a bright flower in her chest and spread down her arms and legs. She closed her eyes and sank back onto the floor with a long, whistling sigh. A deep sob racked her body as tears streamed down the sides of her face and onto the floor.

"You must be getting kind of hungry and thirsty by now, ain't yah?" Alan said without the slightest note of caring or concern in his voice. "Or maybe you want a little more of something else," he added suggestively.

From somewhere in the dark room, she heard a rustling sound and then footsteps as he walked over to where she lay.

"Feel like eating *anything?*"

Sarah opened her eyes when she heard the rasp of an opening zipper. She looked up at the dark silhouette towering above her and whimpered. She saw Alan's silhouette framed against the lighter gray glow of the night sky outside the camp window. Strong hands materialized out of the darkness, reached out, and gripped her. One hand ran down the zipper of her sleeping bag, and folded the thick down-filled cover aside. For the first time, Sarah realized she was naked from the waist down. Alan must have done that while she was unconscious. His hand now slid over her breasts, down her stomach to her crotch, and then began massaging her roughly.

"Maybe you aren't satisfied yet, huh?" Alan said, his voice husky with passion.

313

"No . . . please, I just—just need something to eat right now." She sucked in a deep breath and held it. "If you let me have something to eat, I'll . . . I'll do what you want."

Alan sniffed with laughter. When he leaned toward her, Sarah tensed, thinking he was going to force himself on her again, but he eased his arm around her back and hiked her up into a sitting position, the sleeping bag still around her. Once she was sitting, he pushed her back against the edge of the couch. The impact sent bolts of pain through her, but she forced herself not to cry out.

"I got some beans 'n' franks in a can," he said. He snickered and added, "Top of the line, too—Campbell's. But I ain't about to chance lighting a fire, so they're gonna be cold. About as cold as the beer. Sorry, but that's all I got to drink unless you want to suck on some snow." He laughed again and added, " 'Course, I got something better you can suck on if you want."

He struck his cigarette lighter, used it to light a single candle in a glass star-shaped holder, and placed it on the coffee table in front of her. The underlighting gave his face a sinister orange cast.

"It's freezing in here," Sarah said, her teeth chattering wildly.

"Yeah, well, you're lucky I even lit a candle for you. I ain't about to stoke up the fireplace," Alan said. He went over to a corner of the room and rustled around inside a paper bag until he found what he wanted. Then he walked into the kitchen. Sarah heard the steady grinding sound of a can opener, then the rattle of silverware when Alan opened one of the kitchen drawers. He came back into the living room carrying an opened can with a fork sticking up out of it and placed it on the wagon wheel coffee table in front of her.

"I can't very well eat with my hands tied behind my back, now, can I?" Sarah said.

" 'Spoze not," Alan said sourly.

He turned her around with a rough shove and hurriedly

314

undid the knots holding her hands together. Sarah sighed with relief as she brought her hands around in front of her and shook them vigorously to restore the circulation. The pins-and-needles feeling was soon replaced by a painful burning that intensified steadily until it felt as though her hands were on fire. She fought back the rush of fear that her hands were permanently damaged as she tried to flex her fingers. The muscles and joints were weak and stiff, but finally she was able to open and close her fists.

"D'yah want a beer with that?" Alan asked. Again, he moved over to his bag of supplies, took out a can, and held it up to her.

"I don't think so," Sarah said, shaking her head. As fragile as she was feeling, one swallow of beer would sure as hell knock her out cold.

"Suit yourself," Alan said. He popped the top, leaned back, and took a long, noisy gulp. When he was finished, he smacked his lips loudly and wiped his mouth with the back of his hand.

Sarah tried to control her shaking hands as she reached for the can of food. As soon as her fingers closed around the handle of the fork, her mind filled with the thought of leaping up, rushing at Alan, and attacking him. She imagined herself pinning him to the floor with her knees and using the pointed tines to gouge his eyes out and rip his throat open. The vividness of her imagination startled her. Shivering, she pushed the thought aside and concentrated simply on getting that first bite of food into her mouth and swallowing.

The sour smell of the beans made her gag as she scooped some up and slid them into her mouth. The growling in her stomach was too loud to ignore. She chewed slowly and then swallowed, surprised by the raw gulping noise her throat made.

"I could use a drink of something," she said in a raspy voice. The salty bean sauce felt like acid being poured down the back of her throat.

"Hey, I already told you the choices," Alan said. "This ain't the fucking Bangor House. You can either have a beer or I'll get you some snow to suck on."

"Snow, I guess," Sarah said, still finding it difficult to talk.

Alan sniffed with disgust as he got up and walked into the kitchen. Sarah saw him grab a bowl from the cupboard. He swung the door open, leaned out into the night and filled it, then returned to the living room and slid it onto the table next to the candle.

"Thanks," Sarah muttered. Her hand was trembling as she scooped up a small amount of the snow and slid it into her mouth. It felt like ambrosia as it melted and trickled down the back of her throat, taking with it the sticky sweetness of the cold bean sauce.

Her stomach seemed to be accepting the food just fine. While Alan sat in the corner of the room, guzzling his beer, Sarah ate slowly. She was aware that if she finished off the meal too fast, she might end up puking everything out. Although her grip on the fork was still feeble, she was glad that feeling had been almost completely restored to her hands. By the time she was halfway through her meager meal, though, she had another reason to eat slowly. She wanted to delay because she knew, as soon as she was done, Alan would tie her up again . . . or do something else to her. She racked her brain, trying to think of some way to strike up a conversation to delay that, but the only thoughts that filled her mind were — *Why is he doing this? What does he plan to do with me?*

"You — uh, sure do seem prepared," she said softly.

For an answer, he sniffed before taking another guzzle of beer.

"I mean — you've got food, and clothes — even two sleeping bags."

"Oh, I've been ready. I've been planning this for a *long* time," he said.

Sarah took another small mouthful of beans. The can

316

was just about empty, so she took extra care to stab each remaining bean one by one. Suddenly, a bright pain lanced through her wrist. Crying out sharply, she dropped the can and fork to the floor.

"What the fuck's the matter?" Alan asked, looking lazily over at her.

"I . . ." Sarah began but then stopped herself as she looked down at the thin slice on the heel of her hand. In the faint candlelight, the blood looked as dark as ink as it welled up along the line. Instantly, an idea hit her. If the jagged edge of the can was sharp enough to cut her, then maybe it was sharp enough to saw through the ropes binding her. If she could somehow manage it so Alan forgot about the empty can, and if she could hide it somewhere, say under the couch behind her, then she might be able to use it during the night, once he was asleep, to free herself.

She raised both hands and shook them wildly in front of her face, letting her fingers flap. "Oh . . . nothing. It's just my hands. They still feel so . . . so numb," she said.

In the glow of candlelight, Alan glared at her and smiled thinly. Then he snorted with disgust and looked away.

Sarah smiled to herself as she looked down at her bleeding hand. She popped the last bite of cold beans into her mouth, then placed the empty can on the floor beside her, in the shadow of the table cast by the candle.

Maybe, she thought as she shifted around a little to hide the can with her body . . . *just maybe he's getting careless.*

He finished his beer and, sighing heavily, tossed it into a dark corner.

"Well then, you full now?" he asked, heaving himself to his feet and walking toward her.

Terrified that he would think of taking the can, Sarah searched her mind for something to say. Looking up at him, she licked her upper lip and said, "You know, I was thinking . . . maybe we could . . ." She slid the sleeping bag down far enough to reveal her lower belly.

The cabin filled with Alan's laughter as he stared at her.

317

He reached for his belt and undid it slowly, a triumphant smirk on his face.

"Just this time," Sarah said in a rasping whisper, "please, don't be so rough with me. I—I'll do whatever you want."

"Shut up!" Alan snarled as he kicked off his pants and underwear and stood over her. "I'll do whatever I want!"

Sarah looked up at him, her eyes glistening in the feeble candlelight as he grabbed his penis and said, "Open your mouth. And make sure you go nice and easy. If I feel the tiniest little nibble, I swear to Christ I'll cut your fucking throat. Understand?"

Sarah nodded as she reached up and took hold of him. Her stomach lurched when she considered what she was doing—what she was *agreeing* to do. Telling herself she had to do this, she closed her eyes to stifle a rush of nausea as she opened her mouth wide. Alan moaned as her lips closed around him and he started pumping his hips back and forth. Then he knelt down, spread her sleeping bag open, and lay down on top of her. Opening her legs with his knees, he grunted once, viciously, as he thrust into her. Smiling, he looked down at her and said, "Yeah, now that's more like it. Sometimes it's nice when a bitch is easy, agreeable like this."

For a moment Sarah looked up at him but then closed her eyes again to fight the swirling waves of nausea.

"Yeah," Alan said as he slammed hard against her. "You ain't giving me half the trouble your mother did. And like I said, you ain't getting away from me *this* time."

— 3 —

"They had their chance, and they didn't take it," Elliott whispered to himself as he huddled in the cold darkness on the second-floor fire escape of the apartment building on Water Street. Each of his words was a ball of steam that hovered over his head before dissipating into the night. The nearest streetlight was more than a block away, so its

318

feeble blue glow was no brighter than dim moonlight. He wouldn't have to worry about getting caught, not unless he made too much noise breaking into the apartment.

It was a little past midnight. A dog was barking far off in the distance. Other than that, the only sound was of crunching snow as Elliott stood up, flattened himself against the wall of the building, and started moving cautiously along the metal platform toward the nearest window.

He knew the address was right, but he had no way of knowing for sure if this was Griffin's apartment. All evening, it had been the only one in which lights hadn't come on after dark. Whoever lived here definitely wasn't home.

Elliott had briefly considered ringing the front doorbell and trying to bullshit whichever tenant answered to let him in, but he knew he would be breaking enough laws as it was; the last thing he needed was someone who could identify him later. If Alan was involved in any way with Sarah's disappearance, and if he ever was arrested and brought to trial, Elliott knew he had to be careful how he gathered evidence; otherwise, the case would be thrown out on some bullshit legal technicality. But if the local and state cops weren't going to do something about checking up on Alan before it was too late, then he was going to do it and damn the consequences. The important thing was to find out what—if anything—had happened to Sarah.

Elliott couldn't stop a rush of nervous excitement as he leaned forward to peer into the window. For a heart-stopping instant, as his reflection shifted like a moonlit cloud across the flat, black surface, he expected to see Alan Griffin's pale face staring out at him, pressed against the cold glass. Or maybe he'd see that blond boy, staring at him with unblinking eyes as he mouthed the words *"Help her!"*

Gritting his teeth, Elliott pushed aside such ridiculous fears and looked inside at the darkened apartment. His breath left an oval splotch of fog on the glass that instantly froze.

"Well, no sense dilly-dallying," he said as he fished into his coat pocket, took out a thin, flat piece of metal, and slipped it up under the window sash. He slid it back and forth until he felt it catch on the window lock, then, angling it forward, steadily applied pressure. The metal slipped the first two times he tried it, but on the third attempt he felt a yielding resistance. He pushed harder and then felt and heard the lock click.

"All right," he said, heaving a deep sign as he put the metal back into his pocket, pressed his gloved hands flat against the glass, and pushed steadily upward. At first, when the window didn't move, he was afraid it had been painted shut, but on the second try it went up with a prolonged, ear-piercing *squeak*.

"Nice and easy, now . . . nice and easy," he coached himself as he forced the window up until it stuck a bit more than halfway open. A burst of warm air blew into his face through the open window, carrying with it the stench of rotten garbage . . . or worse. Holding his breath, he swung one leg around and inside the apartment; then, flattening himself against the sill, he squeezed through the opening until he was all the way inside. He stood there for a moment, waiting while his eyes adjusted to the darkness before running the window back down and locking it. He saw that he was behind the couch in a small, musty living room.

"But is this *Alan's* living room?" Elliott muttered as he took a penlight from his pocket and clicked it on. The tiny circle of light darted around the room like Tinkerbell as he tiptoed across the floor, scanning the mess of old newspapers, magazines, empty beer cars and pizza boxes, and assorted other trash.

"Whoever lives here, sure as hell lives like a pig," Elliott said, wrinkling his nose and trying not to breathe too deeply. He walked carefully into the kitchen where the mess was even worse. Food-crusted dishes and pans were stacked up in the sink like the Leaning Tower of Pisa. Dirty clothes were thrown in a corner, and the trash can beside the counter was overflowing with garbage and waste paper, mostly empty six-pack containers. *If this were summer,* Elliott thought, *this place would be swarming with maggots.*

From the kitchen, Elliott wandered into the bedroom. That room was just as bad as the others, but something in the far corner caught his eye: the empty cartons for two Sears sleeping bags. A choking sensation caught his throat as he went over and picked up one of the boxes. The staples that had held the box closed had been ripped off. Sighing heavily, Elliott examined the pictures on the box, all the while asking himself — *Now why in the hell would anyone be buying brand new sleeping bags in the middle of February?*

He tossed the empty box back onto the floor and went over to the closet. A quick glance showed him that there were no women's clothes there — only men's. Although all the shirts and pants were wrinkled and faded, and certainly not any style he had seen on campus, none of them looked familiar; they could have been Alan's or anyone else's.

"Shit," Elliott muttered, grimacing with frustration as he made his way over to the bureau. He quickly searched through each drawer but found nothing except ratty T-shirts, socks, and old underwear. He slid shut the last drawer and was all set to leave when a stack of books and notebooks on the floor beside the bed caught his eye. He went over to them, picked up the top notebook, and flipped it open. There, scrawled in handwriting that looked like a grade school kid's penmanship, was the name and address he was looking for:

Alan Griffin
3 Water Street
Orono

"Bingo!" Elliott said, letting out his withheld breath as he dropped the notebook back onto the stack. "But can you

321

tell me, Alan *scum-bag* Griffin, why the hell you bought *two* sleeping bags, or would you just tell me to fuck myself?" Tense with worry and frustration, Elliott shook his head and added softly, "But now all I have to do is figure out where the hell you've taken Sarah."

— 4 —

Hours later, Sarah still couldn't sleep. She wondered if she would ever sleep again. She lay flat on her back in the frozen darkness, muffled by the thick sleeping bag. Her eyes were closed as she vainly tried to stop the stinging flow of tears, but she couldn't shut off her mind. She couldn't stop it from endlessly repeating — *He's the one who did it. He's the one who killed my mother. He's the one who did it.*

After he had finished with her, before zipping her into the sleeping bag, Alan had tied her hands behind her back again, giving each knot an extra hard tug to make sure she wouldn't try to get loose once he was asleep. After another hour or so, measured by three more beers, Alan had finally blown out the candle and curled up in his own sleeping bag on the floor by the door. Before long, the cabin was filled with the blubbering sounds of his snoring.

She couldn't stop the violent rushes of anger and pain and fear that wracked her as she thought that *this* was the man who had done it. This was the man who had ruined her life, had raped and killed her mother, and now was doing the same to her. She'd never felt such anger and hatred for anyone, and still Tully hadn't come.

"Let me die," she whispered, her voice nothing more than a tormented groan in the darkness. "Please, just let me die."

She opened her eyes and stared unblinkingly up at the square of night sky she could see through the cabin's picture window. The stars were as bright as chips of diamond set against the velvety blue glow of the Milky Way. They seemed as impossibly distant as her hopes of ever getting out of this alive. The cold winter night penetrated the un-insulated walls of the cabin, racking her body with shivers; but she knew she wouldn't have slept even if she had been in a warm, cozy house.

After two years of wondering, I know who killed my mother, and I'm not going to live to tell anyone, she thought. *He's the man who chased me through the woods that rainy night, the man who wanted to kill me just like he did my mother! Now he's got me, I'm trapped, and there's no way out! He says I'm not going to get away from him again, not this time. And all along, to think that I sus-pected it might have been —*

"Tully!"

"So is this why you won't come to me now, Tully?" she whispered. "I know you were there in the woods that night, too. You told me you were. So did you make this happen? Or are you not helping me now so you can get even with me because I said I didn't want you around anymore? Is that it?"

A sudden gust of wind slammed into the house, making the rafters creak.

Sarah lay there, listening to the wind and Alan's steady snoring coming out of the darkness. She wondered if he really was asleep or if he was faking it to see if she tried to escape again. As if he needed any excuses to abuse her, to punish her.

"But I can't just give up," she told herself, trying to find courage in the sound of her own voice. "I have to try. There are still people who love me, who care about me. And — and —" Her voice choked off as a fresh outpouring of grief took hold of her. "And I have to do it for Mom, if no one else."

It was then that Sarah remembered the bean can she had hidden under the edge of the couch. A giddy rush of hope, however slim, filled her. Maybe she could sever the ropes with the sharp edge of the can and either get away or else . . .

"Or else *kill* the rotten *son of a bitch!*" she whispered

harshly.

She waited long, agonizing minutes before finding the courage to start. Holding the top of the sleeping bag with her teeth, she nudged the zipper down with her knee far enough so she could wiggle out. At least Alan had allowed her to put her pants back on before going to sleep. Her only problems would be finding her boots before she left the camp and deciding if she would try to make a run for it . . . or kill Alan first.

Sarah listened to Alan's heavy snoring but still wasn't completely convinced that he was asleep.

He's waiting to catch me trying to get away, but what does it matter? she thought. *So what if he catches me and kills me. I want to die. Death will be a release after what he's done to me.*

Pain lanced her arms and shoulders from the ropes wrapped tightly around her wrists when she rolled back onto the sleeping bag and started fumbling blindly behind her for the hidden bean can. She was just beginning to think Alan must have found it and removed it without her noticing when her fingers bumped against it, tipping it over. It hit the floor with a dull *clunk* sound. Sarah sucked in a quick breath and cringed, waiting for Alan to react, but he slept on undisturbed. After long, agonizing seconds, with her pulse slamming in her neck, she picked up the can and struggled up into a sitting position.

"Easy does it, now," she whispered as she ran her forefinger along the inside lip of the can, seeking the sharpest edge. Although the whole inside edge was razor sharp, it was almost impossible to get the rope up against it with any pressure. Relaxing as best she could, she maneuvered the can into position and began sawing back and forth.

This was going to take a long time, but at this point, it was her only option. She tried not to think about the days and weeks of torture ahead of her if he caught her doing this, but she couldn't stop the vivid fears that filled her mind. She found some courage in the thought that death *would* be a release, and she vowed, if he caught her, to struggle so hard he would have to kill her. Bitter tears flooded from her eyes and washed down her face when she thought about the few people who would miss her after she was dead. She tried to calm her mind, forcing herself to work slowly, deliberately, telling herself this wasn't the time to lose it. She had to maintain control!

Minutes seemed to stretch into hours as Sarah steadily rubbed the rope against the rough edge of the can. Unable to see what she was doing made it impossible to know if she was having any effect. For all she knew, every strand of the rope was still perfectly intact, and all she was doing was wasting her energy. But she gritted her teeth and kept working away, if only to fill the time between now and whenever Alan woke up.

At one point, Alan grunted, snorted loudly, and rolled over in his sleeping bag. Suddenly he sat bolt upright and looked directly at her. Sarah froze in mid-motion, holding her breath until it burned like fire in her lungs. He didn't say anything; he just sat there, staring at her, his face a dark blot against the darker night. Finally, with a sleepy smacking of his lips, he settled back down. Flooded with relief, Sarah went right back to work trying to cut through the rope.

"Why the hell can't you help me with this, Tully?" she whispered harshly to the dark. "Why can't you be here now? Where in the hell are you? Come on, Tully! Jesus Christ! Help me out of this, will you?

There was no answer from the surrounding darkness, just Alan's steady snoring and the low whistle of the wind in the eaves. Sarah wondered how long she could hold back the rising, whining panic inside her before her mind finally overloaded and the last shreds of her sanity slipped.

Still with no idea what she was accomplishing, she kept abrading the rope against the can edge until sickly gray light lit up the eastern sky and gradually blended into the brightness of daylight. Rather than risk getting caught in the act, she finally gave up — for now, she told herself. As

325

quietly as possible, she placed the bean can on the floor, then pushed it as far as she could under the couch before Alan woke up. Her only consolation was knowing that, if nothing else, she had at least taken the first step. She was actively working toward making good her escape, and she was damned well not going to give up until she got herself out of this situation and turned in the man who had killed her mother.

Chapter Twenty-three

Goin' Ice Drinkin'

— 1 —

Sarah was first to see the man out on the frozen lake. She was sitting on the edge of the couch, her hands tied behind her back as she faced the picture window. For several heartbeats, she watched him, not quite daring to believe he was really out there. When she realized he was heading straight toward the cabin, she had to bite back a cry of joy. Alan was kneeling on the floor with his back to the picture window as he rolled up their sleeping bags. He caught her reaction and looked at her, confused by the startled expression he saw on her face. Following her gaze, he looked outside and also saw the dark figure moving against the bright glare of the snow.

"Jesus *Christ!*" he shouted. He dropped to a crouch and, gripping the windowsill, peered up cautiously over the edge of the window. Sarah could see his worried expression reflected in the grimy glass and had to restrain herself from hoping too much.

Squinting against the snowy glare, Alan watched the lone figure another few seconds; then he turned to Sarah, his face set with grim determination. Grabbing his duffel bag, he pulled out a roll of duct tape and tore off a length. He hurried over to Sarah and quickly slapped it over her mouth, smoothing it with the heel of his hand. Once she was gagged, he stepped away from her, lifted up his pant leg, and drew his knife from his leg sheath. Twisting the blade back and forth, he held it up close to her face.

"It looks to me like that asshole's on his way over here," he said, his voice a low growl that grated on her nerves as he eyed her narrowly. Without warning, he suddenly lunged at her. Sarah squealed behind the tape, thinking he was going to kill her right here on the spot before he could get caught. Instead, he scooped her up in his arms and, carrying her like a baby, raced up the narrow stairway to the upstairs bedrooms. She almost bounced onto the floor when he tossed her onto the nearest available mattress.

"Now, I'm gonna have to deal with this asshole," he said. He folded his arms across his chest and, for a moment, studied her with a hard, steady stare, as though analyzing just how much he could trust her. Going over to the bedroom window, he leaned down and looked out over the lake. The solitary figure was much closer now, still heading in a straight line toward the cabin.

"*Christ!*" he snarled. Turning to Sarah again, he pointed the knife blade straight at her, like a gun and said, "If you make the *tiniest* little sound or try to alert him in *any* way, I'll gut the fucking both of you right here. No shit, I'll do it!"

The musty stench of the bare mattress stung Sarah's nose and the back of her throat. Even if she hadn't been gagged, she couldn't have replied. She looked up at Alan with fear-widened eyes and nodded earnest agreement.

"You're goddamned *right* you'll stay quiet!" Alan said, sneering. He leaned over her again and lowered the knife blade until it touched her neck. The cold steel tip dimpled her throat just below her jaw. Sarah didn't dare nod again for fear of sticking herself.

"That's good," Alan said, straightening up. He cast another quick glance out the window before starting down the stairs. Sarah's heart hammered against her ribs as she listened to the creaking steps and then the heavy clump of his boots on the floor downstairs.

Tears stung her eyes, and sweat broke out on her face in spite of the numbing chill in the unheated cabin. She closed her eyes, as if that could make all of this magically disappear; but every sound in the cabin was horribly magnified by her ever-tightening fear. She knew she had to stay perfectly quiet. Alan meant everything he had said and was dangerous enough to do it. Lying on her side on the rotten mattress, choking on her fear, she waited to hear the crunch of footsteps in the snow outside the camp . . . to hear the rusty-hinged complaint of the door as Alan swung it open . . . and to hear Alan's initial greeting to the poor, unsuspecting man.

— 2 —

"Yo! Frankie! You in there?"

The voice called out clear and sharp in the cold morning air and echoed in the stillness. It was followed by a quick burst of knocking on the door that rattled the broken glass.

"Door's not locked," Alan said. He was standing in the living room beside the couch, the knife tucked underneath the coat sleeve of his right arm. He cupped the hilt in his palm. Too late he realized that both of the rolled-up sleeping bags were still on the floor in front of the fireplace. If this intruding asshole had half an ounce of brains, it wasn't going to take him long to realize Alan wasn't here alone. Hell, it was too late to hide the sleeping bags now.

"Hey, Frankie, what's that piece of shit you got parked up there by the road?" the man asked as he opened the door and entered the camp. "Since when have you been driving a friggin'—"

"Howdy," Alan said, smiling broadly at the man as he rounded the corner and saw him standing there in the living room.

The visitor's face clouded for an instant as his eyes

329

darted around the cabin. He took one nervous step backward, alerting Alan that he didn't think things were quite right here.

"Say, where the hell's Frankie? He here with you?" the man asked, still frowning as he glanced around the room, trying to take in the situation. He was an old duffer, at least sixty years old, Alan thought. He was wearing a light blue goose-down parka with black piping. It made him look like the Michelin Tire Man who'd been left out in the cold too long. A black knitted woolen hat was pulled down to his eyebrows.

Alan shook his head and tried his best to adopt a friendly expression. "No, no, Frankie ain't here yet, but he asked me to come up ahead of him to check on things. I think he mentioned something about coming up later this weekend, though."

The visitor nodded, but he was still tense as he studied Alan, running his gaze up and down him.

"I don't believe we've met," he said. He slid off his gloves and tucked them into his parka pocket. "You say you're a friend of Frankie's?"

Alan nodded as he stepped closer to the man. "Name's John—John Stowe." To put the man at ease, Alan wanted to reach out and shake hands with him, but he was afraid the knife would slip from his sleeve if he moved his arm.

"Pleased to meet you," the visitor said, nodding tightly. "M'name's Emmett . . . Emmett Hawkes. Say, did you happen to break that window in the door there?"

Again, Alan shook his head. "That was like that when I got here." He patted the bulge in his left pants pocket. "Frankie gave me the key. I was just fixing to head into town to get some glass to fix that so Frankie won't have to once he gets here. Doesn't look like anything's missing, though. Everything looks okay."

"You say Frankie'll be up this weekend?" Emmett said. "That's funny. I thought he told me he wasn't coming up 'till Monday." He shrugged, still scowling suspiciously

330

as he watched Alan.

Alan still didn't move from where he stood. He wished to hell Emmett would stop looking so damned nervous, but he wasn't going to relax until this old duffer accepted his story. He was also listening for the slightest bit of noise from Sarah upstairs.

"Uh—yeah, that's what I thought he said. Maybe I got it wrong."

"Well, maybe you did at that," Emmett said. "No reason for him to hurry, though. I can't say as the fish are biting all that good." He smiled thinly for the first time as he walked over to the window and looked out over the lake. "Nice view from here, ain't it?"

"Yeah," Alan said. His tension loosened just a notch, but he still kept a careful eye on his visitor. Although he'd rather not, he'd kill this man if he had to. Maybe he should do it now, while the old duffer's guard was down. But whatever happened, whether he killed him or not, Alan knew he had to get Sarah the hell out of here now that he knew the owner—Frankie—was due to arrive soon.

"So, who's up here with yah?" Emmett asked, turning around slowly and, with a nod of his head, indicating the two sleeping bags on the floor by Alan's feet.

"Oh, those . . ." Alan said, chuckling tightly. He scratched the side of his face, trying to look casual, but his mind had drawn a blank. All he could do was curse himself for not ditching one of the sleeping bags before this asshole showed up at the door.

"Oh, I just brought two of 'em along—in case I—in case I couldn't get a fire going to cut the chill here. Lucky thing I had 'em, too. Last night was cold."

Emmett nodded, but his expression didn't waver or soften for an instant.

"So, did you come up here to do a bit of ice drinking with Frankie?" Emmett asked.

For a second, Alan didn't get the joke; then he smiled widely and said, "Ice drinking—that's a good one. No—I

331

don't really care to fish—even in the spring when I wouldn't freeze my tail off."

Emmett snickered softly. "Hell, that's why we call it goin' ice drinkin', 'cause we sure as hell catch more beer bottles than we do fish."

"No—uh, like I said, I was just checking the place over for Frankie. There'd been a couple of reports about some break-ins along this side of the lake, so he asked if I'd make sure things were all right. I—uh, just brought an extra sleeping bag along, 'cause I figured I might have to stay the night."

"Uh-huh," Emmett said. "You know, I thought I saw a light in the window late last night. The other fellas said I must've been seeing things, but that must've been you, huh?"

"Yeah," Alan replied, thinking this old geezer must have the eyes of a hawk to be able to see the glow of a single candle from halfway across the lake.

"Frankie's got plenty of wood stacked up out back," Emmett said. "How come you didn't stoke up the fireplace—or use them kerosene lanterns in the kitchen?"

"Just didn't want to bother, I guess," Alan replied. The tension inside him was intensifying. This guy wasn't going to quit. Alan realized he was going to have to get rid of him—fast—one way or another.

Emmett was about to say something else when a heavy *thump* sounded from upstairs. With a quick snap of his arm, Alan shook the knife hilt down into the palm of his hand and squeezed the handle as both he and Emmett glanced up at the ceiling.

"What the hell was that?" Alan asked.

"Probably a squirrel or something," Emmett said, his eyes narrowing suspiciously. "They get in under the eaves sometimes. Or maybe some of the snow slid off the roof."

His voice sounded casual enough, but Alan knew Emmett still wasn't about to lower his guard. The old man nodded tightly as he shifted his gaze over to the stairway.

The heel of Alan's right hand was getting numb from the tight grip he had on the knife handle, but it tightened even more when Emmett started over toward the stairs.

"You say you checked all around up here, huh?" Emmett asked. "I know Frankie keeps some important papers and stuff upstairs. There's kind of a little hideaway in back of the closet where he—"

"I already told you—"

That was all Alan got to say before Emmett started climbing the stairs, moving slowly from age and the cold. Alan dashed over to him before he had mounted three steps, grabbed the bottom edge of Emmett's parka, and tugged.

"You don't want to go up there," Alan said, his voice low and menacing.

"And why's that?" Emmett asked as he turned and looked down at Alan. His eyes were dark with suspicion and fear. He opened his mouth and was about to say more but then thought better of it and remained silent. His pale, thin lips were trembling as he and Alan locked eyes in the darkness of the stairwell. The silence of the camp seemed to swell, marred only by the creaking of the old stairs beneath their shifting weight. Before either of them could say anything else, another heavier *thump* sounded from upstairs. It boomed through the cabin like a cannon shot.

"You got someone up there, don't you?" Emmett asked, leaning forward and whispering. His hands were shaking as he gripped the railing.

Alan nodded, hoping to delay Emmett while he tried to think of an excuse. "Yeah, I do. That's why I had those two sleeping bags," Alan said, lowering his voice and rubbing his chin thoughtfully. "I—uh, I brought my lady friend along. We were kinda foolin' around when you came to the door. If you catch my drift."

Emmett smiled tightly and nodded.

"Well," Alan went on, "she wasn't exactly . . . dressed when you showed up, so she ran upstairs."

333

Emmett nodded again, his old face breaking out with a wide grin.

"Well, hell!" he whispered, followed by a belly-deep laugh. "Why didn't you say something." Turning to direct his voice upstairs, he shouted, "Sorry 'bout the intrusion, ma'm."

Alan took a few steps back so Emmett could come back downstairs. He twisted his body to one side to hide the knife, all the while staring viciously at Emmett. Although the old man seemed to have accepted his explanation, his eyes were still clouded with doubt and suspicion. Alan wasn't entirely sure he should let this man walk out of here.

"Well then," Emmett said. "I guess I'd best be heading on back to my own shack." His voice sounded high and hurried as he took his gloves from his coat pocket and slipped them on, taking care to tuck the edges under his cuffs. After adjusting his woolen hat snugly down over his brows, he turned and started for the door.

He doesn't believe me. Not for a second. And as soon as he's out of here, he's going to head for the nearest phone to call Frankie and ask him if he sent someone out to check this place.

"Yo, Emmett," Alan said, his voice sounding tight with tension.

Emmett paused in midstep, then turned. As he did, Alan flipped the knife around in his hand and with one quick, powerful, upward thrust drove the point into Emmett's stomach just below the ribs. Emmett's face paled with shock when he looked down and saw blood gushing out over his new powder blue parka. His eyes glazed over as he slowly raised his head and locked eyes with Alan. The look of complete surprise on the old man's face pleased Alan, and he burst out laughing.

Alan quickly grabbed the old man's shoulder with his left hand, and spun him around and away from him so the blood pouring from the wound wouldn't get on his clothes any more than it already had. There was no strength left in the old man, no resistance at all as Alan braced his legs, leaned back, and pulled the knife up and up until muscle and bone stopped him. Only two sounds filled the cabin: a low, wet ripping as Alan sliced through the man's thin stomach muscles, and the fast, labored breathing of both men.

Alan brought his mouth close to Emmett's ear and whispered harshly, "There. Is your curiosity satisfied?" He snorted loudly and spit. "I guess you won't be doing any more ice drinking, huh?"

Gritting his teeth with the effort, Alan moved the knife around inside the wound as if he were stirring a pot of stew. The flow of hot blood over his hand was slippery, making it difficult to maintain his grip on the knife. At last, satisfied that Emmett was done resisting, he let go of him. The old man slipped slowly from his grasp and pitched forward. His knees hit the thin carpet first; then he flopped face-first onto the floor in slow motion. A dull, gurgling sound filled the silent camp as Emmett's blood pumped from the wound, puddling like black ink on the threadbare carpet.

"Hey, you bitch! Did you hear that?" Alan shouted. "You fucking *bitch!* You had to go and make a noise, and I had to kill him! Do you hear me? I had to kill him and all because of *you!*"

Alan stared blankly up at the pine rafters of the ceiling, completely swept up by the heady rush of action. Every muscle in his body was trembling with excitement. Every nerve, every fiber of his being hummed with the pure exhilaration of what he had done. There was no need to wonder, even for a second, if this had been the right thing to do. Sure as shit, Emmett had seen what was going on; as soon as he got out of here, he would have headed for a phone to notify either Frankie or the police that someone who didn't belong there was out at the cabin. Alan couldn't stand for that. And what did it matter that he'd killed this man? The old bag of shit was probably going to die soon anyway. In the greater scheme of things, Alan figured he might have saved old Emmett from a long, painful decline into old age. Next year, the old fart would probably have died a horrible death from cancer or something.

"Fucking-A," Alan muttered as he stared down at the dead man, feeling an amazing detachment, as if this wasn't now — and never had been — a living, breathing human being. Raw excitement tingled through him like an electrical current.

"But *now* what?" he said as he bent over and wiped his blade clean on Emmett's new parka. Glancing up at the ceiling, he clenched his fists and shouted, "What the fuck am I going to do about you, you deceitful little bitch?"

Chapter Twenty-four

Investigating

— 1 —

It was early Sunday morning. Bright winter sunlight poured in through the single kitchen window, warming a small area of the grungy linoleum floor. After only a few hours' sleep following his break-in at Alan's apartment, Elliott was leaning on his elbows at his own kitchen table. He had long since forgotten his cup of coffee as he stared blankly at the cassette tape turning inside the tape recorder on the table in front of him. Since well before dawn, he had been going through Sarah's tapes, which Martha had given to him the day before. He felt guilty, embarrassed at times, listening to Sarah pour out her thoughts and feelings about things he had no right to hear, but he consoled himself with the thought that maybe something she said in her "electronic diary" would help him figure out where she was or where Alan Griffin might have taken her.

But after several hours of listening to her voice — faint and fragile at times, strong and self-assured at others and often nearly breaking from worry and strain, he had gotten few if any clues. What concerned him most were the many comments she made about someone or something called a "haamu," which she revealed her grandmother had told her about. There were also repeated references to someone named "Tully" who, apparently, had been bothering Sarah for quite some time . . . since long before she even came to college.

"What if it *isn't* Alan?" Elliott muttered as he rubbed his face with the flats of his hands and heaved a deep sigh. He knew — so far, at least — that everything pointing to Alan as Sarah's kidnapper was circumstantial at best. Sure, on several tapes Sarah mentioned "that creepy janitor" who was following her around, bugging her by trying to strike up a conversation so he could ask her out; but Elliott knew that wasn't enough to make Alan a prime suspect. He was positive that that honor, as far as the state police were concerned, was still reserved for Michael Shulkin.

"But what the hell does this mean?" Elliott said, speaking into his cupped hands.

A sudden knocking at his door startled him so much he jumped out of his chair and knocked it over. The chair back hit the floor with a sound like a gunshot.

"Just a second," he called out. He snapped off the recorder and righted the chair before walking over to the door.

What if it's that blond boy again? he wondered as a tingle of fear ran up his back.

His breath caught when he peered through the security peephole and saw Devin Lahikainen standing in the hallway. Frowning deeply, Elliott glanced back at his kitchen table and saw the stack of Sarah's tapes.

Oh, shit. What if he knows I have them? Maybe Martha told him about them, Elliott thought. *What if he's come here to collect them?*

He knew he had already dangerously overstepped his authority in this case, but he wasn't about to give up now, even if Sarah's father was here to nail him for meddling with the investigation. Dashing back to the kitchen, he scooped up the tapes and tossed them into one of the kitchen drawers. Then, running his hand several times over his unshaven face, he went back to the door, undid the security chain lock, and he swung open the door.

"What the hell has happened to Sarah?" Devin asked angrily. "I got a call from the Orono police yesterday afternoon, asking me if Sarah had shown up at home. When I told them she hadn't and asked why they were calling, they gave me some bullshit runaround. So I drove up to Orono yesterday afternoon, figuring I'd get some direct answers in person. All the Orono and state cops will tell me is she's missing and they're working on it."

"If they are at all," Elliott said. "I think they're still convinced this isn't a serious situation."

"Well, I'd heard you were working on campus and figured I'd get some straight answers from you, so I found your name in the phone book, and here I am. So tell me, is my daughter in any danger?"

For a fleeting moment, Elliott considered how much if anything he should reveal about what he knew. He recalled with a bone-deep chill the horrifying aftermath of Marie Lahikainen's rape and murder—the pain and suffering he had seen both Sarah and her father go through. Seeing the tortured, worried frown on Devin's face immediately swayed him.

"Yeah," Elliott said softly, "I think something's happened to Sarah."

"What's happened?" Devin yelled, so loudly his voice echoed in the hallway. "I couldn't get a straight answer out of any of those assholes. Just tell me, is Sarah all right?"

Elliott's expression froze as he looked back at Devin and saw his own worry and concern mirrored in the man's eyes.

"I'm not exactly sure," he said, lowering his voice. "You'd better come inside before you wake up the neighbors. Take off your coat, and I'll make some fresh coffee. I'll tell you everything I know . . . and everything I suspect."

"Screw that," Devin said as he entered the apartment and slammed the door shut behind him. "I want you to tell me what the hell we're going to do next!"

For the next half hour, Elliott went over every detail about what he knew had happened and what he suspected had happened. He didn't mention breaking into Alan's apartment. He also saw no point in mentioning the appearance of that pale, blond boy on the stairway Friday night. He did show Devin the pile of his daughter's tapes, and he discussed with him at length how many times Sarah mentioned a person named Tully.

"Did you know that she was doing this, using a tape recorder like a diary, to help her sort out what she was going through?"

Biting his lower lip, Devin shook his head tightly. "I never had a clue." Glancing at the stack of tapes, he smiled thinly and added, "Boy oh boy, and to think I thought I was so close to her . . ."

"Well, I want you to listen to one section here that really has me stymied," Elliott said. He popped a tape into the recorder, rewound until he found the right spot, then pressed *Play*. For the next minute or so there was no other sound in the kitchen except Sarah's voice, sounding tinny and frail.

"Meserve's parents said it was okay to stop on the way home for vacation, so they dropped me off at Valley View to visit Mumu. When I first got there, I thought she was doing all right, you know? She looked great and seemed really on the ball. I thought maybe my father had been exaggerating how bad off she was because he loves her so much, just like I—" Her voice caught with emotion. The sound brought tears to both Elliott's and Devin's eyes because they knew what she was going to say next.

—like I love and miss my mother. It's been over a year now, and I still can't believe she's dead." There were several seconds of silence on the tape, then, after a loud sniffling sound, Sarah's voice resumed.

"But that's not what I want to talk about. What's on my mind right now is what she said to me. I still can't describe how . . .

340

how weird it was. The whole time I was there, she was talking to me, but she was going on and on about stuff that didn't make any sense at all. And whenever she looked at me, I got this feeling like she was talking to someone else half the time. I don't know how to describe it, really, but she was looking over my shoulder, not even making eye contact with me, and talking to someone else. And then, when she started in about the family haamu — What did she say? 'You wanted him! Not the other way around. When you called him, he came.' And then she said if I tell him to go away, he will, but I have to understand that our haamu has a life of his own, that if I give in to my anger, there's no way I or anyone else could stop him. It sure is weird. I've been trying to convince myself she's just losing it, you know? Just rambling along out of her mind, but I have to admit that a few times I got this creepy feeling that Tully was there with us, standing right behind me, and she was —"

Elliott hit the *pause* button and looked directly at Devin. "Who's Tully? The name sounds familiar, but I can't place it."

A look of complete confusion crossed Devin's face as he leaned back in the chair, took a deep breath, and folded his arms across his chest.

"This is absolutely crazy," he said, staring blankly at the floor. Shifting is gaze to Elliott, he said, "Remember that night you took us out to where Marie had been killed? Sarah was talking about Tully then, and I explained that he was her imaginary friend when she was little. But here on the tape, she's . . . she's talking about him as if he was *real.*"

"And do you know what a *haamu* is?" Elliott asked. He tried to block out the stark memories he had of that night but couldn't.

Devin shook his head slowly. Before he could reply, the telephone rang, and both men jumped with surprise. Elliott got up and went over to the phone, but he didn't pick it up right away. The hair at the nape of his neck prickled and a chill danced up his spine as he vividly imagined, as soon as he put the receiver to his ear and said, "Hello," a

341

faint voice on the other end of the line would whisper—

"Help her! . . . You were there that night! . . . I saw you there!"

The image of that thin, blond boy, sitting on the darkened landing on the stairs—his hard, unblinking eyes staring at him and that thin, unsmiling mouth not even moving as he spoke—filled Elliott's mind with a numbing rush. His hand was slick with sweat and his voice was tight and high with tension as he picked up the receiver and said, "Hello."

In the lengthening pause, his eyes flicked back and forth around the small kitchen, past Devin, and into the living room. He was positive the front door was closed and locked, but even so, he couldn't ignore the unnerving feeling that someone else was in the apartment, someone watching him and Devin . . . someone who had been just waiting for this moment to call and whisper, *"You must help her! . . . I can't! . . . She doesn't want me!"*

"Yeah, hello, Elliott," a reassuringly deep, resonant voice said over the phone.

The instant Elliott recognized his boss's voice, the winding fear started to drain out of him, and the tightness in his shoulders began to loosen.

"Yes sir, Captain Avery," Elliott said, surprised by the sharp, formal tone of his voice. "Is there any news yet on that missing student?"

"None that I've heard," Avery replied. "This is something else. Look, Elliott, I realize you're not scheduled to come in until noon today, but I just got a call from Kevin Stewart, head janitor over at the Memorial Union."

"Yeah?"

"Well, there seems to have been a bit of a problem at the union over the weekend. Actually, Kevin wasn't exactly clear on what this was all about, but there's been a break-in of some kind into one of the storage closets."

The word *break-in* sent a cold wave rushing through Elliott, reminding him of his own illegal activities.

342

"Happened sometime over the weekend, probably Friday night. As it is, I'm short-handed this morning and just don't have anyone available to send over right now. I was hoping you could swing by on your way in to work today."

"Sure thing, no problem," Elliott said as he wiped away the sheen of sweat from his forehead with the flat of his hand. He wondered if his voice betrayed the immense relief he felt at not hearing that *other* voice on the line.

"Yeah, well—Kevin said he was going to leave things just the way he found them until someone could get there," Captain Avery went on. "I can't imagine this will amount to much more than a pisshole in snow, but—hey, I appreciate you doing this on your own time."

"No problem," Elliott replied. "I'll be there within an hour."

"Great," Avery replied. "Kevin said he'll be waxing floors up on the third floor all morning. Thanks again for covering this."

"No sweat."

With that, Avery abruptly hung up, leaving Elliott with a droning buzz tone in his ear. As he cradled the receiver, he sucked in a deep breath, then let it out in a thin, high whistle.

"Look—uh, Devin," he said. "I've got to get dressed for work in a bit and I—"

"No news about Sarah?"

Elliott shook his head grimly. "None."

Devin clenched his hands into fists. Closing his eyes, he trembled with pent-up frustration. "What are they *doing?*" he said in a low, broken voice. "What is anyone doing to find my daughter?" His voice broke, and Elliott could see that he was close to crying.

Elliott wanted to reassure him that the police were doing everything they could, but he didn't believe it himself, so he let it drop. He suspected that this incident at the Student Union wouldn't amount to anything, but he was vaguely grateful that he had to go to work; he needed to have something to focus on. Constantly worrying about Sarah Lahikainen wasn't going to help either him, Devin, or Sarah, even if the worst had happened.

"I don't want you to get the wrong idea," he said, "because I'm just as concerned about Sarah's disappearance as you are."

"But nobody's doing *shit* to find out what happened to her!" Devin shouted, pounding the kitchen table with his fists.

"I know. I agree with you," Elliott said, forcing calmness into his voice. "But the truth is, there's no strong evidence that there's been any foul play. My hunches and I aren't going to get any action. Until there are some solid leads, the police aren't going to jump into this whole hog, but I . . ."

He was about to take Devin into his confidence and tell him everything, but he instantly decided that he didn't want or need Devin's help. Putting himself in jeopardy by stepping out of line was one thing, but he sure as hell couldn't drag anyone else in with him. No matter what else, Elliott had to keep reminding himself that he wasn't officially involved with the case; he had absolutely no authority. After filing the necessary reports and pushing all he could with the officials, he was supposed to be out of the picture. As much as he might miss being an active player, he had to accept that he wasn't. He was just a campus cop, and like it or not, the local and state police, working with the FBI if necessary, would take it from here.

Elliott dumped his second cup of cold coffee down the sink. "You know what you could do?" he said, turning to Devin, who looked at him questioningly. "You could drive down to—where is it your mother's staying?"

"Valley View Nursing Home, in Waterville."

"Why don't you drive down to Waterville and talk with her?" Elliott said. "Ask her about this *haamu* Sarah men-

344

tioned and if she knows who Tully really is. Maybe she knows more about this that we realize."

Devin grit his teeth and shook his head. "I don't mean to sound cruel or anything, but my mother's not exactly all there anymore, you know? I honestly don't think anything she might say will do us any good."

"And you and me sitting around here all day bitching about how the staties aren't doing anything won't do us any good either," Elliott said. He came over to where Devin was sitting and placed his hand reassuringly on his shoulder. "Look, I have to drag my ass in to work soon. This will at least give you something to do instead of sitting around all day stewing. Tell you what—meet me back here tonight, after eight o'clock, and we'll see where to take it from there."

Devin looked at him, his face betraying his doubts; but he rose from the table and slowly pulled on his winter coat.

"I honestly think it's the best thing," Elliott said. "We both have to keep busy so we won't go crazy."

— 2 —

"Just what the hell do you think we can do anyway?"

Michael was standing beside his chair in the dining room, his food untouched on his plate, as the fifty or so fraternity members sat down for Sunday lunch. Usually, the brothers waited until the meal was over before making announcements, but Michael was too agitated to wait. He was convinced time was running out, and he wanted to enlist whatever help he could now.

"What I think we can do," Michael said, "is try to find her."

Murmurs and whispers rippled around the dining room tables as Michael looked expectantly from face to face, trying to elicit some sympathetic response.

"Are you sure she isn't just shacking up with someone

345

else?" Ronnie Clark offered. A ripple of tight laughter spread through the dining hall. Michael gripped the back of his chair and glared at Ronnie.

"Yeah," Steve Cote said. "I thought I saw her with a TEKE the other night."

"Maybe you're just losing your touch with the chicks," someone else offered. The room exploded with laughter that brought a flush of red to Michael's face.

"So this is the kind of help I can expect?" he said. He had to fight to control the waver in his voice as he glared at Steve, who had started it all. "*This* is how fraternity brothers stick together, huh? In case none of you realize it, this is serious. My girlfriend hasn't been seen since Friday night."

"After going out with you, I'm sure as hell not surprised she doesn't dare show her face on campus," Paul LaChance said. He looked around, expecting more than the ripple of laughter his comment elicited.

"Seriously, Mike," Steve said, adopting a placating tone. "You said the Orono cops were working with the state police on this, right? So what can any of us do?"

Michael picked up his plate of food, raised it high over his head, and then slammed it onto the floor beside him. It sounded like an explosion when the plate shattered, sending hamburger, French fries, peas, and tooth-shaped shards of glass flying everywhere. Rage and frustration filled him as he glared around the room, mentally ticking off the names of several of his fraternity brothers—his *supposed* friends—all of whom were staring at him in amazement.

"Yeah, well, this sucks!" Michael shouted, close to tears. "This *really* sucks! And I don't give a shit whether any of you guys are going to help me or not. I'm not going to stop until I find her."

He knew he shouldn't let the full range of his emotions show, but he couldn't stop now. He was trembling with tension and repressed anger—anger and hurt. Wasn't it just like these assholes to turn everything—even something as serious as this—into an off-color joke? All this bullshit talk about "brotherhood" and all was just fine as long as it never came down to a real test.

His voice wound up the register as he pointed an accusatory finger around the room and said, "And I'll tell you one more thing." His hand was shaking wildly now, and tears filled his eyes, but he no longer cared. "If anything *has* happened to Sarah, and we could have prevented it by doing something right now, I'm never going to forgive any one of you fucking assholes!" With that, he turned and strode purposely out of the room, slamming the door shut behind him. As far as he was concerned, it would be just fine if he never came back to the Sig Ep house ever again.

— 3 —

As Elliott stood with Kevin Stewart in the narrow confines of the janitorial supply closet, he was swept up by the feeling of again being watched by unseen eyes. It could have been just the close, stale air in the closet, the lack of direct sunlight, but there seemed to be an almost palpable presence in the room, hovering behind him no matter where he turned and looked. It was getting ridiculous now, but no matter where he was, even when he was alone in his apartment with the door locked, he felt as if he were constantly under surveillance.

"You say the door wasn't forced or anything, huh?" Elliott asked, scanning the damage even as the skin at the back of his neck went cold.

Kevin grimaced as he scratched his stomach, which jiggled like a sack of seed beneath his khaki workshirt. "Not that I can see anyway," he said. " 'Course, you guys might have some equipment that can tell whether the lock's been picked or not."

"Yeah, sure," Elliott said, smiling at Kevin's naive as-

347

sumption about the level of technology available to the campus police.

"But whoever the hell it was got in here—and however they did it," Kevin went on, "they sure as shit made enough of a mess."

Elliott had to grant him that much. The area at the back of the storage closet, beside the three overturned trash cans, looked as though someone had staggered through here blind drunk, scooping everything off the shelf and not bothering to pick it up. Bottles of industrial cleaner, opened rolls of toilet paper, and various other items were scattered around on the floor behind the metal storage shelf. Garbage was piled everywhere like a rising tide.

"I know it's a mess, but can you determine if anything important's missing?" Elliott asked. "I mean, other than cleaning supplies, what do you store in here that someone might want to steal?"

Kevin shrugged. "Nothing—nothing at all. 'Course, it might just be some fraternity boys' idea of a prank or something."

"I doubt that," Elliott said as he thoughtfully scanned the damage. "What would be the point?"

As he and Kevin were speaking, he kept shifting his stance so he could keep glancing around behind his back. He still wasn't able to shake the feeling that he was being watched.

"What do you guys use duct tape for?" Elliott asked. There was something about the way the half-used roll of tape was poised on the edge of the shelf with a long, loose flap hanging down that had caught his eye almost the instant he had walked into the room. It struck him as strange; maybe because it was one of the few things still left on the shelf, but the more he thought about it, the more he wondered why the tape seemed to draw his attention.

Again, Kevin shrugged. "I dunno. Probably one of the

guys used it to fix a broom handle or something."

Elliott nodded and continued to survey the damage.

"Well then, can you get me a list of everyone who has a key to this room?" Elliott asked.

"Sure—no problem," Kevin said. "I've got the key list right upstairs at my desk. Lemme run up and get it for you."

As soon as he was alone, Elliott moved so his back was flat against the wall, but even then the feeling of being watched wouldn't go away. If anything, it intensified. Every time he darted his eyes one way or another, for just an instant, he would catch a hazy shadow, shifting across his vision. The effect was unnerving, maddening. Especially in the corner of the room, down by the floor, it seemed as if there was a dark blot on the wall and floor. He glanced up to see if the overhead light was casting a shadow from something high up on the top shelf, but there was nothing up there in direct line.

"Jesus *Christ!*" Elliott muttered as he rubbed his sweating palms together and took a deep breath to calm his rapid-fire pulse.

A tight worry started to wiggle like a fat worm in his gut. What if his eyesight was failing him? Or what if he had something wrong with his head? What if when he banged against the wall that night on the stairwell he had done some serious brain damage?

Whatever it might be, Elliott tried to forget it because it certainly had nothing to do with what had gone on here in the storage closet. Once he checked the list of people who had keys to this room, and if there wasn't anything valuable missing and no serious damage had been done, this incident was pretty much wrapped up. Maybe it was as simple as someone bumping into the metal shelf and knocking all this stuff onto the floor and simply not bothering to pick it up.

After one last look at the mess on the floor, and still feeling as though there was a shadowy afterimage blurring his vision, Elliott was about to head out into the hallway to wait for Kevin when he heard the overweight man, huffing like a locomotive as he came down the hallway. His face was beat-red from the exertion when he entered the storage closet.

"Got the list here for you," he said, handing a single sheet of paper to Elliott, who nodded his thanks as he quickly scanned the list of names. Halfway down the sheet he saw a name that sent a cold dash racing through him.

"Alan Griffin? He'd have a key for this room?" Elliott asked. Even as he said the name and thought, *But this still isn't the proof I need,* the darkness at the fringes of his vision intensified, and a loud *whoosh* sounded in his ears.

Smiling weakly, Kevin nodded and said, "Hell, all the janitors in the building have to have access to these supplies."

"This guy Griffin, though, is he a good worker?"

The smile on Kevin's jowly face got tighter. "Let me put it to you this way: Griffin got hired under equal opportunity. The university didn't have its full quota of assholes."

Elliott silently nodded, not wanting to reveal to Kevin any details about what he knew and thought about Alan Griffin. He was just about to shift the conversation when a loud smacking sound filled the small room. Kevin jumped and Elliott crouched protectively, his hand dropping to where his service revolver would have been if he was wearing one. Both men's eyes were drawn to the back of the room where the half-used roll of duct tape had fallen and were rolling slowly toward the back wall.

"Hey, you know," Kevin said with a short laugh, "maybe we got a ghost or somethin' in here who's knocking stuff off the shelves." He was trying to make a joke, but his wide eyes and the tightness in his voice betrayed his nervousness.

Elliott was staring at the tape where it had finally come to rest on the floor. All around the fringes of his vision was a swirling blackness, as though he were surrounded by churning storm clouds. After a few seconds, his focus shifted from the roll of tape to the surface of the floor. What he saw there made his heart do a cold flip in his chest.

"Jesus Christ!" he muttered, not daring to look away as he felt his way through the mess toward it.

"What?" Kevin said, his voice sounding higher and tighter.

Scooching down, Elliott picked up the roll of duct tape. Holding it loosely in one hand, he pushed aside the debris to clear the large area of the floor. He had never been one to believe in, much less trust, either luck or coincidence; but he had to admit that, if that roll of tape hadn't fallen when it had, he might never have noticed what was on the floor. There was no guarantee Kevin or anyone else would have noticed it either. After picking up the supplies and sweeping the floor, Kevin could just as easily have left, and no one would have ever seen the letters scuffed onto the linoleum.

"Just take a look at this," Elliott said, pointing downward.

Kevin narrowed his eyes and shifted back and forth, but he ended up looking at Elliott, shrugging with confusion.

"Look at what? That's the damned floor."

"It's very faint, but it's definitely there," Elliott said. "Looks to me like someone used—I don't know, maybe the heel of their boot to write this." His hand was shaking as he brought it an inch above the mark and said each letter aloud as he traced them with his finger.

"H-E-L-P-S."

"Helps?" Kevin said, looking questioningly at Elliott.

"No, no! See? There's a space between the P and the S. It looks like it says, HELP S."

Kevin's eyes widened as he looked back and forth between Elliott and the floor. "Do you think—Does this have anything to do with the room being such a mess?"

351

Elliott sighed as he stood up and brushed his knees. Unconsciously, he squeezed the roll of duct tape to stop his hand from trembling as he stared, unblinking, at the crudely scrawled message. The darkness at the periphery of his vision deepened and closed in. So faintly he wasn't even sure if it was a memory or, in fact, being whispered in his ear, he heard a faint, reedy voice say—

"Help her! . . . You must help her!"

"What you say?" Kevin asked, looking at Elliott with a worried frown.

Elliott shook his head. "I didn't say anything."

"I can't! . . . She doesn't want me!"

"I could have sown I . . . Didn't you say something just then?" Kevin shook his head, looking completely dazed.

Elliott grunted noncommittally as he stared at the marks on the floor, checking them from several angles to make sure they were really there. A few times, his vision wavered and he almost lost sight of them, but there was no denying it; those letters were definitely there. He took a deep breath, let it out slowly, and said, "I want you to lock this door and make sure no one else comes in here until the state police have had a chance to check this out."

"Why? What the hell are you talking about?"

"You heard about that student who's been missing since Friday." He realized how nervous he must sound, but Kevin either didn't notice or didn't care.

"Sure did. There was something about it on the radio just this morning."

"Her name is Sarah—Sarah Lahikainen," Elliott went on, fighting the shiver that raced up his back. "I just wonder if maybe, just maybe she has something to do with this."

He finally tore his gaze away and, looking at Kevin, had to force himself to say aloud what he was thinking.

"What if this was supposed to read: HELP . . . *SARAH?*"

A half-hour later, Elliott was at the State Police barracks in Orono, his arms folded across his chest as he paced back and forth in front of Detective Philip Lewis's desk.

"Did you have anyone check out his apartment yet?" Elliott asked.

"As a matter of fact we did," Detective Lewis said calmly. "And we found out something quite interesting."

"What was that?" Elliott asked, his hopes momentarily brightening.

"We registered several complaints from neighbors about someone—identity unknown—who took it upon himself to station himself in his car right across the street from Mr. Griffin's apartment building for most of the afternoon yesterday. You got any idea who that might have been?"

In an instant, Elliott's rage and frustration boiled up out of him.

"You're goddamned right I know who it was! And you do, too!" He clenched his fists and pounded them together but forced himself to take a deep, even breath before continuing, "Look, Phil, I know what happened in the janitor's closet in the Student Union over the weekend doesn't really prove that Griffin has kidnapped Sarah, but you've got to admit that it points that way. Don't you think it goes a bit beyond coincidence that the same man who has been bothering this girl—who now is missing and *presumed* kidnapped—is also on the list of people who have access to a room where obviously something happened over the weekend? And isn't it at least curious that he hasn't been seen around his apartment for the past two or three days?"

"We've got an evidence technician checking out the storage closet even as we speak," Lewis said, sounding a bit snide. "And not just because you're making such an issue of it."

"Believe me," Elliott said. "I *know* Griffin's involved."

Detective Lewis smirked as he stared at Elliott over the rim of his glasses. "You say you know it, but you don't have any proof," he said. He, too, was fighting to control his anger. "Everything you've given me is circumstantial at best. We'll use it because we've got nothing else. I keep telling you we're going to have a talk with Griffin as soon as we find him, but until we have something a little more solid to go on than a feeling, an ex-cop's *hunch*, you've got to back off, all right? I don't think I need to remind you that you aren't even a—"

"I know! Goddamnit, I know!" Elliott shouted, unable to contain his anger. "But you guys aren't doing shit with this! By the time you catch up with Griffin—wherever the hell he is now—it may be too late for Sarah Lahikainen. It may already be too late." He jabbed an accusatory finger at Lewis and added, "And it will be your fault for not believing me!"

Detective Lewis took a deep breath and held it a second as he closed his eyes and leaned his head back. With a noisy exhalation, he glared at Elliott and said, "What the fuck is this, anyway, a conspiracy to drive me bugshit or something? Yesterday afternoon the girl's father shows up and does a tap dance on my head about what the hell we're doing to find his missing daughter and why can't he get a straight answer about what's going on. Christ, I'm still not even convinced she's been kidnapped. She's gonna show up in a day or two, and you're gonna look like a fucking idiot."

"I'm willing to take that chance," Elliott said mildly.

"Yeah, well, I'm starting to get pissed with you barging in here, demanding action as if you're my goddamned superior officer." Lewis sighed heavily, and it was his turn to point his finger angrily at Elliott. "I'll tell you this: I've got one fucking nerve left, mister, and you're standing on it. If you don't lay off—and tell your buddy, Devin Lahikainen, to lay off—I'll have the both of you arrested and put in jail, and you can rot there until this college girl shows up."

"Great," Elliott said with a derisive snort. "Just great. Look, Phil, all I'm trying to do here is help you out with a lead on this, okay? You're not even—" He stopped himself before he said anything more as he straightened up and loosened his stance.

"What you gave me is just a tip, not a lead," Lewis said with a scowl. "Come on, you know the difference. You used to be a cop."

"Yeah—*used* to be," Elliott said. His anger stirred again, but he didn't let it out this time. Instead he turned and strode purposely out of Lewis's office.

He wanted like hell to slam the door but held himself back. As he gently eased the door shut behind him, Lewis shouted to him, "You just make damn sure you keep your nose out of this, Clark! You got that?"

Chapter Twenty-five

Tuonela

– 1 –

The whole time Sarah and Alan sat on the kitchen floor, eating a hurried breakfast of cold cereal straight out of the box, Sarah couldn't stop staring at Emmett's body, sprawled and motionless on the living room floor. In the bright morning sunlight, the pool of blood surrounding him dried and turned to a crusty brick-red. Emmett's face was as white and rigid as the frozen lake ice. Sarah couldn't stop thinking that she was next—*she* was going to end up, facedown somewhere, in a drying puddle of her own blood, discarded like an unwanted doll.

After finishing their meager meal, Alan told Sarah to put on her coat, hat, and mittens. Even as she did this, she still couldn't tear her eyes away from the dead man. An arctic wind circled inside her as she thought:

That poor old man is dead, just like my mother. And that bastard killed them both so casually, so easily, as if their lives meant nothing.

She knew she didn't have long. If she was going to live, she had to act fast; she had to do something. She tried not to think about some of the things Alan might do to her before he finally killed her.

When Alan bent over to pick up the rope to tie her hands again, she made her move. Sucking in a quick breath, she pivoted to one side and kicked as hard as she could. The instant her foot connected with the side of his head, Alan shouted in pain. Sarah heard a satisfying *crack* sound as his knees gave out and he fell to the floor. Without waiting to see if he was dead or unconscious, she turned and ran for the door.

Her legs were weak and wobbly from disuse, barely able to support her as she flung open the camp door and staggered outside. Cold morning sunlight glanced off the snow, stinging her eyes as she looked frantically for a direction to run. She knew some of Emmett's friends must be out on the lake fishing by now, but she didn't want to chance going out onto the vast expanse of the frozen lake. If Alan wasn't down and out, he would easily run her down before she got halfway to the ice fishing huts. Running down the camp road might prove just as futile. She had no idea how far it was to the nearest house that might be occupied during the winter. If Alan figured out that she had gone that way, he'd be able to run her down in his car within seconds.

Numerous footprints in the snow over by the large wood shed caught her attention. Someone had been out to the building, apparently to examine the attached carport that sheltered a canvas-covered boat on a trailer. Maybe Alan had made those tracks yesterday while scouting out the area; or possibly Emmett had come out here to make sure his friend's boat hadn't been stolen. Whoever it had been, he had circled the shed and carport several times, leaving deep furrows in the snow. Taking a deep breath of the frigid morning air, Sarah cast a quick glance back at the cabin and then raced over to the shed, hoping her own footprints would be lost in the confusion of churned-up snow.

Her teeth were chattering wildly as she ducked under the carport and crouched at the back of the boat. The air was heavy with the smell of rotting vegetation. Sarah positioned herself behind the trailer so she could still see the cabin door. Then she commanded herself to calm down and wait.

But it wasn't long before the cabin door suddenly flew open. It slammed hard against the side of the camp, and every windowpane exploded into a shimmering shower of broken glass as Alan lurched out into the sunlight. The side of his face was streaked with blood, and even at this distance, Sarah could see that his left cheek was swollen and bruised. He cocked his head back and forth as he listened; then he hawkered deeply in his chest and spit a glob of bright red blood onto the snow.

"I'm gonna get you, you lousy bitch!" he yelled.

His voice echoed in the snowy stillness as he bent over, pulled his knife from his leg sheath, and held it high in the air. "Just wait! And you ain't gonna like what I do to you when I find you."

His face was a mask of pure rage as he sliced the air several times with the blade. Then, crouching low, he examined the snow near the doorstep, obviously looking for fresh footprints.

Sarah whimpered softly in her throat as she clung to the back of the boat trailer and watched him cock his head first one way and then another as he looked and listened for some indication of which direction she had gone. Then she lost sight of him as he jumped off the step and walked briskly around to the front of the cabin to see if her tracks went out onto the frozen lake. His boots crunched heavily in the crusty snow, sounding like a giant, casually munching on some poor, helpless creature's bones.

"Oh, no," Sarah whispered, knowing that, as soon as he realized there were no tracks leading out onto the lake or up to the road, he would know she was hiding somewhere nearby.

"Don't you worry, Sarah girl," Alan shouted in the echoing stillness. "I'm gonna find you sooner or later. I promise you that much! No fucking way you're getting away from me! Not *this* time."

– 2 –

"Mom, *please*. You've got to try to think clearly. I need your help. Sarah needs your help."

358

Devin Lahikainen leaned against the windowsill, staring earnestly at his mother, who was sitting in the chair by the window, looking out at the cloudless winter sky. Sunlight reflected in her eyes, turning them the color of ice. Her skin looked sallow and cracked; every wrinkle and pore was highlighted by the intense light. Her hands desperately gripped the chair arms as if she was afraid of falling to the floor, although the security strap around her waist would have prevented that.

"Why, I *am* helping you, aren't I?" she said in a high, thin whisper. Her dry lips made little clicking noises as she spoke. "I've been helping you as much as I can. And Sarah, dear Sarah. Why, just last night I was talking to—"

"Mom, Sarah wasn't here yesterday," Devin said, his voice tinged with rising impatience. When Elliott had asked him to come here, he had suspected that this was exactly what would happen. His mother's mind was a confusion of events and people from the past. He wasn't going to get a single coherent statement from her.

"Mom, I need to know what something means," Devin went on. "It may not be important, but I have to know what you said to Sarah about a *haamu*."

Ester's gaze suddenly snapped into focus. She looked at her son with a deepening scowl of confusion and—

Fright, Devin thought. She looks scared.

"What is it, Mom? The last time she was here, what did you tell Sarah about a *haamu?*"

"I was about to tell you; he was here last night," Ester said. Her lower lip began to tremble, and tears filled her eyes. "He came to me before to tell me that Jussi, my brother, had died."

"Mom, Jussi died more than fifty years ago, back in Finland. I'm talking about *now.*"

"He came here last night," Ester said as tears carved glistening tracks across her sunken cheeks. "I know it was last night. He was sitting right there on the windowsill where you are. Clear as can be, I saw him. Just a little boy." She shook her head with deepening sadness. "He's nothing but a scared little boy, but I told her! I *warned* her that's what would happen."

"Are you talking about Sarah?" Devin asked with a deep tremor in his voice.

"Of course I am," Ester said in as close to a shout as she could manage. Tears continued to run down her face. Fighting to control his shaking hand, Devin took a tissue from the dispenser and gently dabbed her eyes. His mother kept speaking all the while. "I told her to be careful, but I didn't mean for her to destroy him. Oh, Devin! You should have seen him! So thin, so pale! He has no strength left."

"Who, Mom? Who the hell are you *talking* about?"

"My *haamu*, of course!" Ester said simply. "Now, the house *tonttu* was different. He could never leave the house because he was such a part of it. But the *haamu* came here with me years and years ago."

"You say he came here?" Devin said, shaking his head in confusion as he looked around the room. "Mom, I don't know what you're talking about. Will you please just tell me what you said to Sarah about this . . . this *haamu*, whatever the hell it *is?*"

"Not an it," Ester said, narrowing her eyes. "A boy, and now—" Her breath hitched in her chest, and pain flashed in her eyes. "Now he will never grow stronger. He's not dying, but he'll never grow."

"Do I know him?" Devin asked. "What's his name?"

"Name? His name is whatever you say it is. *Se tulli tänne.* That means, *he came here.* When I was a little girl, whenever I called him, he always came to me, so I called him the Finnish word for *come — Tulla.*"

"That means *come?*"

"Don't you remember, when you were a little boy? Your father would call for you: *'Tulle, tulle tanne poika!'* 'Come here, boy!' He always came when I called."

"Tulla . . . Tully," Devin said in a whisper so faint he

could barely hear it himself. He shivered in spite of the warmth of the room as he regarded his mother, wondering if what she was saying made any sense at all. Was it coincidence that the Finnish word for *come here* was so close to Sarah's name for her invisible friend? And even if what his mother was telling him *did* make sense, it certainly wasn't going to help him find out what had happened to Sarah. Coming down to Waterville had been a foolish idea, and he began to suspect that Elliott had asked him to do this just to get him off his back for the day. Just like the local and state cops, Elliott Clark wasn't interested in helping him find his daughter.

"But what does all this have to do with Sarah?" Devin asked, unable to keep the edge of exasperation out of his voice.

Ester looked at him, her eyes still glistening with fresh tears. Her voice was distant, and she looked like she was falling asleep as she muttered, "Because she sent him away." Her eyelids drooped, and her focus shifted past her son to the cloudless sky. Her face wore an expression of deep sadness, of infinite loss. "And just last night, Tulla told me that he can't go to her anymore even though she needs him — *really* needs him."

A chill skittered up the back of Devin's neck. "Did Tulla tell you where Sarah was?"

Ester's eyes closed as she took a shallow breath and let it out with a sigh. She nodded her head gently. "Yes," she said, her voice a whisper. "He said she was swimming . . . swimming in the black waters of *Tuonela*, the Lake of Death."

— 3 —

Seconds stretched into minutes, and minutes seemed to stretch into hours as Sarah waited, crouching in the darkness of the carport behind the boat trailer. Several times she heard the heavy trod of Alan's footsteps as he ran back and forth, searching for her. She knew he suspected she was still close by because he hadn't gotten into his car and driven off. But even if he had, Sarah wondered if she would have dared to come out of hiding. How long would she have to wait here—until nightfall? Longer? Maybe until she died, she thought grimly.

Hammering pressure was building up inside her until she felt like she was going to burst out screaming, but she forced herself to stay where she was, shifting as little as possible to relieve the cramps that gripped her leg and shoulder muscles. She bit down hard on her lower lip to keep her teeth from chattering from the cold, but she almost welcomed the idea of freezing to death before Alan found her.

"I know you can't have gotten that far," Alan shouted. "And you're starting to piss me off! You know it's just a matter of time before I find you, so why don't you give yourself up before I get *too* mad?"

His voice echoed in the distance, and Sarah realized that he was on the far side of the cabin, possibly all the way up on the road. Knowing if she worked fast he wouldn't hear any sound she made, she quickly unlaced the rope holding down the boat covering, lifted up the corner flap, and crawled into the boat. Once she was underneath the canvas, she slid the rope back through the eyelets she had undone and pulled it tightly, hopping to hell everything would look untouched if Alan thought to check inside the carport. She had no doubt that he would. Like he said, it was just a matter of time.

The darkness under the canvas was thick, impenetrable. Trying carefully not to shake the trailer, Sarah felt her way to the bow of the boat and squeezed herself in under the foredeck. In such close quarters, her panting breath soon filled the inside of the boat with moisture. The musty smells of old rope and life preservers nearly choked her, but she stifled a coughing fit when she heard footsteps coming nearer.

362

"You can't have gotten very far," Alan called out in a singsong voice. He sounded shockingly close to the boat. Sarah imagined him standing right there in front of the boat, maybe no more than four feet from where she hid. Tears and sweat nearly strangled her, but she held her breath and waited . . . waited to hear him move off.

Suddenly a loud bang and the harsh splintering of wood filled Sarah's ears, making her jump. She guessed Alan must have kicked in the shed door, and this was soon confirmed by the rattling, crashing sounds he made as he searched through whatever assorted junk was stored in there. She crouched in the darkness listening to the destruction he wreaked. Memories of hiding from Alan on that rainy night nearly two years ago filled her with intense, twisting agony. Again—just like that night so long ago—she found herself thinking about—

Tully.

She closed her eyes and chanced to whisper his name aloud, knowing that Alan wouldn't hear her over the noise he was making.

"Tully!"

She hoped against hope that he would answer her, that she would feel him next to her in the darkness; but she realized as certainly as if she were in a lighted room that he wasn't hiding there in the boat with her. Deep cold penetrated her mind when she admitted to herself that Tully wasn't there and he wasn't going to come. As her grandmother had said, she had pushed him away. He was gone from her life.

But I'm giving in to my anger now, she thought as black, horrible thoughts about Alan filled her mind. *Mumu, you said if I gave in to my anger, there'd be no way anyone could stop him. I hate Alan Griffin! I want you to come to me now, Tully! I want you to kill him for me. Kill him!*

A loud banging noise from outside made her jump. Heavy footsteps moved from the shed toward the boat. Pinching her eyes tightly shut, Sarah almost screamed aloud when Alan knocked against the side of the boat with his fist. She tried to make herself melt into the cold wood of the boat flooring as she tracked his footsteps around to the back of the boat. Then she heard him tug on the ropes holding down the canvas cover.

"Goddamn it all!" Alan muttered as he shook the boat violently from side to side. The motion made Sarah knock her head against the side of the boat, but she forced herself not to cry out in pain. Alan was making so much noise that she decided to chance it and pulled an armload of life preservers up over her, hoping that he wouldn't see her if he raised the covering.

Please . . . please, just go away! she prayed desperately.

Her breath caught in her chest like a fishhook when she heard a sudden loud, harsh ripping sound. Her heart felt cold and silent in her chest when she looked up and saw a bright line of daylight shining through the canvas. Then she saw the gleaming tip of Alan's knife, sliding down the length of the canvas.

My throat's next, Sarah thought as the hole widened, and Alan's bruised, smiling face leered at her through the slit. She covered her face with her hands and waited to feel the sting of his blade.

"Well, well, well," he said, his face contorting into a twisted mockery of a smile. "Lookie what I've found here."

Sarah stared at him, gape-mouthed, unable to say a word as he jabbed his knife at her. He pulled back an inch before cutting her hands.

"I should kill you right now," he said, touching the angry bruise on the side of his face with the tip of his knife. "But you know, I don't think I will . . . not just yet anyway. It's too much fun fucking you."

He snorted with laughter as he reached into the boat, grabbed her by the arms, and pulled her to the ground. Trembling, Sarah looked at him, unable to make even the tiniest sound as he pushed her out into the bright, cold air. Grabbing her tightly by the arm, Alan dragged her up the pathway to his car. From the front seat, he took a length of rope and wound it tightly around her wrists. Sarah winced with pain as the rope bit into her hands. She couldn't tell if this was the same length of rope she had tried to cut with the bean can last night. It didn't matter. She was nearly numb with fright, wondering where he would take her next . . . and when he was going to kill her.

"Where are we going?" she asked. Her voice was hollow with defeat.

Alan looked at her with a harsh stare as he knelt down and bound her feet together. Once he was sure she couldn't get away, he made her sit on the car seat behind the steering wheel while he went down to the cabin for their sleeping bags and his overnight luggage. When he returned, he tossed everything into the backseat of his car.

Shivering from the cold and her misery, Sarah looked frantically around at the silent, snow-filled woods and the long stretch of frozen lake in front of the camp, wondering how close she had come. Should she have run instead of hidden? How far away were that old man's ice-fishing buddies? Even now, would they hear her if she started screaming as loud as she could? Where could she have gone? What should she have done to get away from this madman?

The frigid morning air stung her lungs, bringing tears to her eyes as she scanned her surroundings. At the very least, she figured she owed it to poor Emmett to try to remember where this place was, so if—

No! she insisted to herself. *Not if, when I get out of this, I can bring the police back to here . . . to a cabin on Pushaw Lake, owned by a man named Frankie.*

"You know you're not going to get away with this much longer," Sarah said. She forced strength and determination into her voice even though her stomach twisted whenever she recalled how easily Alan could kill someone. She knew he would have no compunction about using his knife on her, too. And she knew why he hadn't done so yet; like he

365

said, he wanted to keep her for the sex. It was just a matter of time.

"I know damn well how I can get away with it," Alan snapped, looking at her with a thin sneer. "But you don't think I'm actually going to tell you my plan, do you? How fucking stupid do you think I am?"

Not stupid—crazy, Sarah wanted to say, but she held her comments back, thinking that she had to lull him, not antagonize him if she ever hoped to free herself.

"And even if you're right—even if I do end up getting caught," Alan continued as he reached down and patted his lower leg where his pants covered his sheathed hunting knife, "I'm gonna make damn sure you're not around to see me fry."

"In case you didn't know, Maine doesn't have a death penalty," Sarah said snidely. "You'll end up in Thomaston for the rest of your life."

Alan's reaction surprised and secretly pleased her. His face paled, his eyes went suddenly blank, and his mouth stiffened into a tight, bloodless line. Anger—or perhaps *fear*—smoldered behind his eyes as he looked at her and clenched his fists at his sides.

"Don't talk to me about Thomaston, you . . ."

One fist began to rise threateningly. Sarah shied back, but before his anger exploded, Alan managed to control himself. Lowering his fists, he said in a low, steady voice, "You know, I think I want you to ride in the trunk for a while. A little tape over your mouth will keep you nice and quiet. And who knows? Maybe a bit of bouncing around back there in the dark will knock some sense into your head." Without waiting to see her reaction, he stuck the trunk key into the lock, clicked it, and raised the lid.

"Oh, come on," Sarah said. Icy fear spiked through her as he pulled her off the front seat and dragged her to the back of the car. The thought of suffocating or choking on exhaust fumes in that confined, dark space filled her with an aching dread. "You don't have to do this."

366

"I know I don't *have* to. I want to."

Looking around, she wished again that she had run instead of hidden. Now, with her hands and feet tied, she didn't have a chance.

"You actually think I'm gonna trust you?" Alan shouted. His eyes glazed, and spit flew from his mouth. "After the shit you pulled back there?" He rubbed the side of his bruised cheek with one hand. "I should have gutted you right away, for trying to let that old man know you were upstairs!"

"I did *not!* I didn't make any noise," Sarah said, shaking her head in violent protest.

"Bullshit you didn't! I heard you knock—*twice.* We both heard you. That's why that old bastard started coming up the stairs. And you know what?" He was wide-eyed, crazy-looking as he slapped his hands against his thighs. "If you hadn't done that, I wouldn't have had to waste that miserable old fuck. *You* killed him; not *me.*"

"I didn't do *anything.* I never heard anything except you two talking downstairs. I never made any noise . . ." Sarah's voice broke with rising terror; just the thought of spending time locked up in the car trunk sent her into a paroxysm of panic.

Alan smirked as he bent down and shoved aside the junk—assorted tools, oily rags, and old newspapers—in the trunk to make room for her. The spare tire was flat, so he lifted it out, set his grip tightly on the rim, and then, grunting, spun around twice before flinging it off into the deep snow under the trees.

"There. All nice 'n' roomy for yah," he said, standing back and looking from the trunk to Sarah. Without any more comment, he opened the driver's door, picked up his roll of duct tape, and came at her.

"Now to make sure you stay shut up," he said as he pulled off a strip of tape.

"No—*please,*" Sarah wailed. "I can't . . ." She looked at the open trunk as if it were the wide-open jaws of death

367

itself.

"I'm not taking any more shit from you, understand?" Alan said sharply.

"I could suffocate in there," Sarah said.

"You think I care?" Alan replied with a hollow laugh. "You'd consider yourself lucky, if you only knew what I have in store for you."

In a move so sudden Sarah didn't even see it coming, much less have a chance to react, he threw a punch at her that landed solidly on the side of her face. Stars exploded across her vision and she started to fall. Alan darted forward, grabbed her by the shoulder, and spun her around before she hit the ground. He held her tightly in one arm as he slapped the strip of tape over her mouth.

"Now, no more shit, okay?" he said, his voice a tortured growl close to her ear.

Sarah could see that her bound hands were level with his crotch, and even through her confusion of pain, she considered trying to nail him a good one; but the darkness swirling inside her was deepening. The last bit of strength drained out of her when she felt his strong hands holding her like she was a lifeless doll. She heard him snort with laughter.

After making sure the tape and the ropes binding her hands and feet were tight, Alan lifted her up and dropped her into the open trunk. Sarah hardly felt the impact as her shoulder banged against the wheel well. She lay there, dazed, with her legs hanging out. Alan smiled wickedly at her before lifting up her legs and cramming them inside. Resting one hand on the open trunk lid, he leaned over her and snuggled her coat collar up tightly around her neck as though she were a child about to be sent outside to play. The snowy glare behind him washed out his features; he was nothing more than a huge, looming black blur.

"It probably won't be as bad as you think," he said. His voice seemed to come from far, far away. "Oh, no . . ." He sniffed with laughter. "I think, once this drive is over, things will be a lot worse!" With that, he slammed the trunk lid down with the finality of a closing coffin lid.

—4—

Sarah had no idea when she finally came to . . . if, indeed, she had ever lost consciousness in the dark confines of the car trunk. She had no sense of time and only a vague memory of hearing Alan start up the car. It didn't matter if her eyes were opened or closed—the same pressing darkness surrounded her, molding around her body like icy black water. All she knew was the steady vibration of the engine and every head-splitting bump in the road. She tried like hell to shut off her brain so she wouldn't have to wonder where he was taking her and what he planned to do with her. Wave after wave of pure, blinding panic crashed inside her as she considered that this was it. She wasn't going to get out of this alive.

Alan's voice rang like a tolling bell in her memory. *"I think, once this drive is over, things will be a lot worse!"*

But as tempting as it was simply to give up, Sarah couldn't let go of life. She couldn't give up and let the swelling darkness claim her. In the core of her heart, even as desperate as she was, she knew life was too valuable to let it slip away without a struggle. As clearer consciousness returned, with it came the keen edge of the survival instinct. Fighting back churning, black hopelessness, she grappled with the panic and clinging claustrophobia. Like a ship-wrecked sailor, she clung to the faint hope that she still might get out of this alive. She *would* survive.

After numerous jolting turns, the road gradually smoothed out. A dizzying sensation of speed and blind turns filled Sarah with a curious disorientation, but she forced herself to stay alert. When the road was smoothest, the tires whined like mosquitoes close to her ears. She guessed they might be on the turnpike. Before long, the air inside the trunk grew stale. She gagged on the cloying exhaust fumes and other, less definable odors. The fear of suffocation pressed inward at her, collapsing her lungs, but it was the watery blackness and her inability to move that were the worst. In spite of the car's motion and repeated reminders to herself that she was in a car, the image of being sealed alive in a coffin wouldn't leave her. And with her mouth sealed shut with duct tape, she couldn't even scream.

After a while, the car took a sharp turn and slowed to a stop. Sarah heard the car door open and shut as Alan got out. Footsteps crunched heavily on the icy road beside the car. A single, heavy *thump* sounded against the side of the car, so close to her head Sarah jumped. A hollow, metal scraping sound was followed by the sound of running liquid. She realized Alan had stopped for gas. Either he or the station attendant was whistling tunelessly as gas sloshed and gurgled into the tank beneath her. Gasoline fumes swirled inside the trunk, bringing fresh tears to her eyes.

Sarah considered making some kind of noise inside the trunk to alert the attendant, but her arms and legs were too cramped to move. Before long, she heard him replace the gas tank cover, get back into the car, and start it up. They were back on the road.

Desperate and crazy thoughts careened in Sarah's mind. She couldn't stop thinking about what Alan had said to her before stuffing her into the trunk. He had said that he had a plan so he could get away with kidnapping her. Sarah couldn't stop wondering what that plan might be.

If he was going to kill her, he certainly would have done that by now. Why bother taking her anywhere when he could just as easily have killed her and left her lifeless corpse on the isolated camp floor alongside Emmett's body? There was no doubt that he intended to continue using her, degrading her physically. She consoled herself with the thought that—maybe—after a while she could make herself immune to anything he did or made her do.

But beneath all these worries and concerns was something else: was anyone trying to find her?

It had been a day and a half since she had been taken. Had Michael realized yet that she was gone? Would he be worried enough to notify the police? Did her father know she was missing? Elliott wouldn't miss her until she didn't meet him on Monday for their morning coffee. What about Martha? Wouldn't she be concerned that her roommate hadn't returned from her date on Friday night?

It seemed like a lifetime ago. With a twinge of guilt, Sarah thought how everything she had lived through — even the horror of her mother's rape and murder — was nothing . . . nothing compared to what she faced now. And the terrifying thought that filled her with a dark, coiling dread was that it wasn't over. And no matter how hard she tried to contact Tully, he wouldn't come to her.

Long minutes or hours later, the car stopped again. The tires sounded like tearing paper as they locked and skidded over thin dirt. When Alan cut the engine, the sudden absence of its steady rumble broke the hypnotic daze that had held Sarah. She listened as Alan got out of the car and walked away from it. She tried to stay alert, but the combination of stale air and mind-numbing fear weighed her down. She couldn't resist the backward, plummeting fall down . . . and down . . . deeper into the blackness inside her mind. Soft, wet darkness folded over her like oily waves. She couldn't get away . . . even if she had tried to struggle . . . but she had no strength left. As she spiraled down, her pain and misery eased . . . her tortured muscles and burning nerves unwound . . . and the sickening stench of exhaust fumes faded. The deeper she went, the more the pain receded until she imagined herself as nothing more than a piece of senseless, waterlogged wood, sinking deep, deep . . . into a cold, silent, black lake . . .

Chapter Twenty-six

"... hungry..."

— 1 —

Alan needed to get Sarah someplace where no one would ever find her, and his first thought was to head south, figuring it would be best to go to Hilton, where he at least knew the area. As he drove down I-95, he made a point of staying just below the speed limit so he wouldn't draw any undue attention to himself. He started having doubts when, as soon as he was on the turnpike, a state police cruiser with flashing blue lights streaked past him. If the police had any idea Sarah had been kidnapped, and if they had somehow gotten the idea that he was involved, maybe because of his previous record or whatever, then Hilton was the first place they would look for him. He got off the turnpike at the Gardiner exit, turned around, and started back north.

"It's like the ripples in a pond when you throw a rock into it," he said, squinting from the snowy glare. "The longer it's been, the further the ripples go." He sniffed with laughter as an idea hit him; an idea so brilliant, so simple, he was surprised he hadn't thought of it until now.

"Shit, I'll stay right where I was," he whispered. "If they think she's been kidnapped, they'd never think I'd dare keep her right there around Orono!" He gleefully pounded his fist on the dashboard. "By Jesus, that's it! We'll stay right in our own backyard. Let the cops look all over the state for us; we'll be right under their fucking noses!"

He got off I-95 in Augusta and drove the rest of the way to Bangor on back roads, figuring he'd be less likely to be spotted—*if* the cops were on the lookout for him. It was still an hour before dark when he drove into Bangor, but he knew he had to find a place to hole up for the night while he thought things through. When he saw the sign for the E-Z Veazie Motel, on Route 2 just outside of Bangor, he knew a dump like this would be perfect, at least for the first night. Because of its shady reputation, most of the locals twisted the name into The Sleazy-Veazie. And, it was close enough to the Interstate so he could get moving fast if he had to.

Alan parked the car far away from the office door, assured by the silence in the trunk that Sarah was either sleeping, passed out, or dead. He put on an air of confidence as he walked into the motel office, but he couldn't disguise the slight tremor in his voice when he asked the bleached blond, pig-faced woman at the desk for a room for the night. His hand was shaking as he hunched over the counter and filled out the motel registration form. The whole time, Pig-face watched him with a steady stare that worked his nerves like a high-speed drill. Her Coke-bottle glasses made her look google-eyed. He wished to Christ she would stop staring at him, go back to drinking her Diet Pepsi, munching her Cheetos, and watching whatever idiotic show was on the TV. It was hard enough making up a fake name and address and everything else without her watching him as if his face were still covered with that old fart Emmett's blood. Maybe it was the swollen bruise on his cheek that drew her attention.

373

Killing that old geezer and getting kicked in the face were the least of Alan's worries right now. He consoled himself by insisting he hadn't *planned* to kill Emmett; he hadn't *wanted* to kill him . . . at least not at first, not when he saw him walking across the lake toward the camp. Everything had just sort of happened. And once he got down to it, it sure had been fun, seeing that crazy expression on the old shit's face when he saw his own blood gushing out of his stomach. That was the second time Alan had gutted someone, and he had to admit that there had been a rush almost as good as sex when he felt their bodies go limp in his arms, while their life seeped away. And sometime soon, there was going to be a third one, but *she* was going to die ever so slowly . . . by inches, if he had his way.

'Course, none of this would have happened if that bitch hadn't gotten away from me the first time, he thought, bitterly recalling that rainy spring night nearly two years ago.

"Sir?"

Alan shook his head and looked at Pig-face, suddenly aware that she had asked him something.

That's not good, he told himself. *Can't let things slip. Don't want to tip her off that things aren't perfectly ordinary.*

"Sorry, ma'm?" he asked, smiling widely.

"I need to know which charge card you're going to use—Master Card, Visa, or Discover."

"Uh, no,—I'll pay cash." Alan said. His hand went to his hip pocket for his wallet.

Pig-face eyed him suspiciously. "That'll be thirty-five dollars, then," she said. "Do you plan on staying more than one night?" Framed by her straw-yellow hair, her eyes looked like cartoon blots of black ink, shifting back and forth behind her thick glasses. "I can arrange for you to have clean sheets and towels first thing in the morning."

"Actually," Alan said, scratching his cheek. "I'm kind of

374

a late sleeper and don't want to be bothered. And anyway, I'll be heading out first thing in the morning."

"Where you headed?" Pig-face asked.

Her question seemed casual enough, but the suspicious undercurrent in her voice warned Alan that she had caught his little slipup; if he was a late sleeper, why was he leaving *first thing* in the morning?

"I—ah, I'm heading down to—umm, to Boston," Alan said. The back of his neck and his arm pits were clammy with cold sweat. "To—ah, see my girlfriend."

Pig-face nodded knowingly. Her eyes narrowed and her head cocked to one side as if to say, *You don't fool me for one second with this girlfriend talk. You're probably going to head straight into Bangor to some sleazy bar, pick up a whore, and bring her back here. Don't try to kid me, Buster! I've seen your type already a hundred times this year!*

"Umm—well, thank you Mr.—" A hint of a smile crossed Pig-face's lips when she read the registration. "Mr. *Smith*. That will be Unit 26. The very last door on your right as you face the office."

Alan smiled and mumbled a quick, "Thank you," as he took the room key from her. Sucking in a deep breath, he turned, pulled his collar tightly around his neck, and walked boldly from the office back out to the car. He knew, if just for the sake of appearances, he should at least check out the room before going out for something to eat. His stomach felt like a cold, hollow pit. Maybe he would try to get Sarah into the room before dark rather than leave her in the trunk much longer. He could back the car up close to the door, carry her inside, and leave her tied and gagged in the room without too much worry. After than, he could head out to Burger King and pick up something to eat. Hell, he might as well see if she's still alive before wasting any money on food for her.

Michael was dog-tired. Ever since Saturday morning, other than for a quick stop back at the fraternity house on Sunday for lunch, he had been out on the road, searching for Sarah. He had no idea where he should start looking, so he simply kept driving around the Orono/Bangor area, hoping against hope that — somehow — he would bump into her. He grudgingly admitted that this tactic was absolutely hopeless. All he was doing was wasting time and gas, but he had to do something to keep busy. At roughly half-hour intervals, he would stop at a pay phone and call the Orono police or the State Police barracks to see if there had been any progress, but he always got the same answer.

No leads . . . no information . . . no *nothing*.

As the bright Sunday afternoon blended into the deep purpose of twilight, the mental strain and two-day lack of sleep started to hit him hard. His eyelids felt as if they were weighed down by tiny lead weights. After not eating much during those two days but drinking way too much coffee, his stomach felt like a cold, hard block of ice.

"Jus' one more time around town, and then it's back to the house for some sleep," he said aloud as he stifled a yawn that brought tears to his eyes.

After making a quick circuit on Union Street, he cut across on Fourteenth, went down Hammond Street to downtown, and then up State Street. As he started back to Orono along Route 2, tracking beside the Penobscot River, a wave of chills suddenly shifted across his back and up his arms. He was wearing a heavy winter coat, and the car's heater was working overtime, but that didn't stop the shiver that violently shook his shoulders. Another yawn made him open his mouth so wide his jaws clicked and his ears popped. When he shook his head to clear it, he caught a glimpse of something from the corner of his eye. His foot tapped the brake pedal, and he tensed as he glanced quickly at the seat beside him.

"What the—" he muttered, positive that, for a flickering instant, he had seen a swirl of darkness beside him in the passenger's seat.

Without thinking, he slowed the car to a stop on the dirt shoulder of the road. He jammed the shift into *Park* and then for several seconds just sat there, staring at the empty seat beside him. For just an instant, he was positive he had seen something, *sensed* someone sitting there. For some reason he thought it was a young man. In his exhausted state, he even half accepted it, as though he had known all along that someone was riding around with him.

Another, stronger shiver raced through him as his gaze shifted from the empty car seat out into the cold night. His headlights illuminated the head-high ridge of dirt-stained snow beside the road. Beyond that, the lights from downtown Bangor glistened above the twisting, black gash of the frozen river. A cold, helpless loneliness . . . a numbing sense of loss filled him as he leaned over the steering wheel and looked up at the night sky. Only the brightest stars shined through the glare from the city, but the eerie sense of loneliness wouldn't go away.

He rubbed his eyes with the flats of his hands as he shook his head from side to side.

"*. . . hungry . . .*"

"Umm—yeah, I sure am hungry," Michael said.

"*. . . eat . . .*"

Michael smiled grimly and nodded. His stomach responded to the suggestion by giving a cold, hollow flip. With a jolt of surprise, he sat up, aware that he hadn't *thought* the words; he had *heard* them, as if someone were . . .

"Jesus *Christ! First I'm seeing things—now I'm hearing voices.*"

377

His eyes darted back and forth, but he was unable to find anything to anchor his gaze. The palms of his hands screamed with pain from the tight grip he held on the steering wheel; his chest hurt from the breath he was holding back because he knew, if he let it out now, he was going to scream. Sweat broke out like dew on his forehead. Again, he was filled with the overpowering conviction that someone else was in the car with him. He slowly shifted his eyes over to the passenger's seat.

For a flickering second, between him and the passenger's window, darkness swirled like a thick column of smoke, as if the night had somehow condensed, taken on form, and seeped into the car. The lights on the far shore of the river were distorted and smoky for a moment before the cloud wavered and then, in the blink of an eye, vanished. He collapsed forward, resting his forehead on the edge of the steering wheel as panic welled up inside him.

It's gotta be that I haven't slept, he told himself as he struggled to push back his churning panic. *I'm hallucinating because I'm tired as hell and I haven't eaten.*

"*. . . yes . . .*"

The word hissed in his mind like wind-blown sand, whistling around the car door.

"*. . . hungry . . .*"

Sweat streaked Michael's face and neck as he sat there, trembling, unable to accept what he had seen and heard—or *thought* he had seen and heard. It took him several minutes to calm down, to convince himself his mind was playing tricks. He slipped the car into gear and pulled back onto Route 2. After driving no more than half a mile, he saw the lights of a Burger King up ahead on the left.

"*. . . there . . .*"

Without signaling, Michael cut across the road and into the parking lot.

As he drove around the side of the building toward the Drive-Thru window, he fished his wallet from his hip pocket. Whenever he glanced to the right, he more than half expected to see someone sitting there in the passenger's seat.

It's got to be from the strain I'm under . . . because of what's going on, he told himself as he pulled to a stop in front of the display menu.

"Make I take your order, please?"

The voice coming over the speaker system startled Michael, making him jump. He quickly scanned the menu and was just about to order a Whopper, fries, and a Pepsi when he glanced up. Directly in front of the car was a man with a large Burger King bag in hand, walking out to his parked car. A spark of recognition made Michael do a double-take.

" . . . him . . ."

The faint voice whispered, but before Michael could respond, the sudden blare of the voice from the microphone interrupted his thoughts.

"Sir? May I take your order, please?"

Michael watched the man place the bag of food on his car roof, fish his car keys from his pants pocket, unlock the car door, and slide in behind the steering wheel. The car — a battered black Mustang — started up, sending a billowing puff of exhaust into the cold night as the driver let the engine warm up, then backed out of the parking space. Bright lights from the restaurant danced and wavered over the car windows, blocking Michael's view of the driver; but with a sudden spark of recognition, he realized it was that janitor from the Student Union . . . What was his name? The one who had been bugging Sarah last fall.

" . . . him! . . ."

The voice whispered again, louder, more insistent as the janitor's car pulled slowly toward the exit onto

379

Route 2.

"Oh my God," Michael muttered, his mouth going suddenly dry. He rubbed his hand over his lips as he watched the car slow for the turn. "Please, sir . . . you're holding up the line," the voice over the speaker said. "Would you please either place your order or else move along?"

Michael stepped down on the accelerator. An overweight woman and two children who were just leaving the restaurant had to jump back onto the sidewalk as Michael came around the side of the building a bit too fast. Through the closed window, he heard her shouted complaint, nothing more than a rasping buzz that sounded like an enraged hornet, but he ignored her, his eyes fastened on the other car as it pulled out onto the road.

"*. . . yes! . . . him . . .*"

The voice hissed loudly in his head as Michael jerked the steering wheel hard to the left and then sped up to close the distance between him and the rapidly receding taillights of the janitor's car.

"What the hell's his name?" Michael asked himself aloud. Seeing no cars between them, he eased up on the gas a little, not wanting to alert the driver that he was being followed.

"*. . . Alan . . . Griffin . . .*"

A shiver raced through Michael when the name popped into his mind. Damned if it didn't sound as though someone had said it out loud! Again, he glanced nervously at the empty passenger's seat.

This is crazy! This is completely wacko! he thought, but he didn't stop following the twin red taillights. He nervously gnawed at his lower lip as he wondered why he was doing this. Why follow some guy's car? What was the big deal? He had seen this university janitor — Alan Griffin — leave the Burger King with a big bag full of food. So what? Why should that make him suspicious?

"... *it's him!* ..."

The voice rasped in the darkness of the car like metal scraping against metal. Michael swallowed several times, trying to get rid of the hard lump in his throat, but it didn't do any good. All he knew was he *had* to check this out.

He was so preoccupied with thoughts and speculations that he barely noticed that Griffin's car was slowing down. Michael almost drove straight into his tail-end before the Mustang took a sharp left-hand turn. Michael hit the brakes hard. His tires skidded on the road, but then, once the car in front of him had made its turn, he hit the gas and sped ahead.

But in that instant, he memorized the license plate number. He drove just a short distance down the road, waited, and then turned back so he could check out exactly why Alan Griffin, with a bag full of hamburgers, would be pulling into the parking lot of the E-Z Veazie Motel.

— 3 —

The light snapped on in the bathroom, blasting into Sarah's eyes like an exploding star. She had no true sense of time, but she guessed it had been at least an hour since Alan had left her lying on her side in the bathtub with her face mashed flat against the cold, white porcelain tub edge. Her arms were jacked up behind her back, and her legs were buckled up in front of her. After she came to, she hadn't been able to change position, so her arms and legs were numb with pins and needles. Now, after so long, she had lost all sensation in her limbs, and the fiery edge of pain was nothing more — or less — than a constant, droning presence.

"Hey, you must be getting kinda uncomfortable in

381

here, huh?" Alan said. His tight laughter echoed weirdly off the close walls of the bathroom.

Sarah tried to look at him but could barely focus; he was no more than a watery shadow. When he knelt down beside her, she could see that he was smiling a wide idiot's grin as he ran his fingers gently through her hair.

"Or are you nice 'n' comfy here, huh?" he whispered almost soothingly.

When he leaned closer, Sarah's vision cleared, and she saw that in his other hand, he was holding his hunting knife. The honed tip of the blade was pointing straight at her. Whimpering inside her muzzle of duct tape, Sarah kept her eyes tightly shut and filled her mind with frantic prayers for no pain, no suffering as she waited to feel the razor sting drag across her exposed throat. In her fear-crazed imagination, she could already hear the slow spiraling echo of her stifled screams as her blood pumped from the gaping wound in her neck and gurgled down the bathtub drain.

When Alan grabbed a fistful of hair and lifted her head, her scalp felt as if it were on fire. The pulse in her neck throbbed feathery hammer blows as the cold steel of the knife touched lightly behind her left ear where her pulse pounded the hardest. The shock of the touch was almost electric. Her body jerked with rigid muscle spasms, and she was close to fainting as the tip of the knife worked its way underneath the duct tape. Then, with one quick, rough tug, the knife ripped up through the tape.

More pain followed, but it was almost a relief to Sarah as Alan jerked her head back and forth and unwound the tape. Just that little bit of motion made blood begin to flow back into her arms and legs. Her skin was stretched, but she ignored the pain in the glorious rush of having her mouth free once again. With a roaring gasp, she sucked in a deep lungful of air.

Once Alan finished removing the tape, Sarah slumped down, resting her throbbing head against the side of the bathtub. A line of drool ran from her mouth to her shoulder as hot tears of relief coursed down her cheeks. Once she dared to, she opened her eyes again and looked up at Alan.

"I guess I'm gonna have to let you up for a bit," Alan said. "Got you some supper here." He was smiling, but there was a wicked gleam in his eyes, and he still gripped the knife tightly as if he was just itching to finish her off now. "You ain't gonna give me any trouble now, are you?" Before Sarah could respond, he reached behind her and quickly untied the ropes binding her. As soon as the pressure was released, blood rushed into her arms and legs with a fiery surge.

Still unable to speak, Sarah looked at him with eyes that felt as if they had been dusted with powdered glass. She feebly raised one hand and gripped the edge of the tub. Gritting her teeth, she tried to sit up as pain sang a stainless steel tune along every nerve, bone, and muscle. She was too weak even to try. After a few seconds, she collapsed back into the tub, her body trembling as though she were freezing to death.

"Oh, what'sa matter? You need help?" Alan asked. "Or are you just so comfortable where you are you wanna stay there?"

Numb with shock, Sarah simply glared at him in silence.

"Come on, then," Alan said. He slid his hands around her back and under her legs, and stood up. Cradling her like a baby, he carried her into the bedroom and lowered her with surprising gentleness onto the double bed. As soon as she felt the firm comfort of the mattress beneath her, she lost control. She shook the bed as she started to cry uncontrollably.

"Hey, your stuff must be pretty fuckin' cold by now," a faint voice said. It reverberated with echo, as though coming from the end of a long, dark tunnel.

Dim consciousness and red, pulsating pain returned to Sarah in an audible rush. She eased her eyes open to mere slits and found herself staring up at a yellowed, water-stained ceiling. For several heartbeats—the only true measure of time she knew anymore—she just lay there, studying the grainy patterns of dirty smudges. Her gaze went unfocused as she drifted back to her childhood, remembering how, whenever she was sick, she would lie on the couch in the living room and look up, imagining what it would be like if gravity suddenly reversed and she could walk on the ceiling.

Where the hell am I? she asked herself, letting the sphere of her awareness widen.

Her arms were like coils of useless rope at her sides. Every joint in her wrists and hands ached dully as her fingers rubbed small circles on the nubbly bedspread. It felt as grimy as the ceiling looked. A high, rhythmic sound, like heavy panting, was coming from somewhere down by her feet, but she told herself not to worry about that . . . at least not until she could sit up.

She had no way of knowing how long she had been asleep—or unconscious. Her body was dishrag limp, drained of everything. Whenever she even started to think about the pain and suffering she had been through over the last—what? days? weeks? a lifetime?—a dark curtain would drop down over her mind to protect her.

But where am I?

She forced herself to roll over. After some violent effort, she managed to swing her feet to the floor and slowly, achingly sat up. The mattress creaked beneath her weight and then started to sway gently from side to side.

Pulsing, black waves of dizziness threatened to throw her back down again, but she struggled to hang on.

"I—" she said, but that was all she could manage. Her mouth and throat were desert dry, and no amount of licking seemed to help. Her hands and arms pulsated with heat as blood tingled inside long unused muscles. She gripped her head tightly, desperately hoping she could stop the room from spinning. Glancing around, she finally realized she was on a double bed in what looked like a seedy motel room.

"If you don't want it, I could probably finish it off for you," Alan said. He was slouched in the single, battered easy chair, his feet up on the coffee table in front of him as he watched a movie on the TV. Sarah's eyes were drawn to the flashing, high-contrast figures moving across the screen, but she couldn't tell what the movie was. It sounded like a raunchy, soft-core porn movie on a late-night cable station. The colors were adjusted much too bright; they made her vision blur as tears filled her eyes.

Alan looked over his shoulder at her, took a sip of soda from a paper cup, and belched loudly.

"You looked so comfortable there, I didn't have the heart to wake you up," he said with a thin smirk on his face. Groaning, as if it took great effort, he dropped his feet to the floor, leaned down, and picked up a crumpled Burger King bag. Opening the top, he looked inside and said, "Hope you like your Whoppers cold." He pulled out a boxed hamburger, a large container of French fries, and a paper cup of soda that was soggy and beaded with condensation. He placed them carefully on the table in front of him.

Sarah looked at the food but didn't move. She wasn't able to move. The steady thump of her pulse filled her head with mounting pressure. Her arms and legs were all tingly and useless. As much as she tried to bring the room into focus, her vision kept glazing over, as if she

385

were looking through a foot-thick piece of plate glass. The mere thought of food sent a knifelike pain jabbing into her stomach. If nothing else, she knew she should eat to try to regain her strength. She couldn't give in. But she was convinced her whole system had shut down. She knew she should be hungry, just as she should have to go to the bathroom; but right now, both activities seemed as foreign to her as flapping her arms and flying.

"No, I'm not—"

Her voice cut off abruptly when something behind Alan caught her attention. In the corner of the room, over by the rusty heater beneath the window, she saw a dark, wavering circle. At first she thought it was just a stain on the wall, but then she realized that it was spreading out across the floor, soaking like a wash of thin ink into the cheap carpet. Sarah watched in amazement, her breath catching in her throat as the hazy blot darkened and spread. Her first panicked thought was that the heater must have sprung a leak of oil or something, but then she realized the darkness had dimension. It was hovering in the air, billowing and expanding like a thick ball of smoke in the space between her and the wall.

Alan didn't notice her reaction. He was too busy digging around inside the Burger King bag, picking up loose French fries and popping them into his mouth like candy. His gaze was fixed on the images on the TV screen.

As she watched the steadily enlarging cloud over by the window, Sarah wanted to scream. She calmed herself and sniffed the air, wondering if the heater was on fire. She didn't want to sound the alarm, though, because she realized this might be exactly what she needed—something that would draw attention to the motel room. A fire would bring firemen and policemen, and she would be found! It was almost too much to hope for.

"No, I—I'm too—" Sarah said, then cut herself off and

groaned loudly before collapsing back onto the bed. She was hoping to draw Alan's attention so he wouldn't notice the smoke until it was too late, but when she glanced over by the heater again, she was surprised to see that the dark cloud was gone. For several heartbeats, she stared at the wall in utter disbelief, but there was no trace of the billowing, dark stain. After she closed her eyes, she realized that it had looked vaguely human-shaped, but by then she was too deep in misery and depression to react.

"Not hungry, huh?" Alan said, casually glancing over his shoulder at her. He made as if to stand up and come over to the bed but then sank back into the comfort of his chair. He made a mental note to tie Sarah up before he went to sleep, but he wasn't overly concerned; she was much too wasted to be any problem right now. Smiling to himself, he turned his attention back to the X-rated movie on the motel cable system and slowly unwrapped the Whopper he had bought for her. Holding it in one hand, he brought it up to his mouth and took a huge bite. A glob of ketchup ran down his chin. His other hand slid down to the hard bulge of his crotch and started to massage gently as he watched the frenzied action on the TV.

Chapter Twenty-seven

Midnight Visitor

— 1 —

The TV was off, and the room was cast in darkness when Sarah's eyes suddenly snapped wide open. A voice whispering close to her ear as she slept had yanked her to instant alertness. Gooseflesh raced over her arms and legs as she sucked in a breath and held it while her eyes widened and shifted back and forth, trying to pierce the darkness.

It must have been a dream, she thought.

She looked frantically around the room. The ethereal details of the dream were dissolving in her mind even as she became aware of the harsh reality of where she was and what had happened to her. She was lying in bed in a seedy motel. The person sleeping soundly beside her on the double bed was Alan Griffin. She was still wearing the clothes she'd been wearing on Friday night, the night Alan had kidnapped her from behind her dormitory. Hunger, thirst, intense physical pain, and mental anguish all vied for immediate attention, but for some reason, she wanted to remember what the reedy voice had whispered to her in the night.

She tried to move, but her hands were bound tightly behind her back. Her legs were also tied. Heaving a

388

shuddering breath of pain and frustration, she began twisting her hands back and forth, trying to loosen the rope. She knew it was hopeless, but she had to try.

The old bedsprings creaked beneath her shifting weight as she worked the ropes back and forth, trying to slip her hands through the loops. She was close to giving up when her fingers brushed against a bunch of knots. Unbelievably, she could twist her hands and get her fingers under one strand of the rope.

You can do it. You can do it, she coaxed herself as her fingertips pushed against a knot. For the longest time, it felt as though she was just wasting energy, but then the knot slipped, and the pressure around her wrists eased.

"Holy shit," she muttered, not quite daring to believe it was true. The rope felt as if it was peeling off a layer or two of skin as she pulled and squeezed her hand and found she could actually move it. Holding her breath and pulling ever so slowly, she slipped first one hand, then the other free.

Maybe this is a dream, too, she thought with a sudden flood of panic. *Or if it isn't, what happens if Alan wakes up?*

Moving as quietly and as slowly as possible, she bent down and began undoing the knots that bound her legs together. Her breath caught like fire in her lungs when Alan shifted position in the bed. Any second, she expected to feel his iron-tight grip clamp down on her shoulder and pull her back down onto the bed.

She kicked and pulled her legs free, and then carefully shifted her legs out from under the covers and sat up on the edge of the bed. The bedsprings complained loudly. She tensed, listening and waiting, but Alan slept on. She knew she should get up and run for the door—just get the hell out of here, but she also knew her body was too weak to move just yet. She looked at the door to freedom; but as much as she tried to concentrate, to focus her mind, her eyes were continually drawn to the corner under the window, beside the heater.

The darkness there did indeed seem somehow deeper, almost as if there were a tunnel there, drawing her attention, gently pulling her down toward it. She remembered now that her dream had *something* to do with that part of the room. But what?

What the hell did that voice say?

Through the drawn curtain, she could see a faint, blue glow, either a streetlight or the motel's sign. She wanted desperately to go to the window and look out. She had to figure out where she was, but she wasn't even sure she had the strength to stand, much less walk.

The room was cold, almost frigid, as she sat on the edge of the bed and tried to piece everything together. It must be late Sunday night or early Monday morning. That would mean she had been missing for two full days now.

"Jesus Christ!" Sarah said, pressing her hands over her eyes and rubbing vigorously. The darkness behind her eyelids pulsated with eerie red light. "Where the hell am I?"

". . here . . ."

The single word came to her as light as a feather touch out of the darkness. A cold shock gripped Sarah as her eyes darted around the room, seeking the source of the voice.

Had someone spoken? Or had the voice been inside her head?

After scanning the pressing darkness, her gaze returned to the soft glow outside the window curtain. Her breath caught like a flame in her chest when she looked down at the floor beside the heater. The darkness there was thickening.

She told herself it had to be a trick of the light — just a shadow cast by the streetlight or the motel sign outside. But down by the floor and spreading up the wall was a blackness so deep it was almost solid, as though the wall and floor were dripping with oil. The window curtain stirred gently. On a cold, winter night like this, Sarah knew the window wouldn't be open, and she could hear that the heater wasn't running, but *something* was making the curtain ruffle gently and bulge outward . . . as if someone were standing behind it, pushing it out.

Her throat went dry, and fear prickled her body like electricity when a face materialized out of the darkness beside the window. At first, it was no more than an indistinct white glow, looming out of the darkness like a dim light seen through thick fog. But with each hammering pulsebeat, the features got clearer and the form solidified until Sarah was positive the dark stain had taken the shape of someone standing there. As a ghastly underlighting got steadily brighter, the features became clearer until she saw

"*Tully!*"

The name burst out of her like a gunshot when recognition hit.

Her fear spiraled upward, whining like a power saw. Sarah wanted to deny it, but the longer she stared, the clearer his pale face became. Scraggly blond hair framed his thin features—flat white skin, icy blue eyes, and tight, bloodless lips. The eerie glow radiating up from the floor cast his features with a pallid lifelessness. His face looked like that of a corpse, all except for the eyes. Tully regarded her with a cruel, unblinking gaze.

Sarah's ears thundered with her rapid pulse as she stared back at Tully, completely hypnotized. She was distantly aware of Alan on the bed beside her, but she didn't even think to worry about waking him up as she licked her lips and said in a low, strangled voice, "Tully! Where the hell have you been?"

Tully's face was fully resolved now, hovering in the darkness beside the window. His lips began to move, but

391

when he spoke, his words came in broken bursts, like a radio signal that was weak and scrambled.

"*I've . . . here all . . . time, Sarah . . . but I . . . help . . . anymore . . .*"

The voice didn't sound at all like him. It made her think of a dead tree branch, scratching a night-stained windowpane, of wet, rotten cloth being torn to shreds. It certainly wasn't a *human*-sounding voice. Hot currents of fear jolted her as she leaned forward off the bed. She wanted to stand up, to go to him, but waves of dizziness threatened to send her spinning back into unconsciousness.

"What's the matter, Tully?" she said, her voice crackling with desperate pleading. He looked so lonely, so sad, so helpless, so powerless. "Why can't I see you . . . the way I—the way I used to?"

"*It's too . . . late, Sarah . . . I can't . . . you anymore . . .*" Each word faded with a curiously diminishing echo.

"Please, Tully!" Sarah wailed. Her ears rang with the haunting resonance of his voice as fresh tears filled her eyes, blurring her vision. Tully's mouth kept moving, mouthing words as his face wavered and then slowly began to fade. The darkness of the room collapsed inward on him, dropping down like a heavy black curtain.

Sarah watched, horrified as Tully's face flickered like a sputtering candle and then dissolved. The hammering pressure in her head made her feel as if she were about to explode. Every nerve in her body was tingling as she wished with every ounce of energy she had that Tully would stay with her.

"Please don't go! *Please!* I need you . . . I need you *now!* Don't you understand that?" she cried. Clenching both hands into fists, she beat them in frustration against her legs, unmindful of the pain.

"*. . . too late . . .*"

Tully's voice warbled from the darkness with a curious

reverberation; then it was gone.

"Tully . . . *please!* Please! Don't go!" Sarah wailed.

Tears coursed down her face as she lurched up off the bed. Her legs collapsed beneath her, and she fell to her knees, reaching out feebly; but her mind told her the truth: it *was* too late. She had gotten what she had wanted all those years. Tully was gone *forever*, leaving behind only a cold, pressing silence. Darkness collapsed inward like an avalanche where he had been. Consumed by misery, Sarah pitched forward face-first onto the floor, releasing her agony in a long, agonized howl that gradually faded as consciousness slipped away from her.

— 2 —

A short way down Route 2, Michael turned around, drove back up the road, and pulled into the parking lot of the E-Z Veazie Motel. Cruising slowly, so he wouldn't draw attention to himself, he went down the line of units until he found Alan's car parked outside the last unit in the complex. In the glow of a distant streetlight, he could just make out the brass numbers of the shadowed door.

"Unit 26," he whispered, resisting the shiver that ran up the back of his neck.

Figuring it would be the least obvious, he parked his car in front of one of the other motel room doors, making sure he had a clear view of Alan's Mustang. He hoped to hell neither the night manager of the motel nor Alan would notice him there as he settled down in the car seat to watch and wait.

"You know this is fucking ridiculous," he said to himself as he slouched behind the steering wheel. He still couldn't shake the feeling that someone was sitting beside him in the front seat, but he pushed the thought away. His eyes grew heavy with sleep. Without the heater running, cold soon penetrated the car, making him shiver and helping to keep him awake.

He couldn't stop wondering why he was even doing this. What he needed right now was a decent meal and a good night's sleep, not to be sitting out here, freezing his ass off, playing private detective, staking out a college janitor who happened to be shacking up in a cheap motel.

What was the big deal? From what Michael knew about the E-Z Veazie, it was just the kind of place a low-life like Alan Griffin would go after picking up some floozy in a bar downtown. It made no sense to be following him — no sense at all . . . except for that voice.

Michael cringed, remembering how clearly the voice had sounded in his ears, first telling him he was hungry and then telling him to watch Alan Griffin. He was positive it had not been his own thoughts. He convinced himself that, although faint and raspy, the voice had *definitely* been in the car with him, not inside his head. No doubt the tension and stress of the past few days had strained his nerves past their limit. He was starting to fall apart, really lose his grip on things. The strain and worry he'd been under would certainly drive anyone crazy.

"It can't be my imagination," Michael whispered.

Sighing deeply, he leaned his head back against the car seat and let his eyes slip slowly shut. A corner of his mind warned him that if he fell asleep now, he probably wouldn't wake up until morning, and by then he might look out and see that Alan Griffin's car was long gone. But it was so tempting; it felt so good to shut his eyes and let the bunched-up tension in his shoulders relax, to feel the stiffness in his neck and arms unwind. As he drifted off to sleep, a voice whispered in his ear.

"*. . . realize . . . she's in . . . there . . .*"

"Umm . . . I figured she was," Michael said dreamily. Eyes still closed, he twisted his head to the right as though looking at someone in the seat beside him. He barely registered the creaking of fabric in the passenger's seat. Opening his eyes to narrow slits, he smiled and nodded at the pale, blond young man he saw, sitting there beside him.

"You have to . . . help her . . . I can't . . . doesn't want . . ."

Michael groaned softly and then shivered as the cold night reached inside his coat. "I think she's all right . . . for now," he replied. The words tumbled from his mouth as if they had originated in his throat with no connection whatsoever to his brain. Heaving a deep sigh, he let his eyes slip shut again.

Pulsating darkness filled the inside of the car like oily smoke, heavy and close. Drifting in a state of semisleep, Michael imagined that the car was somehow magically sealed off from the rest of the world—isolated in its own environment. The wet rasping of his breathing sounded like grinding metal as he drifted deeper . . . deeper into himself. And the deeper he went, the clearer the voice became.

"Michael! Aren't you listening to me? Sarah's in trouble, and you have to help her. She doesn't want me anymore."

Whose voice is that? Michael wondered lazily. *It almost sounds like someone I've heard before. Kinda like Sarah's voice, actually.*

This time he was too relaxed to feel the spike of fear the voice had given him earlier that evening. He didn't care. All he wanted to do was keep floating, drifting deeper and deeper into sleep. It was so calm, so quiet—except for that insistent voice.

Michael's head flopped lazily back and forth against the seat when cold hands that almost passed through him took hold of his coat collar and roughly shook him.

"I'm telling you, man! She's in that room right now! Room 26! I've been in there! I've seen her! If you don't do something to help

395

her, right now, both of you aren't going to get out of this thing alive! Don't you hear me, man?

"I . . . ummm," Michael said, moaning deeply in his chest. "I can't . . . right now. I'm . . . not . . ."

He raised one hand to his shoulder and made a feeble motion as if to swat aside the hands that were shaking him. But the shaking got steadily harder, more insistent. Michael's head lolled back and forth on the car seat. Like a swimmer who had plunged deep into the water and was now swimming up to the sparkling surface, he felt himself being violently tugged upward . . . upward against his will to consciousness. As he got closer to wakefulness, the voice began to fade.

". . . alive . . . if you don't . . . something right now!"

His mind began to clear. Hard-edge thoughts returned and with them cold, gnawing worry, twisted like a knife in his gut.

". . . that room . . . before it's . . . too . . ."

The voice was fading like the long, slow *whoosh* of a car speeding off into the distance in the night.

Michael's body jerked forward as his eyes snapped open. Sucking a huge gulp of freezing air into his lungs and shuddering with stark terror, he looked over at the seat beside him. It was empty.

"What the hell is going on?" he said. His eyes flicked wildly back and forth as he search his memory for any coherent traces of the dream he'd just had. Right here, in his car parked outside the E-Z Veazie Motel, he had seen and spoken to . . . whom? A young man—a blond kid with pale blue eyes and a grim, lifeless expression. But what had he said? As vivid and as real as his memory of the boy was, Michael could recall only fragments of their conversation, which had made perfect sense at the time.

He stretched out his arm and peeled back his coat cuff so he could see his watch. He shivered when he saw that it was midnight. His eyes darted over to the darkened doorway with the number 26.

"You're losing it, buddy," he whispered.

Tight, thin laughter escaped from him, but he found neither cheer nor reassurance in the sound. No matter how much or how little of his dream he could recall, it had left him with one single, clear conviction—Sarah was in that motel room, and he had to do something about it . . . now!

—3—

Sarah came to—she had no idea how much later. All she could see when she eased one eye open was that she was lying facedown on the floor with her arms and legs splayed wide. Her hands gripped the carpet as though she were an insect specimen, pinned to the wall. Pain inflamed every inch of her body like invisible biting insects. The left side of her face—the bruised side—was flat against the floor. Memory rushed back to her as she gritted her teeth and, forcing herself to ignore her pain, rolled over and sat up stiffly. She pulled her legs up against her chest and hugged herself tightly in an effort to stop the violent trembling that wracked her body.

Her eyes went immediately to the wall beside the window where she had seen Tully.

Behind her on the bed, Alan muttered something as he rolled over in his sleep. Tensing, Sarah leaned forward onto her hands and knees, and glanced at him over her shoulder. The shape on the bed thrashed out wildly, rustling the sheets, then with a deep snort, settled back down.

I've got to get the hell out of here, she thought as she stared at the closed door. *Just get the hell out of here and hope to hell I can find help.*

Her knee and hip joints creaked like old door hinges

397

as she eased herself to her feet. The darkness of the motel room throbbed with a subtle strobe effect as she glanced around. The red numbers of the digital alarm clock beside the bed glowed eerily: 12:02.

Sarah turned and cautiously approached the door. Her feet whispered on the thin carpet, but even the tiniest sound sent shivers racing up her back.

Please don't wake up! Please don't wake up! became her litany as she moved closer and closer to the door.

When she reached out and touched the cold metal doorknob, a sharp shock lanced her hand. Her fingers fumbled for the lock tab, found it, and clicked it to the side. She ran her hand up the side of the door until she found the security chain lock and slowly, carefully eased it out of the slot. The chain rattled lightly against the wood, but to her fear-heightened senses, it sounded like a burst of machine gun fire. Her hands were nearly numb as she turned the doorknob ever so slowly. The latch bolt clicked inside the door once . . . twice, sounding like double explosions. Holding her breath, she looked one last time behind her at the bed. Alan slept on undisturbed.

Thank God! Now please! . . . Please! she thought as she eased the door open. Frigid air swirled in through the narrow crack that appeared. Her teeth chattered wildly as she gazed out into the motel parking lot. In the soft glow of a streetlight, everything looked dreamy, unreal. The night was silent and deep except for the far-off whine of a truck on the highway. Several cars were parked in front of the motel, but her eyes were drawn to the peeling painted sign that said E-Z VEAZIE MOTEL.

We're only in Veazie? she wondered. *Why aren't we miles away from Orono?*

It didn't matter. She knew the important thing now was to get the hell out of here. If she could just make it to the motel office, there had to be someone on duty to register late-night guests. All she needed was less than half a minute to get far enough away from Alan so she would be safe.

— 4 —

At first, Michael thought he was dreaming again. Looking over at door number 26, he saw someone step out of the dark room into the night. It didn't take long to realize it looked like Sarah, dressed in nothing more than a blouse and jeans. He sat up straight behind the steering wheel and pinched his cheek hard to convince himself that he wasn't sleeping. It might not be Sarah, but *someone* was sneaking out of that room . . . the same room that voice in his dream had told him to watch.

"Holy *shit!*" Michael muttered when the person stepped out into the glow of the streetlight, and he saw her face clearly. It *was* Sarah! For a frozen instant, he sat, watching in amazement as she glanced furtively around the parking lot.

What the hell is she doing? he wondered as she tiptoed away from the door. For all he knew, she could have been shacked up here all weekend with another man—with Alan Griffin! Maybe *that's* what his dream had been warning him about: maybe Sarah was having an affair with the janitor. That would certainly explain why she had been acting so strange toward him lately.

But then he caught a glimpse of the side of her face when she turned to look at the streetlight. Against the pallor of her skin, he saw the dark stain of a bruise that went from just below her eye to her jaw line. Feeling a gush of sympathy, he popped open the driver's door and jumped out of the car.

"Hey! Sarah!" he shouted. The words came out of his mouth in two cloudy puffs of steam that hung suspended in the cold, night air. His voice echoed weirdly in the

399

stillness.

Sarah froze in midstep and crouched as she glanced frantically around, then looked over her shoulder into the motel room. Michael was moving around the front of the car, watching her intently, still unable to believe it was really her, when he saw the darkness inside the doorway suddenly deepen. Before he could fully register what was happening, two arms reached out and snagged Sarah. In the wink of an eye, she disappeared back into the room, leaving nothing behind but the fading echo of a scream.

Michael blinked his eyes rapidly and shook his head, fighting the illusory sensation that this was still all a dream as he started across the parking lot. The cold night air bit his lungs. He walked briskly at first, then, as panic flooded his brain, he broke into a run toward door 26. Just as he got to it, the door slammed shut with a hollow *boom*. Michael grabbed the doorknob and twisted it viciously back and forth. Through the door, he heard the rattle of the security chain being slid back into place.

"Open up! Open the fucking door!" he shouted as he slammed his shoulder repeatedly against the door.

Turning back toward the parking lot, he cupped his hands to his mouth and shouted as loud as he could, "Someone call the police!" Then, stepping away from the door, he hunched up and rammed into it as hard as he could, shoulder-first. The cheap lock gave way beneath the impact. Pinwheeling his arms for balance, Michael stumbled into the darkness.

"Michael!" a woman's voice screamed, loud and ragged. It didn't sound at all like Sarah's, but it was drowned out by a man's voice.

"You lousy son of a bitch! How the hell'd you ever find me?"

Before Michael could get his bearings, the dark room exploded with three flashes of light accompanied by three

400

ear-crashing explosions. Something tugged hard at his right side, spinning him around. His legs went all goofy and gave out from under him. Spinning in a lazy circle, he crumpled to the floor. If he had thought he was dreaming before, everything turned into pure nightmare as soon as the overhead light came on and he saw Alan Griffin, staring at him with a pistol leveled at his head.

Michael tried to stand, but the icy numbness in his side sent paralyzing waves through him. Sarah was cringing behind Alan, looking at him with fear-widened eyes. Her mouth gaped open, a perfect O from which came nothing but a strangled gasp.

"You *really* fucked up this time, lover boy!" Alan hissed. Michael watched helplessly as Alan turned quickly, cocked his arm, and smashed the butt end of the pistol against the back of Sarah's head. Without a sound, she collapsed onto the bed, bouncing twice before lying still. A steady hammering sound, growing louder with each beat, filled Michael's ears. The ceiling light flickered in time with each pulse, and his vision went blurry as he watched Alan move away from him. He wasn't even aware that Alan had picked Sarah up from the bed and carried her outside until he heard a car door slam shut and then the car start up.

Again, Michael struggled to get up off the floor, but he found that it took too much effort simply to raise his head. His arms and legs flopped around uncontrollably. He felt as if he were mired in glue, trapped like a cartoon fly to a piece of flypaper. The hammering sound in his ears grew steadily louder, filling his vision with thick, red, pulsating swirls.

"I —" Michael said, but before he could continue, his lungs cried out for more air. He tried to take a deep breath. Icy fear rushed through him when he couldn't feel his chest expand. Instead, from down near where the numbness seemed to be centered, he heard a loud, bub-

401

bly whistle. Rolling his head to one side, hoping to clear it, he looked down and saw the bright splotch of blood, seeping out from the circular hole in his coat. Seeing that made him aware for the first time of the hot stickiness covering his side.

Maybe that's the glue that's holding me down on the floor, he thought.

"Hey, you fuckin' moron!"

A growling voice came to him from far away. Looking up, Michael expected to see Alan leaning over him again, but there was no one there. The walls of the motel room looked as if they were reflected in a round fish bowl; everything was distorted, rippling with glassy reflections. Then a face loomed into view.

Who the hell is that? Michael wondered as he stared into wide, ice-blue eyes.

The person leaned over him, a grim smile splitting his face.

"You really fucked *yourself* up this time, huh?"

Michael opened his mouth to reply, but even though he could feel his mouth move, no words—not even any sounds—would come out. All he could hear was that thin, high-pitched whistling noise coming from his chest. His lips—his whole face felt like it was made of rubber.

Yeah, he thought as billowing red waves crashed around him, deepened to maroon, and then plunged into black as they folded in on top of him. *That's the problem . . . I'm made out of rubber and I've . . . I've sprung a leak . . .*

His head fell back against the floor with a resounding *thump.* He was only dimly aware that he was fading, that his life was slipping away. Darkness collapsed over him, embracing him with cold, smothering black arms.

— 5 —

Even through the burning haze of pain that made her

want to shriek, Sarah forced herself to keep her eyes closed, pretending she was still unconscious. By the whining sound of the engine and the sickening swaying motion, she knew she was in the car again, heading God knows where. Her back pressed painfully against the door handle; her head was thrown back, resting on the back of the seat. She opened her eyes slowly, but when she saw the black hole of a gun aimed straight at her forehead, she gave a startled cry and sat up quickly.

"You don't want to make even the *tiniest* fuckin' little move," Alan growled as he glanced over at her. He had one hand on the steering wheel, playing it loosely back and forth as he drove. The other hand—the one holding the gun—was cocked up over the back of the car seat.

"What the hell did you do to me?" Sarah asked. Moving one hand with exaggerated slowness, she brought it up to the back of her head and gently touched the hard knob at the base of her skull. Even a slight pressure sent white splinters of pain exploding through her head.

"Sorry 'bout that. I had to hit you," Alan said. Then, more tightly, he added, "All because of that—that fuckin' *jerk-off* boyfriend of yours!"

Sarah sucked in a shallow breath. So she *hadn't* imagined it! Michael had been there at the motel. And now he must be—

Dead.

The thought was too terrifying to contemplate, but it wouldn't go away. She tried to clear her mind and bring back the details of what had happened, but everything was lost in a tumult of hazy images, fear, and pain. Fragments of the events in the motel room flashed through her mind like a grotesquely underlit slide show.

She remembered hearing Michael shout to her just as she was sneaking out the motel door . . . She remembered looking up and seeing him coming toward her, and not believing her eyes . . . She remembered feeling

403

strong hands grab her from behind and pull her back into the room . . . She remembered choking on her fear as she cowered back behind Alan as Michael slammed through the door . . . She remembered, while the room was still dark, hearing three ear-splitting shots and seeing three bright flashes of light from a gun . . . She remembered the numb shock when she saw Michael lying on the floor of the motel room with a puddle of blood around him.

Other images, less clear, less coherent, rose up in her mind . . . memories of seeing and trying to talk to Tully . . . of him standing in the corner of the room and slowly fading away as he repeated the words—*"Too late!"*

And now—*because of her*—Michael was dead.

Sarah shifted her gaze away from the gun to the road ahead. The headlights pushed back the darkness of a narrow tree-lined road, highlighting the snowplow ridges that lined both sides of the road. Beyond them was nothing but towering, black pine trees, looking like jagged teeth against the dusty night sky. For some reason, what came to mind was the memory of that night almost two years ago, when she had been driving to Westbrook with her mother along a dark road out of Hilton. It filled her with a gnawing sense of dread.

But that was long ago; there was much more recent pain. Tears stung her eyes whenever she recalled her last glimpse of Michael, lying on the motel room floor with blood bubbling from the hole in his chest. She tried hard to believe that he wasn't dead; she couldn't even contemplate such a thought, but it was obvious the bullet had done serious, probably fatal damage. She blocked as much of it out of her mind as she could, finding a slim hope that the sound of the shots or the squealing of tires as Alan sped out of the motel parking lot must have drawn *someone's* attention.

"Where did you . . . get that—the gun?" Sarah asked.

Her voice almost choked off because the image of Michael dying slowly on the floor wouldn't go away. She wanted to cry, but right now, the pure terror of her situation dried up all her emotions.

Alan smiled and gave a casual shrug. "I had it all along. I just hadn't had a need for it . . . till tonight." He gave the pistol a reassuring shake but didn't shift its aim away from her. "Wouldn't have tonight, either, if that asshole hadn't shown up."

You lousy fucking bastard! Sarah thought, but she forced herself not to say it aloud. All she wanted to think about was getting out of this alive and making *damned* sure Alan Griffin paid for what he had done. Her eyes brimmed with tears as she watched him, staring grimly at the road ahead.

"So . . . what are you going to do?" she asked, her voice trembling with fear. "Wh—where are you taking me?"

Alan sniffed with laughter. "Just shut the fuck up, all right? You don't fool me, not for one goddamned minute!"

"What do you mea—" She stopped herself when Alan jabbed the gun toward her.

"I said *shut* the *fuck* up!" He shook the gun on each syllable for emphasis. "I'll use this! I swear to Christ I will! You think I don't know what you're up to? If you keep your mouth shut, I just might let you live . . . at least a little longer."

Sarah tried to ease back in the car seat but couldn't; every muscle and nerve in her body was thrumming. The minutes and miles stretched out as they drove on in silence.

It wasn't long before Sarah realized that they were going around in circles. Apparently Alan had no idea where to go or what to do; he was freaking out, that much was obvious from his tense posture and the grim

405

expression on his face. Maybe shooting Michael had shaken him more than he was willing to let on. If so, then maybe . . . just maybe she could use this to gain the upper hand.

"I'm gonna have to get gas soon," Alan said. He looked from the dashboard to Sarah with a lowered, hostile glance. The pale light from the dash gave his face a gaunt, hollow look. For an instant, the pale image of his face looked more like Tully's than his own.

Sarah shifted as far away from him as she could, pressing her body tightly against the door. She glanced down at the door handle and considered—right now—snapping the latch open and jumping out of the moving car. As if he was reading her mind, Alan chuckled softly and said, "Don't even think about it, all right?" He straightened out his arm and pointed the gun squarely at her face. "I fixed the latch on your door so it can't be opened from the inside."

"I wasn't—"

"I swear to Christ," Alan said, laughing softly as he shook his head. "You must think I'm so ignorant."

Sarah remained silent.

"You never even knew I was on to you all along, did you?" he asked. His eyes kept flicking back and forth between the road and her face. The expression on his face was tight, immobile.

"I have no idea what you're talking about," Sarah said. "All I know is, whatever happens to me, you're never going to get away with this. Not now that you killed—"

Alan cut her off with a burst of laughter that sprayed the windshield with spittle. "Get away with this? Oh, that's rich—that's rich, all right! Won't get away with this!" He almost lost control of the car when, still chuckling, he took his hand off the steering wheel to wipe his mouth. "I know damned well what you, your fuck-head boyfriend, and that son-of-a-bitch Elliott Clark have been

406

doing. You've been setting me up all along so I'd get caught!"

Sarah frowned with confusion and shook her head.

"Come on! Don't play stupid with me, okay?" Alan snapped. "You think I don't know?"

"Well, whatever—You won't get away with it," she said, forcing courage into her voice. "What's tomorrow—Monday, right?"

They locked eyes for a moment, but before Alan could respond, she went on, talking to give herself at least the illusion of hope. "I don't know if you've checked the newspapers or TV, but I *must* have been reported missing by now." His grip on the steering wheel tightened noticeably. "And even if I haven't been, as soon as they find"—her voice choked for a moment, but she forced herself to continue—"as soon as they find Michael, the police are going to talk to the motel manager, and they'll get a description of you and your car."

"I'll hot-wire another car, then," Alan said, snorting as he wiped his nose with the back of his hand. "And anyway, do you honestly think that bloated sow at the desk could describe me? She probably couldn't describe her own goddamned father." He tried to sound snide and self-assured, but Sarah could tell by his deepening frown that he was bothered by what she said.

"Then what about work?" she asked, hoping to enlarge the tiny gap in his facade. "You know damned well, as soon as you don't show up this afternoon, the police are going to put it all together. A description of you and your car will go out to *every* police station in the state."

"That's it!" Alan said, snapping his fingers and looking at her with a wide grin. "Thanks for the suggestion. All I need to do is buy some time, right? A couple of hours at the most."

He looked at her and smiled widely. His face looked sickly yellow in the dashboard light as he gritted his teeth and stepped down on the accelerator. The car growled like an angry beast as it sprang forward into the night.

"I can steal another car easy enough, so all I gotta do is make sure I get to a phone booth and call in sick sometime this morning. Then we'll head on up to Canada. Once we cross the border, they ain't never gonna nail me for *anything* I did. Talk about not getting away — *you're* the one who ain't gonna get away."

Chapter Twenty-eight

Pursuit

— 1 —

Late Sunday night, a little after midnight, Elliott was sitting on the battered couch in his apartment, nursing his fourth or fifth beer. Who was counting? He stared vacantly at the old-time movie on TV. His mind was occupied by what had—and *hadn't*—happened today. The police still hadn't located Alan Griffin for questioning. If they were following any leads or had any suspects, they certainly were keeping it a secret. Sarah Lahikainen was still missing. No phone calls; no ransom note; no nothing. And nobody was telling him what—if anything—they had discovered about the break-in at the Student Union or those tracks in the snow that indicated a struggle of some kind. Elliott was convinced they were connected with Sarah's disappearance, but the police were stonewalling him, telling him only that they were investigating *every* angle.

So that left things pretty much where they had been all weekend, except for what Devin Lahikainen had told Elliott about his visit to his mother in Waterville. After describing what Ester had said, neither man could figure out what to make of it. They both agreed that, in all likelihood, Devin's mother was far gone in senility, but they found many things she said—especially about Sarah being in danger and near death—unnerving. This talk about a "family ghost" and invisible friends struck Elliott as pure nonsense, but he had to admit that it all bothered him.

Around eleven o'clock, Devin had gone back to his room at the Black Bear Motel. Elliott knew he should get to bed; he had the early shift in the morning. Problem was, he wasn't the least bit tired. In fact, he felt wired. He couldn't stop wondering and worrying about Sarah, and he couldn't control the angry waves of frustration inside him. He wanted to *do* something, but all he had reached were dead ends. Every avenue of action was either exhausted or else roadblocked by the police.

From the kitchen, the police scanner occasionally squawked with voices and bursts of static, but there was nothing of interest coming over the air tonight. Elliott tried to convince himself he should just forget about it—go to bed, get some rest. One of the local cops had hinted that they were going to bring the FBI in on the case, but Elliott still wasn't satisfied.

"What the hell can I do?" Elliott whispered harshly.

His stomach bubbled with sour acid. His hand holding the beer can tightened involuntarily, caving in the flimsy aluminum sides. Sighing heavily, he looked around the darkened apartment, his gaze darting like a frantic dragonfly from dark corner to dark corner. He forced a tight laugh when he realized he had expected to see that thin, blond kid again, sitting in the corner, staring at him with those weird, unblinking eyes of his as he whispered—

"Help her! . . . You must help her! . . . I can't!"

Elliott shivered, recalling the dull, emotionless timbre of the boy's voice. He tried not to think it, but it was exactly what he imagined a dead person would sound like . . . if a dead person could speak.

"Who the hell *is* that kid anyway?" Elliott asked him-

410

self, grinding his teeth in frustration. "Better yet, *what* the fuck is he?" Devin's talk about ghosts made him think along lines he simply couldn't accept. He had never believed in the supernatural, but almost against his will now, he was starting to wonder if perhaps that kid might have been some kind of ghost or apparition that haunted the apartment building. Or maybe he was this *haamu* Sarah kept talking about on her tapes. Was something like that even possible?

Probably not, Elliott concluded. More likely, he had hallucinated after a few too many drinks. But whatever the hell he was, the memory of that night — and his pale face . . . his glowing, unblinking eyes — sent chills tingling up and down Elliott's spine. He was so lost in thoughts and speculations that he missed the beginning of the report that came in over the police scanner.

". . . is correct. We have a ten-forty-nine at the E-Z Veazie Motel on Route 2, reported at zero-five hours. Rescue has been dispatched to the scene, and a medical examiner has been requested. Suspect or suspects, apparently a Caucasian male and female, have fled in a late-model black Mustang. Over."

"What the . . ." Elliott shouted. He jerked forward and sat on the edge of the couch, tensing as he listened to the crackling static that interfered with the report. A ten-forty-nine was a possible homicide, and a request for a medical examiner, a ten-forty-seven, meant *someone* was dead — or dying. Elliott got up and walked quickly into the kitchen to hear the exchange of radio voices.

"Car 5 to HQ. Do you have any further details? Over."

Elliott held his breath and waited for the reply.

"Not many details at this point," the dispatcher said. "The victim is a young, male Caucasian. Ethel Gustafson, the motel manager, found him with two bullet wounds in the chest and he appeared not to be breathing. We have only a partial ID of the registration num-

411

ber. The last three digits, according to the witness, might be 3-3-7. That's 3-3-7. Do you copy? Over."

"I copy. Over."

"Bingo! That's him," Elliott said. His mind felt razor-sharp as he focused every bit of his attention on the glowing red light of the police scanner on the kitchen counter. He didn't need to hear the other numbers of the license plate; he knew exactly what they were. The color and make of the car matched the description of Alan's car, which he had given the police yesterday. This was no longer just a hunch or coincidence; it *had* to be Alan Griffin.

"Suspect's vehicle was reportedly seen leaving the motel at a high rate of speed, heading north on Route 2. We don't have any confirmation, but we figure he's heading for the Interstate. Wait a second . . ."

Elliott tried to swallow the hard lump that had formed in his throat, but it wouldn't go down. He rubbed his hands on his pant legs as he stared intensely at the scanner, willing the dispatcher to come back on and give him some more information.

"All right, you son of a bitch, you've gone and killed someone," Elliott muttered. He felt mild relief, knowing that it wasn't a woman; there was a chance Sarah was still alive.

"Either way, I'm gonna nail you," Elliott muttered as he waited for voices to break into the radio static.

"I just got a complaint from a motorist who was forced off the road in Veazie. A vehicle answering the description of the suspect's car has been seen heading north on I-95." A loud *click* came over the airwaves, and the police dispatcher continued, "Attention all units. Be on the lookout for a black Ford Mustang, late model, with a license plate ending 3-3-7. That's a ten-thirty-two. Suspect or suspects are armed and considered dangerous. Over."

"HQ, this is car 5. I copy," the patrolman replied.

412

"State police have been notified," the dispatcher said, "but all available units are tied up with a trailer truck that jackknifed out on I-95, south of Bangor. I'll radio up ahead to the Howland police. Hopefully they'll be able to get someone out there. Over."

"Ten-four. I'm on my way to the E-Z Veazie," the patrolman said. "ETA under three minutes. Over and out."

Elliott yanked open the kitchen drawer, grabbed his gun and car keys, pulled on his winter coat and gloves, and raced down the stairs and out to his car. Though it was against the law for a civilian to have a police scanner in his car, Elliott had one; he also had a CB and would be able to call for help if he needed it. Right now, especially because there was no available police units in the area, his only thought was to get out to I-95 and see if he could run down that son-of-a-bitch Alan Griffin before he killed anyone else.

— 2 —

Once they were heading north on the Interstate, it didn't take long for the high, steady whine of the tires on the road, working in combination with her pain and exhaustion, to lull Sarah into a dreamy daze. Leaning her head back against the seat, she closed her eyes and willed with every ounce of energy for everything simply to disappear. She concentrated on her pain, mentally picturing it as nothing more than faint flashes of lightning on the distant horizon.

Memories came rushing at her in jolting, distorted bursts. The image of Michael lying on his back on the floor in a widening puddle of blood got steadily sharper, more horrifying. She imagined Michael staring up at her with silent, gape-mouthed anguish. The bullet hole in his chest no longer made that high-pitched whistling noise as the air escaped from his punctured lung; the wound

413

turned into a blood-filled, distended mouth that screamed and *screamed* as thick red bubbles foamed up out of it and popped like gore-stained soapsuds. Sarah clearly pictured Michael's dying face, his agonized features shifting and changing until they finally merged into the thin, pale face of Tully.

"Oh, Tully," Sarah whispered as she rolled her head back and forth on the seat. "Tully . . . why the hell can't you come when I need you? What's the matter with you?"

Sarah squinted as she concentrated hard, trying to focus every ounce of mental energy into calling to Tully, willing him back into existence; but she knew it was futile. She tried to convince herself that she could feel him close by, a dark presence in the car with her, trying to reach her . . . wanting to help her, but when she glanced quickly into the backseat, she saw that it was empty.

"Please, Tully," Sarah whispered. *"Can't you tell how much I need you?"*

The only sound was the whining of car tires on asphalt. She glanced over at Alan, who sat stone-faced behind the steering wheel, his eyes focused straight ahead at the road. Looking through the rear window, Sarah could see the dark highway pulling away with a nauseating, backward glide. There were no other cars on the road, either in front of or behind them. That struck her as strange, but she let it go for now. All around her, the steady hum of the car's engine created a soothing background noise that wavered and gradually diminished but never quite disappeared. She leaned her head against the seat and closed her eyes. A cold, muffled silence filled the car. For a moment Sarah had the disorienting impression that her ears were packed with cotton.

I should have listened to them, she thought bitterly. *To Tully and to my grandmother. If I had listened to them, this wouldn't be happening.*

414

Her grandmother's words rang in her memory with a lonely, desperate echo—

"You wanted him! Not the other way around. When you called him, he came. Now, if you tell him to go away, he will. But you must understand—our haamu has a life of his own. If you give in to your anger, there's no way you—or anyone else—will be able to stop him."

"But I tried," Sarah whispered as tears formed in her eyes and ran down her cheeks. "I wanted him to help me, so I tried like hell to give in to my—"

A sudden flash of white light exploded across her vision accompanied by a loud, wet smacking sound. Her head filled with a loud *zing* that rapidly shot up the scale like a dentist's drill. Her head slammed against the side window. On impact, another blinding bolt of light filled her sight as a booming voice roared out, "He ain't never gonna help you! There ain't *no one* gonna help you!"

Her head was screaming with pain as Sarah eased her eyes open. In an instant, everything came back to her with a roaring rush—the night, the headlights on the road ahead, the pain and exhaustion that wrung her body, and Alan, driving grimly with one hand on the steering wheel while his other hand held a gun aimed straight at her forehead. A frightened squeak escaped her as she twisted around in the seat, trying to get as far away from him as she could. She moaned softly as she brought her hand up to the back of her head and felt the hot, sticky trickle of blood where he had hit her with the butt of the pistol.

"Don't you go trying to get away from me!" Alan said, his voice low and measured.

Sarah could barely hear him above the ringing in her ears, but she could see clearly enough that the gun was still aimed straight at her head.

Go ahead, she thought. *Pull the trigger. Do me a favor.*

"D'you understand me?" Alan snarled. "Don't give me

any more trouble."

Unable to speak, Sarah simply grunted and nodded. Dejection and hopelessness filled her as she turned away from him and gently pressed her face against the cold glass. She stared silently out at the roadside slipping past her.

"I already pushed him away," she whispered, her breath fogging the glass and blurring her view as tears flooded from her eyes. "And now it's too late."

"What did you say?" Alan snapped.

"Nuh—nothing," Sarah replied. Her throat was on fire, and her breath hitched painfully in her chest when she turned and looked at Alan. His face—a harsh, dark profile against the deeper blackness outside the car window—looked as if it were carved out of stone. She knew she would never find any pity there.

"Well, I've had just about all I can stand from you," Alan said, snorting with disgust. "If you're gonna just sit there, mumbling to yourself like some fuckin' idiot, I swear to Christ, you're gonna end up in the trunk again before you drive me out of my goddamned mind!" His eyes widened crazily as he shifted them back and forth between the road and Sarah.

Even the dim glow of the dashboard instruments was too bright; it stung Sarah's eyes. Everywhere she looked, she saw spinning, watery circles of light. The ringing in her ears was starting to fade, but it still warbled up and down with high-pitched frequencies.

"Yeah, well—and don't think I don't know who you're talking about," Alan said, snickering softly under his breath. When Sarah looked at him again, his eyes were fixed rigidly ahead as the muscles of his jaw flexed and unflexed.

A cold prickling ran up the back of her neck. She didn't dare turn around and look, but she couldn't ignore the unsettling feeling that someone was sitting in the

416

backseat of the car, watching her . . . and waiting . . . and listening.

"If you still think that asshole partner of yours is gonna get you out of this, you're crazy as a shithouse rat. You don't, do you?"

Sarah shook her head even though it sent a surge of pain through her.

Alan's snickering broke out into loud, lunatic laughter as he faced her. "You must take me for some kind of fucking *idiot!*" he shouted. A spray of spit flew from his lips, splattering her face. "I've known all along what you and Elliott Clark were up to!"

"Elliott Clark? What . . . are you talking about?" Sarah said weakly.

Alan almost replied but stopped himself. He was sick and tired of her half-assed chattering, and she was starting to drive him crazy! Rather than talk any more, he decided he had to do something about her—right *now*. He had to shut her up—permanently. When he saw the sign for the rest stop area up ahead, he made his decision. Gritting his teeth, he slowed the car as he approached the entrance. With a crunching of tires on sandy gravel, the car fishtailed as he slammed on the brakes and jerked the steering wheel hard to the right. The Mustang spun around 180 degrees and then jolted to a stop in the middle of the parking lot.

"Yeah," Alan said in a low, mean-sounding voice as he looked around at the night-rimmed area and then turned to face Sarah. "Nice and deserted . . . I think this will do just fine."

– 3 –

Elliott took Gilman Falls Avenue out of Old Town to I-95. As soon as he hit the highway, he nudged his car up to seventy-five miles per hour and headed north. He

417

was absolutely convinced that Alan Griffin was involved in the shooting at the E-Z Veazie and was now hightailing it north, up the Interstate to Houlton and the Canadian border in a desperate attempt to save his ass. Even if what had happened at the E-Z Veazie had totally unhinged him, Alan would be smart enough not to go tearassing up the highway at ninety miles an hour and draw attention to himself; so as long as Alan didn't get off the turnpike and lose himself on back roads, Elliott figured he'd be able to catch up with him by staying just a bit over the speed limit.

Elliott wished to hell he had a siren and flashers so some overzealous town or state trooper wouldn't pull him over and delay him, but he would just have to chance it. He knew he had no authority to be out here in pursuit in the first place, but he told himself this was different because Sarah was involved.

He wanted more than anything to believe that she was still with Alan and alive, but he couldn't stop wondering if she, too, had already been killed. And as he drove, other doubts intruded as well. What if Alan hadn't even been involved in the incident at the E-Z Veazie, unless he was the person who had been shot? What if someone else had stolen his car? And even if that wasn't the case, there still wasn't even any direct evidence connecting Alan to Sarah's disappearance. But something powerful inside was telling him that it *had* to be Alan, and Sarah *had* to be with him!

The police scanner crackled with static and garbled messages, but no further reports came in on the shooting at the E-Z Veazie. Elliott considered using the CB to call the Orono police to get a positive ID on the victim, but he decided against it to keep the channel clear. Within fifteen minutes, he passed through Howland but heard nothing more over the radio to indicate that they had responded to Orono's request for assistance. He figured once he was closer to Medway, he'd call ahead to the police there and ask if they had received any communication from the Orono police. With an all points bulletin out on Alan, it shouldn't be too tough to get some cooperation, even if he did have to bullshit about his involvement with the case.

Other than a few sixteen wheelers, there wasn't much traffic moving north or south this late on a Sunday night. The highway north of Howland unspooled like a black ribbon in front of Elliott's headlights as he nudged the car up to eighty miles per hour. Finally, about five miles north of the Howland exit, just to satisfy his curiosity, he gave in to the nagging worry that he might be on a wild-goose chase and decided to call Orono for a positive ID on the shooting victim. He was just reaching for the CB microphone when he crested a small rise and saw the dull glow of taillights up ahead.

"That's gotta be him," Elliott whispered harshly to himself. His voice sounded foreign to his ears, and he had the unnerving sensation that someone was sitting beside him, whispering to him in the dark. He shivered, imagining for an instant that the thin blond kid was riding with him.

Elliott immediately slowed down and dropped back until the taillights disappeared around a bend in the road up ahead. He snapped off his headlights, trusting in the faint glow of moonlight reflecting off the snow to show him all he needed to see of the road. This way, he could narrow the distance between them, get right up close to the car without the other driver knowing he was even there. He pushed the accelerator to the floor and within seconds rounded the curve and started to close the gap between him and the car. In the dim moonlight, he could see that it was indeed a dark-colored Mustang in front of him, but that was all. His hands went clammy with sweat, and a hard, dry lump formed in his throat. With

419

just a bit more pressure on the gas, he got close enough to read the license plate number.

"Maine registration number 7-2-4-3-3-7. Bingo!" Elliott whispered as a smile twitched the corners of his mouth.

"Now please . . . *please* let her be there and be all right," Elliott said as his eyes darted back and forth between the car up ahead and the CB microphone. Satisfied that Alan wasn't going to get away from him now, Elliott eased up on the gas enough so the Mustang moved out ahead of him. He realized he had been holding his breath and let it out in a long, slow whistle before picking up the radio microphone and clicking it on to Channel 9, the frequency monitored by the state police.

"Ahh—breaker, breaker. This is Big L. I need to get in touch with some state bears, preferably Orono. Over."

He waited tensely as a burst of static filled the car; then a woman's voice, weak with distance, came over the speaker. "Roger that—was that *Big* or *Baby* L.? This is Darlin' Dolores out of Milo. What's your 'twenty'? Over."

"I copy you loud and clear, Darlin'," Elliott said.

He knew right away that Dolores must be one of the many CB buffs in the state who spend most of their time at their radios, following police and rescue action. Some people criticized them as nothing more than technological ambulance chasers, but in the line of duty, he had been grateful for their help more times than he cared to count.

"Don't even consider calling me *Baby* L., Darlin'. I can't give my 'twenty' in case my rabbit has his ears on. I'm the hound dog on the trail of that ten-thirty-two the boys in the blue suits are looking for. You copy all that? Over."

He felt a bit silly slipping into jive CB lingo, but he didn't want to reveal too much over the airwaves until he was sure there were going to be police units up ahead and behind, to block off all of Alan's possible escape

420

routes.

"I copy that," Dolores said. "Been following that MP over the weekend. Ask and ye shall receive, Big L. Over."

Elliott was elated to realize that she deduced from his chatter that he was being cautious with what he said in case Alan Griffin had a CB radio in his car.

"Darlin' I'll be forever indebted to you if you get on the horn and give Orono and Houlton each a buzz, see if they can get some bubbletops heading out my way. You're local. Let's say I'm an eye-niner-five who's past my howlin' days and am getting on the cold side. You savvy that? Over."

"Haven't seen any log jams yet, have you? Over."

Elliott smiled, knowing Dolores knew he was heading north on Interstate 95, past the town of Howland, and was asking if he had crossed the Penobscot River in Medway yet.

"That's a negatory on that one, Darlin'. If you raise the bears and get my rabbit in the trap, I'll make sure you get your face on TV. Over."

"Big Roger on that, Big L., but I don't want to risk breaking too many hearts out there in TV land. I'm switching over to Ma Bell. I'll be comin' back at 'cha real soon. This is Darlin' Dolores, over and out."

Elliott smiled grimly as he clicked off the CB and replaced the microphone. As long as Dolores had truly understood his coded messages, help should be coming from both ends of the highway. All he needed to do now was keep his speed up enough to catch a glimpse every now and then of Alan's taillights and make sure he didn't get off at Lincoln exit up ahead. But just as he was feeling satisfied, he saw the Mustang's taillights flash red. His heart skipped a beat and his stomach did a cold flip when he realized that Alan was pulling off the highway into a rest stop. He couldn't stop his hand from trembling slightly as he pulled over to the side of the road, picked up the radio microphone, and snapped it on.

"Breaker, breaker. This is Big L. calling you again, Darlin' Dolores. You copy me, sweetheart? Over."

He listened to the crackle and snap of static for a few seconds, then repeated his message, fighting to keep the nervous edge out of his voice.

"Big L. to Dolores. Come on, honey. Get your ears on! You there? Come on, Darlin'. I think I'm gonna need some bears out here *real* soon! My rabbit's gone to ground. You with me, honey? Over."

Still nothing but static came over the airwaves. There was either a mountain or too much distance between him and Dolores. He realized with a sour sinking in his gut that there would be no more communication until the state police were close enough to pick him up on Channel 9. Elliott was confident that Dolores had understood his message and that help was on the way . . . but when? he wondered. He tried to fight back the sickening waves of frustration and worry as he stared up at the dark road ahead.

If Sarah was still alive in the car there with Alan, he wasn't about to sit here and wait for the state police to show up. He couldn't risk it. For all he knew, Alan might be planning to get rid of her now before continuing on to Canada. Elliott felt for his revolver under his coat, but it didn't provide half as much reassurance as he would have liked as he stared ahead at the turnoff into the pitch-dark rest area and knew he was going to have to go up there . . . alone.

Chapter Twenty-nine

Full Circle

— 1 —

"I've had just about all the shit I'm gonna take from you," Alan said with a snarl. He rammed the gear shift into *Park* and leaned over across Sarah, his weight mashing her against the car seat. Her first thought was that he was going to hit her again, so she closed her eyes and cringed, waiting for another bright bolt of pain. Alan's weight pressed her down even harder, and she feared that first, before he killed her, he was going to rape her one last time. She was trying so hard to shut down her mind so she wouldn't feel a thing that she barely noticed the blast of cold air when he snapped the door latch and swung the door open.

"By the way," he said, laughing, "I lied to you about the door latch not working. Now go on! Get out!"

His face looked bloated and horrible in the dim light of the car as he pushed her roughly toward the open door. "I said get out of my car!"

Nearly numb with panic, Sarah wiggled out from under him. She rolled off the car seat and stepped out into the night, stumbled, and almost fell down. Her teeth chattered from the cold as she pulled her collar tightly around her neck and hunched her shoulders. Her legs felt as if they were going to collapse under her at any moment as she staggered away from the car. Glancing fearfully around at the wall of trees illuminated by the car's headlights, she knew this was the end of the road for her. She wondered if she should try—one last time—to make a run for it.

Run where? she wondered, shivering. *Just like at the camp on Pushaw, how far can I get before he catches me?*

Alan was muttering to himself as he killed the engine, got out the driver's door, and walked around behind the car. The taillights underlit his face with a baleful red glow as he slipped the key into the trunk lock and raised the lid.

"Get your ass over here!" he shouted. His voice was stern, but it almost broke with rage. He kept the gun aimed steadily at her, never wavering. If it wasn't for the gun, she told herself, she would have run.

"No . . . please!" Sarah pleaded. She took a lurching step backward. "Please don't make me get back in there."

A blazing tongue of yellow light flashed simultaneously with an ear-splitting blast. The bullet whined like an angry hornet as it ricocheted off the road inches from Sarah's feet. The rolling echo faded into the still night. Choking on her fear, Sarah shut her eyes tightly and waited with bated breath for the next shot . . . the one that would send a bullet slamming into her. Her legs were trembling, ready to collapse.

"I *said,* get your ass over here—now!"

Sarah stumbled a few steps forward and had to grab on to the side of the car to keep from falling.

"I promise you, the next one won't miss!" Alan said, his voice sliding higher up the scale. "I'm not going to listen to any more of your bullshit and lies!" Stiffening his arm, he drew a steady bead on her. "And I'm not gonna say it again."

When the second shot didn't come immediately, Sarah started moving cautiously forward. All the while, Alan stared at her down the length of the gun barrel. There was a cold, hard look in his eyes and a sick smile on his face as

424

he fished around inside the trunk until he found what he was looking for. Sarah saw that he was holding a roll of duct tape.

"I need to stop for gas at the next station I see, and I don't need you screwing things up any more than you already have!"

"I promise . . . I won't do a thing. I won't say a word," Sarah said, fighting back her tears. She couldn't stop wondering what had made him snap like this. Was it something she had said, maybe while she was asleep? Or was he starting to lose it because of the shooting back at the motel? Maybe, after killing that old man at the cabin and then shooting Michael, the reality of how bad things were was finally sinking in.

"You're damned right you won't!" Alan said, followed by a high, crazy laugh. He slipped the gun into his coat pocket before bending down to pull his hunting knife from the leg sheath. He tore off a strip of duct tape and held it up high, dangling, so she could see it as he came toward her. When Sarah tried to dart away from him, Alan snagged her by the wrist, spun her around, and jerked her hand behind her back, up between her shoulders. She let out a sharp yelp of pain.

"Ahh, I'm awfully sorry I did that. Did it hurt?" he asked in mock sympathy.

Before she could answer, he gave her arm another vicious pull upward. Sarah bit into her lower lip to keep from crying out as fiery pain lanced her shoulder socket and neck. The salty taste of blood filled her mouth. She had to hold herself back from spitting into Alan's face when he turned her around, grabbed her by the coat collar, and yanked her so close to him their noses almost touched.

"You should thank me for letting you live as long as I have," he said, his voice lowered to an animal snarl. His heated breath poured over her like sour liquid as he brought the edge of the knife up to less than an inch from her throat. "I should just kill you and leave you here for the

425

crows to eat. That'd solve all of my problems. Yours too, far's I can see. Is *that* what you want? I can do it now if you want."

Sarah let her head drop back, exposing her throat. She wanted to answer him but could only grunt. Pain inflamed her shoulders and neck. When Alan dragged the honed edge of the knife lightly across her throat, it sent an electric tingle racing through her.

Yes, she pleaded in her mind. *Do it. Do it now!*

"You know," Alan went on, "now that I think about it, maybe I will." His sick smile twisted his face as he pulled away from her. His eyes went unfocused for a moment as he looked up at the night sky and inhaled deeply, his breath shuddering like a machine gun. Then, shaking his head as though clearing it, he slapped the strip of tape roughly across Sarah's mouth and smoothed it with the heel of his hand. Deep laughter rumbled in his chest and then burst out in a rising wail. Every time she swallowed, Sarah nearly choked on the blood flowing from her cut lip.

That laugh, she thought, feeling wave after wave of pounding terror. *He laughed just like that the night he killed my mother.*

Terror as sharp and as clean as a scalpel cut into Sarah when she looked up at Alan's face so close to hers and remembered him calling to her on that rainy, terror-filled night—

"Come on, little girlie! I know you're around here somewhere, and you know I'm gonna find you . . . You know, the longer I have to wait, the sorrier you're gonna be once I do find you . . . I'm losing my patience with you! You know I'm gonna get you!"

Caught in a maelstrom of fear, Sarah's mind tried to shut itself down, but she couldn't lose herself in the sweet oblivion of unconsciousness. There was no way to escape what was happening until it was over. Every sense dimmed like candles sputtering feebly in a high wind, threatening to wink out. All resistance and hope left her. With a strangled cry, she sagged forward into Alan's arms. Her eyes narrowed to mere slits as she looked dazedly up at him, but she could no longer see his face.

Satisfied that she was past the point of giving him any trouble, Alan grabbed a fistful of her hair and pulled her head back so far her neck crackled. Letting the knife graze against her exposed throat, he shouted through his laughter, "You know—I've got another idea, though." His voice was tight and twisted; it drove into Sarah's ears like a spike. He took the edge of the tape and ripped it viciously from her mouth. The pain brought tears to Sarah's eyes.

"I think I'd like one last fuck before you die," he said, his voice crackling with twisted laughter. "You know what they say: if you gotta go, go with a smile!"

Sarah sagged lifelessly in his arms, but he shook her viciously, like a dog with a rat in its jaws. "Come on, now. Don't go passing out on me. I want to hear you *scream* before you die!"

—2—

Elliott hated indecision. All his life, especially in the line of duty as a police officer, when lives hung in the balance, he had taken pride in his ability to size up a situation, see the solution, and act on it swiftly. Even that night at the White Crane restaurant, the night that had led to the death of Lester Lajoie, the imprisonment of Alan Griffin, and his own resignation from active police work, Elliott was proud that he had acted correctly, on reflex. When he saw Lester make a threatening move toward Henry Hartman, he hadn't waited; in less than a second, he had aimed his gun and squeezed the trigger.

But now, sitting in his silent, dark car, his eyes straining to see through the trees up to the rest stop area, Elliott wasn't sure what to do. If Darlin' Dolores had gotten through to the State Police, then units should be heading this way. But if Sarah was still with Alan, every second he delayed could mean the difference between life and death for her. He was on a deserted stretch of highway, alone with a homicidal kidnapper and—quite possibly—his intended victim.

"God *damn* it!" Elliott snarled as he shifted his car into *Park*, killed the engine, and got out. He zipped his coat up tightly and, grasping his revolver firmly in hand, started down the road toward the rest stop entrance, hoping like hell that, if some Staties did show up, they'd realize right away what was going on. As he got closer, he could see the dull glow of Alan's headlights through the bank of pines. In the darkness, he saw figures moving in eerie silence, illuminated by the red glow of taillights. Elliott strained to see what was happening. He felt a slight measure of relief when he saw two people. If Alan didn't have an accomplice, then Sarah was still alive.

Keeping his eyes fixed on the dull red glow up ahead, he kept to one side of the road where the shadows of the trees were deepest. The night surrounded him with silence and cold. A faint breeze shifted the tall tops of the pines, whisking them against the starry sky. Elliott's boots crunched loudly on the snow and ice along the roadside, so he moved slower than he wanted to. He had to maintain the element of surprise until he was within striking distance.

"You know—I've got another idea, though."

The voice echoed, faint with distance, but the words hit Elliott's ear like a solid one-two punch. His grip on his revolver tightened.

That's Alan Griffin's voice, all right, he thought, fighting back his impulse simply to charge up the hill like the rescuing cavalry.

The voice rang clearly in the cold night air, rising high with laughter. "I think I'd like one last fuck before you die. You know what they say: if you gotta go, go with a smile!"

Higher and higher the maniacal laughter rose, whining and spiraling until it blocked out every other sound . . . every other sound except a voice whispering from the darkness close behind him—

"You were there that night!"

"Come on, now. Don't go passing out on me. I want to hear you *scream* before you die!"

Elliott broke into a run, knowing there was no time left. As he ran, the blond boy's voice filled his ears like the wind, hissing in the trees. The pit of his stomach filled with an icy ball of fear.

"I saw you there!"

The night thickened, squeezing in on Elliott from all sides, making him shiver wildly even as he ran. Every movement felt sludgy, as though he were running in slow motion.

"You must help her! . . . I can't! . . . She doesn't want me!"

"Jesus *Christ!*" Elliott muttered. In spite of the freezing temperature, sweat had broken out on his forehead.

That has to be Sarah up there, he thought through his rising swells of panic.

His grip on his pistol was so tight he lost all feeling in his hand as he ran up the hill. His feet skidded noisily on the sand-covered road, but all he could do was hope—hope to *hell* that Alan was distracted enough not to hear any noise he made until it was too late.

— 3 —

"Tully!"

The word burst from Sarah the instant she saw something—a dark shape sweeping soundlessly out of the night, racing straight toward them up the road from behind Alan. Through pain-dimmed eyes, she tried to track the thing's motions, but everything dissolved into a swirling, black blur. For all she knew, Alan had already severed her windpipe; it would just be a matter of time before her brain registered the stinging pain and the gush of lifeblood. A warbling echo in her dimming mind told her that she *was* imagining Tully in one last, desperate hope of clinging onto life. Any second now, the dark void would slip open beneath her and suck her down into it.

Surprised by her outburst, Alan glanced over his shoulder. He stiffened when he saw that they weren't alone. The steady *slap-slap* of feet on pavement froze him for an instant as he peered down the road, trying to figure out what was going on. Then, in the feeble glow of the taillights, he saw that a man was closing the distance fast.

"This is the police!" a voice boomed in the night. "Hold it right there, Griffin!"

The words drove into Sarah's awareness, dragging her closer to consciousness.

It isn't Tully, but I'm not dead.

She felt oddly divorced from her body as Alan grabbed her arm and spun her around, using her as a shield between himself and the approaching person. The night was a whirling riot of darkness and shattered, watery images as Sarah watched the figure draw closer. With one hand, Alan pressed the cold knife blade hard against her throat while he held her tightly with the other hand.

"Stop right there!" he shouted. "I swear to Christ, I'll kill her if you take another fucking step closer!" His mouth was close to Sarah's ear; the shrillness of his voice deafened her.

"I have backup coming in," the voice from the darkness called out.

Alan snickered. "Yeah—sure. You expect me to fall for that one?"

"Griffin, you've made enough mistakes already. We already found that boy in the motel. Don't make another one now 'cause it will be your last!"

"Yeah, well, *fuck* you!" Alan shrieked. He glanced behind him, judging how far it was to the car door. Should he kill her now and make a run for it, or should he hang on to her as a hostage? If he could get the car door open, get the little bitch inside, and start up the car, he just might be able to run this asshole down before anyone else showed up.

"Sarah! Are you all right?"

430

"Elliott? Is that? Is it really you?" she called back feebly. Her voice sounded as raw as a crow's cawing, and she couldn't believe that she had actually heard Elliott's voice.

"Just shut the fuck up!" Alan hissed close to her ear. The tip of the knife jabbed into her throat, jolting her with pain. Blood began to flow, but instead of driving the knife deeper, Alan eased his hold on her and reached for the gun in his coat pocket. As soon as she realized what he was doing, and knowing this was her last chance to get out of this situation alive, Sarah pushed herself away from him with a desperate surge of energy.

"Look out, Elliott! He's got a gun!" she screamed.

Then everything seemed to happen all at once.

Elliott dodged to one side just as Alan raised his gun and fired. The blast ripped the night, the bullet ricocheted off the road with an ear-piercing *zing*. Dazed by the gunshot so close to her ear, Sarah still had the presence of mind to ball her hand into a fist and drive her elbow back as hard as she could. It caught Alan squarely in the gut. His arms jerked backward, sending the gun flying off into the darkness as his body snapped forward. On pure reflex, Sarah spun around on one foot, leaned forward, and rammed her knee solidly into his crotch. Doubling over with pain, Alan made a sickening noise in his throat that sounded as if he was going to throw up.

"You—" he sputtered, glaring at her as he pitched forward onto the ground. Surprised that it had been this easy, Sarah was immobilized for an instant. She just stood there, staring down at Alan as he writhed in agony on the ground.

"Get the hell away from him!" Elliott shouted, crouching defensively as he took several shuffling steps forward.

His voice cut through Sarah's confusion. Shaking her head, she looked up at him and the gun he had braced in both hands, aimed squarely at Alan. As she slowly backed away, she allowed herself a smug feeling of satisfaction that, at last, Alan was on the receiving end of things.

431

"You're under arrest, asshole," Elliott snapped. His feet scuffed in the dirt on the road as he moved nervously back and forth, all the while keeping his gun pointed steadily at Alan's head.

Lying on his side, his hands clutching his groin, Alan looked up at Elliott. His eyes glowed strangely in the faint red light of the taillights. A thick string of blood-stained saliva ran from the corner of his mouth to the road, but he didn't wipe it away as he writhed in pain on the ground.

"Sarah," Elliott said sharply. "My car's parked down a little bit away from the turnoff. The keys are still in the ignition. Think you can make it down there and drive up here?"

"Yeah," Sarah gasped even as pain lanced through her.

"As for you, you miserable fucking asshole," Elliott said, addressing Alan again. "If you move a muscle, I'll put a fucking hole in your gut the size of a goddamned basketball!"

"Can I at least stand up?" Alan asked, looking up at Elliott. His face was pinched tight with pain as he hugged his stomach tightly.

"Just take it nice and slow," Elliott said, nodding as he took a cautious step backward. Alan brought his knees up under him and then, keeping his hands pressed tightly against his gut, rocked forward and started to stand. The low moaning noise he was making sounded like a ghost, howling deep in the surrounding night.

Sarah could barely bring herself even to walk past Alan where he was struggling to stand. The instant she finally dared to take a few steps, she heard a rasping scuffing sound. Alan was nothing more than a blur of motion as he leaped up and made a rush at Elliott. She screamed as the two men collided, but the sound was lost beneath the blast of Elliott's gun. The night filled with a loud, bubbling shriek. For a frozen instant, Sarah waited, expecting to see Alan fall to the ground from a gunshot wound; but then, to her horror, she saw Elliott stagger backward. His legs wobbled and then gave out from under him. Grasping the side of his neck with both hands, he leaned forward and dropped to the ground. Near fainting, Sarah stumbled back a step and fell down when she saw the wicked flash of Alan's knife in his hand.

"You actually thought you were gonna get the best of *me?*" Alan shrieked, his laughter soaring high as he cocked back his foot and planted a solid kick in Elliott's ribs. The cracking of bones sounded like cellophane paper crinkling. With a quick sweep of his foot, he kicked Elliott's hand, sending the gun skittering off across the road into the darkness.

Alan's laughter pealed shrilly as he nudged the fallen man with the toe of his boot. Then — very deliberately — he brought his heel down hard on Elliott's hands as he grasped his throat. In the glow of the taillights, Sarah watched with numbed detachment as dark blood flowed from the knife wound in Elliott's neck. She was frozen into silence as Alan dropped to his knees beside Elliott and raised his knife high into the air.

"I want to tell you one thing before you die," Alan said in a high, twisted voice. His knife hand trembled as he prepared for the final, fatal stroke. Turning toward Sarah, who was cowering beside the car, he shouted loud enough so she could hear, too.

"I've been on to you — the *both* of you — ever since you started. You must've thought I was a fool not to know, but neither one of you ever fooled me." Turning to Sarah, he said, "Did you know that this — this asshole here, is the jerk who sent my ass to Thomaston for a year? Huh? Oh, yeah — 'course you did! You've been working with him all along." He snickered softly. "I just think this is fucking hilarious how it's all coming around full circle, don't you?"

He burst out with a spray of laughter. "The great thing about this is the way it's all turning out. Now fuckhead here will never nail me for what I did to your mother." Leaning close to Elliott's pain-racked face, he hissed. "Oh, yeah! You've been trying. You both have! And I think it's maybe even a little bit sad that you won't get to put me away for killing the bitch's mother. Don't you? But—hey! Them's the breaks."

Elliott tried to answer, but the only sound that came from him was a thick, choking sound as blood filled the back of his throat. Sarah knew what was coming next. Alan would kill Elliott and then her. It was all over. In a last desperate effort to save herself, she started crawling backward, away from Alan and Elliott. At first, when her hand brushed against the gun on the ground—the gun Alan had dropped when she elbowed him in the stomach— she didn't even realize what it was; but her fingers curled around the pistol handle as firmly as if someone standing beside her had thrust it into her hand. Nearly in shock, she looked down in disbelief at the gun.

"Well, asshole," Alan said gleefully as he settled himself and gripped the knife with both hands, preparing to plunge it into Elliott's chest. "I guess it's about time to say good-bye. But you can die knowing that I fucked her mother and then I killed her . . . just like I'm gonna fuck and kill her as soon as you're—"

"No you won't!" Sarah screeched.

Alan spun around and looked at her. His expression froze when he saw that she was pointing a gun straight at him. He was about to speak when he saw something else— something moving behind Sarah. At first, it was like a moon-cast shadow, shifting against the night like a passing cloud; but in the space of a heartbeat, it twisted into a black shape that looked vaguely human but remarkably large. Cold hands clutched Alan's throat, silencing him as he stared in horror into the glowing red eyes that materialized out of the night as the dark figure reached from behind Sarah and apparently gripped her hands to steady her aim.

"Jesus Chri—"

Her words were cut off by a deafening blast when, almost against her will, Sarah's fingers squeezed the trigger. She watched, horrified, as the impact of the bullet knocked Alan over. He fell down and skittered around on the ground, howling with pain.

"You bitch! You lousy, fucking *bitch!*"

Getting up onto his knees, he started pawing around on the ground, seeking his knife. With a tight, rising wail, Sarah, knowing that he was still intent on killing Elliott, stood up and charged him. She hit him hard and low, like a football player, and knocked him back down. Straddling his chest, she pinned him to the ground with her knees.

"No, it's *you*, you *bastard!*" she screamed. *"You're* gonna die because you killed her. This is for my *mother . . .*"

With a rising shriek, she raised the gun high above her head and brought it butt-first down hard against his nose. Her face twisted into a half-smile when she heard the satisfying *crunch* of bones and felt his nose shift to one side as though it had suddenly detached. His body bucked beneath her.

"And for *Michael!*"

Again, she smashed the gun into his face. A black splash of blood shot into the air and landed with a dull *plop* on the ground beside him. She saw his left eye pop out of its socket and slide down his cheek like a slimy, glistening marble.

"And for *Elliott!*"

A third time, the gun smashed into Alan's face, this time with a crunching sound as his skull caved in. Swept away in a frenzy of anger, she continued to pound the gun into Alan's face until his face was nothing but a bloody pulp and he was no longer recognizably human. At last, exhaustion claimed her, and her raging blood-lust was satiated. She pitched off him, stood up shakily, then leaned over and vomited when she saw Alan's body twitch violently before finally coming to rest. Then the silence of the night was broken only by her heavy breathing and one other sound — the loud, gurgling noise of Alan's blood, pumping from his ruined face onto the road.

Immobilized by the full terror of what she had done, Sarah stared in disbelief at the blood-smeared pistol and her hands, dripping with Alan's blood. She leaned her head back, stared sightlessly at the night sky, and let it all out in one long, anguished cry that originated in the core of her soul. The sound echoed dully in the cold night until a faint groaning noise snapped her back to attention.

Whimpering softly, she dropped the gun to the ground and staggered over to where Elliott lay. It took an incredible effort on her part even to move, and all the while she kept glancing over her shoulder, expecting to see Alan's eyes suddenly snap open as he rose from the ground and went for her throat. Her body was wracked by dry, hitching sobs as she sat down and cradled Elliott's head in her lap, gently brushing his face with the flat of her hand. She barely noticed the wide, bloody smears she left on his face. Elliott's eyes were glazed with pain as he looked up at her and forced a weak smile.

"My . . . car," he said, no more than a sputtering gasp. "There's a . . . radio . . . in . . . my . . ."

Sarah didn't want to leave him there; she didn't dare to, even for a second; but she knew, if he was going to have even half a chance of surviving, she had to call for help with the radio in his car. Shivering wildly, she took off her coat, bunched it up to form a pillow, and eased Elliott's head gently down onto it. All around her, the night was spinning in a wild vortex of black shadows and eerie, glowing light. Her legs trembled and almost gave out from under her as she stood up slowly and took a deep breath. Waves of dizziness threatened to drag her under, but with tears carving tracks across her blood-streaked face, she forced herself to go down the road to Elliott's car.

Once there, it took her an agonizingly long time to figure out how to turn the radio on. She wasn't even sure she was broadcasting as she depressed the button on the side of the microphone and ran through the channels. Her voice trembled, broken by sobs, as she cried out for help. At last, a man identifying himself as Trooper Citro came on. Sarah blurted out her story in disconnected snatches, barely aware of his calmly spoken instructions. When she realized she was unable even to tell him where she was, the trooper reassured her that he had a rough idea from a phone call he had received earlier that evening. He told her to leave the car lights on, go back to Elliott, and wait there while he radioed for a rescue unit.

Miraculously, Elliott was still breathing when Sarah got back to him. Telling herself she had to be strong—if only for him—she sat down beside him. Her body quaked with shivers as she gently stroked his face. The soothing motion and her soft, crooning words lulled her and seemed to calm Elliott, who lay there, staring up at her with a distant, glazed expression. His breathing was shallow but steady, and he was smiling. After a while—she had no idea how long—she heard the warbling wail of sirens far off in the distance . . . and getting closer.

Chapter Thirty

Liberation

— 1 —

A week after the events in the rest area out on Interstate 95, the police and the FBI had pretty much wrapped up all the loose ends in the case, including a trip out to Pushaw Lake where they located the cabin owned by Frank Ranieri and found the frozen corpse of Emmett Hawkes. Sarah's father took a leave of absence from work and got a room at the University Motor Inn in Orono so he could visit his daughter at Eastern Maine Medical at least six hours every day. The strain of the weekend and of the following week, watching and worrying by Sarah's bedside as she recovered, wore heavily on him. As soon as she was released, he planned to take her home to recuperate. The doctors consistently expressed amazement at how strong and fast Sarah was recovering from the physical trauma of the experience. She was being counseled to help deal with the rape and abuse, and knew enough not to ask how long it would take her to get over the psychological trauma. She almost even accepted the idea that, like her mother's death, it was something she might never recover from.

Even if the horror of what had happened to her eventually faded from memory, she knew in the core of her soul that she'd never forgive Alan Griffin for what he had done to her and her mother. And even though she knew her mother's killer was dead, none of the grief and misery she thought was behind her was expiated, even by the joy and exhilaration she had felt when she had killed Alan. It struck her as almost funny, in a way, how after so many years—her entire childhood, really—of feeling guilty and haunted because she felt responsible for so many deaths, the one time she was *positive* she had done such a horrible thing made her feel so free, so cleansed.

On the advice of her doctor, she made arrangements to see a therapist. She knew she would have to be completely honest with her new therapist, but even before her first visit with Dr. Costello, she was mentally debating how much she should reveal to him about Tully. For the first time in her life, she didn't feel haunted all the time; there was no shadowy figure hovering nearby, out of sight— watching her and acting out her angry impulses. She wasn't quite sure she knew how to handle such a feeling, but it didn't matter because she knew that Tully was gone—if he had ever really existed at all.

Elliott was also hospitalized for several days, recovering from his broken ribs and the knife wound to his neck. Alan's blade had cut cleanly through his neck muscles on the left side, but—luckily—it had been deflected by his collarbone and missed his subclavian artery by a fraction of an inch. His five broken ribs caused the most pain; but with his chest well-taped, he was on the mend soon enough. The doctors were concerned about the possibility of infection, so they kept him in the hospital a bit longer than he thought necessary. Several times a day, both before and after she was released, Sarah and her father came to visit him. Elliott figured time was going to be the best healer for her, so he never talked directly to her about what had happened . . . especially when her father was present.

Needless to say, none of them attended the funeral services in Hilton for Alan Griffin.

The weather was bright and sunny but below freezing on the morning Elliott was to be discharged from the hospital, the same day Devin and Sarah were planning to return to Hilton. Sarah asked her father to let her drive alone to the hospital to pick him up. After an inordinately long delay trying to find a doctor to sign the release forms, Elliott was finally allowed to get dressed. He felt curiously disoriented as he put on his regular street clothes for the first time in a week. It seemed as though he had been away from the world and its mundane concerns for months . . . or years. Just as he and Sarah were ready to walk out of his room, the attending nurse insisted, in spite of his protests, that Elliott use a wheelchair to go from his room to the hospital door. Hospital regulations. He grudgingly sat down in the wheelchair, and Sarah rolled him out into the corridor.

"I still can't get over how you found me," Sarah said. "I mean—what are the chances?"

Elliott turned his head stiffly because of the pain in his chest as he looked back at her. He was happy to see that color had returned to her face, and in spite of the padded bandage on her left cheek, her eyes sparkled with a light that made her look young, vivacious, and alive. Just being with her made him feel infinitely better.

"Well, you know," he said, "the plain and simple truth is, I knew it had to be Alan all along, but when I saw that message, I knew you had left it for me."

Sarah drew the wheelchair to a stop. The sudden motion send a jolt of pain like a hot wire through Elliott.

"What do you mean? What message?" she asked.

A faint smile twitched Elliott's mouth as he looked up at her, but after a moment, he saw by her expression that she wasn't joking; she honestly didn't know what he was talking about.

"In the storage room in the Student Union. Where Alan kept you that first night."

She bit her lower lip and she shook her head slowly from side to side. The memory of that horrible night was hazy.

Elliott looked nervously up and down the corridor, then locked onto her eyes with an intense gaze. Lowering his voice, he said, "I know the doctors didn't want us to talk about . . . what happened—at least not while I was still in the hospital. I just thought—"

"No, tell me," Sarah snapped, kneeling down in front of him and looking at him earnestly. "Tell me." She took his hand and gripped it tightly as she searched his eyes for the truth.

"I didn't think it was any big deal, really. When we got the complaint that someone had trashed the storage closet in the Student Union, I went to investigate it. Underneath all the trash there, I found where—well, I thought it had been you—but someone used the heel of their shoe or something to scratch HELP S on the floor over by the wall." He shrugged helplessly. "I assumed you had done it."

Even before he'd finished speaking, the image of a thin blond boy rose in his mind. The boy stared at him with icy blue, unblinking eyes as he whispered—

"Help her!"

Elliott couldn't repress the shiver that raced up between his shoulders.

"Well," Sarah said, exhaling loudly and shaking her head, "I didn't." She stood up and, gripping the wheelchair handgrips tightly, continued down the corridor. Her eyes clouded for a moment as she tried to recall that night. She found it difficult, almost impossible to allow certain memories to surface. "No . . . I couldn't even see in there. And I don't know what you mean about the closet being trashed. I don't remember that at all."

"Well, I have no idea *how* it got there." He looked back at her again, walking behind him, and had to fight a strong impulse to pull her around, grab her, and hold her close to him. "But it did confirm my suspicion that we were after Alan Griffin. Otherwise, the police might not have re-

441

sponded to the report on what happened at the E-Z Veazie."

"And then, as it turned out, you didn't even need their help," Sarah said with a thin laugh.

"No, just yours. If they hadn't heard you on the radio, I would have bled to death out there on the Interstate."

Sarah's expression tightened, but then it broadened into a smile when she stopped the wheelchair in front of a closed door at the end of the corridor.

"Well, here we are," she said, beaming at Elliott as she rapped her knuckles lightly on the door and then swung it open. Elliott looked nervous, as if he didn't want to enter, but Sarah guided the wheelchair inside the room. Her face softened as she wheeled Elliott over to the silent figure lying in the bed and said, "Well hello, bucko. Look who's getting out of here today!"

Michael's eyelids fluttered for several seconds; then his eyes opened and he looked up from the fluffy well of his pillow. His face was whiter than the pillowcase as he turned to the side and focused on Elliott's face. He smiled weakly, and his lips moved; but if he said anything, it was lost beneath the hissing sound of the respirator to which he was attached.

"Mike, you can't believe how happy I was to hear you made it," Elliott said. He made a move as if to get up out of the chair, but Sarah gently pressured him to remain seated. He leaned forward and lightly patted Michael on the shoulder.

Michael's eyes widened with acknowledgment as his head bobbed weakly up and down.

"I was following the reports of the shooting there at the motel over the radio, but you know, I never even suspected it might be you."

"I thought . . . for sure I . . . was a . . . goner," Michael said, chuckling dryly. His voice was raspy from all the tubes that had been stuck down in his throat, but Elliott took comfort in the brightness and the will to live he

442

saw in the young man's eyes.

"Well, I gotta say you had us pretty worried there for a while," Elliott said. He glanced over at Sarah and saw tears filling her eyes as she looked back and forth between the two men.

"You know . . . though," Michael said, licking his lips. He tried to sit up in bed, but the effort proved too much, and he collapsed back down. "It was the . . . the weirdest damned thing . . . when I—when I—"

"Don't strain yourself trying to talk, honey," Sarah said. Elliott looked at her in surprise; she sounded tense, almost angry, as if she didn't want to hear what Michael had been about to say.

Michael's gaze got lost in the distance for a moment as he focused on the wall behind Sarah and Elliott. He licked his lips furiously before continuing, "No, really . . . I gotta . . . tell you . . . it was the strangest thing." He took a deep, shaky breath and tried to force his voice louder. "You know . . . I never felt the pain when the . . . bullet, hit me. It didn't hurt like you'd . . . expect it would. But then I—I . . ."

"Don't push yourself," Sarah said as she leaned over the bed. As comforting and concerned as she appeared to be, Elliott still had the impression that she was trying to block his view of Michael so he wouldn't listen to him.

"You just take it easy," Elliott said, looking past Sarah at Michael.

"But you . . . know," Michael went on, as if he wasn't even aware of them. "The weirdest thing about it all was . . . after I was . . . was shot . . ."

The effort of speaking was obviously taxing him. Elliott started to regret coming to visit him, at least not until he was stronger; but there was an intensity about Michael and what he was trying to say that held his attention. He stared intently at him while Sarah busily tucked the sheet up around his neck, all the while casting nervous glances over her shoulder at Elliott.

"When I was . . . lying there . . . on the floor. It's so confusing, but it was like . . . like even before the ambulance came, there was this . . . this guy . . . there . . . in the room, sitting on the floor next to . . . me."

A rush of chills rippled up Elliott's back as Michael stared at him with vacant, unblinking eyes. There was stark terror in his gaze, but something more — as if he had seen something that he could never forget.

Is that what it's like, Elliott wondered, *when you've been right out there on the edge and faced death? Or is it something else? Is it the way Michael's watching me . . . as if, even in his weakened state, he thinks I understand something he doesn't fully comprehend yet?*

"It was so . . . weird," Michael went on. He shook his head weakly and his eyes snapped back into focus on Elliott's face. "This skinny little blond guy — almost a kid, really . . . looked like he was close to — to dying himself. He leaned over me and he never — never really touched me or . . . or spoke to me, but I felt this . . . this strength come into me . . . like I was a glass, and he was cool water . . . filling me up. So even — even though I knew I might be dying . . . I wasn't afraid. It was like — like I also knew nothing was going to hurt me, ever again . . ."

Elliott was struck speechless as he stared at Michael. For just an instant, his sight blurred, and he wasn't looking at Michael Shulkin at all. Another face was superimposed over his, and Elliott found himself staring at the pale, thin face of the nameless blond boy.

"You must help her! I can't!"

The words hissed like crinkling paper in his mind.

Tension wound up so tightly inside Elliott he was positive he wasn't going to be able to control it. Gritting his teeth, he grabbed the wheelchair armrests for security.

"Well, you just get some rest now and get your strength back," Elliott said. His whole body was shaking as he gripped the wheels and turned himself around. He squared his shoulders in spite of the stinging pain in his chest and,

444

taking Sarah's hand, directed her gently toward the bed. Taking Michael's thin hand, he joined their hands, smiling as they intertwined their fingers.

"And don't you worry, Michael," Elliott said, forcing strength into his voice as he propelled himself away from the bed. "Her dad and I are gonna take good care of her until you're out of here."

Michael's expression went blank for just an instant; then he shook his head as his eyes filled with a light as bright and intense as the winter sun.

"You'd better!" he said, closing his eyes and settling into the bed. "You damn well better!"

— 3 —

"I got another letter today from Michael," Sarah said. She was sitting in her bed, in her bedroom in Hilton, speaking softly into her tape recorder. "That makes three already this week."

She smiled mildly and glanced at her reflection in the mirror over her dresser. Although the skin under her left eye was still puffy and prune purple, her face was looking much better. The snowy glare of the winter afternoon reflecting in the mirror hurt her eyes, so she turned away and focused on her hands, holding the tape recorder.

"It sounds like he's getting back on his feet, though. I sure do miss him. I can't wait for this weekend. God, I wish I could see him right now," she whispered. "I don't know if it's love or not." She paused and took a shuddering breath. "But whatever it is, he sure does make me feel like no one else has ever made me feel."

She cut herself off sharply when, in the corner of her eye, she caught a shifting motion of light in the mirror. A cold tingle ran up her back when a single word — a name — popped unbidden into her mind —

Tully!

"Yeah," she said hoarsely, shaking her head and resisting

445

the shiver that ran up her back. *"You* made me feel like no one else ever has, too, . . . only in a different way."

Hot tears formed in her eyes, surprising her as she turned and glanced around the bedroom. Her father was at work, and the house was filled with a dusty, empty silence. Through the window, she could see the bright winter sky and the lacy black line of trees down by the river. Slanting sunlight poured through the glass onto the cushioned seat of her rocking chair and cast long, blue shadows across the floor. A hollow feeling of loneliness, of abandonment swept up inside her.

"Tully . . ." she whispered, her voice as soft as rain as her eyes darted around the room. Her gaze kept coming back to the empty rocking chair by the window. For the first time in weeks, that same old, unnerving sensation of being watched filled her, making the skin on the back of her head crawl. The cold loneliness inside her got stronger.

"Tully," she repeated, more forcefully now. "If you're here . . ." Tears choked her as she stared through blurred eyes at the tape recorder in her lap. "If you want to talk to me now, I'd like to—to see you . . . one last time."

Just at that moment, a cloud passed in front of the sun, momentarily washing everything with dull gray light. Sarah glanced at the rocking chair for a moment; then, shivering violently, she turned ever so slowly to look at its reflection in the mirror over her dresser. She both wanted and dreaded what she might see there.

"You know, I really—"

Her voice choked off suddenly when her eyes snapped into focus, and she saw—nothing. The rocking chair was absolutely empty, with not even a trace of a gray shadow there. Sighing deeply, Sarah wiped her hand across her face and finished, "I really don't miss you. I'm glad you're gone, Tully."